D1265687

THE BELL IN THE LAKE

Also by Lars Mytting and available from ABRAMS

NON-FICTION

Norwegian Wood: Chopping, Stacking and Drying Wood the Scandinavian Way

LARS MYTTING

THE BELL IN THE LAKE

Translated from the Norwegian by
Deborah Dawkin

THE OVERLOOK PRESS
New York, NY

This edition first published in hardcover in 2020 by
The Overlook Press, an imprint of ABRAMS
195 Broadway, 9th floor
New York, NY 10007
www.overlookpress.com

Abrams books are available at special discounts when purchased in quantity
for premiums and promotions as well as fundraising or educational use.
Special editions can also be created to specification. For details,
contact specialsales@abramsbooks.com or the address above.

This translation has been published with
the financial support of NORLA.

Library of Congress Control Number: 2019938601

Printed and bound in U.S.A.

1 3 5 7 9 10 8 6 4 2

ISBN: 978-1-4197-4318-4
eISBN: 978-1-68335-819-0

To my mother

"And this also," said Marlow suddenly, "has been one of the dark places of the earth"

JOSEPH CONRAD, *Heart of Darkness*

CONTENTS

First Story

THE INNERMOST LANDSCAPE

The Girls Who Shared a Skin

THE BIRTH WAS HARD. THE HARDEST EVER PERHAPS, and that in a village where many births might compete for that title. The mother was large, but not until the third day of her confinement did they realise she was carrying twins. The details of the delivery, how long the screams reverberated in the log farmhouse, or how the womenfolk actually got the babies out – all this was forgotten. Too ghastly to be told, too ugly to be remembered. The mother tore and bled to death and her name vanished from history. For ever remembered, however, were the twins and their deformity. They were joined from the hip down. But that was all. They breathed, cried, and were lively.

Their parents were from the Hekne farm and the girls were baptised Halfrid and Gunhild Hekne. They grew, laughed a lot, and were never a bother, but a joy. To each other, to their father, to their siblings, to the village. The Hekne twins were put before the loom early, and sat for long days, their four arms flying in perfect time between warp and weft, so swiftly that it was impossible to see who was threading the yarn through their weave at any one moment. The pictures they wove were uniquely beautiful, often mysterious, and soon their weaves were traded for silver and livestock. At that time nobody thought of putting their mark on such craftwork, and later there were many who paid a high price for a hekneweave even when it was uncertain that it was genuine.

The most famous hekneweave showed Skråpånatta, the Night

of the Great Scourge, the locals' version of the Day of Judgment, loosely related to the old Norse prophecy of Ragnarok. A sea of flames would turn the night into day, and when everything was burned up and the night darkened again, the earth's surface would be scoured, leaving nothing but bare rock, and come sunrise both the living and the dead would be swept to their doom. This weave was given to the church and hung there for generations, before it vanished overnight through locked doors.

The sisters rarely left the Hekne farmstead, even though they got about better than folk might think. They walked in a waltz-like rhythm, as if carrying a brimful water-pail between them. The slopes below the farm were the only thing that defeated them. Hekne was situated on a very steep incline, and in the winter the slippery paths were treacherous. But since it was a sunny slope, the spring thaw came early in the year, sometimes by March, and then the twins would come out with the springtime sun.

Hekne was among the earliest settlements in the valley, and the family had of course chosen one of the best spots for a farmstead. They owned not one, but two seters – summer farms – further up on the mountainside, each boasting a fine milking shed and dairy, and a herd of well-fed cows that grazed on the deep-green grass all summer. The farm also had easy access to Lower Glupen, a rich fishing lake with a handsome boathouse built with the thickest logs available. But the true measure of a farmer in Gudbrandsdalen was how much silver he owned. This was their bank vault, a visible and accessible reserve. No farmstead was worth the name, if it did not have cutlery for eighteen, and with their trade in weaves the Heknes had accumulated enough silver for thirty.

The Hekne twins were young women when one fell ill. The thought of what this might mean – that the survivor would have to drag her sister's corpse around with her – was unbearable. So their father, Eirik Hekne, went to the church and prayed for them to be allowed to die together.

His prayer was heard by the village pastor, and presumably by God. Death did claim the girls on the same day. As the end neared they demanded to be alone. Their father and siblings stood waiting by the door, and inside the girls' chamber they heard them talking about something that must be done. That day they finished the weave of Skråpånatta. They had started it a long time ago and now Gunhild would complete it alone, with Halfrid dead at her side and her arms no longer a help. Their father left Gunhild to work in peace, for when it came to the twins there was always something greater at work, something he and the others who scarce saw above the rocks or water's surface would and never could understand. Late in the evening a cough was heard, then the loom-comb fell to the floor.

The family entered and saw that Gunhild was close to death. She seemed not to notice them, for she lay with her face turned to her sister and said:

"Ye shall shuttle wide, and I shall shuttle close, and when the weave be woven we two shall return."

She took Halfrid's hands and folded them in her own, made herself comfortable, and thus they lay with their hands clasped, as though in two-voiced prayer.

Later, the family disagreed over what Gunhild had meant, since the local dialect made for ambiguity. "Shuttle" might refer to their weaving but also to their moving fast. When the weave was donated to the church, the pastor wrote Gunhild's last words on the back of the wooden mount, but the complexity of the original was all but ironed out: "Ye shall go a long way, and I a short way, and when the weave is done we shall return."

The girls were buried under the church floor, and in thanks for their dying together Eirik Hekne had two church bells cast.

They were named the Sister Bells, and they rang with a unique richness and depth of tone. Their sound carried from the stave church across the valley and to the mountains, where it echoed against the rocks. When there was black ice on Lake Løsnes, below the church, the bells could be heard in the three neighbouring villages as a distant harmony over their own bells, and in the summer, when the wind was right, some folk even claimed they could hear them all the way up in the seters.

The first bell-ringer went deaf after three services. A wooden platform was erected at the bottom of the tower for the next to stand on, who stuffed his ears with beeswax and wound a leather strap round his head and ears.

The Sister Bells had neither a sad nor fearful ring. At the core of each chime was a vibrancy, a promise of a better spring, a resonance coloured by beautiful, sustained vibrations. Their sound penetrated deeply, creating mirages in the mind and touching the most hardened of men. With a skilful bell-ringer the Sister Bells could turn doubters into churchgoers, and the explanation for their powerful tone was that they were *malmfulle* – that silver had been added to the bronze when the church bells were cast. The more silver, the more beautiful and resonant the chime.

The skilfully crafted moulds and bronze had already cost Eirik Hekne a fortune, far more than his twin daughters had ever earned with their weaves. In the madness of his grief he went to the melting pot and threw in all his silver cutlery, then shoved his big working hands deep into his pockets and threw two fistfuls of silver dalers into the boiling alloy, coins that stayed on the surface surprisingly long, before they melted and the bubbles rose.

The first time the Sister Bells were said to warn of danger was during a big flood in the valley. That year, the mountain snowmelt came suddenly and violently, heads throbbed beneath the black Pentecostal sky, and on the night that the river found a new path the villagers were woken by the church bells ringing. The rain set in, and the inhabitants of two farms only just managed to escape before their houses were swept away by the flood. Massive log buildings were flung over, their timbers strewn like twigs along a watery gash in the landscape. And out on the lake, white bundles were seen to float, low and heavy in the water – sheep. Only later, when the villagers stood in the pouring rain trying to account for everyone, did they find that all the members of the bell-ringer's family were present, and that he had not been in the church. And when the priest went down to check he found that the church door was, and had been, firmly locked.

Eirik Hekne had been dead for many a year. There is nothing to indicate that he ever regretted melting his silver, but so much had gone into the Sister Bells that the farm teetered several times on the brink of a forced sale. Were it possible to divide Hekne into two farms, it would have been done, but the land was too steep and narrow. In the next few years, the bailiff took Lower Glupen, two crofts and the largest seter, and later generations paid for Eirik's excesses. They managed to keep the rest of the farm in the family, heirs begat heirs, and they all had an opinion about their forefather. Few felt that silver was better spent on church bells than on fields and barns, yet they took it as a reminder that hardship was easier to bear than sorrow. Every Sunday soothing chimes floated up to the farmstead from the bells that Eirik had once called the Daughter Bells, a custom and right that had died with him.

The Stave Church

For centuries the Sister Bells rang out across the village. They rang for the living, the dying and the dead, for marriages and Christmas Mass, for baptisms and confirmations, and sometimes for forest fires, floods and landslides. Folk rarely moved to or away from the village, those who did leave never came back, and many children believed that all church bells must sound like the Sister Bells, just as those who live near a magnificent view take it for granted.

The bells hung safely in the tower until 1880, when they and the village were the subject of sudden changes and unbending wills. One of the bells would even finish up under water and be hauled up again, and the only person who would have any power over their fate was a young girl of Hekne lineage. Her sacrifice was no less than that made by the Hekne parents centuries ago, but hers had to be made in secret, and for some time only one man would remember her for it. Those who might have *wanted* to remember would have found it hard to understand her actions without knowing the story of the stave church and the village she called home.

The Hekne farmstead was in Butangen, in a side valley between Fåvang and Tretten in Gudbrandsdalen. About a thousand souls lived in the village at the time, divided among some forty farmsteads and the crofts they controlled. The place name itself had a long story attached, not that it was often told, with so few visitors to tell. The village had got its name from an area on the shore of Lake Løsnes, a very long stretch of deep water, lined with dense forest and huge boulders, which offered only a small headland – a *tangen* – flat enough for a *bu* – a shack. It was here that early settlers built their boathouses and moorings, calling it Butangen. Nobody ever set up home here, but since it gave vital access to the main cart-road on the other side of the lake, by boat in the summer and sledge in the winter, the whole village was named after it. The church itself was built higher up the side of the valley, partly for the view, but also because the villagers knew from Fåvang what a flood could do to a cemetery.

All along the valley, families clung to the patches of land their forefathers had claimed. Some farms were built on such precipitously steep, rocky land, that even after three generations they only managed to clear three small fields. But, by way of compensation, the piles of rocks found new life as stone walls, so high that not a single sheep was ever taken by wolves in Butangen.

Change came slowly. The village was twenty years behind its neighbouring villages, which were thirty years behind Norway's towns and cities, which were fifty years behind the rest of Europe. In part this was due to the journey there. The curious, if they existed, had to head north along the winding River Laugen, and then, at Fåvang church – if they could find it and were still determined in their quest – they had to go up the valley side and follow a narrow mountain pass near Okshol farmstead. From there the trail crossed a rocky terrain and disappeared from view. Here many turned left and found themselves in the barren and uninhabited Okshol Valley. Only if they turned right did Butangen come into fine view, with its church high on the slope and farmsteads around it. But then, looking down, they would see the deep waters of Lake Løsnes and the treacherous marshes. Most turned back here, and the rest gave up when, having failed to find the trail, they stood knee-deep in marshland with the night closing in, being devoured by mosquitoes so that their skin looked more like an animal pelt.

A few did make it round the lake, or were lucky enough to get a boat ride from some dour villager who had put out his nets. When they finally arrived, they would either get married or be stabbed to death. A slight exaggeration, of course – Butangen was, in fact, a good place to live. The River Breia which carved this valley out was fed by many streams that supplied the farms with water. There was a bashfulness about the landscape, as the countless sharp twists in the river and streams created an eternal shift between lush sunny banks and mysterious shadowy slopes, before the river made one final, abrupt turn and spilled out into Lake Løsnes. Despite its steep inclines, it was a pretty, sun-drenched little valley, and on walking further you could enjoy a little social interaction with the locals, with a nod and a wave from afar.

Transport was slightly easier during the winter. When Lake Løsnes froze over, you could just speed across the ice and marshes, and then take the cart-road downhill to Fåvang. Thus village life followed a six-monthly rhythm. Winter was the time to visit others, to arrange marriages, to trade ploughshares and gunpowder. Some villagers longed to be some place else, but those who had been to this "some place else" could confirm that folk there did the same things, maybe a tad differently, but not in a way that was superior. There was no prospect of anything but drudgery, and drudgery could be found just as well at home, where it was borne among relatives and familiar faces.

Strangers and foreigners never got to pour their more exuberant genes into the Gudbrandsdøls' pot here in these valleys, as they did along the coast – where the dour character of the locals was diluted by shipwrecked Mediterranean sailors, who, when they waved farewell at their emergency harbour, left little gifts in the girls' bellies, gifts that sprang out as fiery-tempered kids with jet-black hair. The valley folk lived out their lives within their stone walls, in a slow and steady dance with the seasons. Each farm was a self-sufficient kingdom, and the valley sides were like ramparts separating them from the outside world. The tall barrier of pine trees strengthened their belief that it was better to collect moss in the old way until they dropped dead, than to change the direction of their lives. They were content to spend days at a time in the mountains, and to toil in the sleet and rain, and they preferred shovelling snow to digging the clod because it was lighter work, and the grand folk and humbler folk never mixed, generation after generation kept to the same farms. Time was irrelevant; they carried on the work that others had died doing, which they knew an unborn child would continue, and with the use of the same skills and often the same carts the ancient piles of rocks grew larger. And all these things bore upon how they spoke and behaved, even upon their sensing and feeling.

When Christianity came to Norway, the Butangen folk built an elaborate stave church, a masterpiece in ore-pine, with ornate carvings, dragon heads and a proud spire. Since everybody had enough food and no notion of time, months and years could be devoted to the most painstaking work in wood and stone. The church was completed during the reign of King Magnus V, and the year 1170 was carved into the foundation log. The staves and framework were made from the giant pines that grew in Gudbrandsdal back then, and, as was the custom in Norway, Butangen church was richly decorated with motifs from the ancient pagan faith. It became a kind of Viking chieftain's hall with a veneer of Christianity, and the woodcarvers spent long summers decorating it with serpents and other familiar ornaments from the Norse times. The exterior of the weapons porch was adorned with long-necked lions, and a gigantic carved serpent curled itself around the main door. On either side of the altar were wooden staves decorated with bearded faces, ancient gods with fearsome eyes and no pupils. All offering protection against the terrible powers that the Norsemen had battled against for centuries. The carpenters worked very hard to please all the gods, just in case Odin and Tor were still active.

In the centuries that followed the church was neither altered nor plundered. Just as the villagers' character avoided dilution by strangers, so this hidden medieval masterpiece remained untouched by fads or fashion. The decorations were not wiped away when the Reformation stripped God's houses bare, and Pietism never set its claws into the furniture and fixtures. The eight dragon heads continued to snarl towards the sky, and the outer walkway and walls released the fragrance of centuries of thorough tarring.

The story of the church bells and the Hekne sisters was barely known beyond the village. Once, in the early 1800s, an artist had come to the village and made drawings of the church, but he made little impression. Soon afterwards there had been another visitor – probably unconnected to the artist – who seemed to have some hidden agenda, and who quizzed a villager about the story of the Sister Bells, but he too was never heard of again, and soon nobody was sure whether either man had been there at all.

Churches no longer got financial support for their maintenance, it had stopped long ago when Catholicism was replaced by Protestantism. Utterly reliant now on what their own parish could raise, God's houses soon became a measure of good times and bad. Gudbrandsdal was a severely impoverished district throughout this century, plagued by overpopulation, flooding, frost-ravaged harvests, alcoholism and potato blight. The small windowpanes still cast their delicate light over the church pews, but they grew loose and let the north wind blow straight in on the Eucharist. The wooden roof tiles started to warp, and the rain seeped into cracks that became increasingly difficult to find. The only items able to withstand the elements were the two church bells. All around them the decay continued. Water constantly sought new pathways in the intricate framework of beams, and when it froze the ice swelled and widened the cracks, and dry snow came in through the gaps. Over the next few decades the dragon heads were taken by the wind and rain, one by one they fell to the ground, jaws snapping helplessly between gravestones, and the whole church seemed to slump a little without them, as though it looked with dread upon dark times ahead.

The Sound of Silver

These dark times were heralded by the Sister Bells when they rang for Mass on New Year's Day, 1880. The sound carried up to the stables at Hekne, where it fuelled a squabble between two of the eight Hekne siblings.

"Osvald!" said Astrid. "Ye mun drive us now!"

Her brother replied that she had been too slow in asking for a ride.

"Cocky good-for-nowt!" she said. "Stop quibbling and prepare the sledge!"

Osvald got to his feet and held out a broken neck rein and a brow-band with its buckle missing. "The sledge would have been ready if Emort were man enough to admit he wrecked these yesterday."

"We has more harnesses! Ye be making up excuses!"

Balder, the Døla horse that usually took them to church, snorted in his stall. Astrid brushed straw off her Sunday-best skirt. Osvald moaned. "Listen to ye!" she said. "Always moaning. With everything we mun do to get this farm back on its feet. And ye canna even prepare a sledge!"

"If it be broken, it be broken."

"Ugh! I can walk!" said Astrid, turning. "Though I mun walk with old Klara."

Osvald flung the harness aside.

"'Tis nay bother to me," Astrid went on. "It'll be Father ye mun answer to. 'Tis him they shall gossip about, when I'm not taken by horse to Mass."

She hurried across the courtyard. The snow creaked, and she pulled her shawl tighter about her. The minute she had opened the front door that morning, Astrid had noticed that it was not just cold, it was *very cold*. Typical of new year, the bitterest time of year. The wind lashed at her face like a taut switch, the air in her lungs grew thin and sharp. Truth was, she was dreading going to church. She had attended morning song on Christmas Day, and it had been so cold in there that her toes had not stopped burning until the fourth day of Christmas. The reason she had to venture out again was that Klara Mytting – an elderly parish pauper – wanted to go to Mass and needed someone to hold her steady on the slippery paths.

The powerful sound of the Sister Bells continued to ring out between the wooden houses. This was just the first round of chimes, calling the congregation. The church was not far from Hekne, but it was small, and space was limited, and to be late meant a lack of choice. In actual fact Astrid, as the eldest daughter of a farm like Hekne, was under no obligation to venture into the cold to help a woman like Klara. But there can be many reasons for attending church beside the singing of hymns, reasons that might just require a front-row pew.

Astrid hurried past the Hekne *stabbur*, the food storehouse, and along the narrow path that had been cleared of snow down to the cowshed, where Klara lived with the cows and some of the farmhands. The snow was unusually heavy that winter, and Astrid could hear the farm cats fighting up by the barn. They were bored and irritable, like everyone else, now that the snow had made their hunting grounds impassable, and all they could do was slink along the walls of the houses.

The church bells paused. Since childhood Astrid had noticed that they sounded different when the snow was deep. The village resonated less, the echoes from Lake Løsnes and the mountainsides were muted, as though she stood closer to the bells themselves, at the vibrating heart of their silver-chime. She was familiar with the story of the silver coins that had splashed into the melting pot and sent the farm into bankruptcy, causing her father and brothers to cast resentful looks towards the boathouses at Lower Glupen on their way to Imsdalen, where the fishing was open to all, but which was a full day's march away and never yielded as much.

Astrid was twenty years old, and among the few family members to be proud of her ancestor's insane great deed, although she was not the type to go padding about in a graveyard talking to the dead. She had a restless mind, and her thoughts seemed always to race ahead of her. Her grandmother said she ought never to have gone to the summer school, since the knowledge she had gained had only made her hungry for more, and everyone knew there was no prospect of a village girl pursuing such desires.

Nobody could keep up with Astrid Hekne as a child, scampering about and sticking her nose in folk's work, asking why things were done *this* way and not *that*. She clambered up onto the dry stone walls and ran along them so the grey rocks clattered, a disrespectful habit that left everyone fuming, but she ran on anyway, kicking up the moss as she went, down to the bottom of the fields, where the wall ended abruptly on the edge of a sheer drop into the valley below. From here she could see across Lake Løsnes, and through the gap in the mountains she could just about make out Fåvang and Losna.

She liked to gaze towards Losna because she knew what was on its way over there. In a few years, at set times, there would be a ribbon of steam and coal smoke, the result of the colossal endeavours of the railwaymen who were, inch by inch, laying narrow iron tracks, probably no wider than her arm, a stretch of incredible length – some folk claimed it reached all the way to Kristiania and from there to Sweden and maybe even further.

It seemed beyond belief, to the young Astrid, that there were beasts of burden in this world that needed no rest at night, and she often imagined herself on this train, and never tired of this one thought: that real life was happening elsewhere, that everyday life was just a delay. But she had no idea where she wanted to go, these dreams were just a ladder that went up and up and ended in thin air. Her thoughts transported her to different places every day, and the only thing she knew was that she was searching for something, and that whatever it was, it was not in the village. As each day approached evening it brought her a sense of loss, for nothing new ever happened here. And as she fell asleep, a grain of sorrow would land in her mind, and she knew that these grains would add up, and in a few years make her like other girls, heavy and old before her time.

As an adult she had turned down two suitors, good suitors from fine farms, Nordrum and Lower Løsnes. It was some time now since anyone else had given it a shot, something folk put down to her restlessness and sharp nature. Both of which rendered her incapable of falling for the charms of the young men from the farms around there, all of whom were typical Gudbrands stock – big, sturdy hard grafters who cultivated dumb silence. Besides, her appearance was unusual. Even though someone had to be truly ugly not to get married in this part of Gudbrandsdal, there was a strong preference for a well-built woman, wide in the beam, preferably with big breasts and with a good, strong back. Astrid was long-limbed and bony, with a thin face and dark, curly hair, and in another village she might have been reckoned pretty. The right man would even have said that she was beautiful and appreciated the unusual slant of her eyebrows, the way she jutted her chin out, and her arms that bronzed in the sun. But common opinion about the eldest Hekne girl, after these two rejections, was that she was mulish and impossible to discipline. Tradition favoured girls with coarse hands who toiled silently as the grindstone turned, who gave birth without fuss and returned to the milking shed with the afterbirth still steaming behind them.

As she supported Klara out of the barn, she saw that the old woman was better dressed than usual, for another villager had lent her a skirt and boots. They walked down, both in their heavy woollen shawls and skirts. Each time a horse-drawn sledge passed by, Astrid stared stiffly ahead. Klara seemed not to notice the cold, she trundled on steadily, repeatedly pulling on Astrid's sleeve and asking – far too loudly – the names of those who rushed past. Astrid was unable to name them all. Families never had enough space on their sledges for all their children, and the road was a jostling mass of boys and girls. It was impossible to see who was who, their faces either hidden in big shawls and scarves, or disguised by the thick frost that sprouted from their eyebrows and noses. They were barely halfway to the church, but Astrid's earlobes already stung, reminding her of the agony that awaited her when she got back home and her frozen limbs would start to thaw.

Astrid overheard someone saying that it was forty degrees below zero. They no longer had a thermometer at home. It had burst one night when they forgot to take it into the warm, which, from what her teacher had told them, proved that the temperature outdoors was lower than minus thirty-nine degrees, since that was mercury's freezing point.

The cold was inescapable. Hekne might seem comfortable enough from afar, but it was still in the grip of the seasons. The *stabbur* was huge, but was rarely filled with enough supplies to keep them going properly until spring. There were fewer and fewer trees in the forest for firewood, and they only ever had enough wood to heat one floor. Darkness fell early in the afternoon, and each evening the family would huddle around the hearth for warmth and light. The menfolk carved small tools and ladles, regularly sweeping up the shavings and throwing them onto the fire so they burst into flame. The bairns were a throng of noise and bickering, stealing or tugging at each other's sheepskins, coughing and sneezing. Worst for Astrid was the lack of any opportunity to *get away*. She was scolded if she sloped off with a tallow candle, such a costly item was to be shared. The village was coal-black in the winter, filling even the stoutest heart with fear. Which was why she too joined the heaving mass around the fire each evening, enduring the little ones' farts, the old folks' interminable reminiscences, her great-aunt's humming and her mother's stern orders for quiet "soon".

No, she thought often, that's what's wrong: there is no distance. No light.

The bells rang again, these were the chimes meant to hurry folk up. The great sound vaulted over the mounds of snow, past them and towards the mountains, each chime returning in an echo that merged with the next.

"The old bell-ringer, he were a good 'n," muttered Klara, when it was quiet enough again for them to hear each other.

"A good 'n, ye say? In what way?"

"Gave folks the Holyblight he did. Oh aye. Got permission from the Bell-Witness, then scraped it off and gave it to the sick."

Klara Mytting came from the farmstead of the same name, where things were even worse than at Hekne, so that she and her younger sister became paupers, dependent on the parish, and were finally taken in by the Heknes. Klara was a little slow, unsure even of the year of her birth, though she was definitely old, since her sister had been sixty-two when she died. All through her life Klara had been a frail but good-natured creature, unable to do much, other than carry water or sit at her knitting when her arthritis allowed. She ate like a bird, and had violet circles round her eyes.

"What ye be saying makes nay sense," said Astrid. She straightened her headscarf and went on walking. "What did ye call it?"

"The Holyblight. It grows inside of the church bells."

"That be nowt but rust."

"Rust? Nay. There be good powers in't. The bell-ringer scraped them with a knife with a cup under, and when he came out in t'light with that cup, there be dry crumbs in't. Good powers in that powder. Good powers. Aye. In the olden days folks mixed it with grease. Rubbed it on wounds, they did. Ate it too, some folk. Made everything good again, it did. Astrid, can ye ask the new bell-ringer? If he can go up and fetch me some Holyblight. So I may be cured of the arthritics. Please."

"I canna promise, Klara," said Astrid.

"The bells be tolling, eternity awaits," Klara said.

Astrid shuddered and asked no more. The "new" bell-ringer had been ringing the church bells for over thirty years now. Klara was as steeped in the old folklore as Astrid's grandfather had been, but her mind was so chaotic it was impossible to separate what belonged to tradition and what she had simply made up. She spent much of the day crossing herself over the milk pan, or secretly slipping porridge remains to the dark elves, and generally trying to keep the old powers satisfied. Despite her peculiar ways, she was treated with kindness and respect, since many of the villagers, Astrid's grandfather among them, believed that every human being was allotted an equal number of talents, it was just that they took different forms and some were harder than others to recognise or understand. Bairns whose speech was unclear might make outstanding fiddlers or woodcarvers, the blind could calm horses, and lunatics were generally in contact with greater powers, which one did well to respect.

Klara was busy muttering to herself, as they approached the church with its familiar red-painted spire. The north-facing walls were black, while the sun-facing walls were deep umber and golden-brown. These rich tones now gleamed beneath a veil of white frost, and smoke streamed from the pipes that stuck out from the walls.

Was *he* already in the church? Astrid asked herself. Feeling as cold as she did?

She knew the church so well, and the parsonage even better. She had worked there as a maid for two years. One of the few places respectable enough for her as the eldest daughter of a farm like Hekne, which could, in better times, have afforded to let her be a lady of leisure. Two years of sewing, cleaning and furniture-polishing, and then, from last spring: her heart had beaten harder and harder as she sewed, cleaned and polished. Until she was hastily dismissed that autumn and forced to return to her farmwork at Hekne.

Astrid and Klara stamped the snow off their boots and entered the porch, but just as they were about to cross the threshold Klara gave a deep curtsey, muttering something about a "Door Serpent". Astrid, who was holding Klara by the arm, assumed she was falling and tried to pull her up.

"What? Will ye nay curtsey to the Midtstrand-bride?" said Klara, shuffling through the doorway with an awkward bend in her knees.

Astrid looked hastily around her; she could see nobody from the Midtstrand farmstead.

"Straighten up, Klara!" Astrid hissed. "Folks be staring!"

"Ye must greet the Midtstrand-bride nicely now," said Klara. "Every time. Or she can get angry."

"Shh!"

"The Door Serpent is nay longer here, yet 'tis here all the same."

Astrid dragged Klara in with her. She had no idea what the Midtstrand-bride or Door Serpent were, or if they were one and the same thing, nor was she about to stop and ask. It was typical of Klara to come up with something like this, and it would be even more humiliating if she continued with her muttering.

Once inside, they discovered that the church was already full.

The Heknes' no longer owned a permanent pew. They had been forced to give it up one year when they fell behind with their shoe tax, and their name had been painted over and replaced with another. There was still some space on the right with the menfolk, but women were meant to sit on the left, where only the draughtiest places were now free, next to the wall. Apologising, Astrid pushed Klara in along the pew, while folk turned their knees and stared at the ceiling.

"Nay, but Astrid, must I sit *here*?"

"Klara! Just sit down," whispered Astrid, between half-closed lips. "Ye can see for yersen that there be nowhere else free!"

"Aye, but what about *there*, nearer the front?" said Klara loudly, pointing to a place that was indeed better, but which they had overlooked, and which was about to be taken by two girls from Framigard Romsås.

Astrid shoved Klara towards the draughty wall. She wanted to change places with her, but the old woman was already seated and muttering and nodding.

The bells rang, drowning out what Klara was saying. A few stragglers came in, a family of eight, they divided in the aisle and two girls were rude enough to squeeze in at the end, forcing everyone to shunt along, so that Astrid and Klara were squashed up against the wall. Astrid could now feel how emaciated Klara was, her shoulder and hip bone poked through her clothes.

Folk shivered, exhaling white breath. The tallow candles cast their light over the aisle, all that could be heard were the hushed whisperings of the congregation and the restless shifting of coarse woollen garments. Only the grander folk who could afford large animal-skin rugs sat at ease.

Astrid liked the stave church, but only when the weather was warm. Christianity made little impression on her, but when she was not gripped with the cold, she could dream and picture herself there, back in time; she constantly found something new in the carvings and decorations, things of *beauty* but no practical use, and she liked to spell out the peculiar epigraphs in their swirly lettering.

The door to the porch was now closed. No doubt the churchwarden had been desperately stoking up the huge wood-stoves since five that morning, but the warmth had not penetrated the walls.

Still, she would endure the cold. That, and the memory of a vanished hope that was about to step into view. She would endure it the way she endured the rest of her life. This was the life allotted her, like it or lump it. There was no changing things. There she sat, on the coldest day of the year, in what must be the coldest House of God. She wanted warmer clothes, but had none. She wanted a man to love, but doubted she would ever get him. And she wanted the summer. At least that would come eventually. Unlike love, or fine clothes. And in fact, the summer compensated for both. The warmth of the sun, the rustling of the aspens, getting scrubbed up clean, walking barefoot and free.

The prayer bells rang. Three sets of three chimes before the service began. The old priest had been Danish, and the bell-ringer still followed the Danish custom of starting Mass with these nine chimes. When they were done there would be silence, until he stepped forwards.

But in the silence Astrid knew that a familiar old suitor would come first, who would cling about her and sneak beneath her clothes.

The frost.

And there it was. Invisible, but cruel and merciless, a sharpened knife. She tried to shrink from it, but the draught crept up through the floorboards, seeking her knees, her fingers, her toes.

Astrid knew what awaited her. This was a cold that went deeper than skin and muscle, it sank into the very marrow of your bones. Yes, the marrow – just like the marrow they sucked on after the annual sheep-slaughter – would actually be chilled. And once the icy cold had taken hold, it stayed in your skeleton, leaving a stiffness it took days to drive out.

He made his entrance at last. He did not walk, he glided. From a private chamber at the back of the church, past the altar, full of anticipation, as though he had been in the church since dawn. Cassock, Bible, wide-open eyes.

Kai Schweigaard.

He cleared his throat and the service began. But Astrid soon saw he had more to get off his chest than usual. The undue length of his sermons was the only failing in the "new pastor", as the villagers would call him for many years to come. Schweigaard spoke plainly, intelligibly, and with suitable solemnity. His services had proved very different from the sleepy efforts of his predecessor, a stuffy man who had never lost his mumbling Danish accent – the coloniser's accent – and only ever preached about Christian duty and the rod of correction.

Yes, there was a *fizz* in Kai Schweigaard, fizz as in a bottle of Yuletide brew. He had a tanned face, rolled up his sleeves so his forearms could catch the sun too, shaved daily with a knife, was lithe in his movements, determined in his gestures. He was direct and unpatronising, and happy to splash in the baptismal font when babies were fractious. He conducted himself very differently from other pastors, not that this caused his status as a Man of God to be doubted. The local council appointed him as chairman of the Poor Law Board, and he was quick to call on the poorest cottages in the village, where families of ten cooked, ate, washed and slept in one room.

And it was this that the villagers knew him for.

She moved her head to see him better. He had arrived in the village last May, when, dressed in her apron, she had lined up with the other servants outside the parsonage waiting to welcome him. They had known he would be young, but not *so* young, and they had expected him to arrive with a cart-load of furniture, a well-dressed wife and flock of young children; but instead, out of the carriage sprang a black-clad, cheerful man carrying two suitcases and little more.

It was then that Margit Bressum had spied her big opportunity. She was a garrulous, self-satisfied widow with huge pendulous bosoms, who until that day had only ever held a minor position in the household. The old priest had taken the best servants with him, and on Schweigaard's arrival she made sure she was first in line to greet him and, exuding bristling efficiency, introduced herself as Oldfrue – a title generally conferred upon a head housekeeper.

Thus began a new epoch at the parsonage. Oldfrue Bressum held forth about having picked out new curtains for the living room, asked the new pastor if he liked blood pudding and liver for supper, and was there anything more they might do for him? The old pastor had had a family of six, and it took days before Schweigaard put a stop to Oldfrue Bressum's notions of running a grand household, and a lavish kitchen supplying rich sauces and cream puddings. Butangen's modern Man of God explained that he was not married, and after the briefest pause, as he let his eyes drift over the servants, he added: "for now". Little slips of this kind would prove typical of Pastor Schweigaard; he could say something quite innocuous, but because even during sermons he allowed his gaze to roam among folk, his words took on unintended meanings. Whatever the case, he had no plans for a busy social life but for a "thrifty and modest enterprise". The only thing he desired for himself was to follow the recent trend for chicken eggs at breakfast. A farmhand fenced off a corner of the barn and got him some poultry, otherwise things went on as before. Margit Bressum's ambitions of ordering about a whole bevy of maids were eventually reduced to the organisation of his three simple daily meals. She kicked up a fuss about this, but continued to call herself Oldfrue, even when she was left with only a handful of servants to order about.

Astrid continued with her tasks – sewing, cleaning, tidying the parlour, planting and weeding the flower beds in the garden. A little hasty and heavy-handed in her work. An occasional sideways glance at the new priest, who just nodded back briefly and vanished with his coat-tails flapping. Always at a distance, until the day she spotted a copy of *Morgenbladet* on top of the polished chest of drawers in the hallway. Schweigaard had the newspapers delivered to him in little bundles every week. Each day he only read one, no matter how curious he might be about what was happening in the world, or how many days the post had been delayed.

Today a newspaper was lying on the chest of drawers. Folded into four, with tightly packed print running down in five slender columns. She went closer and gave it a sniff. It must have come off the press recently, since it gave off a faint aroma like fresh mushrooms. She quickly looked around and opened it out. *Morgenbladet* consisted of two large sheets, the first crammed with the same Gothic lettering as in her textbook from the summer school, but the second was divided into little blocks of writing, which she initially took to be in another language until she recognised the new letters, which her teacher had called "Roman" and dismissed as "vulgar and garish".

Astrid found them neither vulgar nor garish. Not in the least. These blocks of writing must, she concluded, be advertisements. The entire page was like a building with little open windows, through which came streams of fresh air and exciting sounds. In Kristiania there were raffles of paintings, auctions, dance classes, concerts, and oranges from Valencia for sale, even hatching eggs from English ducks. There were violin strings made from pigs' intestines, decorative plants in pots, shrink-proof underclothes, and something she had only the vaguest concept of – the latest French corsets.

She saw an advertisement for a lecture about the North Atlantic expeditions, which was to be held at seven o'clock, and just then the grandfather clock struck seven. She heard the front door go, quickly folded the newspaper and put it back, but as she was about to leave the new pastor entered, and the breeze from the closing door lifted a corner of the thin newspaper and their eyes met.

They had only been on nodding terms before, but now Schweigaard started – with no hint of impropriety – to give her the paper after he had read it. And as he did so, he would question her about the village. About the farms and their names, the living conditions, the children, the connections which he clearly had difficulty putting together. An unusual trade; he wanted the narrower view, and paid with a wider view. She read and grabbed the outside world with both hands, but when she had read the newspaper and returned to her sewing needle, she felt – more and more – that she was in the wrong place and wrong century. And eventually, the wrong bed.

Each Sunday she followed Schweigaard with her eyes. At the end of Mass he usually set some time aside for "an overview of world events", in truth just a roundup of news snippets from Kristiania and abroad. But since she had been allowed to borrow the newspaper, she knew what he was likely to say, and all week she felt a tremor of suspense, as though she and the pastor shared a secret.

Margit Bressum must have seen that this secret might grow into something bigger. Nothing had ever happened, or been tried, or said. But it might not be long before something was tried or said. One day Margit Bressum caught her with a newspaper in her hand. "Ye shan't have time for *that* when the new pastor's wife arrives," she said.

Astrid's lips quivered and Oldfrue twisted the knife. "He's spoken for, ye know."

It was then that she realised that where folk saw a threat, there must be an opportunity.

At last it was time for a hymn. Astrid nudged Klara, who rose stiffly to her feet. It's wrong, mused Astrid, to think that we stand up in church to honour the Lord. It's to give us folk who are blue with cold a chance to wriggle our toes and get the blood flowing.

Klara breathed through her nose, the moisture causing her nostril hairs to turn white with rime. She needed help to find the page in her hymn book, she liked to hold it open despite being unable to read. The service continued, and during the next hymn everybody's teeth were chattering so hard that the words were incomprehensible. The floor was so cold now that Astrid felt as though she was standing there barefoot, and she could soon feel nothing even when she screwed up her toes.

The baptisms began. It was popular to baptise babies on New Year's Day, and there were nine in the queue. They had been wailing and crying at the start of the service, but now the cold had subdued them. The first child was brought forwards. But nothing happened.

She heard muttering near the front.

Craning forwards, Astrid saw Schweigaard shift the baby's position in his arm, and bring his knuckles down to the font. A cracking sound echoed around the church as he broke the ice on the water. Then he baptised the boy, declaring him now one of God's number.

The next babies were presented, their names given in unsteady, shivering voices. The rites were swiftly completed, and it seemed that some folk purposely omitted the middle names they had chosen. The last baby was a girl from Tromsnes, and Astrid knew they had planned to call her Johanne after her grandmother, but her father was shaking so hard with the cold that he swallowed the first syllable and Schweigaard christened her Anne Tromsnes.

A storm was brewing outside, and the congregation shivered yet more. All the stoves had burned out and the churchwarden could not interrupt Mass to add more logs. A blast of wind made the walls creak, penetrating them so the altar candles flickered.

Schweigaard went on. He seemed unaffected by the cold. On the contrary, he appeared to take strength from it. Astrid thought of the time they had folded a tablecloth together. She remembered how his face had come close to hers, how with each fold he became less priest and more man, how the trembling of their arms had gone through the fabric, making the tension between them visible like waves that rippled towards each other and met in the middle.

Astrid looked around her. The pews were filled with villagers, all concentrating hard on holding out. They were used to holding out. Life's torments were always out to get them, and they never gave in because of a toothache or gout or painful knees. So they sat there in their church pews, and held out. Held out until their faces turned white, and then blue. Soon even the children were staring emptily ahead, some losing control over their frail bodies, rocking involuntarily from side to side, as though on a ship on rough seas. When the time came to sing another hymn, the organist's fingers were so cold that nobody recognised the tune, and several parishioners sang the next hymn on the board instead.

The only folk not shivering now were Hallstein Huse and his children. He was a bear hunter and wore a heavy fur coat, and had spread a large animal pelt over his four precious sons. Klara Mytting, however, had failed even to get up, but Astrid decided to let her sit on in the shadows.

There was another long, thundering blast of wind, stronger than the last.

"The Night o' the Great Scourge," whispered Klara. "She be coming soon."

Astrid just nodded. The old woman leaned against the wall and rested her head.

Then it began to snow inside the church. Chalk-white grains tumbled over the congregation, onto the crucifix and altar, down onto Schweigaard's Bible, and for once he lost his place in the reading.

People looked up at the ceiling from where the snow was coming, and soon realised that it was not snow, but the rime formed from their breath. The last gust of wind must have shaken the loft floor, causing the rime to scatter in a snow-like shower.

The last white grains floated towards the floor. Some hit the tallow candles, which spluttered for an instant, then flared up again.

Kai Schweigaard looked over the congregation. He threw his arms open and said loudly:

"Thanks be for this ordeal, which we now bear together! This is a sign from God, like those Moses received, and I promise you:

by next winter our circumstances shall be improved. Already this spring, I say, something great shall pass, to free us from this misery."

His voice was unsteady as he resumed the reading. Astrid wondered what he meant. She had seen him like this once or twice before. Fired up, overexcited, usually before a visit from the mayor or some other smartly dressed men.

She gazed over the shivering mass of people with frost on their shoulders and hair. Few were capable of listening anymore, and those who had heard had probably already forgotten what he said.

Up in the pulpit, Schweigaard hesitated. Barely halfway through the list of hymns on the board, there was another blast of wind, and he had to blow snow from his Bible again. He started to make cuts to the service. The organist got confused, and Schweigaard was forced to say straight out that they would skip four hymns.

The final fifteen minutes saw a display of the strength Kai Schweigaard could take from adversity. He made God's word vibrate between the staves and turn to flames of faith and fortitude. In the end he sang alone, while the candles flickered.

When the Sister Bells rang at last, the congregation headed out as fast as its frozen knees allowed. Astrid pushed folk on and rotated her ankles and hips to loosen her tight muscles. It felt as if the church pew itself was stuck to her backside, the tree's growth-rings pressed into her skin. Standing in the aisle, she realised that Klara was still in her seat. She rushed back to her and tugged her sleeve.

Astrid's life changed in that moment. Grains tumbled into her head, coloured by the blue ink of despair. And an image fixed in her for ever, so vividly did it burn its way in, the image of what happened when she tugged on Klara's arm. The old woman had tipped forwards and hung there, one cheek firmly frozen to the church wall. Her last moist breath must have been exhaled onto the frozen timbers, and she hung there for a long time, until her skin came loose with a ripping sound and her head slammed into the pew before her.

The churchwarden heard Astrid scream and rushed over to her, and moments later Kai Schweigaard was there too. Meanwhile, oblivious of all this, the bell-ringer continued to ring the Sister Bells, and between their deep chimes Astrid only caught fragments of what the pastor said.

"When the spring comes," said Kai Schweigaard, putting his arm round her shoulders, "then you, and everybody else, shall be liberated and spared such suffering – Astrid."

A Leaky Boat on Stormy Seas

On the 3rd of January, and again on the 4th, the churchwarden tried to open a grave for Klara Mytting, but the frost in the ground had gone so deep that even two days of bonfires could not thaw it. The churchwarden stood in the rising steam between the falling snow and smoking embers, hacking away with his pickaxe. The image – as though the graveyard were built over hell itself – made Kai Schweigaard order him to give up before it attracted village ridicule.

"We'll have to give her a funeral in the spring," said Schweigaard.

Again he was confronted by the very thing he found most painful in his pastoral role: having to see the spiritual defeated by the practical. As a pastor he was visited daily by both, and when it came to a battle between the two, the natural forces always won, and mounting the coffin they did a victory dance that threw long, flickering shadows. This was not how he wanted things, he wanted to make death more beautiful, more serene. To keep the soul pure, free from the corpse.

The churchwarden nodded. "As the Pastor wishes," he said, leaning on his pickaxe. "But folks is unlikely to hold off from dying afore then."

"Neither you nor I control death or the cold," said Schweigaard. "As his servants, we shall postpone any funerals until the spring."

It was a painful decision. His first major volte-face in Butangen. Though he avoided phrases like "we must do as before" or "we must return to the old ways". Statements Kai Schweigaard would never make.

He was one of a hundred and forty-eight young men who had been ordained in the previous year. They had no choice about where they would serve. The lazy or inadequate among them were sent to miserable outposts where the flames of faith scarcely burned, where they either got a hold on themselves and their congregation, or succumbed to liquor and loneliness. The brooders and the romantics, those who were too good-hearted or too bombastic, were given parishes where their defects were worn down by the colossal workload. A few in the litter – the so-called "poets", the wimps, with delicate appearances or beautiful singing voices – such radiant lights of piety were sent to assist a pastor in a city. Meanwhile, the average novices were appointed as chaplains; some blossomed in the task, the rest shuffled through it, leaving no mark.

Then there were the chosen few. Distinctive, energetic, but rough at the edges. They generally seemed older than they were, and often an intensity simmered beneath the surface; their spelling could be wanting, but each was born with a rare gift, various talents that were observed and noted, and they were sorted from the others with a knowing nod. These men were cast from tougher stuff, they were explosively enterprising, with a steely determination, often with a little flaw in their personality that would, with age, develop into a large personality. These few were immediately made pastors in medium-sized villages populated by stiff-necks and drinkers, or where poverty, and often superstition, ruled. It was into these places that the bishops sent their brightest, longest lances, and such a weapon was Kai Schweigaard.

He had been sent to Butangen by Bishop Folkestad in Hamar, and they both knew why. Assuming he made a good job of it there, he would soon be offered a better post. Since some of these young men – despite being difficult to identify through examination – would actually end up as bishops.

Under the old pastor, and presumably those before him, no-one in Butangen had ever been buried in midwinter. But in November, as he approached his first winter in the village, Schweigaard had shocked everyone by ordering that the church's store of well-dried cordwood be used to thaw the ground in the cemetery. He was told that the villagers had, since time immemorial, kept their dead on their farms through the winter, frozen stiff in their coffins, even the bodies of children and babies could lie there for months, as everyday life carried on about them. Besides, the old pastor had shown scant interest in funerals. Like most priests of his time, he only attended the wakes of the wealthiest farmers, gave a graveside eulogy only when paid, and a ceremony inside the church cost even more. Which was why folk usually took things into their own hands. They made the coffin themselves, held the vigil at home, sang to the corpse on its way out, walked in a procession to the cemetery and dug the hole themselves, in a plot that was hopefully free. Meanwhile the old pastor sat behind his curtains like a dull sleepwalker, content just to scatter a bit of earth during the next Sunday Mass. But by then the coffin was already deep in the earth, and occasionally he even got a name wrong, though nobody ever dared or bothered to correct him.

Schweigaard had had to deal with the outfall of this already that spring, when, in his first weeks as pastor, he regularly had to rush down to groups of unregistered mourners wandering about with spades and pickaxes, and holding their own funeral services. The cemetery itself looked like a rough patch of newly cleared land, rugged and uneven. And since few villagers could afford more than a plain cross or wooden marker, hardly anyone knew who was buried where. Schweigaard immediately ordered that all deaths be reported, and instructed the churchwarden to ensure that the graves be opened in advance. Schweigaard himself would then come down to the cemetery to see the coffin lowered and scatter the earth. The villagers, however, made it clear to him that they did not like change, or authority when it weighed in uninvited. Although by autumn the piercing silences and hard looks became less pronounced. Folk began to nod when he spoke, and gradually the mourners seemed to appreciate it when he shook their hands and offered a few words of comfort.

Then the snow had come, and he had felt driven to uphold the law that the dead be buried within eight days. But the quantity of wood it took was colossal, as was the exertion it demanded of the churchwarden, and now, finally, as they stood there with Klara Mytting's body, they were forced to admit that the midwinter freeze had defeated them.

The churchwarden kicked the smouldering wood into the snow where it hissed, gathered the charred logs into a sack, and muttered "well, well" as he rubbed the soot off his spade and pickaxe.

"There'll be no more digging during the winter," Schweigaard said. "But we must build a mortuary chapel." He put his hands on his hips and looked around him, as though searching for a suitable plot. "The villagers must be relieved of this torment."

The churchwarden looked doubtful and took his leave.

Schweigaard stood alone before the open wound of ashes and turf. There was a little trickle of meltwater, but it didn't go far before it froze. Thankfully, a little snow fell and spread a thin white blanket over the shamed earth.

Winter, he thought. This wretched winter.

And death.

The New Year service had been one long disaster, crowned with a death in the church itself. The next few months would take its toll on his congregation. Endless, dark days in which nothing good happened, and the icy beak of winter pecked where humans were at their weakest. In grief, in hunger, and the frozen marrow of their bones.

Yes, he said to himself. A mortuary chapel was needed. A simple and effective solution. Remove the dead from the farms. But before anything else he had to sort out that frightful church. He'd had a long conversation with Bishop Folkestad before his inauguration, and was prepared for the church to be old, but not for it to be a relic from the early Middle Ages. He had, from the very first day, been troubled by the monstrous carvings, by the traces of the old Norse faith, by the organ bellows which were regularly torn, so that the chorals died out in strangled tones. This was not a *functional* church. It could not serve his plans. Norway was facing unsettled times and major changes. The newspapers published articles on inventions and changes in politics, a new era was on its way. This new era, this seismic shift in the times, required sound leadership, firmness and spiritual health. This monstrosity of a church was like a leaky boat setting out on stormy seas.

He looked up at the church and a shudder went through him. Yesterday he had come down here and let himself in, and sat in the empty, dismal gloom. He had sat in the pew where Klara Mytting had died, and prayed for the parish and himself. Now he felt the urge to go in again, to return to that same pew, to send up another prayer, to beg for a helping of God's strength.

"No, Kai Schweigaard," he said half-aloud, straightening his back. "You do not have time for such womanish mewling. The Lord's lance must be sharpened each night. You must be active now. Find new tasks for the churchwarden. Maintain the momentum to bring the plan to fruition."

The plan.

He had been on the verge of revealing it to his congregation during the service when the frost had floated down onto his Bible, but had bitten his lip just in time. He had rehearsed the words so often, and was so excited about telling them what was to come. But it was too soon, a vital signature was still missing, and there were a few aggravating issues yet to be sorted, although these were mere details that he hoped would be resolved in the letter he was expecting from Dresden.

Fortunately, he was not alone in it all. He had been to Vålebrua several times and talked to the mayor, and the director of the Commercial and Savings Bank was heartily agreed that something had to be done. But the parish never had the necessary money.

Until he had come up with the plan.

Schweigaard gave himself a shake and headed back towards the parsonage. There too he had made a careful assessment of what was and was not necessary. The house was too big, too old, its floors too cold, and he only required an office, bedroom and study. He had asked Oldfrue that summer to cut the number of maids and other staff, never expecting that Astrid would be one of those Bressum would eventually let go.

He kept his farm manager on. He had a family of six and a few labourers. They tended the land and animals on the estate, and occasionally went up into the mountains to set traps. All Schweigaard asked of him was that he take care of the horse and carriage and provide ingredients for the kitchen.

Still, he thought, it's absurd – twenty people to keep one priest alive! The empty bedrooms upstairs were a continual reminder that he was expected to get a wife and children. But he was in no position to marry, not now, not here! Their engagement was still on, but if Ida Calmeyer were to come here, from her embroidery to this wilderness, dragged away from her snippety friends, she would waste away and die.

Kai Schweigaard trudged on, still in a fury about having to give up on Klara Mytting's funeral. He had told no-one, but he had seen the burial of this unfortunate woman as the perfect opportunity to introduce a truly modern funeral service, which made no distinction between rich and poor. He wished Astrid Hekne was still around, so that he could ask her how this new custom was likely to be received. She was the only person he could really *talk* to, who was of any real help when he tried to grasp the workings of Butangen. The other maids floated off like so many feathers whenever he entered a room, while Oldfrue Bressum stomped about giving orders.

Astrid Hekne had never been like that.

She was not the type to sit with her head bowed, or walk with her gaze fixed to the floor, she wanted to know what was happening around her. Early on he had felt a delight in making her happy. A paltry old newspaper was loaned to her, and she lit up like the moon. Initially he had seen this as an act of public enlightenment, the nourishment of an impoverished mind. But he soon discovered that Astrid's mind was far from impoverished. On the contrary. She was curious, hugely capable, and had an unerring instinct for what was right and honest. Eventually he wished their brief meetings could be longer. Her smile was never submissive, but a little probing, and he saw that understanding and human empathy did not always have to flow in just one direction, from him to her – she too had much to offer.

Yes, he *saw* her, and not merely with the eyes of a pastor.

In the beginning they had discussed trivial, everyday things; then he began to ask about certain individuals and families in Butangen, carefully seeking her advice so as to understand the locals better, and she probably came to see that for a pastor Butangen was one of Christianity's loneliest outposts. He remembered one conversation in particular, after a Mass during which he had berated the villagers for working in the fields on a Sunday. She had been pretty feisty, saying they only did it at ploughing and harvest time, when food had to be got in for the winter.

"And it be the crofters mostly. Especially them as has no horse. They work on the bigger farms all week, so it be only on a Sunday when the rain holds off that they can work their own bit of land."

"When the rain holds off?" he asked.

"Aye, when the clod in't too soggy."

Kai Schweigaard insisted that he found work on Sundays to be morally offensive, to which she replied: "Well, happen it be best not to take offence then – that way the Pastor will save himseln a good deal o' bother!"

He was stunned. Scratched his head. She had said it in such a way that it could not be taken as an insult. Pointing out that he had all the power, and was the one to wield that power. But also that she was his equal, with the right to have her say.

"There aren't *that* many holy days," he replied. "Not *now*, under Protestantism. Do you know why the Norwegians were so opposed to Christianity?"

"That must have been afore ye came," she said.

He had no idea what she was getting at. "I'm talking about St Olav's time. When Christianity was first introduced here. The farmers weren't resistant just because they wanted to keep Odin. Back then, you see, the church wasn't Protestant but Catholic. And the priests wanted thirty-seven fixed holy days."

"On top of Sundays?" said Astrid.

"Indeed. Thirty-seven in addition!"

"So many? That comes to nearly ninety, with Sundays."

"Quite! For an entire quarter of the year nobody was permitted to work! People might have accepted that in warmer and more easily cultivated lands. But it was unworkable up here."

She nodded, scooped up his dinner plate and cutlery and put them on the silver tray with a decisive clatter.

That clattering sound.

It told him that this was how she would clear the cutlery if he sat at *her* table. He knew she came from a quite large farm, a farm that had been connected to the church for generations, which had donated church bells and other gifts, but was now – according to Oldfrue Bressum – "as good as bankrupt".

"Godliness is well and good," Astrid said as she left, "but hunger and sound wits always win out."

A statement that seemed self-evident to her, but which left him pondering.

He started to turn a blind eye to Sunday work in the busy seasons. And perhaps it could be explained by his isolation at the parsonage, but his encounters with Astrid made him relinquish some of the Lutheran grey of his mind, and visit a little room where his heart beat against the walls, a room that might be filled with the love of a spirited and vivacious woman.

A room that was never quite warmed by Ida Calmeyer.

A room out of which he had once stumbled. Through the door of the harlot in Pipervika, doubtless ten years older than him, who whispered: "You're not yet a priest." For a long time he tried to deny that it had happened. How he and his student-friends had parted company one evening, deliriously excited from a one-off dalliance with opium in some bed-sitting room, and joked about visiting a brothel in Fjerdingsgate. He had reeled along the road, giddy and laughing, open to anything and everything. A smile in a doorway. Did someone want him? Small talk first, as she asked what he was studying, followed by his utter defencelessness as she held his hand and caressed his cheek, her unwholesome erotic insinuations, his shock when he realised that his desire was stronger than his will, so that he followed her up to the dismal garret, where she kissed him and pressed her fingers playfully against his pelvis before she undressed them both, sat astride him, clamped his hips between her thighs, enveloped him so entirely that he felt he was being born again, the momentary trance when his body lost all contact with his brain, the wet patches on the yellowed bed sheets, and then the coins, "One more, yes, one more of them big coins," then the shame and aimless wandering through the streets as the opium rush faded, followed by all the desperate prayers for forgiveness and the nightmares when he saw his crotch covered in huge boils.

It was only two years later, after making large detours around Pipervika whenever he had to return to the area, that he managed to think about the experience with any clarity, and tried to call her a "lady of the night" instead of a whore, but meanwhile, in the grips of his ascetic remorse, he had followed his mother's advice. Advice? No, it was a *command* – to offer his hand to the milky-white Ida Calmeyer, who accepted his proposal politely, before continuing with her embroidery.

Ida. She was part of his life's plan. That he would soon be posted to a town parish, then promoted to dean, and then in a few years his voice would sound at bishopric meetings. And at his side: Fru Schweigaard, born Calmeyer. A little pale perhaps, but chaste, loyal, and a support in his ultimate goal – his life's mission. A notion of great import in the Schweigaard household that trumped everything, and was far superior to "happiness".

Even when he was a child, his mother – always the most imposing, blackest-clad widow at any Christmas event – had impressed upon him the importance of having a *mission* in life.

She had picked out the young Frøken Calmeyer at a social event, Kai himself had watched it all unfold; his mother's narrowed eyes alighted on the young girl sitting at the piano, she made a quick calculation as she lifted a delicate porcelain cup to her lips, and by the time she had put it down in the saucer she had decided that a match between Kai and Frøken Calmeyer would be advantageous, most advantageous.

It would be a sensible marriage, an alliance between dynasties, a plug in a hole, a hole created by her somewhat directionless and hot-tempered youngest son Kai, who had never quite applied himself to his schoolwork, and who lacked the stature of his uncle, the renowned parliamentarian. Nor was Kai suited to anything that might require diplomacy; when irritated for long enough, he could fly into a rage without warning. He had little sense for the roots or complexities of history. What was the point of discussing things? Best to act single-handedly, be stubborn, get things done! The rural districts in Norway were still governed by priests, and he decided on an ecclesiastical career. Where his uncle reformed Norway with railroads and schools and a telegraph service, Kai Schweigaard wanted to bring about change from within, shape the nation's soul, open the minds of its people in preparation for the new times ahead.

His mother was livid about his posting to a little backwater in Gudbrandsdal, but calmed down when he explained that Butangen was, in fact, the steepest career-ladder with the largest gap between its rungs, and that its top was, practically speaking, already propped up against the office window of the ageing dean of Lillehammer.

Better to be king in a little kingdom, than prince in a big one! Therefore the ordeal by fire: Butangen.

Where he had learned, through Astrid Hekne, that a woman was *not* most useful when she nodded and agreed. He had never felt lonelier than he did here, despite having grown fond of his parishioners. They cultivated their eccentrics and fiddlers, and they all pitched in, no matter if it was pelting with rain or the workhorse was lame. But their dialect was impenetrable and their ways were often an enigma, sometimes purposely so. They never gave a clear yes or no, and instead of voicing refusal they pretended to be stupid, although the instant a problem was resolved they would set to work quickly and intelligently.

One day he asked Astrid why fewer folk came to church when it rained. She explained that it was because many of the poorer villagers shared shoes. He also wondered why some families never attended Mass on festival days. "It be the folk that is ashamed of their clothes," she told him, adding that it was on such occasions that these differences showed most. Later he expressed surprise that nobody ever sat in the back pew of the church.

This time she was slower to reply.

"Well – naebody wants to sit there," she said.

"Because it's draughty?"

"Nay, because – well, the Pastor mun excuse me."

"Tell me!"

"'Tis the bastard-kids pew."

"The what? Really – the bastard—?"

"The old priest called it summat worse."

"What?"

"The 'whore-pew'. He used to point at the girls and tell everyone what they had done. 'To put the fear of God into them,' he said, 'and to warn against sin in the village.'"

"What are you saying? I didn't know this."

"He set awkward questions for the youngsters he didna like. So they couldna get confirmed, and couldna wed. And all the unwed mothers had to sit there at the back. Happen at the start they sat there so they could go out and suckle their babbies. For they was alone with them, with naebody to help look after them. But when he started to point the finger, they just stopped going to church."

"A pew of their own? Mocked and humiliated? That's the *opposite* of what I'm looking for in a church. Illegitimate children and fornication are serious matters, of course, but our message must be forgiveness! A church should be a place of purity and light, with room for everyone."

Little by little he got a grip on things, and services, baptisms and weddings became easier to handle. But the vagaries of the poor-relief system and his other welfare duties could leave him totally baffled. Nevertheless, he took on task after task. The last time he had gone to Vålebrua to discuss the church with the mayor, the sheriff had dropped by and asked whether he might be willing to distribute the bounty payments for the killing of predatory pests. It was actually the responsibility of the bailiff or the sheriff himself, but since the office was so far from Butangen, mightn't it be more practical if Schweigaard took on the task? It was, the sheriff said, quite usual in the remoter parishes now, as it spared the poor, malnourished hunters a long journey and raised the odds against the gluttonous predators that preyed on farmers' livestock and poor folks' wild game. But Schweigaard had no idea which skins or claws belonged to which animals or birds. Hunters presented him with claws that clearly came from a variety of birds, but they all insisted that theirs were the talons of a golden eagle, for which the bounty was equivalent to many days of a farmhand's wage. On one occasion a hunter brought him a wolfskin, and although it seemed rather small Schweigaard paid him, and he was worried that he – and worse still: the priesthood – had been made a laughing stock. A week later another fellow came with the brown-black pelt of a wolverine. This time he instructed the hunter to wait, saying he needed to go "into a room with better light".

He dashed across the hallway and went into the workroom to find Astrid.

"Tell me," he whispered, closing the door behind him. "Is this the hide of a wolverine?"

She dug her fingers deep into the fur and rubbed the hairs against each other.

"Nay, this here be a Spæl sheep. 'Tis much too soft. Ye can tell if ye run your fingers against the fur. Like this. Nay, like this!"

Schweigaard returned to the con man and sent him packing without any payment. Later a man showed up with two lynx hides, and again the pastor took them off to be inspected in a room with better light.

"Lynx?" said Astrid. "Nay. 'Tis a young fox. With her brush taken off."

"Brush?"

"Her tail. They mun have pulled her fur off the wrong way, snipped off her tail and pulled the skin forwards to make it stand up in a point. But 'tis a fox."

He tried to rub the fur in his fingers as she had done.

"How do you know all this?" he said.

"I shall tell ye one day. Who be after this bounty?"

"Some fellow from that croft they call Gardbogen."

"Hm," she said.

Schweigaard went back and studied his visitor. The man's trousers were worn thin and shiny, his face was frostbitten. He felt tempted to pay out for a lynx, despite the bounty being much higher than for a fox. He said gently that the hunter must have been slightly mistaken today, but here was money for two foxes and he was heartily welcome back with his next catch.

Eventually word spread that the "new pastor" could tell the

difference between the claws of a hen and a hawk. But more important than that, Astrid had helped him to understand how poverty drove folk to cheat the bounty system. She was a veritable ship's lantern shedding light on the Gudbrandsdal peculiarities, and her light shone ever brighter.

Until the day she put out the wrong tablecloth.

It was autumn. Schweigaard was expecting a visit from the mayor and director of the bank to discuss the church. The dinner table was to be laid with the customary colours of the church calendar, but, coming down into the dining room, he had to point out to Astrid that she had put out an advent tablecloth, and that the guests were about to arrive.

"Then give me a helping hand, Pastor, and we can get it shifted!" she said.

He did as she bade, without a thought for its being women's work. Going to the head of the long table, he took one end of the cloth, and together they began to fold it. She had a nifty method of doing it that he tried to imitate: she gripped the cloth tightly, then loosened it between her thumbs as she stepped forwards, throwing the folds in towards herself, he managed this, but they had to hold each other's gaze so as to mirror each other precisely, or the purple advent tablecloth would drag on the floor.

They drew steadily closer.

Then he had to shift his hold, she lost her rhythm, the tablecloth tightened and instantly began to quiver. A trembling in his arms rippled through the fabric in waves that flew towards her, as though in a wind, before they ran back, equally strong, but tighter, he swallowed hard, unable to stop the vibrations, and now the gap between them was closing, and the shorter the cloth grew, the tighter it got and the more it quivered, and he saw his own desire drawn in the fabric, and this went on until they were so close that he could smell her, she must have used a new soap, and for a moment they stood eye to eye, before she snatched his half of the tablecloth and disappeared. Only then did he notice Oldfrue Bressum standing in the doorway.

The following day Astrid was gone. It being in Oldfrue Bressum's mandate to appoint and dismiss staff. To get Astrid back he would have to *demand* her return. He would have to state his reasons for such a request, and his reasons could not be said aloud, and if he mumbled some other excuse, his guard would fall, and his servants would see that beneath his robes a priest wears ordinary clothes, and beneath those he is naked.

He pulled his coat tighter about him and headed towards the parsonage. His thoughts returned to *the plan*, and he wondered if this week's postal delivery might include a letter from Dresden. In his haste he left his usual path, and took a shortcut through the uncleared snow. The dry, powdery snow whirled around his tall leather boots as he waded on. Entering the courtyard, he saw a stranger standing by a horse and cart talking to his tenant farmer. Schweigaard went in, and had barely closed the door behind him before Oldfrue Bressum informed him that he had "a visit from them Hekne folk". He took off his hat, laid his coat on the arm of a chair and leaped up the stairs two at a time. Sitting on the stool outside his office was Astrid Hekne, alone.

The Secret of the Mountain Elves

Gerhard Schönauer had just come out of a lecture on Moorish decorative art when he received a message that Professor Ulbricht wanted to speak with him. A portly and rather pedantic man in his mid-sixties, Ulbricht was Gerhard's favourite lecturer on art history. And he had, on several occasions, visited the professor's dark-brown, smoky office in the west wing. The word "office" was presumably just an administrative label, since one of the many privileges that came with his professorship at the Dresden Academy of Art was the huge floor space put at his disposal. The "office" was a studio, a teaching room, an exhibition space and a salon all rolled into one, so spacious that a horse could stand in it without seeming out of place. It was joked that in Ulbricht's case it would always find something to eat too. He was granted six metres' ceiling height – essential when instructing students in the painting of palatial murals. Around the desk were shelves filled with old leather-bound books, stacks of documents and drawings and yellowing rolls of paper. Propped against the walls there were countless wooden boards covered with drawings and paintings, so many that they ate up half the floor space. Ulbricht had even covered the ceiling with pictures, mostly reproductions of Flemish masters, but also the occasional Arab and Persian work. It was quite a feat to make such a huge space seem cramped; Gerhard could hardly move without looking down, for fear of treading on some obscure treasure that the professor had picked up on his travels.

"*Gesundes neues Jahr*, Herr Schönauer, a happy New Year!" said Ulbricht, before reverting to his usual stiff manner: "I don't have much time, so I must be brief. I've taken a look at your work and find that you have an outstanding, nay, a first-rate understanding, of both the decorative arts *and* architecture. Which are, in truth, two very distinct disciplines."

Gerhard recognised the professor's tone. This was an overture, and now he expected a polite nod, which was duly provided.

"The time's coming for you to make a choice," Ulbricht said. "Let me ask you: which would you rather pursue: painting or architecture?"

"Erm, it's hard to tell . . ." murmured Gerhard.

"Well, that's precisely what I want you to do now! Tell me!"

"*Vielen Dank*. But I'm just not very good at talking like that – on the spur of the moment."

"Ha, then try! Between us, Herr Schönauer, there are enough braggarts in these corridors. It might be good for you to weigh up your talents. You're a rare bird! But possessing a multifaceted gift has its drawbacks. The risk is that you'll waver, never really getting good at any one thing."

"Architecture is what I like best. But it's probably also the most daunting."

"And why is that – on a deeper level?"

"*Everybody* sees architecture, they *have* to see it. But if I truly mastered it, then . . ."

"Then?"

"I like the idea that people might walk past something every day that I have created. That, even though they don't look at it closely, its sheer presence gives them *pleasure*, without costing them anything. That they could pass this building knowing that it will still be there in another hundred years. A painting is deeper in its intensity perhaps, but a beautiful villa, an apartment building, a town hall – they all impact life itself."

"And decorative art?"

"Well . . . that's just a thing of the moment, to be viewed close up."

"Hm! Listen, Schönauer. The calendar's telling us that the study trips are coming fast upon us. My question is simple: have you secured yourself a grant?"

"I want to go back to London," said Gerhard, "to study the architectural works of Wren and Jones again."

"Yes, but my question was whether you have financed the trip?"

The words cut deep. College fees were sky-high, and most of Gerhard's fellow students were funded by their wealthy, art-interested families. The gap showed itself in their travels. The well-off students outdid each other with lofty plans to stay in Florence or Milan to make studies of the classical sculptures, with the bonus that they could quaff wine all day, and – as they would brag later – make excursions to the cheap, but first-class, bordellos of Lombardy.

"When were you in London?" asked Ulbricht.

"A couple of years ago, but only briefly. Just two weeks. And then two weeks in Cambridge. Extremely enriching, however."

"Which family covered your costs?"

Gerhard twisted his lips. "None, Professor. I paid for it with the sale of a few portraits that I painted in the evenings. Not very good, but adequate."

"Impressive, nonetheless! So – you don't have any benefactors?"

"Unfortunately not."

"I understand you're from East Prussia? Königsberg?"

Gerhard was taken aback. There was no obvious reason for these questions about his hometown. It could only mean that Ulbricht had been making enquiries about him.

"A little further east, actually," Gerhard said. "My family lives in Memel."

"Aha! In the very east. Tell me – you have a rich tradition of building in wood there, is that right?"

"Yes, absolutely. We even have our own variation of the Russian peasant style – walls built with huge logs, joined only at the corners."

Ulbricht nodded. "Tell me, young Schönauer: are you ready for a challenge?"

Gerhard said "yes" and tried to look excited, adding that no *true* art student would answer no to such a question, although he could hear how hollow this sounded.

"That's the attitude!" said Ulbricht, slapping Gerhard on the back. "I need the right man for a trip to a very exotic place, in the service of architecture."

Gerhard mumbled that he'd love to go, but—

"Ah, I can see straight through you!" exclaimed Ulbricht. "Don't worry about your expenses." He leaned forwards and whispered: "They'll be covered by the Saxon royal family!"

Gerhard did not understand. The Dresden Academy of Art was a royal institution, enjoying the official approval of Albert I, but from the way Ulbricht was talking, it seemed the plan was known to the regent himself.

"*Vielen Dank*, Herr Professor, but—"

"In fact, you'll be paid for your efforts. *Most* generously! But the trip will be a whole seven months long, since it involves taking goods across the ice during the winter! Ha ha, now you're curious! Well then, if your answer is yes, we can meet here tomorrow."

"But . . . where are you sending me?"

"To the Norwegian part of Sweden!"

"Nach Norwegen?"

"Yes. The far north. Don't worry, there are maps."

"But Professor . . . apologies, but . . . surely there can't be much in the way of architecture up there? Isn't it an underdeveloped country, dominated by very basic agriculture? I mean, this region wasn't even mentioned in any of our lectures about European architecture?"

Ulbricht chuckled.

"Then you've not been listening closely. I *did* mention Norway once. It's a poor country, true enough, but these mountain elves are hiding a little secret."

Ulbricht stepped over some plaster heads on the floor and retrieved his overcoat from the broken arm of a statue of Salome. On her head was a hat set at an angle, and draped about her neck a vermilion scarf. He unwound the scarf. "I'm busy today.

Ten o'clock tomorrow, Schönauer. Sharp," he said, lifting his hat from the statue's head.

"By the way – do keep this to yourself."

Gerhard did not manage to keep it to himself. That very evening – though not before she had put her clothes back on – he told Sabinka that he was going to Norway.

"Norway? You'll freeze to death. That's right next to Greenland!"

"No. It's a part of Sweden apparently. A couple of days from Hamburg by boat."

"Hmm. For how long?"

"Oh, two months. Three perhaps."

"Three? Three whole months? I could barely hold out when you went to England!"

She was telling the truth, he knew that for a fact. A fellow student had let slip that she had indeed *not* held out, while he was away for that one short month in London and Cambridge to study urban architecture. The whole truth – that he was going for *seven* months – would have to come later, otherwise she'd move on to fresh pastures right away.

"I won't be travelling until April," he said. "And this time there'll be some money in it. Big money."

"You and your money. Don't let that be all talk. And go, before the others come."

Sabinka took life lightly. She was the sister of a life model from Mähren, one of those girls the students were warned not to speak to or contact, but whom the more enterprising among them had tracked down anyway. Gerhard had gone home to his parents for Christmas, but had travelled back to Dresden to celebrate New Year's Eve with Sabinka, and they had gone to a wild party at the Lindenkrug – a tavern where the clientele looked over both shoulders before entering, filled with the laughter of women who didn't care what people said, and with men who liked such women, but never considered marrying them.

Sabinka was heavier and more buxom than her sister, with chapped hands from working in a laundry. He drew several portraits of both sisters in pencil and charcoal, but always held back when drawing Sabinka. Her face was pretty enough, but she was inclined to get fat. Her breasts were so large that they were cold in the winter, and he was worried they would lose their beauty with time.

But now she was young, he was young, and they were young together in Dresden.

He said goodbye to her, headed towards his lodgings in Antonstadt, made a detour past the pink baroque church, turned into the promenade lit by two rows of gas lamps, then stopped by the Elbe and looked at the magnificent buildings reflected in the water below. All the fountains, the statues on the roofs, and the fine facades that tolerated being painted mint green, pink and blue.

A breeze swept up from the river and stroked his cheek. Behind him came the clatter of a horse-drawn cab, and an exquisitely dressed couple stepped out.

Dresden. The entire city was an artwork. The sum of thoughts too big to be conceived by one person alone, greater than anything an entire generation could conceive. Europe's most beautiful city – the only one that might match it was Florence. Each building was the culmination of ambition, taste, money and toil. Nothing had any value if it did not take a minimum of five years to build. Hewn granite, bricks, plasterwork, copper, lime and paint. Each new thing that was built had to be the most beautiful, until – in the following year – someone would set out to surpass this again, so that with each century the city became more exquisite.

He wandered on aimlessly, past the opera house, past museums, churches, concert halls. Someone opened the kitchen door of a restaurant to let out the odour of frying food. Back in his rooms he had nothing but dry biscuits.

One day he would eat and drink whatever he wanted, wherever he wanted. His table would be set with clinking cutlery, veal steak in a steaming sauce would arrive when his beer glass was half-empty, and he would nod when the waiter asked if he and his company would like more.

Gerhard Schönauer turned back to the Elbe and listened to the lapping of the broad, slow river. The city lights glowed, and so did he. The *chosen one* was heading north, and he wondered which Norwegian city Ulbricht would send him to.

Church Bells Shall Still Ring

Astrid Hekne stood up and curtseyed, and Kai Schweigaard said: "It's very nice to see you again, despite the circumstances."

Moments later they were in his office, sitting on either side of his desk. In the middle of the otherwise empty tabletop stood a little brown bottle with a handwritten label: *Giktsmurning* – arthritis salve.

"Klara only ever got to use half of it," said Astrid. "So we reckoned the liniment ought to go to someone that needs it – as Herr Pastor sees fit."

Kai Schweigaard took the bottle. In it the contents sloshed stickily. He had no idea what the salve contained or whether it was of any real use. But he remembered having done his best, that summer, to ensure that Klara Mytting got some for her pain.

Astrid was being terribly formal – "Herr Pastor" indeed. What was the reason for her visit today? If her excuse was this *giktsmurning* then her actual errand must be of gigantic proportion. He looked into her eyes and the long tablecloth came back into his mind. She shifted on her chair and straightened her shawl, he cleared his throat and focused his thoughts where they should be, on the shrivelled old woman who had died in his church.

"She was a frugal woman," said Kai Schweigaard, placing the bottle on the table, slightly closer to himself, signalling his acknowledgment of its return to the Poor Law Board.

"Klara owned nowt at all," said Astrid. "So 'twas enough with just the one trip here."

"Yes. Indeed. And you're keeping well – up there – on the farm?"

"Well enough, thank you. It were better before."

He nodded, though he didn't understand her. When before?

"Where's Klara been put?" asked Astrid.

The shine of her hair. The curve of her eyebrows, the mystery in her gaze, the sharpness of mind that was almost tangible. The tablecloth started to quiver again.

Astrid cleared her throat, and asked again where Klara was.

"Oh. In the carriage shed. In a coffin, of course. A person who dies in the House of God must surely be allowed to await their burial in – well – in one of God's houses."

"We have come to fetch her up to Hekne. Me and a farmhand."

"Oh, so *that* was who I saw. Right. Well, I'm afraid there's been an unexpected turn of events. We'll have to postpone the funeral until spring. The churchwarden can't hack through the frozen ground."

"Oh," was all she said.

"This isn't how I wanted things to be," said Kai Schweigaard, pleased that his statement allowed for what they were both thinking, that Klara had frozen to death during his service. "Not least because the plan was for Klara to be buried in the new way."

"New way?" she asked, and Kai could hear that she was faintly elated. Yes, he thought, *that*'s the difference with folk here in this village. Their reaction to this phrase. As though it were almost shocking!

"From now on I intend to hold funeral services inside the church," he said. "For everyone. Not just the well-to-do farmers. And Klara shall be the first of her . . . rank."

Astrid inclined her head. "Are the dead to go inside the church now?"

"That's been usual in the towns for some years. I see no reason for the custom not to come to the countryside."

He saw her squirm. "What's the matter, Astrid?"

"The skirt," she said.

"The skirt?"

"Klara borrowed the skirt and boots she had on that day. She wanted to look nice for church, like we all do."

There they were again; the hard realities. Each time he came up with a good plan, along came the cold or poverty and kicked the legs from under it. It was as though he was being followed by some sceptical goblin, in breeches and clogs, who picked his teeth and tittered at any new idea.

Borrowed shoes. A best skirt. Firmly stuck to a corpse. He pictured what the task would involve. Klara had to be semi-thawed, the clothes peeled off, then a shroud wrapped round her, ready to be laid in the carriage shed again.

"I'll see to the clothes and shoes," said Kai Schweigaard, pleased with the brisk tone of his words. That was how he wanted it to be, there must be no baulking when the Church faced extra duties! "*You* shan't be burdened with such things, Astrid," he continued eagerly. "You can come and collect everything in three days. I'll have it all washed and folded."

Astrid looked surprised, and with joy he realised how radical – and modern! – he had been. That *others* might take responsibility for folks' lives was unheard of, perhaps it was improperly forward. But he also registered that this desire to act might not be wholly honest, that it might not come from as selfless a vein as it should, but from a masculine need to impress.

"But about this new way," said Astrid. "Will there be ringing for them that has passed? Of the church bells, I mean?"

"Of course. That's part of it. It's the least we can offer. And there'll be no charge!"

"But what of the poor souls that takes their own lives?"

He was flummoxed by the question. Not because he lacked the answer, but because her thoughts went off at such a tangent. "Well, Astrid, the law is very clear on that. Nowadays they can be laid in consecrated ground, but there can be no speeches or scattering of earth. Although a moment of reflection for the family might be permissible and . . . well . . . I'll give it some thought."

He must have left a little question mark hanging, because she nodded, and said: "I see. It were just summat that came to my mind. 'Cos Herr Pastor knows that some folks can na' hold out."

Schweigaard scratched his nose. He had no idea what to say. There was an awkwardness between them today.

"But considering . . . hmm . . . the *nature* of the matter at hand," he said, immediately regretting his tone, "this would have been the perfect opportunity for this new funeral service. I mean with Klara having died . . . er . . . away from home. It left a situation that's rather . . . delicate."

Astrid looked at him blankly.

"What do you think?" he said.

"Is it nay just a fond cruke?" said Astrid. He felt a certain irritation, and also a faint excitement, at the impertinence of her exchanging his word "delicate" for some dialect word he did not understand.

"It musna come too sudden," she said. "Herr Pastor musna forget that they like the old ways here. They be accustomed to giving folk a good send-off. With Klara, we thought we should have the old schoolmaster sing her out afore she were laid to rest."

"It'll still be a good send-off," said Kai Schweigaard. "But within the firm framework of the Church. And for the poor too."

He was aware that families took a lot of trouble over their dead. The problem was that they stirred all sorts of dubious rituals in with their wakes. They burned the corpse's straw mattress and read the future from the direction of the smoke, and when the coffin was about to set off everyone watched the horse drawing the carriage or sledge: if it raised its right hoof first, the next person to die would be a man, if it raised its left, the mourners looked around wondering which of the old women would be next. He had heard about wakes that lasted for three days and degenerated into wild dancing and card-playing, before ending in a drunken brawl, with the womenfolk hurling insults and pulling each other's hair, while the menfolk brandished their knives, inflicting injury on themselves and others. But worse still, in Kai Schweigaard's opinion, was the custom of forcing the reality of death onto young children. Often, during these wakes, they were ordered to see and embrace the dead, while the master of ceremonies' lamp danced and threw shadows on the wall. Kai knew that a little girl in the village, who had been rude to the deceased and not apologised, was dragged to the corpse to kiss it and make her peace. Apart from the danger of infection and the pools of liquid that oozed from the corpses, these events attracted beadsmen who chanted and performed strange ancient rites, far outside any Christian practice. But from now on . . .

"I were wondering," said Astrid. "Be the Holyblight mentioned in the Pastor's books?"

"What did you call it?"

"Holyblight," she repeated.

"No, I've not come across that," said Kai Schweigaard. "It must be some sort of strange superstition."

"Klara said it grew inside the church bells, and that it were a remedy for all kinds of sickness."

"Oh, I see. That's the sort of notion I'm keen for us to be rid of. One of my goals for Butangen is to stamp out all forms of superstition and folklore."

"Oh aye, but them things in little caskets," said Astrid, "that the old pastor taught us about at confirmation. The remains of saints. Toenails and locks of hair and knuckles."

"Oh, relics! Yes, that's largely a Catholic thing. Hm, that kind of thing is, well—"

"So what be the difference betwixt them and the Holyblight? Who decides that one counts whilst the other do not?"

"We'd need to have an awfully long conversation to get to the bottom of that one," he said.

She looked straight at him, and her lips pursed into a tiny smile, accompanied by a little flutter of her eyelashes, and without her uttering a word he got the feeling she wanted to answer: "Happen a little cup of coffee would na' go amiss then?"

But a thing like that could not be said, by him or by her, nor did she say it. He cleared his throat, she cleared her throat, but something had happened. They had shared a moment, encountered an obstacle together, and each of them knew that the other knew it too.

He shot a glance at the grandfather clock, hoping Oldfrue Bressum would not burst in on one of her flimsy pretexts.

"That time, in church, at the end of New Year's Mass," said Astrid Hekne carefully, "Herr Pastor said summat about change.

That the village would be 'released from suffering'. Or 'set free', I think it were."

Set free? thought Kai Schweigaard. Did I say that? Whatever the case – she had been following closely!

"Well, I can say this much," he said. "We must do something about our church. This isn't something I want gossiped about, but the fact is that the church is, by law, too small."

"But surely it be the sheriff that's in charge of the church?"

"No, not directly – or yes, in fact the sheriff is. The law states that there should be room enough in a church for one third of its parish. I have studied the numbers. We don't have room for one tenth in our church. This is an old law, introduced in 1842. It's only by the mercy of fate that we've been able to go on here."

He paused, uneasy at his use of the word "mercy", which was generally reserved for the Lord to dispense. "When I first came here I studied the church records. The number of children born to each family has grown enormously. In sixty years, the population of the village has doubled, despite the recent emigration to America. But there's been no change in land usage, and the crops don't provide enough food for everyone."

"But surely the law canna do anything about the number of folk? Or that they go hungry in the winter?"

Kai Schweigaard could not make her out, she seemed almost to toy with her own curiosity, and yet it was fenced in by a melancholy, a melancholy he recognised in many of the villagers, about the fact that life was so hard and that there was scant prospect of it ever being easier.

"Christianity should lead to progress," he said. "But the church itself is too dilapidated. People as far as Lillehammer are talking about how someone froze to death during Mass. It's best you keep this to yourself, but I can give you my promise that you'll never have to experience such a thing again."

"So does Herr Pastor plan to rebuild the church?"

"Please, Astrid, don't address me in the third person."

"Because we be just two here?"

"I mean that you can speak directly to me – you don't need to say 'does Herr Pastor this' or 'does Herr Pastor that'."

"Right. So, Kai Schweigaard, is the plan—"

"I meant you could just say 'you' – 'do you plan'. Let's allow ourselves to use more modern forms of address."

"Aye, I understood. I were just teasing."

"Well anyway, something must be done with the church."

"But it be a secret?"

"Well, it's . . ."

"'Tis nay trouble," she said. "I be good at keeping secrets."

He felt he was on the point of doing something. It was rare for him to be alone with a woman, and something vigorous was kicking to get out of his secret room, it felt reckless, and yet so agreeably natural. He managed to keep his eyes turned from her, but then the urge burst out again, the urge to draw her closer to him, to let her into his world, and he told her that although the funeral must be postponed, she shouldn't worry, because he was thinking of building a mortuary chapel. She seemed not to take this in, reacting with neither questions nor surprise, as though she merely registered that he was speaking, without it having any relevance to her. She still had her outdoor clothes on, and he wondered if this was because she had intended this to be a quick visit, or because she was cold.

"Are you cold?" he asked.

"I have been far colder. But ye already know that."

He got up and fetched a woollen blanket with deep green and black stripes, a Scottish tartan design, and walked over to her. He knew how things were on the farms. People slept under rough animal skins, surrounded by the acrid odour of sheep or goat or calf. She could use this blanket both as a shawl and a blanket. It was richly woven, with fringes at the ends. An exquisite article, as refined as the parsonage itself, which despite its slight shabbiness was elegant, with its painted floors, polished furniture, panelled windows and veranda, and he was suddenly gripped by an idea – by a desire to see Astrid Hekne in another guise, here in these surroundings, improved, refined, like a handsome table of raw pine, planed smooth and painted.

For a second he fumbled. This was a gesture of kindness, nothing more, it must not be interpreted as an act of intimacy, and he stopped at an exaggerated distance from her, and had to lean towards her and stretch his arms out to give it to her.

"It's my travel blanket," said Kai Schweigaard. "My mother gave it to me. You can have it until spring. I'm not planning on going anywhere. And, by the way, I've got a newspaper here, you can take that with you too. Keep it!" He bit his lip. "For a while. I collect them in the archive. But hold on to it and the blanket for as long as you like."

He glanced at the headline on the front page. The steamship *Finmark* had been caught in a hurricane and almost grounded. She stroked the blanket. A long, delicate movement, her slender hand barely touching the soft wool, as though she were stroking his forearm, making the fibres lie towards her.

"Thanking ye kindly," she said, placing the blanket and newspaper in her lap. "But ye mun take care not to introduce too many new things at once."

"Thanking *you*!" said Schweigaard. "But we must move with the times. It'll be good for us all. No – I may as well tell you, loud and clear! What's happening, Astrid, is this: we're to have a new church!"

Astrid leaned forwards in her chair.

"I recognised the need for a new church the instant I arrived in Butangen. Our good Bishop Folkestad in Hamar agrees that the greatest material obstacle to religion lies in these cold, rickety churches. As he said in a letter to me, 'God's servants ought not to be sent to an outhouse, which is the case in far too many places in Gudbrandsdal.'"

"But do the bishop have any money?"

"No. And there you've hit the nail on the head, Astrid. I've had meetings with the local council and the mayor. We're all in absolute agreement. But there's never been enough money. Not before now, at least."

She inclined her head, inviting him to tell her more, but he managed to hold back, saying that things weren't quite in place yet. "But," he said, clearing his throat, "church bells shall still ring across the village."

She left shortly afterwards, but showed none of the excitement he had hoped for. Rather, she appeared more grown-up and less amenable. There was a sourness in their exchange as they parted, more probing than warm, and she did not put the blanket over her shoulders, but clamped it under her arm so she could open the door herself.

Kai Schweigaard listened until her steps faded in the hallway. He went to the hatstand and rummaged in his overcoat pocket for his pipe and tobacco pouch. "Shall still ring." Why, at the very end, had he said something so blatantly obvious? Without filling his pipe, he opened a drawer in his bureau and took out a copy of his latest letter to Dresden.

God's Finger Pointed at Norway

Gerhard Schönauer was so nervous the next morning that he nicked the corner of his mouth shaving, and his tongue kept returning to the wound as he walked towards Ulbricht's office. He was shown in and introduced to two men who stood at a slight distance from each other, inspecting the artworks on the walls. One, who had an extraordinary moustache and smelled strongly of pomade, was named Kastler, and Gerhard wondered if he had misheard when the professor introduced him as a royal courtier sent by the queen. The other seemed impatient, and barely bothered to acknowledge Gerhard, who ascertained only that he came from the office of the burgomaster.

"Let me begin, gentlemen," said Ulbricht, leading them with short, careful footsteps to a round table, "with something you may not all know." He stopped, and with a sweep of his arm he directed his visitors' eyes around the room. "This room," he said, "once belonged to Professor Dahl. Yes, the famous Norwegian. Johan Christian Dahl was his full name, although you will know him as J. C. Dahl. I was among his students, and later I had the pleasure of working closely with him. On his death in 1857 I took over both his office and his professorship. Dahl was a formidable force in landscape painting, but a lesser known aspect of his work was his study of medieval churches in his homeland, and the culture from which they sprang. And this coincides with one of *my* passions, namely the study of the roots of the old Germanic culture."

With a deliberate, almost ceremonial gesture, he rested his hand on a large, leather-bound book, and suddenly Gerhard recalled that Ulbricht had given a lecture on Norse decorative arts in the Middle Ages, and that he had mentioned one of his personal possessions – a precious book of drawings produced by Professor Dahl, which had been printed in a tiny edition, but which showed the most magnificent carvings and architecture.

"Gentlemen," said Ulbricht, and Gerhard knew by his tone what was in store – a long and pompous lecture. The professor was so erudite that he no longer possessed everyday language. As one of Gerhard's fellow students had remarked: "Even when he talks about the weather, he's like an encyclopaedia."

"*Meine Herren*, we stand before a crisis in art history, in the *philosophy* of art itself," said Ulbricht. "The last remains of the finest European medieval architecture in wood are in the process of being destroyed – wilfully! I am, of course, talking about the stave churches in Norway. In its time this dark mountainous country had over a thousand such churches. Wondrous buildings, unique in the world."

"What? In Norway?" exclaimed the burgomaster's representative. "You enjoy a little joke, eh?"

"I, too, was surprised when I first heard about their existence," Ulbricht went on. "Although it would be more accurate now to talk about their *past* existence. There are only fifty left, and the madness has only intensified – large numbers are being torn down each year. This wouldn't be so catastrophic if the stave churches were the simple, pragmatic buildings we imagine them to have in this impoverished land. But there is a paradox here! Today's Norway is a very different country to that which built the stave churches. Today it is a poor and overpopulated land, but it was not always thus."

"So we have a responsibility here," said the burgomaster's representative. "I recognise your story from other fallen, degenerated kingdoms. Take Egypt or Persia, to name a couple. The instant a society ceases to produce surplus to its basic needs, its respect for its cultural history starts to suffer. For centuries Egyptian grave robbers have sold off their country's ancient treasures; such is the passage of history that it only takes *one* individual's hunger pangs to be stronger than his sense of principle, and – poof! – four-thousand-year-old shared assets are surreptitiously sold off at the bazaar. And I'm not ashamed to say that our museums are among the world's foremost precisely because we have stepped in and saved such treasures in their hour of need. Dresden both *is* and *will* be the bank vault of culture!"

"Quite!" said Ulbricht. "And right now we have just such a case, call it 'Egyptian', in Norway. A thousand years ago, the Norwegians had a high culture, but now they breed like rabbits, without a thought for how they'll rear their offspring, and they starve because their agricultural methods are medieval. Incidentally, the situation is worse than in Egypt, since in Norway we're talking about the *systematic* and *intentional* eradication of cultural monuments. The authorities have even introduced a law that sets a *minimum size* for churches, and this, in parallel with population growth, has led to a demolition-mania in the name of modernisation! The idea seems to be that all the old churches must go, and they've come a very long way to achieving that goal."

Courtier Kastler nodded stiffly, as though to endorse Ulbricht's words thus far. He rarely said anything, but behaved as though his opinion alone might cast disfavour on even the humblest request. He wore an exquisite double-breasted suit, and hanging on the hatstand was a glossy hat and an overcoat with a high collar.

"Norway," continued Professor Ulbricht, "was once Europe's leading shipping nation. More than that, Norway was an empire! The mainland had the longest coastline in the entire civilised world, and they ruled over the Faroe Islands, Iceland, Shetland, the Orkneys and most of the Hebrides, as well as a few narrow strips of Sweden and Greenland's best stretch of coast. Despite the occasional axe-murder of a king, and various intrigues in the court and bedroom, they held dominion over the North Atlantic, and their earls and nobles had deep links with Europe's royal houses. They were rolling in money. And this was before our own appalling times, when wealthy people put their money in the bank to make *more* money. Interest rates didn't exist at that time. Money had to be used there and then, on something visible. The product of money, power and the desire to go down in posterity, gentlemen, *is art – and architecture*!"

Ulbricht cleared his throat. He had yet to open the book of prints. Gerhard guessed that the professor intended – in the spirit of a good lecture – to build the suspense further before the grand conclusion, and he braced himself for an even longer monologue.

"Let me give you a clearer idea of why the stave churches are as they are," said Ulbricht. "Christianity came to Norway late, and the chieftains opposed it. But the pope was determined to establish a mission in this seafaring country, because of the power it wielded internationally. The problem was that the Norwegians were a stubborn and ferocious people, who were determined to hold on to their highly developed and eagerly practised natural religion, founded on a world of aggressive, warring gods and a plethora of creation stories and legends, which we too recognise from our own Germanic past. But there was money in the Vatican to promote Christianisation. God's finger was pointing at Norway! And with this came an interesting contiguity between geography, Catholicism and architecture."

Ulbricht opened an atlas, turned to the page headed "Norwegen und Schweden", and then mumbled something to himself – a habit Gerhard recognised as his usual prelude to firing his final cannons.

"Take a look. Norway is a vastly inaccessible land mass. The forces of nature have carved it up like a labyrinth, like a fortress, with treacherous mountain passes, endless fjords and seething rivers. It wasn't enough for Christianity to be paraded in the coastal towns," he said, pointing at Trondheim and Bergen. "No, it had to penetrate deeper." He traced his index finger across the map, past an area marked "Dovre", where the place names became increasingly sparse, before he finally landed on Gudbrandsdal. "It had to reach *here*, the centre of darkness, where paganism was still the norm. Yes, for Christianity to take proper root in Norway, it had to get a firm foothold like a goat on a mountain slope. Which is why so *many* churches were needed – often small, but numerous."

"Very interesting," said Courtier Kastler, crossing his arms.

The professor mumbled, cleared his throat again, and continued: "The material available to them was timber. Vast quantities, in fact, of tall pine. Excellent, sturdy, durable material, ideal for the crafts which these fierce people of the north had mastered to perfection, in the form of shipbuilding, carpentry and intricate woodcarving. The old Norse religion was highly visual, they were not afraid to show the faces of their gods like the Muhammadans – no, Norse ornamentation was rich and spectacular."

"Hmmm," said Kastler. "*Und wertvoll.*"

Ulbricht nodded eagerly. "Yes! Very costly indeed – when calculated in terms of labour. And – well, this is the strange thing. The Catholic Church accepted a *liberal* transition between the old and the new faith!" Closing the atlas and putting it aside, he explained that the papal authorities had accepted – perhaps because it represented the path of least resistance in the face of the truculent Norwegians – that the old Norse faith should take its place side by side with Catholicism.

"And now you all know where I'm going with this," said Ulbricht. "The world of the Norse gods has much in common with our own great myths. The fabulous tales about the Valkyries, about Odin, Thor, Loki, the roots of Wagner's magnificent Ring Cycle – our whole Germanic-Nordic culture – all lived on in these churches. The beliefs were not promoted openly, of course, but stayed in the background looking on, like some sort of shadow religion! It manifested itself in carved reliefs and sculptures, in hidden runic inscriptions and decorated wooden portals. Most of these churches were gradually stripped of their

Norse elements. But a few," he added, secretively, "went on until today, serving two gods simultaneously, and as such these are the oldest preserved illustration of the ancient German faith."

"And all this is now disappearing?" asked the burgomaster's representative.

"Not just that!" said Ulbricht, flinging out his arms. "It's being desecrated! Church spires are torn down with ropes, wrought-iron hinges are melted down to be made into horseshoes, sacristy doors are used as barn doors, leaded windows are fitted into outdoor privies, decoratively painted timber walls are split for firewood. Everything that was once a triumph of building techniques and artistry is being smashed up across all of Norway. It is our duty to— well, just take a look at this," said the professor, finally presenting the huge book of prints so that they could see its long title inscribed in gold letters: *Stave Churches – Examples of the Highly Developed Art of Building with Wood from the Earliest Centuries in the Innermost Landscapes of Norway*.

He leafed through the stiff, yellowing pages, and opened the book to reveal the first plate.

"Prächtig! Phänomenal!" exclaimed Gerhard, breaking the awed silence that had descended. The drawing was a masterpiece, proof that a truly good pencil drawing could take the breath away of even the most hardened art connoisseur. But it was clear, too, that the artist had taken a subject befitting his talents; the Borgund church offered a magnificent, perfectly balanced composition of steep angled roofs, decorative detail, tall spires and gaping dragons. Its style was as foreign to Gerhard as any Persian palace, but it was without question a masterpiece, utterly different from the stately buildings and mansions he had dreamed of designing. Yet this church touched a nerve in him, something deep, it was a link to a wild and smouldering world, to the time of the sagas, of bonfires and drawn swords, surrounded by the powers of the night and the sea.

Professor Ulbricht turned to another drawing, entitled "Urnes church", saying: "Note the signature here. These are not drawn by Dahl, but by one of his students, a certain Franz Wilhelm Schiertz."

Then, looking straight at Gerhard, he related the story of how a Norwegian church had been taken down under Franz Schiertz's supervision, and transported to Berlin, where it was to be rebuilt – before the plans were changed, and it ended up in the Riesengebirge in Silesia. Ulbricht said that this task had proved immensely difficult, but that the church was still standing to this day. "In this, Dahl succeeded. Although he was extremely disappointed by the reception of his book. Very few people bought it, and not one Norwegian library wanted a copy."

Ulbricht turned carefully back to the preface now, and read a passage from Dahl's account of his many travels in his homeland: "When I visited Norway again in 1834, several of these ancient churches had disappeared and been replaced by new, distinctly unremarkable, wooden buildings. And now, sadly, the axe is laid at the root of these trees."

The professor explained that Dahl had even greater plans for his project, but a lack of time and money meant that it was never completed. Looking Gerhard Schönauer in the eye and pausing for dramatic effect, he fished out a large portfolio. "But now, gentlemen, like the genie of the lamp, let me present for your delight: Dahl's *unpublished* drawings."

First came two drawings of Ringebu church and Lom church, which Gerhard would have liked to linger over. But Ulbricht moved quickly on to a drawing of a church resembling the one in Borgund, and announced, in a tone of absolute rapture:

"Here it is. One of the most beautiful. The church of Butangen. In a secluded place in the innermost part of the country, surrounded by bears and wolves. Utterly untouched."

The group leaned over the table, shoulder to shoulder. Kastler let out an appreciative "mmm", as if, after a long wait, a napkin had been wrapped round him and a fine dish set on the table. This church was even more dramatic than the one in Borgund. Its angles were sharper and the dragon heads were not just flat timber cut-outs, they were hefty, three-dimensional sculptures that hissed at all four corners of the heavens with long, rippling tongues. But the thing that really made this church special was its decorative features. The covered walkways were crammed with carvings, and the jewel in the crown was the portal, decorated so exquisitely that a full page was dedicated to a detailed study of it. Such carvings were worthy of being cast in gold, wild fantasies made manifest with consummate precision, they were among the most febrile artworks Gerhard had ever seen. Every surface thronged with mythical beasts, lizards with shells on their backs, and, running around the door, a giant serpent, its jaws snapping.

"This portal," Ulbricht continued, "is a beautiful example of how the old Norse faith was adapted and used. The entrance is low and narrow, barely bigger than an attic door. These marvellous carvings were supposed to prevent any evil powers from sneaking into the church – very pragmatic – the spirits were too frightened by these figures to wheedle their way among the congregation. The Norsemen were unconvinced that a crucifix or even the *andreaskorsene* – St Andrew's crosses – that were such an intrinsic part of the construction of many stave churches, were up to the job. It required a brute of this magnitude," he said, pointing at the fearsome serpent.

"Heavens preserve us, that's impressive," said the burgomaster's representative. "I've never seen anything like it. Such a concentration of faith and originality. We can't allow this to be lost."

"The only thing I can compare these with," ventured Gerhard, "are the nightmarish creations of Hieronymus Bosch. And they've managed to achieve it with ordinary woodcarving tools. *Absolut fantastisch*!"

"Added to which," said Professor Ulbricht, "this church offers something else of great value: two church bells that come with their very own legend attached – such things cannot be measured in money."

The three men fell silent. Courtier Kastler stared into Gerhard's eyes. There was something hypnotic and reptilian about his gaze, although Gerhard instantly dismissed the idea, thinking he must have been too deeply affected by Dahl's lizard drawings. Kastler had still not told him why the Saxon royal family was taking such an interest in the project, and Gerhard realised that he was expected to work this out for himself.

Yes, of course, Gerhard nodded to himself: the Queen of Saxony, Carola von Wasa, was Swedish. So this stave church was in her native country – or were they in a some sort of union – Norway and Sweden?

"*Jawohl*, Student Schönauer ..." said Kastler, smacking his lips. "You'd better start to learn Norwegian as soon as possible."

Gerhard spent three evenings a week with a rather corpulent private teacher in Leubnitzer Strasse. Herr Lorentzen was Danish and spoke a language "similar to Norwegian". They focused on a working vocabulary that covered buildings (window, ceiling, wall) and labour (faster, working hours, too expensive), horse and carriage (harness, horseshoe, hay) plus the essentials for social interaction with the locals (good morning, herring, cheers!), and very soon Herr Lorentzen was applauding him for his excellent progress and, in particular, for his pronunciation.

Gerhard's optimism was further boosted when he managed to get hold of the latest edition of *Meyers Dänisch–Norwegischer Sprachführer für Reise und Haus* – a well-edited cross between a travel guide and a pocket phrase book, with beautiful fold-out maps and hard-wearing covers of brown board. Meanwhile, aside from attending his lectures at the academy, he read up on Norse mythology, studied Wagner's operas, received money for warm clothes and drawing materials, and travelled to the Riesengebirge to look at the stave church there, whose reconstruction, he concluded, had largely been based on someone's imaginings. He asked Ulbricht if it would be advisable to invite a photographer to record the stave church at Butangen.

"A photographer?" the professor bellowed, causing Gerhard's stomach to turn with each syllable. "These so-called cameras can only see what the eye sees. You will discover the building's innermost soul. Accentuate it with care, guide our eye to what is essential. Your pencil strokes must be pure, precise, true. Good-quality paper from Leipzig's best presses, and Faber's graphite pencils, hard or soft, whichever you find appropriate – that's all you need!"

He was being promised a generous salary. "But more important than that is the prestige this project brings with it," said Ulbricht. "From next year, the name Schönauer will be remembered. This is a historic rescue mission!"

He saw less of Sabinka. Their embraces were no longer so close, so lingering, so naked. Their conversations often ran dry, and in the end there was nothing to say. She found another lover, spring came, he gave back the keys to his lodgings in Lärchenstrasse, and left. Just hours after a shining locomotive had pulled out of the Berliner Bahnhof in Dresden-Friedrichsstadt, he alighted in Hamburg, where in the evening he boarded the steamship bound for Kristiania. Two days after his departure he had dry land under his feet again. Surrounded by the odour of modern transport – raw sea, machine oil and coal smoke – he took a moment to look around and muse: I am standing here now with three suitcases, and I shall leave with a stave church.

Kristiania turned out to be a touchingly small town, and it took him just ten minutes to stroll from the harbour at Bjørvika to the Søstrene Scheen's guesthouse in Prinsensgate, where his room was unsurprisingly austere and the mattress hard, but the floor, chamber pot and washbasin were well scrubbed and smelled of salmiac. On his departure, he was given a receipt, written in such beautiful handwriting that he kept it. This receipt would later play a part in a mother's decision, but neither Gerhard Schönauer nor the Scheen sisters could possibly know that beautiful handwriting might occasionally determine the fate of a human being.

Reliable travel information and time-keeping were increasingly rare the closer he came to Gudbrandsdal. The train shuddered and wheezed its way into Hamar, where he had hoped to buy a ticket for the paddle steamer bound north. But Lake Mjøsa was still frozen over, and he had to shiver all the way to Fåberg on a horse-drawn trap, where he spent the night in a cramped room which was equally cold. The local authorities had introduced a regular stagecoach through the valley, in an attempt to establish a more permanent route. But it was late in departing and the roads worsened with each mile, the spring thaw had turned them to mud, and the stagecoach skidded about so violently that at one point the luggage fell off. His fellow passengers, two English surveyors with droopy moustaches, took out a bottle of White Horse and offered him some, but generally sat in silence, as they joggled on through narrow, shady passes. Suddenly a wide valley opened out, and acres of farmland filled the slopes that rose from the riverbanks up towards the mountains. A sharp sun hung over the fir trees on the horizon, blinking over the mighty, frozen river that had shaped the landscape, which was more impressive with each turn. And a fevered thought entered his mind: he must be the first of his family to see this place. As each new view emerged before his eyes, he got the urge to jump off and start sketching, but then another even more exotic landscape would open up, and he realised he could spend years here and never be done.

The sun was paler now, the sky turned grey. Later that afternoon he was set down near the church in Fåvang. It had been arranged that someone from Butangen, doubtless the pastor himself, would meet him there with a horse and carriage. It was terribly cold now, he had not eaten for hours, the door into Fåvang church was locked, and there was no priest in sight. The church must have been restored recently, it was austere in style, just as he imagined the churches on the American prairies.

Gerhard stood in the slushy snow wondering whether he was in the right place. His suitcases began to soak up water. Eventually, he found a farm that also served as a coaching inn, but the only person he met was a little boy who kept telling him that somebody would come "soon". But still nobody came.

Finally a bright-looking young fellow appeared, and Gerhard asked him how to get to Butangen. He had to repeat the question four times, and started to doubt whether his Norwegian classes had been worth the expense. Eventually the man pointed up towards a narrow mountain pass and drew a big arc high in the air. "Gå råket," he said, "gå råket".

Gerhard wasn't quite sure what "råket" meant, but he got the gist. Butangen was on the far side of that mountain pass. It's getting late, he thought, but what the hell, things are as they are! I'll eat snow. And it's not really *that* cold. The best treasures are hidden in caves and guarded by Cyclopes. This is merely a tough initiation. An ordeal that will make a good story some day, for a lecture tour about the stave churches entitled "Die Norwegische Mittelalterkirche", an amusing anecdote about bleak weather, backache and sweaty feet.

*

An hour later Gerhard Schönauer's enthusiasm for a "tough initiation" was fading. The road was difficult; bad weather had set in, so that at moments the path ahead disappeared from view. It was madness to have brought three suitcases. After taking a wrong turn at a field of rocks he wandered about helplessly for ages, before finally turning back. Higher up on the slopes the snow had melted, but here in the shadows he walked across crusty snow. There were no signposts, although he noticed there were little heaps of rocks at regular intervals along the way.

Then the path vanished altogether. He stood there, gripped by terror, darkness closing in about him. He heard the sound of voices coming up behind him. Two women hurried past, each bending down to pick up a rock as they went, which they threw onto one of the piles. They nodded when he said "Butangen", but did not stop. Walking quickly, they were soon a fair distance from him, but he noticed that they continued to throw rocks onto the smallest piles, and he realised this was a way of marking the path, and also, perhaps, meant to bring them good fortune on their journey. He followed them until the horizon suddenly opened up before him – and there it was – it had to be Butangen, there on the other side of that long stretch of water below! A deep-blue light hung over it, a light he had never seen before, which he would later find out the Norwegians called "blåmørket" – the bluedark – and he felt giddy with the desire to capture it in paint.

Up on the valley slopes he could see small farms. It was an extraordinarily tranquil place, only a few buildings had lights in their windows, tiny glints of yellow, and in the background the snow-clad mountains loomed. But *there*, was that— was that *it*? Yes! On a little plateau above the lake he could just about see a dark, angular building.

It had to be the church!

He lost sight of the two women and took a long time to find

his way around the lake. The darkness thickened as he struggled through the forest, but then, as he began his ascent to the village, he could see the church spire faintly etched against the night sky. He would not visit it yet, he wanted to save that moment for the daylight. With his back covered in sweat and his arms stretched to aching, he headed for the nearest group of buildings, hoping it was the parson's estate. Here he did as was customary in his native land, assuming it to be the done thing here too; that is, arriving at a farm late at night he slept in the barn rather than bothering folk and waking them up. It was also probably best, he thought, to postpone his first meeting with the pastor – who he had heard was "very helpful" – until he was fresh in the morning!

He was right about his night stay, but wrong about the pastor.

Gerhard woke up freezing cold and stiff, and as he stumbled out into the courtyard, picking strands of straw off his coat, he saw the pastor come out of the door wearing his cassock and collar.

After a brief, bony handshake, Gerhard said in Norwegian: "I delightedly look forward to beginning these important works."

The pastor looked thoughtful, as though he were querying the result of a sum. Gerhard felt useless, he had spent an age practising this sentence, and now he realised his pronunciation and grammar were lacking.

"Alone I must come here," he continued. The priest smiled, and the rest of their conversation was conducted in German.

"You must be frozen," said Kai Schweigaard. "Go inside, and I'll make sure you get some warm food, and that you can change your clothes. A cup of broth? Soup? We eat a lot of porridge up here, you'll get used to it."

"That'll be fine! But I intend to start work immediately. The church is empty, I take it?"

The pastor tilted his head, and said there must be some mistake.

"I've some funerals right now, but we'll talk properly afterwards," he said. He set off down the slope, but stopped, turned: "Are you really the only person they've sent?" he asked, in a precise but toneless German.

Gerhard nodded. "Yes. I'll be here until the winter. Unfortunately, there was nobody there at the appointed meeting place!"

Kai Schweigaard thought for a moment, then politely pointed out that Gerhard was four weeks early.

"What? *Four weeks*?"

"Yes, there must have been some misunderstanding. But that means you'll have plenty of time." He asked Schönauer to "hold off for now", apologised for being "sehr beschäftigt" – very busy – and disappeared out of the gate.

Gerhard Schönauer was left standing in the courtyard.

He was astonished at the cold. Spring came late in Germany, but it would clearly be even longer before winter released its grip here. He could see five or six farms from here, low log cottages that seemed sunk into the terrain. The main house on the parsonage estate was timber-framed with horizontal cladding. White, two stories and double-fronted. Featureless. Without any attempt at ornamentation, apart from a few twiddly bits around the windows.

He went inside, was shown to a room by a large, brusque woman, changed his clothes and went back down to the bare entrance hall. There, on a chest of drawers, he found a steaming cup of thin broth and a cracker.

The Norwegian idea of hot food.

Gerhard drank down the broth in one. Four weeks early. The church in full use.

He opened a suitcase, took out his sketchbook, easel and drawing materials, and went out. The church was hidden behind a ridge, but he could see the end of the long lake from here. This place was quite unpretentiously idyllic. Each log cottage, each steep field, bore witness to the fact that nature had reluctantly made way for human beings, and that a settlement had been reached.

Hooves clattered nearby. Three horses approached, folk dressed in black seated in carts, and some way behind them others on foot, also in black.

A funeral procession. He followed them with his gaze, waited a moment, and walked behind them.

Then it came into view.

The stave church.

Standing free in the landscape. Dignified, ancient. Black-brown like a forest bear, intricate as a queen's crown, stubborn as a pilgrim. Waiting, in some way, like a castle whose monarch was away on a never-ending journey. More impressive even than Dahl's drawings. A little more dilapidated perhaps, but *what* a building! Not very big, but an absolute triumph, the result of daring skills combined with wild fantasy, nurtured through the generations. Until these skills and this fantasy had, he knew not why, died out.

He moved closer.

It was the structure of the roof that was most striking. Like a myriad half- and quarter-houses, all assembled in one beguiling whole, no single surface allowed to dominate or become boring before it was interrupted by another. He had never seen anything like it before, and the thought of it being torn down sent a shiver through him. What sort of human being could suggest such a thing? He wanted to shout: "You can't destroy a thing like this!" But drawing closer he also felt a thief-like urge to say, "But, you know, it's only a church," and to smuggle this jewel away. In his head he was already writing his first report for Ulbricht, he wanted to say how different this church was to anything else. As if two powerful trends in architecture had gone their separate ways: two brothers with equal talent, one had a wish to lay stone, the other to fell a tree, and so they parted at a crossroads, one went to Notre Dame and the other came here, and they never saw each other again.

But ... something wasn't quite right. He looked again, and was aghast. The dragon heads were missing! A tragedy! It had been these that completed the wild lines of the roof, that hissed at the evil powers, and, when the sun was down, created a dramatic silhouette against the night sky.

Nearly all the mourners were in the church now, and as Gerhard walked towards the stone wall, he tried to reassure himself that the dragon heads had been removed for safekeeping, to be kept dry and secure. And that, if the worst came to the worst, a skilled woodcarver could remake them.

Suddenly he jumped, cricking his neck. Three massive booming sounds caught him unawares, so mighty they could only hail from the cosmos itself. Only when the sound was repeated, three times over, did he realise it was the chiming of bells, metaphysical in their power. The echoes bounced against the mountains, returning in a fainter tone than the original, where they merged with fresh chimes, minor in tone, before they travelled out into the world again, like sunlight in a prism, weaker each time, yet multiplied. After nine chimes the reverberations subsided, died away like dissolving mist. But the base notes had beaten a message into him.

"You have been warned."

Her Own Winter Bird

Why was a stranger standing there painting Klara Mytting's funeral? Astrid craned her neck to see over the heads of the other mourners. The stranger was oddly dressed, in a long, fox-brown coat with huge pockets and figures of eight embroidered around the buttonholes. A lock of chestnut hair hung over his brow, and tied at his throat was a piece of blue fabric. He seemed totally unaffected by the presence of the Hekne and Mytting mourners, who were mumbling a hymn only thirty metres away. Instead, he was staring right through them, as though he were alone in the cemetery. Working behind a large easel, the stranger occasionally reached out for more artist's materials from a fold-up table.

From the forest, gentle sighs could be heard as snow slid from the spruce trees. A faint odour of smoke rose from the bonfire that had thawed the last of the frozen ground.

Kai Schweigaard stood with his Bible in one hand and an old wooden bucket filled with earth in the other. He always looked so strong and stately from afar, but now, closer up, there was a lost look in his eyes. And he, too, stole an occasional glance at the stranger. Surely the pastor hadn't paid an artist to make a painting of the first of these new funeral ceremonies? Something to hang in a gilded frame in his office to commemorate the beginning of the new era?

For three long months the travel blanket had lain in a sack under the roof in the barn, so that neither the mice nor any inquisitive siblings could meddle with it. Occasionally she would sneak away from the others, creep in there and put a ladder up against the rafters. But even when it was at its coldest, she never used the blanket indoors, not because she was concerned about the smell of old cooking and boots – although, yes, it was folk's habit of *sniffing* things out that worried her. Kai Schweigaard had no idea how deep village curiosity could dig. Anything that stood out was instantly the subject of village gossip, weighed and considered, as though it were as vital as finding the way out of a forest fire.

But she liked to sit wrapped in the blanket reading the newspaper, imagining that it was still fresh and crisp and she was sitting up in the parsonage. And, more than this, she liked to think that its contents related to her, that it mattered what *she* thought about Norway's union with Sweden and the extension of voting rights. These dreams were partly a game for which she was too grown up, partly a chance, which time would soon rob her of, to contemplate the possibilities for her and Kai Schweigaard. An icy chill emitted from the walls of the room she slept in with Oline, her little sister, and at night, when she was too cold to sleep, Schweigaard's face would come to her with the warmth she imagined the blanket would have offered, and thus they became interchangeable, the warmth and Schweigaard.

Sometimes these daydreams strayed over soft, sun-warmed marshlands. Because even if he was the pastor and an oaf when they talked, Kai Schweigaard was a sinewy young man with flaxen hair. And she would wander further, to a situation where they were married and lay close in an after-supper laze, to where he was a man who smelled good and had a knowing smile.

In bed. How would it be? And were men different from each other? Did he lie in his own room, and then come to her? Did he wait at her door, perhaps, and did he say something first or was he meant to come right in and take his place? And would it be warm and exciting and liberating, as when she let her own fingers slide down, or mechanical and soundless, like when the bull covered the cow, who continued to gobble up grass as he mounted and shoved into her?

These had been the winter's thoughts of a future summer, but now the chill spring was come. They had been seedling dreams in the hope of blossoms, but now she stood at a funeral. And he was betrothed and had been this whole time, and would continue to be so.

That spring the *stabbur* was almost bare, she felt hungry and grey and without prospect. It seemed Kai Schweigaard felt the same way. Standing a few metres from her singing, he looked gloomier and thinner than when she had last seen him, dressed in his cassock he was as black as a winter bird. He kept glancing over at the strange painter, and she found herself doing the same. His arrival was the oddest addition to an already very odd day.

The spring thaw had set in. The sun had made the remaining snow wet, and two bullfinches sat perched on the roof of the walkway. But the churchwarden had failed to fetch enough grit from the stream in the early winter, so the path the mourners walked on was icy and wet. They clung to each other, not from grief, but to avoid going head over heels.

The villagers talked about the "new pastor". They grumbled about the new ceremony and his plans to drag the dead into the church. Poor folks' coffins, in particular, were often made lovingly but crudely, not fit to be seen in a church. The corpse would now lie for ages with nobody around. And the villagers would no longer get to carry the coffin round the church three times. No, folk would lose contact with their own, and they were particularly aggrieved that their dead would no longer be walked from their homes with a beautiful dirge, but get a pathetic hymn sung at their grave by a miserable, shivering crowd. Nor could folk choose the day for a burial, to fit in with their duties on the farm. Sven Giverhaug, an old travelling schoolmaster, who had sung in his sonorous voice for hundreds of the village's dead over the years, had let rip in the pastor's office, and it seemed then that there might be a doubling-up of rites, with everyone continuing quietly as before, while the pastor did his own thing when the coffin got to the church. How could he, a pastor who knew nothing of the deceased, who had never seen them as a child or at work or in times of adversity or celebration, say anything worthwhile? How, and why, would an outsider worm his way in and take over at the very end?

But Schweigaard had been as unmovable as a mountain. The new rites were introduced, and first out was Klara. The ceremony in the church was overshadowed by scepticism and hostility. Although Astrid sensed that only the stubbornest stiff-necks, of whom there were many in the congregation, failed to see that Schweigaard had honoured Klara as a proper human being. His brief speech about her life was a little muddled and idealised perhaps, but nonetheless he created a beautiful memorial to the arthritis-ridden life of this elderly parishioner. But was what he said true? Astrid wondered. Did Schweigaard preach about life as it really was? He had even said, presumably rather thoughtlessly, that "she died in the faith of her Saviour". A little "hmm" had erupted among the silent mourners, who sat row upon row with one noticeable gap at the wall end of one pew. Nobody wanted to sit where Klara had frozen to death.

But Kai Schweigaard had reined himself in again.

"Klara never got to see the world. Her work was to fetch water. And she did it steadfastly, at least thirty times a day, walking the hundred metres to the stream and back. From that I calculate that Klara walked six kilometres each day, which is a good two hundred Norwegian miles a year, so that she could have travelled to Moscow each year if she'd headed east, or to Paris if she'd gone south. But Klara never even crossed the stream. She stayed here, in Butangen, and it is this woman's toil that we honour and remember today."

Klara's kinfolk swallowed. Old men nodded, and even Astrid's mother wiped away a tear.

The ceremony ended in confusion, since nobody quite knew what should happen next, whether more should be said, and if so by whom. Schweigaard's presence made it difficult to talk, and folk began to squirm in their pews and look around. Then the Sister Bells started to ring, and the pastor beckoned some men forwards, and eventually the coffin was carried out to a pealing of bells, so loud that it was impossible to hear whether there was any suggestion of doing things otherwise. The Myttings had brought shovels along in case they were needed, but Schweigaard said no: the grave was already open.

It was over at last. Schweigaard scattered earth on the coffin and shook everyone's hands and bade them farewell. Astrid curtseyed to him as if he were a stranger, and the mourners went their way, feeling strangely incomplete. The pastor had taken the sting out of death, and surely life had to have a sting, or there was no difference between a wasp and a harmless fly.

Astrid told her father that she wanted to go home alone. She waited until all the horse-drawn carts had gone. Then she walked beside the stone wall, and stood watching the painter from afar. Suddenly Kai Schweigaard came out of the church. He marched over to the man by the easel, who continued his work, despite Schweigaard flinging his arms about in seeming displeasure. There seemed to be no meaning or sense in their exchange, until she realised they were speaking a foreign language.

A glimmer of light and a flash of warmth. A beam from a sun behind the old familiar sun, a sun that vanished again no sooner than it had warmed her.

The stranger was a foreigner. The first human being she had ever seen from the outside world.

Schweigaard went back up to the church, clearly in a hurry. Astrid remembered that there was to be another funeral soon, and that tomorrow four more would be laid in the earth, the winter's collected dead.

Astrid went over to the man with the easel. She wanted to approach him from the side, but had to walk round a pile of snow, and came into his view from in front.

The stranger stepped to one side, his fringe followed his motion, he moved elegantly, obligingly, as though performing a dance step with easy grace; then shifting the grip on his pencil, he held out an open palm towards the easel, his fingers pointing a welcome towards the large piece of cream-coloured card that was securely fixed there against the wind.

It was not a painting, but a drawing, and it was not of the funeral procession, but the stave church. She met his gaze, he was perhaps twenty and a bit, his skin slightly more tanned than that of the men from these parts; he was curious and proud. At the bottom of the page he had drawn some sort of scale bar. The walkway and the decoration on the ridge of the roof were finished in fine detail, and he had come a long way with the spire. With immense precision he had drawn each individual wooden roof tile, transferring the reality and claiming it for his own.

Except the church was not real any longer. It looked newly built, its timbers fresh-hewn, instead of dark and dilapidated like the church that stood before them. What was more, the drawing included something that did not exist, namely eight dragon heads that sprang from the gables, jaws snapping into the empty air. And there were no untidy grave mounds around it, instead the ground was smooth and grass-covered, and at the far right the artist had added a non-existent stream.

They both became aware of further movement up by the church. Kai Schweigaard had come out again. He observed them for a moment, then carried on towards the parsonage. The stranger and Astrid exchanged glances again, he bowed and said something to her in stilted Danish. She inclined her head, to indicate that she did not understand.

"The bells," he repeated, pointing towards the church. "Strong ring!"

With his words came the aroma of something fresh and sour, and he pointed towards the fold-out table. Lying there, among his drawing materials and a portfolio inscribed "Gerhard Schönauer", was a crumpled sweet-cone, from which some amber-coloured drops had escaped. She helped herself to one, very slowly, giving him time to protest if she had misunderstood his gesture, then left.

Crumbling Centuries

Gerhard Schönauer stared after the girl for a long time. Her features made him want to draw her, there was a unique quality about her. She was quick and less reserved than the other villagers he had met that morning. The description in Meyer's seemed to sum them up precisely: "The Norwegians are a proud and strong race of Germanic descent. They are more stoic and slower than the Swedes, but not as phlegmatic as Danes. They can seem very closed and sceptical, but once one has earned their trust they are loyal and open-hearted, and they are outstanding seafarers, with the world's best maritime pilots."

He put down his pencil and waited until the girl was out of sight. The funeral party had gone, and now he was waiting patiently for two men, the bell-ringer and churchwarden perhaps, to leave too. The pastor had left some time ago. He had been churlish to the point of rudeness – and just because he had started drawing!

But now – now he was alone! At last he would see the portal. His anticipation of this moment had helped keep his spirits up during the entire gruelling journey here. The building as a whole was one thing, but the portal with its mythological animals and ancient gods – an artwork fused with a building to ward off evil spirits – was like a giant bag of camphor drops to his artist's brain. He would need time to take such a sight in.

Besides which, he needed time to calm down. When the bells had rung they had shaken him to the core. Like cannon blasts. But when they had stilled, his unease had continued, and it dawned on him that it was an *absence* that troubled him. The absence of noise. For years he had lived surrounded by the raucous din of Dresden, the rumble of iron-clad cartwheels on cobblestones, the cries of market vendors, this broad frequency of noise that enveloped him the instant he stepped out into town. All this was muted here, so traceless that he might be fooled into thinking that Dresden had never existed. Only the sounds of nature now. The whinnying of horses in a stall, the squelching of mud as a boy came running. And deep in the forest the chopping of an axe.

During the funeral he had set up his easel and sketched in the first lines of the church. He listened to the sounds from within. The sermon in that rough-edged Norwegian, the hymn that slowly gathered pace, sounds that were an inspiration and felt natural to his work, and his first sketch of the stave church was promising.

He left his easel and walked up to the church, he ran his hand along the warm sun-facing wall. Never before had he touched such old timbers. They were twisted and cracked, and left a trace of yellowish powder on his skin, which he knew to be the remains of old tar, the dust of ruins, the crumbling centuries in solid form. Age left no trace in stone, for that the stone itself was already too old, but it made its mark in wood as in a human face. The bottom logs had sunk over the stone foundation wall, and their profile was squashed. The colour of the wood was richly variegated, in some places it was like the coat of a chestnut horse, in others a coal-black horse, all according to what nature had exposed it to, baking sunshine or deep shade, rain or snow, and the endless layers of tar which oozed down the walls each summer and hardened again with the winter.

He walked slowly along the covered walkway, to the stone steps that led up to the open outer door. In his head he estimated the distance, counted the number of footsteps and turns he would have to take to reach the main entrance, then with his eyes closed he carefully walked up. He stepped before the portal which he knew was inside the porch. There he stood, eyes tight shut, free of disturbance at last, this was the moment he would describe with huge gravitas in his lecture on "Die Norwegische Mittelalterkirche", his first impression of the portal that even Hieronymus Bosch would have been shocked by.

He opened his eyes.

But—

There was no portal!

He was staring at a pair of large double doors. Painted black, they were fixed in a coarse door frame surrounded by a wall of plain, tarred timbers. The wrought-iron hinges were long and roughly forged. There was no trace of the carved wooden panel that Dahl had once drawn. The mythological creatures had been driven away, without leaving so much as a hoof-print.

He tried the door handle.

The pastor must have locked the main door to the church.

The Barbed Word

Astrid still had the sweet in her mouth when she reached the iron gates of the parsonage. Camphor. As exciting as sailing ships in the sunset. She occasionally had camphor drops when they went to buy supplies, but, for reasons that turned slowly within her now, she chose to let the sweet dissolve completely before going into the parsonage.

Memories emerged through the tingling taste. Had she been ten years old? Twelve perhaps, no more. Her father had been secretive after supper, he had fished out a little brown sweet-cone, then walked the length of the table putting one sweet before each child and their mother, and, with the bag now empty, had told them to wait. He took none for himself. At first Astrid had thought they were going to get rock candies, but glinting against the long, scarred tabletop was a row of golden drops. Her father had returned from Stavsmartnan earlier that day, and had clearly eaten his drops there and asked the vendor how they were made – since, when they were finally allowed to take their drops and eat them, he said that camphor oil was extracted from trees that grew in French Indochina, that the wood and leaves were ground and boiled, and that the steam was somehow caught in a container, where the oil formed droplets and then thickened.

That evening when her father had said the words "French Indochina" had been the only time she had seen a dreamy look on his face, the only time he had forgotten to be bitter about Lower Glupen and the old Hekne farm.

"I want to go there!" Astrid had shouted. "And make lots of camphor drops. There, in Indo—"

But she was too eager to express her joy, and swallowed the camphor drop, so fresh that its edges were still sharp, and she felt it scratch its way down to her stomach, where there was no sense of taste, just grey intestines that absorbed nourishment, and everyone laughed at her as they continued to suck their drops, including their mother, who tucked hers safely under her tongue, smacked her lips and said:

"That'll learn ye to be content with what ye have."

*

Astrid felt the drop grow smaller and smaller on her tongue. Round and smooth, like a small pebble plucked from a stream, then the size of a wheat grain, then gone, with only the taste living on. She pushed the gate, but then changed her mind and headed quickly towards Hekne. She soon caught up with the mourners who had not got a seat on any of the carts, and hurrying past them she walked up to the farm, where she sneaked into the barn and took out the sack that held the newspaper and travel blanket. Through the gaps in the timber walls, she saw her mother and father making their way back to the farmhouse, while the farmhands loosened the horses' harnesses. Astrid was hungry and had a headache, but this had to be done *now*.

They were turning this way and that, her thoughts about Kai Schweigaard. He had not been his usual self at the funeral, as he steered them towards these new rites; God's big man in priestly robes. She had always thought he was so honest, so straightforward. Now something was out of joint.

A betrothed priest lent out his mother's travel blanket. A new church was to be built, but no matter how hard she looked she could see nowhere for it to go. A foreign painter was drawing the old one. And that queer thing he had said: "Bells will still ring over the village." That sentence gnawed at her. Well – he had set up the perfect excuse. Something borrowed must be returned.

She stuffed the blanket and newspaper under her shawl and left the barn. She felt the warmth of the blanket, superfluous now that it was spring, and wondered if that was how women survived without men.

Soon she was standing outside the parsonage.

Two floors, a cellar and a loft. A flagpole, rows of panelled windows; the white-painted face of power and faith in Butangen. Death and burial, baptism and the holy cross. All through Kai Schweigaard.

He fitted in with this building. With everything this building was. The kitchen garden behind the house, barren after the winter, waiting for the spring to come. Old trees with bare branches, patches of snow on yellowy-brown grass. The house itself seemed to be waiting for a woman to move in.

These daydreams. It had been so delicious to let her thoughts run free. But it was foolhardy, plain *stupid* to think he might be interested in her, and even if he were, the pastor could never ask a girl from Butangen to marry him.

Not now, at least. Perhaps in times gone by. Hekne had been in the family for more than four hundred years. Long ago, the farmhouse had stood well tarred and proud, with crafted wooden roof tiles and high foundation walls, more admired than the parsonage itself. From a distance the farm buildings were still impressive, up close they were rundown and rickety, and the silverware in the parlour would barely stretch to a small gathering.

Astrid's little sisters wore her hand-me-downs, and she herself had only two sets of Sunday best; otherwise, during the week, she used the coarsely woven skirts, which had been given to her – one a year – while she worked at the parsonage. But it was her headscarf that folks' eyes were drawn to, bought in Lillehammer, brilliant white with a border of blue checks. Like many other girls in the valley, she had started wearing a headscarf despite being unmarried; she always kept it starched and clean, and just as her scarf sat proudly over her curls, so too did her pride in the Hekne tradition: speak clearly and honestly, never speak ill of others. Do not mistreat your crofters, take in paupers without question. Be mild in your manner, never belittle anyone. The true legacy – honour, the firmness of a promise, the honesty of a handshake – could not be measured in money nor diminish in value, so long as each and every Hekne conducted themselves well.

She pulled herself up straight and entered by the main door.

The problem now was how to get past Oldfrue Bressum. She clamped the travel blanket under her arm, slipped along the hallway, caught a glimpse of the old lady's back in the larder, crept up the stairs and knocked cautiously on the door.

He must have been in deep thought, because although he said "come in" he seemed surprised when she did.

Astrid put the blanket on a chair by the door, saying that she didn't need it anymore, now that the spring had finally come, and here were the newspapers he wanted for his archive, and she must thank the pastor for his *charity*.

She had chosen this word on her way down. "Charity". There were many words she might have used, she could have thanked him for his generosity, for his kindness, for the loan, or simply let the words "thank you" stand alone. But she wanted it to be slightly barbed, to give him pause for thought.

Schweigaard paid no attention to the word "charity". He just sat there, looking pale and distracted.

Astrid stood there in silence. The office walls were painted a dull green, on one hung a small framed picture of Jesus on the cross. He was painted grey, eyes rolling upwards, mouth drooping at the corners. That's not how dead people look, she thought. That's not how they look at all.

She wondered whether the same thought ever came to Kai Schweigaard when he looked at this painting. Whether he ever doubted that his faith bore any relation to real life, or whether he perhaps turned a blind eye to the fact that its teachings differed so widely from reality.

He still said nothing. Perhaps the word "charity" had been too cutting, he was clearly struggling with something.

"It were a fine funeral," she said at last. "Quiet, but that were because folk didna know what to say. The part about the stream were especially nice."

Schweigaard got up and gave her an impenetrable look,

before crossing to the window that overlooked the cemetery. His shoulders sank.

"At last!" he said, his breath settling in a mist on the window for a second before it cleared. "He's packing his things away. That man is vital to us, but I had to make him see that it simply wasn't appropriate."

Astrid did not move from the door, but craned her neck to get a view.

Schweigaard turned. "Did he say anything to you? I saw you walk over to him."

She shook her head. Through the window she could see the stranger put his easel over his shoulder. She assumed that he had finished his work, that he'd filled in the decorative details and the walkway.

"Who be this painter, precisely?" Astrid asked, shutting her lips quickly, not wanting Schweigaard to catch the smell of camphor.

Schweigaard squeezed the root of his nose. An idea flashed through her, a vague notion of the effect she had on Kai Schweigaard, that she aroused feelings in him that he found difficult to deal with.

"He's come much too early," he said. "He wasn't meant to be here for another four weeks. I was planning to announce the building of the new church during our next service. But then suddenly he was standing there waving his drawing materials about. And the rumours will soon be flying."

"Aye, they be flying already," said Astrid, although no gossip about the church had actually reached her.

"Oh, well," said Schweigaard, looking at her. "It'll be announced soon anyway." He seemed to shake off the burden. "Listen now, Astrid. This painter fellow – well, he's actually an architect – he's part of the work for this new church. That we lacked the money for. But now here at last are the *glad tidings*."

He went over to the bureau and took out a roll of paper. Astrid stepped out of the little puddle that had melted from her shoes. Schweigaard unravelled the paper. It was a line drawing of a large building with a long row of windows. Simple, bare, without any decorative embellishments; she wondered why he was showing her a drawing of a storehouse, until she saw the little spire at the end.

"This will be big enough," he said. "More than big enough. It'll comply with the law, with some to spare."

"But, tell me – why did ye get a foreigner to draw the old one?"

"Because it's going to be torn down."

She stood there dumbstruck. He might as well have told her Lake Løsnes was going to be drained.

"*Tear our church down?*"

"Yes, Astrid. It has to be done."

"But surely, 'tis just to build a new one somewhere else? Then ye can have two to choose from, and—"

Schweigaard interrupted her gently, and she could tell that he had spent nights going over this in his head. Foreseeing resistance, he took on the quarrels in advance, formulating answers to the bullish questions he put to himself when he stood in the opposition's shoes.

"We did consider that. But when you study the layout of Norwegian villages, you find that the oldest buildings always occupy the best spot. The land on which our present church stands is too narrow for two churches. It would be an insult to the parish to build the new church in some shady corner elsewhere. Especially in a village as hilly as ours. It simply wouldn't be right."

She stood and pondered. Before the silence became unbearable, she said:

"Our church doesna have any dragon heads."

"Hm?"

"He drew dragon heads on our church, though it doesna have any."

"Oh. Did he? Well, no doubt he's already started to plan the restoration work."

"Herr Schweigaard, ye say *restoration* – an uncommon word that I have nay heard ye mention afore in your story."

She was startled at the way this strange sentence burst out of her, and realised it had matured in the small hours, when, pressed against a cold wall, she had wondered how a pastor's wife spoke when the Sunday sermon was tried out on her.

It seemed to have taken Schweigaard by surprise too, he cleared his throat and started to roll the plan back up, and then instantly smoothed it out again and waved his pencil over it vaguely, with no intention of writing anything.

"Astrid. When a church is demolished, the materials are usually sold at auction, stave by stave. But this never generates much money. When you were here last, I was in the midst of an exchange of letters about our old church. Although I myself have a preference for simplicity, for things that are – let's say "practical-minded" – I am not blind to the fact that an old church has some kind of inner value. There has to be a better ending for it than as firewood."

"Aye, she could stay where she be."

He looked at her and shook his head. "This is the deal: we've sold the church for five times the usual price, if not more. This means we have the funds to build a fine new church here."

"But what be the use of him drawing the old one?"

"Well, it's to be moved and then put up again! Yes, it's true! In Germany. He's come here to draw the church, inside and out. Every single beam and plank will be marked as they take it down, and when the ice settles it will all be transported to Saxony, where the church will be rebuilt. It'll be a long trip!"

"To where?"

"Saxony. To a city called Dresden. I can understand that this sounds . . . rather fantastical, but churches have been relocated many times before! Not just between villages here in Norway, but over very long distances! Our old church will get a new lease of life, it'll practically get a new congregation down there."

"But what'll folk think of her there? That she be strange? Summat to scoff at?"

"No no. These are Germans! Men of culture. Thinkers and composers. It'll be both a church and a museum. Have you ever heard of—"

Schweigaard stopped mid-sentence, she saw he was nervous about embarrassing her, as she would have to answer: "No, I've never heard of that, I've never been outside Butangen, and don't ever expect to go anywhere else."

He offered her a chair and, standing with his back to the bureau, launched into what she assumed – by his intensity of tone and choice of words – to be the rough sketch of his "glad tidings". He talked about a painter named Johan Christian Dahl, who had been made a professor in Dresden, and almost single-handedly aroused interest over in Germany in Norway's culture, particularly its stave churches.

"But where I and the Norwegian Church heartily agree," said Schweigaard, "is that Dahl's romantic notions about these worn-out churches were of little use for our mission. In 1840 the parishioners in Valdres were all looking forward to getting a new church. Dahl got wind of it. At first he tried to halt the demolition work and put forward various outlandish proposals that were all thankfully rejected, so then, using his own money, he bought this wreck of a church. It, too, was rebuilt in Germany, in a place called Silesia. So everyone was happy."

Astrid looked at him and thought: it is *now* that a good pastor's wife smiles and nods encouragingly. Fetches coffee in thin porcelain cups, says "how interesting", and invites him to go on. Which was why she said, "And so?"

Schweigaard swallowed.

"Listen to this! A friend of mine is the pastor in Valdres now. We correspond. He wrote to me about this curious event in 1840. And I thought: well? Why not repeat this? My friend assured me that there are scholars at the Dresden Academy of Art who continue to study Norway. Interest in our country is still huge down there. Some Germans even come to Norway simply to see the nature."

"And to go hunting perhaps?" said Astrid. "They surely can na' just walk about and look around?"

"Oh, but they do," Schweigaard said. "Some even just sit on the ship's deck and gaze at the coastline."

"And they do *nowt*?"

"No, they call it 'going on holiday'!" said Schweigaard. He gripped the back of the chair; his knuckles went white when he was tense, and they did so now.

"Well, them that can," said Astrid. "Have ye ever done that – gone 'on holiday'?"

"No never. Unfortunately. Nor does it seem I can ever go on holiday, with so much to do here. But one day, you never know," he said, his knuckles regaining their colour. "It could be fun."

His knuckles tightened and turned white again: "Anyway, Astrid. I found out that Dahl had actually been here and drawn our church once. I took a direct approach: I sent a letter to the academy, made sure my schoolboy German was tolerable, contacted a professor there, and after some negotiation they made us a generous offer, which we have accepted."

"So Herr Schweigaard has palmed off a battered old church onto foreigners. Well, well, well. I mun say."

She said it to buy time. Something was niggling at her, the

echo of what he had said about "church bells still ringing", that runaway sentence that had realised it was in the wrong place, tripped and hidden itself, unsure whether it had escaped notice.

Schweigaard set about explaining how easy such a move was, although this was hardly surprising to Astrid. Log buildings were often moved in the village. Their turf roofs were blithely torn off, each timber was marked at its end with a Roman numeral, knocked loose and piled onto a cart. The cowshed and the barn at Hekne both had such marks chiselled into their corner joints, and it was said that the *stabbur* had been sold and moved twice before ending up on their farm.

"We must adjust to the times," Schweigaard said. "Just look around you, look how people are suffering in these ruins from the past. In an hour the funeral of that poor woman up at Solfritt will begin, you know, the crofter's cottage."

"The woman who died so horribly in childbirth?"

"Yes. She already had six little ones. Her husband and children see nothing beautiful, nothing dignified, in her being remembered in a church where birds flap about under the ceiling. People's basic needs have to be covered before we can preen ourselves in the past. We need to be warm! Well fed! Safe."

She noticed how he shifted between a speech prepared on paper and a normal conversation where he listened to her – right now he had slipped back into the old Kai Schweigaard who gave speeches: "Conservation is undoubtedly a noble idea, but it is often more beautiful for the onlooker than those to whom it relates. Our country is at a turning point which requires all the power of human thought, and Christianity is the only true light in this web of confusion. We cannot nurture our faith behind the warped timbers of heathen times. And besides, our church is too small by law. Full stop."

Astrid looked again at the painting of Jesus on the cross.

Something inside her shifted, she thought of the stranger with his easel, a man who was able to draw the world exactly as it was, but who added dragons that did not exist.

"May we ordinary folk ask how much the Germans be paying?"

"A little over nine hundred kroner, when the money's been changed."

"*Nine hundred kroner*?"

"Yes, it's a lot of money! And they'll cover the transport costs themselves. It's an excellent deal. Garmo church is going to be demolished soon. It's been valued at just two hundred kroner, including the altarpiece, pulpit and baptismal font. The church in Torpo has been sold for two hundred and eighty kroner, and a church in Ål has been put up for six hundred, but hasn't been sold."

Astrid swallowed hard. She had earned seventy kroner a year when she worked at the parsonage. "But how—" she began.

"That was the price I demanded! A round figure in German marks. Though this German fellow's already coming up with objections – he was in here a moment ago complaining that the church lacks a portal."

"A what?"

"Some kind of door frame. Supposedly decorated with twirling shapes of some kind. Mythological creatures and a terrifying serpent, from what he said. No doubt the door was replaced with a bigger and better one at some time – an improvement of course. But anyway. This is a joyous moment for us! We get enough money for a *functional* church, a *warm* church, with four wood burners – and the carpenters plan to do something very clever: they're going to make hollow timber walls and fill them with wood chips so that the church stays warm. The windows will be big and easy to clean, not like those bumpy glass panes high up on the walls. I want us all to *see* each other!"

She was lost for an answer. He was so excited, so eager, so – happy!

"I reckons they mun search for the Hekneweave," she shot in. "When they take down the church."

He asked her what that was, and she told him all she knew. "It shows the Day of Judgment. As the pastor here, ye mun surely know about the weave."

"Yes, absolutely, Astrid. I'll get someone to look for it. That's a promise!"

He talked on, but she had stopped listening. Suddenly everything had fallen into place, with resounding clarity. She remembered the drawing of the new church with its pathetic little spire. If the Sister Bells were hung there, they would ring straight in the ears of the entire congregation. And there was no separate bell tower or other place to put them.

And something else occurred to her. This price – five times more than what was normal – must surely have been paid because the church came with a dowry. A very valuable dowry.

The Serpent That Vanished

Gerhard Schönauer tried many times that day to have a proper conversation with Kai Schweigaard about the vanished portal, but the pastor seemed not have any useful answers or time. *Haushälterin* Bressum made herself understood by repeating Norwegian words louder and louder, until Gerhard nodded and retreated. She said the pastor had begun something that led to nothing but *merarbeid og vanskeligheter* – "more work and trouble".

Gerhard was wandering about aimlessly, when he noticed the

camphor-drop girl coming out of the parsonage. She seemed cross about something, and moments later the priest came out too, looking glum. Shortly afterwards Gerhard found that the door to the church was open again. He got a little glimpse inside, but only just managed to see that the altarpiece was in place, before a group of mourners came shuffling in and Schweigaard took him aside again to tell him that it would be unseemly to draw now.

Walking round the church, he pondered the piles of smouldering embers in the cemetery. And seeing a row of open graves he worried whether some sort of plague had broken out, before realising that they had been prepared for the day's funerals.

He headed straight back to the parsonage and shut himself in behind locked doors. Well, well! He wasn't allowed to draw inside, and with the pastor holding funerals from the crack of dawn to nightfall, he couldn't draw outside! Nor was there to be any proper welcoming dinner, the priest had to go out that evening, he said, and would be busy with funerals again from breakfast tomorrow.

Gerhard's only comfort was that he fell in love with a small log cottage near the parsonage's *stabbur*, partly hidden behind some tall birch trees – the perfect studio. Oldfrue Bressum, who declared herself to be in charge at the parsonage, got the servants to clear out the rubbish, old timbers and cartwheels. They carried in a rough-hewn table, a bed and a sooty whale-oil lamp, while a farm boy made a log pile by the front door. Soon smoke was rising from the chimney, and a young girl got going with a mop. The water she emptied into the snow outside was worryingly grimy, and when Gerhard poked about in the gritty hollows made by its heat, he found two dead mice.

He settled himself in, but still felt uneasy. Back in Dresden everything had seemed so doable. He had ventured that this might be too big a task for just one person, especially a student, but Ulbricht had reassured him.

"No need to worry!" he had said. "Herr Schiertz was alone too. It's perfect for a final-year student. Such things happen only once in a lifetime. When you become an architect, Schönauer, you won't have the time to immerse yourself in one thing for months on end. As to the practicalities – you shan't have to touch a single timber. Your main task is to bring us drawings of the stave church. Lots of drawings! Quality drawings! Of every nook and cranny, exactly to scale, so that the carpenters have a precise guide to go by during the reconstruction. Oversee the demolition, establish a system for the identification of each part, take a summer vacation wherever you fancy, return to Gudbrandsdal when the winter comes, accompany the goods here, and assist our carpenters on your return."

Ulbricht was expecting regular reports on his progress, and Gerhard sat down now with a pen and ink. His stool was too low, and he had to ask for another. The windows were too small and gave a poor working light, but if they cut down the big tree outside the sun would come in.

"I find it hard to believe that a work of art like the portal could have been discarded, although sadly I fear this may be the case. The Norwegian people's cold pragmatism is exactly as you described, Professor Ulbricht. Modernisation seems to trump everything."

He wrote that he would look for the missing dragon heads, but did not mention the pastor's reaction to his arriving four weeks too early, choosing instead to convey some pieces of good news from Butangen – not least:

"*Die Schwesterglocken sind intakt* – the Sister Bells are in perfect working order and sound like the voice of God himself."

What joy the Sister Bells would bring. They would have no problem in drowning out the noise of Dresden. Every time they rang, they would inject a moment of reflection into the city's clamour. Inspire spiritual obedience. Enrich the minds of the good inhabitants of this cultured city.

He finished his letter, but resisted putting it in the envelope. Luckily he caught sight of the pastor out in the courtyard, and ran out and thanked him for his cottage – studio and lodgings in one.

"That's excellent," said Schweigaard. "You'll get everything you need, Herr Schönauer. Let's discuss things over dinner tomorrow – right now, I have another funeral to prepare."

"This can't wait."

"I'll have more time tomorrow."

"It's about the portal that I mentioned. When can you look into what happened to it? Whether it's somewhere else, for example?"

Schweigaard flung out his arms. Did they understand each other right? Was it a door, or a portal? With serpents and mythological beasts? He excused himself and went back in.

Gerhard went back into his little cottage, made a quick sketch from memory of Dahl's drawing, caught the priest on his way out again and showed it to him.

Schweigaard shook his head. "No such portal exists," he said, walking on. "It's not been here in my time at least."

"*Aber* Herr Schweigaard, how could Professor Dahl have drawn it, then?"

"I'm afraid I can't answer for what Dahl did fifty years ago," said Schweigaard, without slowing his pace. Suggested, in a slightly milder tone, that Dahl might have confused it with another church.

"But Dahl's other drawings all correspond perfectly," said Schönauer. "There's just a tall double door there now."

They were nearing the church. Now they saw that not just one, but *two* funeral parties, each with a coffin, were standing at the entrance, and confusion had broken out. Schweigaard strode on, and Gerhard Schönauer struggled to keep pace.

"You're probably years too late," said Schweigaard. "Practically all the old church doors in Norway were replaced between 1830 and 1860."

"What?"

"We had a terrible fire in 1822, during a Whitsunday Mass in a church in Solør, further south. More than a hundred and thirty people died in the flames, because the church had a ridiculously small door which swung inwards. In the years that followed, all the churches were required to rebuild their entrances, with bigger doors that opened outwards, though I expect it took some time here at Butangen. I would guess, and it's only a guess, that the portal you're looking for would have been pulled down in about 1850."

"But . . . that's a tragedy!"

Schweigaard stopped in his tracks.

"What is? Tell me! A fatal fire or the disappearance of a portal? We can't have people trapped in flames!"

"But perhaps the portal has been kept somewhere? Do you have any idea?"

"No, I don't! Nor can I tell you how many bears will be born this winter, or how old the mayor of Madrid will be on his next birthday, or what Napoleon ate for lunch on a certain date in 1804!" said Schweigaard, marching over to the two funeral parties who were waiting.

Gerhard Schönauer cut a piece off his pork chop, and rubbed a pattern into the gravy. Kai Schweigaard cleared his throat and said:

"I'm sorry we got off to such a bad start. Really, I am. My mother always said it was a weakness in me. The tendency to be abrupt. *Entschuldigung*."

Gerhard Schönauer accepted his apology with a nod. "I was probably also a bit – *mürrisch.* What would the Norwegian word be?"

"Er – *grinete* – grouchy. No, don't give it another thought, Herr Schönauer. We can all forget ourselves when things get difficult. And I had something of a confrontation in my office, but anyway . . .". He leaned forwards in his chair. "As soon as I get a moment, I'll examine the accounts and records to find out what happened when the portal was removed. But the archives are in a mess. I fear the door may have disappeared for good."

They ate on in silence. Schweigaard offered him the rest of the peas, and said, "How about we alternately speak German and Norwegian at supper? That way we'll both improve our skills?"

"Excellent idea."

"I'll admit something to you, Schönauer. Since coming here, I've longed for a more worldly visitor, who might enrich my mealtimes with his learning, with a wider perspective."

"I can understand that."

"More beer?"

"Thanks. *Das ist gutes Bier.*"

"Haha. You're closer than you might think! This is called *godtøl* – 'good beer', or 'best beer'. Brewed in Lillehammer. Rather better than what we call *husholdningsøl* – 'household beer' – the everyday, standard beer."

A little later the cork popped off a fifth bottle of beer.

"I have a somewhat . . . lonely task here," said Kai Schweigaard, topping up their glasses. "Demolishing the church is likely to stir up emotions round here. It's a good thing there are two of us now."

"Aha," laughed Schönauer. "You've been wanting a fellow conspirator? An accomplice? Well, here I am!"

Schweigaard lifted his glass to his guest again. Schönauer went on:

"Since you're going to build a new church, let me ask you a question that may seem strange to you. What are the door handles to be made of?"

Kai Schweigaard smiled. "I've no idea. Iron, I expect."

"Not brass?"

"No – why brass?"

"Because it has a unique property: it prevents disease. So-called bacteria. It's a recent discovery; German metallurgists believe that a light electric current is triggered when hands touch brass. Which kills these bacteria. So the disease doesn't spread when people gather in numbers."

Kai Schweigaard lit up. "But that's wonderful! It's precisely the sort of thing I'm after. I suspect that diseases spread when people cough into their hands and then shake hands, as they generally do after the service. I'll give instructions for all the handrails and handles to be made of brass!"

Taking another swig, he remarked on how impressed he was by the handsome tape measure Schönauer had with him.

"Yes, it's made of stretch-proof canvas from a specialist textile factory in Leipzig. Thin, but robust. It reaches to a hundred Saxon feet."

"Saxon feet? But surely the metre is well on its way into Germany too? It poses a problem, does it not – that a foot is not a foot? That its actual length varies from place to place? We went over to metric measurements here in Norway a few years ago. I must say that the idea of an international system has a lot going for it."

"Indeed, and the *Kaiserreich* has converted too. But my client insists on using the old measurements. Many people believe that the metric system isn't so well suited to construction work. The old system is in better harmony with art and carpentry, where we operate with wholes, halves and thirds – just think about the golden ratio. At one time, there was even an agreed model for sorting out any disagreements over the Saxon measurements."

"Oh? Tell me!"

"Four reputable men, who had never met before, would, on the king's orders, gather on a particular Saturday and spend the night travelling to some randomly chosen church. They would wait outside and, when Mass was over they'd pull aside the first sixteen men who came out and tell them to remove their right shoes. Then they'd take all these shoes and line them up toe to heel – in the order in which the men had emerged – and stretch a thin rope along the entire length of the shoes, cut it and bring it to the king. The rope would then be folded four times, and the resultant sixteenth part would be the new standard foot. A perfect average! And no outside interests would affect the result. Clever, eh?"

"Very clever! Ingenious!"

Another bottle of *godtøl* was emptied before Schweigaard rang the bell for Oldfrue and asked for coffee. After which Gerhard left for his own lodgings with an oil lamp dangling from his fist. The ground was slippery with the evening frost, and Schweigaard sent him off with a walking stick. He laughed as Gerhard hunched over, pretending to be a doddery old man.

But deep down Gerhard was still unsure of the priest's volatile nature. He had finally got a key to the church, a gigantic object of worn-out iron, heavy as a revolver; but equally heavy were Schweigaard's admonition to stay away while the funerals were in progress, and when Gerhard had voiced his objection, saying that he must draw the church, cracks had appeared in the priest's veneer. The stuff beneath it was abrupt and intractable, not something that any amount of brass could quell.

It Was a Wolf Before

"They be here after money again, with their claws and skins 'n' such."

Oldfrue Bressum was standing in the doorway. Kai Schweigaard finished the sentence he was writing and looked up at her. "Their skins *'n' such*". It was this way of saying things that irritated him most. That folk seemed unable to take things for what they were. Always putting themselves on the outside and looking at things obliquely. "I couldna get that malt chocolate 'n' such." "Will the Pastor have some cinnamon 'n' such on his porridge?"

"Yes, I know they're on their way," said Kai Schweigaard, who had a bit of a headache. "Ask them to wait until twelve."

"They do nay have pocket watches 'n' such."

"No, but there's a grandfather clock in the hallway – oh, never mind. Who's first?"

"The next eldest brother to that Evensen fellow, the cotter at Lindvik – Kåre, if I remember right. Nay, Karsten."

"Yes, yes, alright. As I said, ask him to wait."

He counted the cash in the grey tin box. His pocket watch was standing upright near the inkwell. Half past eleven. He dreaded these meetings with the village's huntsmen. Alone against them. The shifty looks. The inscrutable smiles. The card-game moves. The smell of sweat and forest. There would be many today. A turn in the weather had made the snow hard further up in the mountains, and he knew that man after man had fetched his scissor traps and snares and gone off to hunt.

He would do better to see to their demands now, but only *she* had the capacity to rid him of this feeling of helplessness. Only *she* could state categorically that this was not a wolverine, but a black Spæl sheep. Only *she* could scoff and say that those were actually the claws of a cockerel.

He grabbed his pencil and noted down the week's events. Two whole pages' worth.

Another woman had died in childbirth, she had been buried an hour ago, and her husband and nine children had stood around the coffin. Three wearing shoes that were much too big, clearly borrowed. Their father had a tortured face. He was a logger. Away for most of the winter and timber-floating during the summer. From now on the oldest girl would have to take care of the others. There would be no more school for her, Schweigaard thought.

The village midwife, known to everyone as Widow Framstad, was undoubtedly skilled, but it got harder for women to give birth as they grew older. Recently, he had been discussing public health with the doctor, and was unable to drink his coffee when they started on the subject of birth. The doctor told him that when things went wrong, they went very wrong, and that Herr Baumann, the doctor in a neighbouring village, had once undertaken an operation that involved taking the baby out through its mother's stomach. "There was no other way," said the doctor, "her soft parts had fused after a previous pregnancy."

He said that all the mothers who were opened up like this died, but that to everyone's surprise this woman had survived. She had lived for twenty-six days, but died when she tried to get up, presumably from bedsores or blood clots. "No other woman in Norway has lived that long after such an operation," said the doctor. "It was very near here. In one of the crofters' cottages in Øyer. Back in 1856. She was quite young, well under thirty. Everyone remembers. Not least Baumann. He never did it again."

Schweigaard went home, lost in thought. The next day he laid *Morgenbladet* aside, he wondered if the foreign news reports were from another planet. Telegraph lines, railways, daily postal deliveries, vaccinations against smallpox. Some day even childbirth might be easier. *Life* would get easier here in Norway. But when? It hit him, again and again, that here, in Butangen, he was struggling with the stubborn relics of a bygone age. Rationality and change were coming from Europe, but the pulpit and the meagre poverty-relief fund were his only weapons in the battle against cold and poverty, food shortages and tuberculosis, darkness and scepticism.

Perhaps it was his despair that had aroused his anger, when he had laid into Schönauer. The anger he thought he had put behind him. Already at the funeral, he had regretted his crazy comments about Napoleon's lunch and bear cubs in the mountains. Schönauer was polite enough, but desperate to satisfy his employers. He had handed Schweigaard a letter that he wanted posted, and had warned him that the purchase price might be reduced now that the portal was gone. The contract was conditional, he said, upon the church being "in dem selben Zustand wie auf Dahls Zeichnungen" – as it appeared in Dahl's drawings.

Schweigaard put the letter in a drawer and decided to forget about it until the next postal collection. The portal was one thing, worse was the matter of the church bells. Now and then he had heard claims that they could ring of their own accord. Clearly one of those banal stories folk entertained over the supper table. The bishop put it simply: "Bells that can warn of danger? A greater power than God? You can hear for yourself that these bells just attract and feed superstition. Get rid of them. We'll arrange for you to have the old church bells from a chapel in Gausdal, they've got some spare!"

He went to the iron safe in the corner and took out the *kirkestol*. As a student he had often wondered why the church accounts book should be given this mysterious name – literally the "church seat". And for a long time he had imagined that it came from a time when the priest's robes and other valuables were kept hidden under a lid in the priest's chair in a locked room. But this theory had been punctured by a teacher who told him that *stol* was simply an old German word for "a sum of borrowed money". The records in Butangen's current *kirkestol*, in which he kept his own accounts, went back as far as 1798. Whole chunks of his predecessors' entries were indecipherable. Few had stayed for long in the village, and the information was often chaotic and contradictory. There were frequent gaps of a year, or even two, during which a priest had written nothing at all. He browsed through the maze of entries, looking for evidence of the portal being replaced, although he was more curious about the church bells. Not forgetting that Astrid had mentioned something about a weave or tapestry, the so-called Hekneweave.

Returning to the safe, he took out an older *kirkestol* and knocked on its thick leather binding with his knuckles. Gothic handwriting, old, brownish ink. Begun in May 1662. The paper was ragged at the edges, had been eaten by mice and smelled of mould. On the first page was an overview of the church's contents and fixtures. "Two church bells (olde). In Memorie of the vertuous joind sisters from Hekne Farme."

Hmm. "Olde". So they were cast long before 1662. "Joind"? What could that mean? Unfortunately, the *kirkestol* that would have covered the years when they must have lived had disappeared, but there, in a later list of church fixtures, he found mention of a "weave" from Hekne. He leafed further forwards through the centuries, during which the church's inventory was recorded only every twentieth year or so. What was their relationship to time in those days? He skimmed through the entire book and then went back to the most recent *kirkestol* again. The weave still appeared in a list made in 1799, but not in one dated 1823.

But then, in an entry for the year 1844, he found: "October. New entrance door for the church."

Nothing else.

Irritated, he went back to the safe, and rooted through some other tattered notebooks. A musty cover bore the inscription *Prestens Optegnelser*. This set of priests' personal notes had been kept systematically until 1810, at which point one of the messier priests seemed to have taken over, using it for draft sermons and anything else that came to his mind, its pages filled with a mass of random ideas and thoughts.

The pastor ploughed steadily on, and there, in 1844 – finally!

"Offered a new entrance door by the king after the fearful church fire in Solöer in the twenties. Tall doors. Outwards swing. 4 speciedalers for materials and 1 speciedaler for wages. Old door and surrounds with diverse pagan figures given to carpenters Bergli and Hallum for fuel-wood. ⅛ daler deducted from their wages."

Burned! How could the priest be so short-sighted?

There was a knock on the door. Oldfrue told him that it was now twelve o'clock. Standing behind her was a lively-looking youngster holding some black claws.

"Got two ravens yes'day!" he said. "In the scissor trap."

Schweigaard grabbed his pen and said, "Karsten Evensen – was that the name?"

"Knut Evensen, if ye please."

Schweigaard nodded, jotted it down in the journal and looked up at him. "Well, let me see these claws."

The boy laid two pairs of black claws on the table and stared at the ceiling.

Ravens? thought Kai Schweigaard. "These seem rather small," he said.

"Young birds," said Evensen.

"Young birds, so early in the spring? You didn't bring any wing feathers?"

"Nay, just cut off their legs, then slung the rest of the ugly buggers away."

Kai Schweigaard rose. "Listen, the raven, the wolf and the wolverine are God's creatures too. Although that sets up a bit of a conflict, of course. You know Moses' Law?"

The boy tilted his head, in a way that said neither yes nor no.

"I take it you're confirmed?" said Kai Schweigaard.

Evensen nodded.

"Well, it says be fruitful and multiply and fill the earth," said Kai Schweigaard. "And that means people. Not ravens." He consulted the sheriff's chart and paid the crofter's son for two ravens, then put the claws in the bottom drawer of his desk.

Next came a middle-aged man, with a pair of yellowish claws. "Eagle," he said simply. Then, shoving his fist into a bag, he pulled out the head of a bird of prey with a powerful beak, followed by a brown wing. Schweigaard took the wing between his thumb and forefinger. It was badly frayed and broken. The eagle must have struggled for hours, beating its wings hundreds of times, before dying with its beak down. Brought here to God's representative in Butangen so that its killer might be rewarded. These methods of extermination had nauseated him from the first. Trapping was the most common form of hunting, and birds and animals starved to death before they were picked up. Eagles and hawks were trapped on tall posts up in the mountains; the birds took them to be good viewing points, but they proved to have snap traps on top of them.

He tried not to think about it. Folk died here as miserably as these creatures, and their deaths were often equally prolonged. But, just as he was about to pay out, he stopped. The claws. Weren't they remarkably small? And that eagle's head seemed very dried out. Hadn't he been offered a similar head a couple of weeks ago by another trapper?

He looked up at the man. His jacket sleeves were too short and he had two front teeth missing.

"Alright," said Kai Schweigaard, slinging the claws in the drawer and opening the cash box.

The next trapper was from Røen. He had the pelt of a wolf cub.

"A wolf?" said Kai Schweigaard. "Congratulations!" He took the hide and dug his fingers in against the direction of the fur, rubbed it as Astrid had shown him, and went over to the window. "Hmm," he said, frowning. "This is the skin of a wolf, you say?"

"Aye, it be a wolf alright."

"The thing is, Røen, it seems more like a mountain fox to me. A white fox. Which only has a bounty of four kroner, not twenty."

"Oh."

"But it's the same amount for a cub as for an adult. Their life's plan is the same, after all. Comfort yourself with that."

"I were sure it were a wolf when I took it," Røen said.

"Unfortunately, I'd say it's a mountain fox. The fur is too short. And soft."

"Oh, aye. Happens it in't easy to tell the difference betwixt them when they're so small. So it in't a wolf then?"

"Sadly not. And Røen," said Kai Schweigaard, pointing at his desk, "you see that notebook there?"

"Aye. I do."

"That's the journal in which I record all the bounties paid. And, having inspected this hide closely, something else is coming back to me. These little spots – right here – you see them? Well, they're in exactly the same place as on a hide for which I paid Jan Brenden a bounty. He was paid for a wolf, but I realise now that that was a mistake. There's not been a little mix-up, has there? Or maybe these mountain foxes came from the same litter? Where did you trap this one?"

"Up near Øverlihøgda."

"I see. Well, Røen. I'll let it pass this time. It may be from the same litter. I usually clip two claws off each paw to show that the bounty has been paid, but Herr Brenden told me he'd skinned it without its paws, and I see you've done the same."

"Oh, aye. Wi'out the paws."

"Maybe that's a kind of – skinning-tradition round here?"

"Oh aye. That be how we does it here, right enough."

"Well, listen very carefully now, Røen," said Kai Schweigaard, laying out the hide on the desktop. "You see this rubber stamp? The cross shows that this is the church's stamp. Now, I'm dipping it into this red ink, and – there – I'm stamping the skin on the back. From now on that's how we'll do it. I've acquired a type of ink with a very high level of tannin, so that it will hold even in the rain."

"Right y'are."

"So, you don't have to worry about it getting wet, or that it might be confused with someone else's catch, when they've already claimed the bounty."

"Nay, quite right."

"Here's the shot bounty, Herr Røen. Congratulations. Do you need a little leather bag to put your coins in?"

"There be space aplenty in me wallet, but thank you, Pastor."

"And we'll see you in church on Sunday – yes? The whole family?"

"Ye may do."

"Herr Røen! Tell me: might we, or *will* we?"

"Oh. Aye. Most likely."

"I'll see you on Sunday then. Have a safe trip home. Use the money wisely. Greetings to your family."

Afterwards, his desk littered with feathers and fur, he sank into his chair. It may well have been the same hide, in which case he had paid for the same mountain fox twice over, and on the first occasion it had been a wolf. But it had been a risk worth taking. The man was emaciated, and no doubt his children were in much the same state. The bounty payments came from the county council, all he had to do was issue a receipt, and more would arrive. It was a good arrangement. It gave the poor an income, while eradicating the guzzling guests in the Lord's larder. The stamps on the back of the skins would help. But they would soon bring him the claws of a bird he had never seen. The trickery would continue.

To whom would he turn for advice?

It was obvious.

Be honest now, he thought. It never really stopped. The glimpse of a pearl of sweat on her brow, the vibrations in the long tablecloth, the stirring in his loins when he saw the throbbing in the hollow of her neck.

He was not, he told himself, some castrated monk. Nor should he be. A pastor needed a wife and children to fulfil his mission. And she was strong. With a strong mind, and a strong will. A will that matched his, that could challenge the status quo in the village.

Astrid never said that "malt chocolate 'n' such". And never would, either. "Malt chocolate!" she would say. As if everyone had the right to taste it.

Now and then he glimpsed what she liked: she liked action. She was the sort to relish *riddersprang* – the knightly deeds of legends. This new church: hadn't he put it in motion to impress, not only the bishop, but her?

In the midst of all this Ida Calmeyer seemed increasingly distant. Grabbing a piece of letter paper, he wrote: "My darling Ida."

He sat and looked at these three words.

They did not ring true.

Just Two Squirrels

They sat down at the long table to eat *soll*, flatbread crushed into milk. Her father was silent. Earlier in the week he had been obliged to kill a horse, a fine mare named Mira. She had been kicked in the head by a young filly they had borrowed, a tragedy as big as tragedies came. But although the *stabbur* was nearly bare, they did not eat horsemeat, only heathens did that, and a workhorse was only just lower in rank than an *odelsgutt*, the first-born son. So they had dragged Mira down the slope furthest from the stream and covered her with rocks.

Astrid gazed down the long table. Her father sat at its head, in his coarse woven black trousers and white shirt. Maybe he was still thinking about the mare. He was marked with heavy toil, but when the world blossomed around him in the summer he became another person. This morning he had combed his bushy eyebrows and trimmed his beard, which was greying even though he was barely over forty.

Astrid's mother set the milk jug in front of her father. After that it would be passed to Emort, the *odelsgutt*, and then on to his younger brothers. Only when the smallest boys had taken their share was it the turn of Astrid and her sisters.

But Emort's place at the table was empty today, and it was to the sixteen-year-old Osvald that her father passed the jug. Osvald had edged further up the bench, well into the space left by his older brother, who lay in bed with a fever and snotty cold, after running around too thinly clad. His mother had been furious when she saw him, and snapped: "The spring be a dangerous time, as I have said! Ye can get lung sickness and die!"

On the other side of the table there was a crunching of flat-bread between the teeth of Osvald and his brothers, Laurits and

Ivar and Hjalmar. At last the milk jug was travelling up the table again, Astrid took a little and passed it to her sisters Oline and Mina. It was the only jug on the table that day, and they all knew it would not be refilled. But nobody said anything, and Astrid was glad there were no strangers to see this.

But Osvald could not hold his tongue. "Weren't more than a splash," he said, nodding towards the jug.

"Can ye expect owt else when ye feed the horses with the fodder what's meant for the cows?" said Astrid.

"Hush at table," said their mother.

The jug was sent on. Astrid's sisters were eagle-eyed as they watched its progress, making sure nobody took too much. As soon as they had their share, they no longer looked right or left, just gobbled their food down. Yet the tabletop remained spotless, for hungry folk never slopped their food.

A suspicion nagged at her all through that day. Was Schweigaard really planning to send the Sister Bells away? It felt as though all her ancestors, as far back as Eirik Hekne, had risen from their graves and agreed that she must act as their messenger, and she had already prepared what she would say: "Pastor Schweigaard, I shall ask ye now – and there be Bibles and crosses enough in this room for ye to answer me true – ye surely have nay sold the Sister Bells?"

And he would doubtless answer casually: "Well you see, it's like this . . ."

To which she would say: "Are ye raving mad, Pastor? They were a gift from us up at Hekne!"

Later she calmed down. Surely, he couldn't be so slippery as to keep something like that back? It must just be the building itself that was being sold. The font, the altarpiece, the Sister Bells, such things would surely be kept and reused. Besides, something else had started to go round in her thoughts: the things he had said about a portal. Twisting designs. Mythological creatures. A terrible serpent.

Later that day she saw her father strolling across the courtyard. He was returning from the blacksmith, but hearing her footsteps he slowed down to let her catch up.

"Tell me," said Astrid. "Did grandfather ever talk of the Midtstrand-bride or the Door Serpent?"

"Not as I can remember. Where d'ye get that from?"

"Klara did talk about them."

"And what be this – how did ye call it – this Door Serpent?"

"Summat in the church porch."

"Well, lass, Klara said plenty of queer things. All I knows about the porch is that the door were shifted long ago. For one that were taller."

"When?"

"Happen it were when I were so small, that I didna need to bend. There in't been a time I couldna walk tall into the church, and that be all that bothers me. More important now 'tis that Emort has worsened."

She followed her father into the farmhouse. In a little room all to himself lay Emort. Pale, drenched in sweat, he said he had an itchy throat. He had been laying traps when he came down with the fever, hoping, he said, to catch some pine martens. But his father shook his head, said it was daft to go fur trapping when the snow was melting, since the animals would be moulting. Nor were there any bounties on pine martens, and besides it was nigh on impossible to understand Emort's feverish description of where he had set his scissor traps.

"I'll fetch 'em in," said Astrid. "I can find them."

Next morning she woke up early, when the sky was still grey. She lay at the foot of the bed with her face under the window, where she was usually roused by the dawn light. But there had been no need for that today, she had been too restless to sleep any longer. Little Oline was still deep asleep, a bundle under the sheepskin in the neighbouring bed.

Astrid pulled her skirt on and headed through the dense spruce forest between Hekne and Syverrud. There was very little of this kind of ancient forest left, most of it had been cut down, the mountainsides were bare, the farms needed timber for building and firewood, for tools, boats and fences. She soon found Emort's tracks, faint prints in the dirty patches of remaining snow.

It was easy for her to get into her brother's head, and to know which trees he might have chosen for his three scissor traps. Emort had forged them himself, intricate and painstaking work. They also used deadfall traps that had been in the same place for years. Heavy logs were suspended on sharpened sticks that were placed in a figure four, and when an animal sniffed round the bait and disturbed the trigger, the log came crashing down. It was quite random, what they got in their traps: martens, stoats, magpies and squirrels, and once a domestic cat – which, luckily, they did not recognise.

With the sun glinting through the treetops, she lowered the scissors traps and opened their blades. Two squirrels. Not a great catch, but fine for a muff if you had eight or nine, and the meat wasn't too bad. The last squirrel had gone in recently, it was still twitching, she held it firmly around the belly and struck it dead. She put the animals in a canvas bag and sat on a fallen tree.

The spring melt was well under way, most of the fields were now bare, but at night the water droplets froze on the conifer trees, and now large, sparkling ice spheres lay on the needles. Gently she snapped off a twig and took it between her lips. The ice melted instantly, imparting a faint taste of pine needles. She stuck her hands into the canvas bag and warmed them against the squirrel that was not yet cold. Up in the air were two crows;

they did not notice her, but landed on a heap of snow nearby and searched for something edible.

A little further down was the church.

The night-chill still clung to her, and her sense of unease refused to lift. No, he was not interested, not in *that* way. A newspaper was just a newspaper. A travel blanket was just a travel blanket.

Behind her, snow slid from a branch. Relieved of its burden it sprung brightly up, and with a cloud of water droplets celebrated its freedom from the tyranny of winter, coming to rest at a sharper angle.

The crusty snow crackled under foot as she walked out of the forest. She took a detour towards Lake Løsnes to see whether the ice would melt soon. The northern part was frozen over and grey, the area to the south was open, black and steaming. The actual reason for this was that the water to the south was so deep that it retained its heat, but Klara had always insisted that the southern end of the lake was bottomless and lay over hell itself.

"Hell must be very small then," Astrid had replied, "since the northern end freezes solid." To which Klara had retorted: "The frost and flame be good friends."

She had been so intolerant towards Klara! So judgmental and scathing! Just because she went about curtseying and muttering her nonsense. Yet again Astrid heard the noises. The horrible sound of her skin ripping. The thud as her head hit the church pew. Like a huge hard-boiled egg.

She missed Klara now, just as she missed her grandfather, missed their untrammelled beliefs. After he got too arthritic to work, Grandfather would usually sit by the stove with the cat, running his sore joints deep into her warm fur, and was grateful to anyone who was ready to listen to him. Astrid rarely abandoned his stories without having been nagged at least twice to get back to work.

He was sad that so few folk wanted to listen to what he called "the wonders of times yore", a chance to ponder what lay behind everything. He remembered all the stories of the past, but was always careful not to mix truth with untruth, even if it might make for a better story. Astrid's father was only interested in things that were practical, and useful to the tending of the animals and land. Her grandfather excused him: "In hard years folks be hungry and they canna think big. We had time to muse over things. To study the order of things as happens. Just as ye and I be doing now, Astrid."

He had taught her the constellations and weather-signs, and when she was ten he told her that the *busemann* and the evil giantess Kari På Vona did not really exist; they were just scary inventions she and the other children were told about from the moment they could toddle around. Farm work was busy and it was impossible for the adults to keep track of where the children went to play, so they let these creations guard the dark lofts and cellars and deep wells, then when their bairns were tempted to venture close or peer in, they did at least hesitate and keep their distance.

Other things, stranger than these, he held to be true, and he often mentioned the joined girls, the Hekneweave and the Sister Bells.

"Sad that they has all gone," said Astrid. "The sisters' weaves, I mean."

"It were a long time ago. They was sold all about. Folks put them over the cradles of newborns, 'cos they said they made sick babbies whole again. Some folks called it Flemish tapestry work. Made cushion covers too, they did. Over the years these mostly got worn to a thread. But happens there still be a few around. I heard that a rocking chair up near Dombås were decorated with a hekneweave, and that nobody were ever allowed to sit on it."

"So we do nay have any here?" asked Astrid, casting her gaze around the room, where there were odd pieces of handiwork left by the generations before them: woven coverlets, embroidered cushions, objects decorated with intricate carvings or the stylised paintings of flowers.

Her grandfather shook his head and explained that he had only ever seen one weave that he was sure the Hekne sisters had made, because it had been donated to the church and hung near the baptismal font. "It were the weave that showed Skråpånatta," he said. "Ye remember, The Night of the Great Scourge?"

Astrid nodded.

"It were their last," he said. "Folk just called it the Hekne-weave. I saw it when I were a lad and remember how it frightened me. Later it vanished wi'out anyone knowing how."

Astrid asked him to describe it.

"It were rectangular and very big. In strong, bright colours. And showed folks running from summat. In the sky there were birds with human faces that spat fire. The folk came out of big, queer-looking houses. In one corner the sisters had woven a picture of their selves."

"Were it the birds that frightened ye?" said Astrid.

"Nay, not really. It were mostly that I knew how the weave came into being. Y'see, Astrid, 'cos the sisters was joined they shared some of their senses. What one touched, the other could feel too. What one saw, the other could see. They must have had a good laugh when one sister covered her eyes, while t'other stared at summat horrible to make her shudder. I asked the doctor once if it were possible, and he said it were. Happen that are why they could make such fine weaves. They was one human as much as they was two. But that in't why I was afeared to look straight at the weave."

"No?"

"It were because I knew about the day it were finished. The girls knew they was dying and they wove together till the moment the first one died. But t'other lived on for a good few hours more."

"And she wove on with her sister dead?"

Her grandfather nodded. "Aye. And since they shared their senses, among them sight, she could see into the kingdom of the dead and into the future too perhaps."

He started to talk about the powers of the Sister Bells. "They do nay ring for petty things. They donae ring to warn of forest bandits or a little earthslide. They ring when folk mun wake up and choose wisely. Or to warn of a disaster as they did in 1814."

On the 5th of August of that year, he told her, the bells had rung of their own accord, and on hearing them the villagers had gone out, one by one, into their yards. Preparations were made, watchmen put into place, muzzle-loading rifles fetched and gunpowder flasks filled, keen-eyed men went up onto the mountainsides, and young girls stood ready to blow warning horns, the rest lay awake. But nothing happened. Not for the first few days, nor the next. The village began to relax, and some wiseacres went down and inspected the church's foundations and claimed that it had sunk slightly in one corner, a sideways movement that had travelled up to the spire and caused the bells to ring.

Six weeks later the sheriff arrived with a message. Earlier that year, fifteen village men had been ordered to join the war against Sweden, and on the 5th of August – the very day the bells had rung – there had been a battle near Matrand. All fifteen men had survived the fighting, but died later from dysentery in the field hospital on the Vinger bulwarks – four each day, then three on the last.

Her grandfather believed that the bells had also been warning of the terrible years ahead. Since they did not ring later for the famine that reduced folk to eating bark-bread, or the barren summers that followed. The crops froze and grain could not be bought at any price. "If they had rung for that time of misery, they would have rung every single day."

"But how can the bells know what kind of danger is coming?" asked Astrid.

Her grandfather let the cat down from his lap.

"When the bells were cast, it weren't just silver that Eirik Hekne threw in. He threw in a lock of each girl's hair and a piece of her nail. Thus the bells got the talent of seeing into the future, just as the girls had done when they looked into the hereafter. But nobody knows how far into the future the sisters saw nor how far the bells will see. Some say till the end of time, all the way to Skråpånatta. But happen we donae fully understand the truth of Skråpånatta. If they could find the weave, we might know more. With each age we understand summat new, but with each age we lose understanding for the times yore."

Astrid sat in silence for a while. "Their mother died, is that right?"

"Aye. In the worst way possible. It were said Eirik had saved some of his good wife's hair and got the ropemaker to plait it into the bell ropes."

"What were her name?"

Her grandfather went quiet.

"The mother of the two girls?" Astrid repeated. "His wife?"

He looked at her and shook his head. "Happen her name's been forgotten," he said. "But some folks say she walks up in the belfry."

Astrid was fifteen when her grandfather died. Carried down to the cemetery by a silent procession of mourners and buried under the family tombstone, and the old pastor demanded payment for the Sister Bells to be rung for him.

Astrid approached the church. In the hazy early morning light she could see the burial place where her grandfather lay. Fathers and mothers before him and before them again.

She noticed that the side door of the church was open. She stepped quickly over a stream of brown meltwater, climbed over the churchyard wall and went over to the church, put down the scissor traps and sack with the squirrels, and walked calmly in and past the altar.

It was the first time she had been alone here. In the awe-inspiring silence, in the cool, high-ceilinged church room, embraced by the smell of ancient dust. Her eyes found nothing to focus on, she moved in the half-dark, hearing the echo of the wind outside.

Kai Schweigaard did not seem to be there.

She found her way to the font, though it was too dark to see where the Hekneweave might have hung. In the aisle hung a faint corpse-odour, left from the last funeral.

She walked on, thought about the pastor, and asked herself what she actually felt. Not religiosity, at least. Only shame at her confusion and her stupid infatuation. Mortified, she forced herself onwards to the pew where Klara had died. Far ahead she could just make out the crucifix.

Time passed, although it was difficult to say how much. She thought she felt a presence close by, but she was unafraid.

Her eyes were growing accustomed to the dim light, but it still felt dingy and murky in the church, the only hint of colour was in the grey strips of light that came in through the narrow slit windows high up. And where was the pastor? Had he just forgotten to lock up?

Suddenly she felt Klara's bony shoulder, her rough woollen shawl against her hand. Then Klara was gone.

Again, she had no fear. This was no ghost. Just a memory in physical form, an imprint of the past making itself known against her body.

But now she sensed that there *was* someone else in the church. A living person.

Norwegian Incense

That same morning Gerhard Schönauer had lain awake while the wind whistled around the house corners. Six days had passed since his arrival in Butangen, and each night he had lain as he did now. Freezing cold, sweating, nervous.

He got up from his bed. The cold floorboards burned the soles of his feet. There were no rugs in the cottage, so he spread his coat over the floor, set his feet on it and rested his head in his hands.

Sabinka. The laughter, the warmth in bed, the breasts that slapped his face. The playfulness and freedom from obligation, the Bavarian beer and the Academy of Art.

He lit the tallow candle and fumbled his way to the chamber pot. Then he returned to bed, only to find that his bowels were waking up. He pulled on his overcoat, tottered outside into the icy morning air and into the privy. The unfamiliar food made his own stool smell strange, as if someone else had done their business before him, and the idea of such intimacy repulsed him. Back at home he would occasionally ask himself a question, a question too embarrassing to be shared, namely why the odours of his own bodily waste – the sweat, the stools, the farts – smelled intriguing and not disgusting, not while they were fresh at least, while other people's smells were always abominable and made him back away. Must be linked to the marking of territory, he thought. Scent-tracks from a primitive past, before God had decided whether man or *Canis lupus* would be the most highly developed species. Something that we, when we had better noses, left behind us to say: this is mine, anything else has the stench of my enemies.

And now my own odour is strange to myself. He stood at the door of the privy. It's the dark, he muttered. It's just the dark.

The daylight will be back again soon, and then I'll get a grip again. Herr Schiertz did it in 1840 and I'll manage it now.

But his hope was egg-like; the instant it was left to stand it rolled over.

Day was dawning. He dressed and walked down towards the church. There was nobody else to be seen, and no sound but his own steps crunching on frozen grass.

He had contented himself over the last few days with making sketches of the church from afar, and going back into the cottage to finish them. But then he would realise that they were woefully inadequate. He could sit for hours tinkering with them, but when he looked at these abysmal sketches, something snarled in his guts, his fingers refused to work and all determination deserted him. Everything that had helped him before to overcome life's difficulties had gone, he doubted whether he'd ever had any talents. There was something up here, beneath the mountains, at the edge of the forest, a heavy, stifling force of unknown shape and dimension.

Suppers with the pastor had become brief, sombre affairs, the silence only interrupted by the occasional squealing of knives against porcelain. Yesterday the pastor had shown him a frayed old book, in which it was apparently written that the portal had been torn down in 1844, and that it had probably been burned.

He unlocked the door to the church and went in. His nostrils quivered with tar and dust and mould. The tiny windows high up in the walls took on a hint of colour from the morning sun, but the light was far too weak for him to draw in. He could barely see more than halfway into the church.

I'll never understand its construction, he thought. This church is one single intertwined mass, dipped in a secret-recipe varnish that hides any trace of method or craft, not a single splice or butt joint reveals the thoughts that were behind its making.

Looking up he glimpsed the cross beams, all the joists were

at angles, forming a riddle about what was resting its weight on what.

He went into the sacristy and over to a window. Its frame was crumbling and there were stains on the decorative paintwork where water had trickled down. Back in Dresden he had assumed he would just take a good look round, to understand the church, and then produce some architectural drawings.

The problem was that this church had not been erected according to any architect's plans. It had been built free-hand and measured by eye. More carved than carpented. Trees stripped of their bark, and joined using long-forgotten skills. There was no trace of a saw anywhere – only axes, scraping-irons, and cutting tools. Even the floorboards had been cleaved and levelled. The smell of tar danced in his nostrils. They did not use incense in the churches here. Tar was the Norwegians' incense.

"Consider yourself a saviour, a man on a rescue mission, student Schönauer."

He shook his head. He did not feel like a saviour, but a grave robber. He looked up at the magnificent altarpiece. That, too, was bound for Dresden. And he wanted solace, an embrace, but got nothing. At the other end of the church, just visible in the scattered light, painted in the yellowing-grey of an aged bone, hung Christ, but the Saviour looked the other way, silent.

I can't do this, Gerhard said to himself. Nobody can. If the church is taken down it'll never be made whole again. There's more here than I can ever understand. The most important thing of all, an inner essence, will disappear when we demolish it.

But another anxiety gripped him too. An anxiety that had started when, on that first day, he had heard the church bells. Now he got the distinct feeling they disliked him. They were somewhere there above him, where they *lived*, free in the air, in fragile balance. Watching, aware of the least movement here below. He should probably go up to see where they hung, but he was afraid he might bump into the bell rope, one wrong step and they would answer with a reverberating boom.

The night-chill still hung in the church, and he sat torturing himself with thoughts of desecration for a long time, until he finally got up and flung the side door open. The morning air and light streamed in, but still it did not reach into the corners.

It would be another hour before he could start drawing. The floorboards creaked as he walked further into the church, where the darkness was most dense.

He thought he could hear the voices of the men who had built the church, and shutting his eyes he tried to see them. Through a dusty light he glimpsed bowed figures from another time, who joined timbers with nothing but axes and knives, masters of forgotten trades, whose workdays were measured by neither clocks nor calendars, but by the daylight. These men built their reputations and fame slowly, without diploma or title, the scars on their leather aprons the mark of their experience.

Something moved here, something *greater*, something that could never be confined to a curriculum at the academy. Something existed beneath these arches that could never be dispersed by the air, or divided into explicable constituents. It was the secret soul of hallowed wood, a smoky figure that had grown out of many centuries of grief and hope. Out of the longings of hundreds of souls, long dead, longings so strong as to be unendurable in their time, but which, liberated by death, had gathered here to float for ever.

Something passed through the square of light from the side door. A thin figure drew close, almost weightless, a faint creak of floorboards, barely visible, a mere shift in the density of shadow.

The person stopped, perhaps to accustom their eyes to the gloom, then moved quietly, almost floated down the aisle, and sat on the inside end of a pew.

The Midtstrand Bride

"So beautiful," said the man.

The voice was thrown about the church, and Astrid looked around without seeing him. He stepped forwards, in the semi-dark between the church pews, the German painter, with a sketchbook in his hand. He spoke in a strange and stilted Danish, apologised for disturbing her, asked her a question, which she did not understand, but which he repeated:

"Were you sitting here in prayer?"

"Nay. Only sitting."

"At home, in my country, it is common for people to sit in the church and pray. In the early morning, often, after a bad night."

She had no answer. It was too dark for her to see his facial features. He kept turning his head, and he moved like a person who thought someone else might come.

They sat there in the church as it gradually grew lighter. He began to draw. Bowed, concentrated. Suddenly he tore off the sheet of paper, screwed it up and threw it into the aisle.

"Impossible!" he said.

"What's impossible?"

This was not a theatrical gesture. He was clearly distressed. She walked past him and stood sideways to him, so that he could not view her from behind, then, gathering up her skirts, she bent down to pick up the ball of paper.

She had never seen a finer drawing. The pulpit and the altarpiece. A sight she was so familiar with, but had never seen in this way. It bore his understanding within it, and that seemed somehow . . . trustworthy. It reflected something of her own view of all things old: that time did not only erode, it also ennobled.

He stopped drawing. Seemed ashamed. She asked why he was unable to draw something that was standing right in front of him, and he replied that he had to draw that which was invisible. She had no difficulty in understanding what he meant. She wanted to go on watching him work, but he had clearly lost courage.

Astrid! she said to herself. This is the man who will take away the bells! Take the church itself!

Just as *I* might pick up a pretty stone, she thought, I am nothing more to *him* than an ant beneath that stone.

He went past her, heading for the porch, and she got up to leave.

"It is *tragisch*," she heard him say.

He stopped by the entrance to the porch.

"What is?" she said.

He was standing on the very spot where Klara had curtseyed. "Wrong door!" he said. "Much too tall! No carvings! No portal! All gone! All destroyed!"

Suddenly Astrid understood. Klara had not curtseyed when she walked in, but stooped down, as though she were still walking through the old door, as she must have done countless times when she was young.

"The door itself is not so important," he said. "But the carvings around it are. The carvings that stopped the evil powers from coming into the church!"

"But what did these carvings look like?" she asked.

The German snatched up his sketchbook again, and soon a beautiful drawing ran from his pencil.

Astrid was stunned. Both by what the drawing showed, and because it was such a stark illustration of the difference between Kai Schweigaard and the stranger. What Kai had called "twirling shapes" became, in the hands of the German, a precise reproduction of the most masterful and fantastical woodcarvings.

Pencil lines and layers of shade emerged methodically on the paper. Second by second the portal was resurrected before

Astrid's eyes. And with its gradual resurrection she understood what Klara had meant.

The church door had broad hinges of decorative wrought iron and an arched top. Around it were large reliefs crammed with carved figures. The main carving was of a serpent that curled itself around the door, a monument in itself, thick as a log, covered in scales that resembled the church's roof tiles, and high above the door the serpent's head and tail met, each dangerous in its own way, and more so together, with a snarling and flicking and a glutenous snap of jaws.

This must be Midgardsormen, the Midgard Serpent, she thought. She had seen pictures of it in the *Skilling-Magazin*. And reading about it she had asked herself whether folk had really once believed in this creature that encircled the earth and gobbled up ships that sailed too close to the edge. Her father had said that coastal dwellers probably thought differently to those who lived in the valleys, who could always see the other side of a lake.

Gerhard Schönauer's drawing grew steadily more detailed. Writhing around Midgardsormen were a myriad other mythological creatures, recognisable even when he described them with just a few strokes. A whole vine of animals emerged before her eyes, creatures with tendrils, with scaly bellies and horns and fangs, lizards and wolves and birds, with snarling jaws and vicious claws, all closely entwined. He drew a dragon that clung to Midgardsormen and stared deep into its eyes, almost trustingly, almost lovingly – or as lovingly as a dragon can look at a serpent, at least.

Was this what Klara had been talking about? Was this Klara's "Midtstrandbrura" – the Midtstrand-bride? And had she muddled up Midtstrand, the name of a local farm, with Midgard, the Norse Middle Earth? She must have believed this dragon was the bride of the great serpent, Midgardsormen. It made sense;

Butangen had certainly been Klara's entire world, and she probably had no idea about dragons.

Astrid pointed to the dragon, and asked the German if this might be the story behind it.

"What? The dragon? A bride? Not at all." He explained, sounding rather too self-assured for her liking, that he had studied the ancient Norse beliefs very thoroughly, and had never seen any mention of a dragon. "It must be a product of local imagination!"

He tore the drawing carefully out of his sketchbook.

"You keep it!" said Gerhard Schönauer.

"Nay, I canna take this!"

"It is yours! Heartily! Just a sketch!"

She stood with the sheet of paper in her hands. It was as though the pencil strokes were still alive.

The drawing told her something else too. This man, who signed himself as "G. Schönauer", was no common grave robber. No-one could draw such a thing without true affection for the subject. She *also* knew that no-one from the village would have destroyed anything as magnificent as this portal.

Glad Tidings

He heard the bells ring, but sat on at his desk. His sermon had been finished the day before, but he was still polishing it, and whenever he tried to read it aloud, he repeatedly fell into thought, because each time he said the words "happiness" or "gladness" or "joy", he found himself wondering how they related to his own life.

It had taken him weeks to understand what he saw in Astrid Hekne, and more to accept it. Night after night he heard voices from the secret room within him, from the dark place where he confessed his own desires. And each time he ventured into this innermost chamber, he shone a light, and in its glow he saw Astrid Hekne. Sometimes he would venture inside and close the door behind him, and there he would stay until the dreams turned to animalistic imaginings, but when he re-emerged God was watching him, and Astrid had taken on the face of the prostitute in Pipervika.

This unseemly desire filled him with shame whenever he saw her, making him clumsy and childlike. Yet at the same time, it was incomprehensibly and intensely pure – just as there was only one God, it was enough for him to be taken by the blazing flames of one love.

He forced himself to consider what he really wanted. He had always imagined himself marrying a kind, quiet soul who inhabited the corner of the living room. Devoted, selfless, in agreement over all the big questions. Ida would be compliant in all things. But rarely did he imagine how she was beneath her clothes. She was amiable enough – little nods, feigned interest, the odd comment about good housekeeping, or the value of faith.

Never on her lips: "That's not how the world looks, Kai." The challenge, which he had to admit, forced him to rethink; so that after a period of arrogant huffing and puffing, he came up with a better, sharper solution. But this need he felt for Astrid was so wrong. She was utterly unsuitable to being a pastor's wife. Far too feisty. Too much a woman. With too many imperatives. She lacked the one quality essential in a clever woman: the ability to get her way by making a man think he'd come up with the idea himself. His mother had let him in on this secret, and as far as he could tell she had benefited from it all her life.

He dared himself to contemplate marriage with Astrid, and a shiver of excitement went through him. Oldfrue Bressum would boil over like a pan of milk. Light entertainment, compared to the catastrophes that might await him when important visitors came. Astrid in a neat black dress with a lace collar, curtseying to the bishop and lowering her gaze? Unthinkable. No modesty, politesse would soon be abandoned: "Tell me what's going on!" A minute later the inevitable, embarrassing scene. And later, if she were to gain a certain status, how would she be then? Even quicker on the draw, she might even overshadow his mission.

The bells rang again. He got up, gathered his papers and went out into the kitchen garden. It would look bad if he arrived together with his congregation, so he lingered by the wall, taking in the fresh air and waiting for the last stragglers to go in.

And what would they say back home? An earthquake! He barely dared contemplate the walk up the front steps to meet his mother. She only had to hear the trace of a country dialect, and she'd uncork the arsenic bottle.

Of course, Astrid lacked sophistication. But that was how she was *now*. It must be possible to shape her, to get her to see that different worlds have different rules, and that if she wanted them changed she couldn't break them all at once. She was more than sharp enough to understand that. After all, there was a touch of cynicism in her, an ability to calculate, to aim high. Enough perhaps for her to put aside her dialect too?

Kai Schweigaard shook off these thoughts and stood looking over Butangen, and realised he wouldn't stay here long. Even Bishop Folkestad couldn't live for ever. And the demands on a pastor's wife would grow with his rank.

Ah, well.

Schweigaard quickly headed down, opened the sacristy door, sat down and checked that his papers were in the right order.

Waiting-time. A lonely waiting-time during which he imagined exchanging looks with two women.

On the other side of the wall the old organ dragged into action. A hymn rose. Landstad. "*Syng høit*. Sing aloud of God's mercy . . ."

Ida Calmeyer was and would be the safest bet.

But he already knew that, in flights of fancy from larger and larger oak desks, he would regularly be transported back to Butangen, and wonder what she was doing; whether she was dragging about with a flock of children, with backache and callouses and a dream she kept locked away.

With her, he would be an altogether different man. They could do so much good. It was certain that *together* they made a greater whole, and that life was bigger with Astrid Hekne.

But he was a priest, he couldn't swan about and seduce and play games. A solid offer of marriage. And, after that, let loose within the safety of wedlock. Then he could rid himself of the shame, erase the face of the prostitute, show Astrid the true Kai Schweigaard, easy-going, playful.

But what could he tempt her with? Her only weakness seemed to be her fondness for great deeds. For one's duty to family. For history. That was her blind spot.

It was silent behind the wall now, and he went out to deliver the "glad tidings".

"This wonderful new church will be with us by winter!" he said, gazing over his congregation.

The muttering spread. Today's Mass was well attended, and after the sixth hymn, when he usually slipped in his brief notes on the world news, he said he had an announcement to make, cleared his throat and told them that the church was going to be demolished, and a new, bigger and warmer one would be built in its place.

Astrid Hekne was sitting near the front. They caught each other's eye, but he tore his gaze free, cleared his throat again, looked out over his parishioners and explained that their old church had been sold and would be rebuilt in Germany, "as a memorial".

He thanked the bishop, the mayor and the chairman of the Savings Bank, and heard a polite "hmm!" spread its way back over the pews. He went on to explain that the church would be finished by Christmas, and that in the meantime weddings, baptisms and funerals would be held in a temporary chapel in the parsonage parlour.

"By the way," he said, "the young German gentleman with the easel who's been wandering about here for some time was sent here by the purchasers of the church. He will oversee the demolition and reconstruction of the church. Be civil to him."

That was all.

He gathered his papers. The church was quiet, apart from the usual muted sounds of a congregation; fidgeting in seats, rustling of hymn books, old women wheezing.

He looked around, waiting for reactions that did not come. He spotted Astrid's father near the back, he must get hold of him afterwards, outside the church, for a brief chat, to explain the formalities surrounding the church bells.

It was time for another hymn. Earlier in his sermon he had praised the work of John Engh, a missionary from Gudbrandsdal who was taking the Christian message to faraway Madagascar. And now they joined their voices in his honour – "*Ber no bod til heidningland* – free the prisoners of the Devil".

The Sister Bells rang out, and he noticed that Astrid was slow to get up. He thought that the bells sounded different, gloomier, as though they were warning him of his own folly and defeat.

The Wedding Gift

Porridge. Not much of a Sunday supper, but it was still spring, and at least there was enough to go round. Astrid finished half of hers, leaned across the table, looked along the table at her father, and said: "What did the pastor want?"

The chewing stopped around her. Her father did not answer, and everyone carried on eating.

Eventually her father finished his mouthful, and said:

"He wanted to know if it were true that the bells were a gift from us. 'From the Heknes', he said."

Osvald was the only one who was still eating now.

"Happen he knew that all along?" said Astrid.

"It didna seem so," said her father.

"Then he were bluffing."

"Enough now!" her mother said, rapping her spoon on the table. "'Tis Sunday! Do nay sit there badgering yer father!"

Her father laughed. "Aye, let us finish our supper. Come up afterwards, lass."

"Up" was the room on the first floor where her father had a small table, a chair, a bookshelf, a map of the forests, and the receipts from the bailiff. "Up" was also the room where, when they were little, they were beaten if they had been naughty or cheeky. Then it was "up" and the door was closed, while the other siblings stood, gawping, at the bottom of the stairs. Inside the little room a bunch of birch twigs hung on the wall, worn with use. Astrid had been eleven when she last got a birching, for cursing when she spilled a pail of milk. But from the age of ten, it was no longer her father who beat the girls, putting them over his knee to birch their bottoms. From then on it was their mother they answered to; she pulled up their skirts and hit the back of their thighs, harder than their father ever had.

They finished their porridge, thanked their mother for supper in dutiful chorus, "Takk for maten", then Astrid and her father went "up" together. It was she who closed the door, and she stood for a moment staring at the birch twigs. Her father had a habit of folding his eyebrow with his fingers when he was thinking, and he did so now.

"Ye'll understand when ye've bairns of your own," he said, nodding towards the birch twigs. "And I hope that be soon. Ye'll make a good farm-wife, lass. When ye have put aside your wild notions, this . . . contrariness."

Astrid said nothing.

Her father sat down. "The pastor said this: that the bells shall go where'er the church goes. He reckoned as they belonged together."

"That in't for the pastor to say."

"He sounded most decided."

"They be a gift."

"Aye, there's the nub of it. They be a *gift*. The receiver can do whate'er he please with a gift. Back in those days, so long ago, naebody thought that the church would ever be torn down."

"And ye'll let that happen?"

"I've enough struggles without falling out with the pastor."

"Father! Listen to yersen! Ye be sending those bells out o' the family!"

Her father leaped to his feet. And there they stood, until she lowered her gaze. Then he blinked and sat back down.

Rather too quickly, she thought. Eirik Hekne would have torn the church down over Kai Schweigaard's head and carried the Sister Bells home, even if he broke a vertebrae with each step.

Astrid walked over to the small shelf behind the desk. She took a pipe with a curved mouthpiece out of a basket. Lying beneath it was an old notebook. It was the only thing left of her grandfather's. She weighed the pipe in her hand and put it back.

Alongside the basket was a whole year's worth of the *Skilling-Magazin*, the weekly illustrated periodical, which her father had received as a prize when his teacher reported him as an outstanding pupil. Its handsome binding was embossed with a golden royal crown, indicating who the benefactor was. She had read every issue many times over, studied the plates and revelled in all the various stories, and felt pride over the golden crown. But her father kept it up here, not down in the living room with the Bible and the few other books they owned, which was how she knew that her father and the Hekne farmer were not necessarily one and the same.

Their time had run out.

Her father sighed, took out a ledger and said that he must record the week's outgoings.

"Mun ye do that right now?" asked Astrid. Her father nodded, saying he had to do it every Sunday while the past week was still fresh in his memory, or he'd get in a dreadful muddle. "I get that from my father. He did the same. That aside, he were a very different man to me. That difference must be my wedding gift to ye."

"What d'ye mean?"

"To let you marry someone like your grandfather and not me."

She was lost for a reply.

"The bells may be taken away," he added, as she headed for the door. "But I shall make sure Hekne be in this family well after I be dead."

Astrid fetched the yoke, her mother barking after her to be quick about it, and headed for the stream. Water-carrying was actually a job for the new pauper-woman, whom they had taken in after Klara, but she was ill and vomiting, despite there being little in her belly to vomit. "Reckons ye almost mun do it, my lass," said her mother. "So it be done with."

Astrid did it without protest, mostly because her mother said "almost" and called her "lass". A lot was said in those few words. Their fall in status, from grand to ordinary folk. From farmer's daughter to housemaid, and from there to water-carrying. Her mother was not kind, but nor was she bad. She had a way of curbing unrest by putting folk to work. Her children and the farmhands sprang from barn to pigsty. No-one complained. Whining was punished with a clip around the ear, because grumbling did not fill anyone's belly, it only poisoned the will to work. Her mother was a good organiser, "done with" was her favourite phrase, and they ate their fill at table, and thus life on the farm was much better than if she'd been kind.

Astrid went to the stream, filled the water pails, emptied them into the barrel in the house and went for more. Klara could never carry more than two half-full pails, and year after year she had walked the same path all day long, slopping water as she went. These were proud, unbending womenfolk. Not a single new recipe had been tried out in the kitchen in Astrid's lifetime. Nor any new working methods. If I were in charge at Hekne, Astrid thought, I'd get someone to run a long copper or lead pipe down from the stream. It's possible to picture it, she thought, so it must be possible to do. A long pipe, going downhill, to some barrels near the farmhouse and barn, so that when the barrels are full they'll run over into another pipe.

But copper was expensive, and women's work did not show in the accounts, and her father would never make anything that risked falling apart, not when all that was needed was to send an old woman out to carry.

Astrid filled the pails again. The yoke weighed heavy on her shoulders, and the cold water splashed over her skirt making the hem slap against her legs. Osvald was standing outside the farmhouse. He nodded towards the stables.

"Bring up four pails for Balder after. He mun go out."

Astrid continued walking straight towards him, but only when she was right in front of him did he step aside.

"Emort said Balder ought to stay in till they get new hindshoes on him," said Astrid, as she passed.

"Emort is sick. So I be in charge now."

She didn't turn, but walked on.

"If Hekne's gonna be summat again," said Osvald, "we canna let the workhorses stand around as decoration."

Then she turned.

"Ye be a grimy-tongued louse, ye know that? Talking ill of folks who be sick."

"And what about ye? Ye canna act the lady now. Not like when ye swanned about the parsonage in a new skirt every year. And what about the pastor?"

"Aye, what of him?"

"He ogles ye."

"Well, let him ogle. And fetch yer own water."

She turned and walked to the farmhouse. There she emptied the pails and headed back to the stream. Up at the stables Osvald was with their father now, and they had taken Balder out.

Gottfred Fyksen, the wheelwright, was down by the gate. The hubs on several of their cartwheels were worn out, Astrid had heard her father say they could only afford to repair two.

Astrid turned the pails upside down and knocked on them with her knuckles. A silly custom that was meant to stop the underground spirits from hiding in them, and which she did now in remembrance of Klara. She knelt beside the stream and drank from her hands. A strange ripple winked at her in the water.

Where had it gone, the wild streak in her family? The wild streak in Eirik Hekne? Everything had always been controlled by fathers, or priests. Always men. Every kroner passed through their hands. They never reached out for anything that wasn't useful. Everything free and great had disappeared through fingers that were numb with the cold, drowned in the daily bellowing of cows and clucking of hens. The spinning wheel spun as it had always spun, but fine embroideries and weaves were unthinkable.

Astrid thought about a girl from the neighbouring farm. She was the eldest of nine, and her mother had worn herself to the bone and fallen down dead beside the laundry tub when she was forty-two. When Astrid popped by the day after the funeral, her friend was standing beside the same laundry tub, wearing the same expression on her face as her mother. She was too busy to talk, and not long afterwards she accepted the first marriage proposal that came her way. Four years later, she had two children and a third on the way, and spoke through gritted teeth.

I shan't, said Astrid to herself. I refuse.

She stood for a moment thinking about the church bells. They may not be *hers* exactly, but they were more hers than anyone else's in the village. With them, existence was greater, poverty more worthy. Their sound offered comfort during times of deprivation and famine.

Schweigaard was visible to her again, both with and without his priestly robes. Suddenly it was as though her directionless love was gaining heat, it began to boil and turn to anger, but between the bubbles she saw something that glinted and glowed. Suddenly she felt like Eirik Hekne. Throw caution to the winds, let the silver coins splash into the cauldron, take a wild *riddersprang* – like Sigvat, who risked all for love.

She left the yoke and water pails.

I must go there, and right away. To throw my own silver coins into the cauldron. For perhaps all of this can be gathered in one blow of the sword. It may be rash, but at least I will have known what it is to kiss a man.

Just an Old Wives' Tale

The letter from Bishop Folkestad had arrived earlier that week, but Kai Schweigaard had avoided opening it until now: "I am so glad that the demolition plans have been made public now. Exercise all the influence you can so that further work may be done without delay. The new House of God must be finished by December, preferably before."

Schweigaard put down the letter and considered what word to use in his reply. "Disconcerted" was too mild. The bishop was not going to be happy that the price had been lowered because of the missing portal.

The door was flung open and in marched Astrid Hekne. And stomping up behind her in the hallway came Oldfrue Bressum, waving her arms and muttering breathlessly that she had "tried to stop her".

"Stop this ruckus," said Schweigaard, getting up. "It's alright, Margit, thank you. Sit down there, Frøken Hekne."

He went over to close the door himself, and waited until he was sure that Oldfrue was actually going back down the hallway.

"You can't just barge in here like that," he hissed at Astrid. "I'm a . . ." He shifted from one foot to the other, and began again. "You must respect my position as a pastor."

"The Pastor *mustn't* sell the church bells. He gave them as a gift to the village!"

"Who?"

"Eirik from the farmstead, our farmstead. My forefather, from long ago. But now the painter's going to take them, and—"

"Now, listen to me—" Kai Schweigaard started. But Astrid continued over him: "And I reckons as ye shall regret it!"

Kai Schweigaard blushed.

"Astrid, I . . . that was two hundred years ago. More."

"Ye stood right there, and showed me those plans. For the new church. But ye said nowt about the bells going away."

Kai Schweigaard tried to explain that he hadn't known the full story, but his explanation was skidding on ice, and he heard how foolish he sounded when he said "and they *are* just made of metal".

"There be many kinds of metal," said Astrid. "But that probably means nowt to ye! All our silver is in those bells!"

Kai Schweigaard was rattled by her rudeness, but, controlling himself, he said: "Admittedly, they have a story around them, a memory of something that happened a very long time ago ..."

"Well, Herr Pastor earns his living from a story about summat that happened nearly two thousand year ago!"

"That's enough!" said Schweigaard, raising his palms as though to ward off some spectre. "I'm trying – I really am trying – to be sensitive. Take care, Astrid. What you said just now is ... is ... *blasphemous* – yes – an abomination! What I was trying to say is that the bells are a sort of ... a memorial. But what's really important here, is that Klara died in a freezing-cold church."

"Aye, the sermon were long enough to freeze her alright."

"But I had to finish Mass! Should I have sent everybody out halfway through? I did in fact omit three or four hymns when I saw how cold people were." He flung his hands out. "And the bishop agrees. I told him the story of the bells. His reply was—"

"The bishop, eh? Donae go blaming the bishop! He in't never even been here. And how did these Germans get to know the bells were worth owt, unless ye told them so?"

He was about to reply, but she interrupted: "Did ye tell them the legend? Oh aye, ye be a fine one! Ye sold the bells even though ye knew what they meant to us up at Hekne. I take it ye donae mean to stick around in this village too long, the pair o'ye!"

"What do you mean – pair?"

"Your betrothed and ye!"

He got up and banged his fist onto the table. "That's enough! Stop there! You have no idea what I want with my life! Or about the priesthood! I want to do good! So you will not – will *not* – bring her into this. Will everyone just stop pestering me!"

They both gasped for breath, each on their side of the desk. He was the first to force himself down onto his chair again. The inkwell had tipped over and a dark blotch was seeping into the wood.

"I'm sorry, Astrid. I get . . . heated. I can't always control it. It usually passes quickly."

He rubbed his neck hard, walked to the door and opened it to see if Oldfrue Bressum was listening in.

Nobody there.

"We had nine children baptised at the New Year's service. Since then, in these few short months, I have baptised thirty-two more, fifteen of them illegitimate, and three have since died from disease. The farmworkers' cottages are overcrowded, the land here can't feed everyone. The population is rising sky-high, and, at this critical moment, the House of God is unusable. What this parish needs is enlightenment, reason, guidance! You're a clever woman, Astrid. Surely you can see for yourself that *that*'s what's needed here? Think of it this way instead – that your family's gift is being put to a greater purpose, namely to promote the conditions in which God can be truly celebrated."

"Folks need summat beautiful too. Summat . . . fine. Not like an ornament. But beauty they can feel inside of them."

"Yes. Yes, of course."

"I wonder what *he* would have thought," she said.

"Who?"

"Eirik. The father of the Hekne sisters. Happen as naebody thinks like him nowadays."

"Poverty robs people of pride," said Kai Schweigaard. "It's

a long time since I saw a fifty-øre piece in the collection box. Most of them throw in a one-øre coin. Probably, if I may compare, because it has as good a ring as a fifty øre. But that doesn't really help."

She was calmer now, he could see that. Her fingers wrapped around the armrests. Her feet neatly together.

"And now I have a problem with this missing portal. But what does Schönauer expect? That I go back in time and extinguish the flames that burned it up?"

He lifted the inkwell and slipped a small saucer under it. His fingertips went blue.

Schweigaard cleared his throat. "Astrid. I wish . . . I wish we could have met under different circumstances. Better circumstances, freer circumstances."

Astrid frowned quizzically.

"Where I wasn't a pastor. Or where I was a pastor, but my work didn't destroy something you love. Then we could have gone for a . . . yes, a stroll, for example."

He bit his lip as soon as he had said it. A stroll. With the pastor. That would be a public statement.

Astrid Hekne got up. She walked towards him, loosened her shawl, took another step towards him, but noticed she was under the crucifix, and sat down again, fumbling. It was as though she had prepared something, planned something, but that it was now impossible to carry it through.

They looked at each other as they had looked at each other across the tablecloth long ago. Silence filled the pastor's office. Jesus hung on the wall and stared at the floor.

She shifted in her chair.

"Well, Herr Schweigaard, a stroll would have been to my liking too. But 'tis most unlikely now. Unless ye upturn this deal. Then happen we could take a stroll."

I'm losing her now, he thought. I'm losing her.

"I've no choice. I must let reason dictate," he said. "The new spire is far smaller, and the bells will come lower. If we hang the Sister Bells there, the congregation will be deafened. We've already been given a replacement of two smaller bells, left over from a chapel in Gausdal."

"But how will they sound?"

"Just as good, no doubt. I've not seen them. They're stored in a barn down by Lake Løsnes along with some other materials for the new church."

Astrid rose without a word; she headed for the door but stopped halfway there and turned.

"As good? That in't possible. Remember the silver in the Sister Bells. The silver that gives them that special ring? That silvery sound?"

Schweigaard shook his head and knew that the clear organ-pipe sparkle in her life was about to die, and he already saw his own life shrivelling, so emaciated that it could never be fattened up.

"It's the *bronze* that gives a bell its sound, Astrid. Silver does not make it ring better. That's just an old wives' tale."

From a Long-ago Funeral Mass

Astrid Hekne headed down to the church, straight for Gerhard Schönauer, who had set up his easel between two crooked tombstones. She knew she could be seen from the pastor's window, and did not turn, but just carried on down, sick of everything, sick of his rigidity, his coldness, his insistence on reason, and the kiss that would fortunately never happen.

"The key," she said to Gerhard Schönauer. "Give me your key." She pointed towards the church and made a turning gesture with her hand.

He muttered something incoherent and reached into his pocket. Soon she was closing the sacristy door behind her.

I'm going to see them, she thought. It's my right to see them before they disappear. She walked along the aisle, up a staircase that ended in an empty loft space, went down again and opened a door behind the organ. There she found a steep ladder, and above a platform, faintly lit by a narrow slit window, she saw two thick ropes dangling in the air, worn smooth by the sweat of hands.

Then another ladder in the half-dark. She gathered up her skirts and continued upwards. Rough wooden structures, heavy beams secured to each other. The only light in here came from the little gaps in the timber walls. It was as though she was in another building entirely, not just colder and smelling differently. Other thoughts ruled here, this place was never meant to be understood by anyone but those who had built the church.

She had an answer prepared for Kai Schweigaard, should he follow her here: "Ye be tearing this church down anyhow, so what be the harm in my coming in here?"

She stopped and listened for sounds. None. Just the creaking and sighing of old timbers. She continued to feel her way upwards in the gloom, her hand tracing beams covered with bird dirt and dust, and was reminded of her childhood fear of nearing a loft she was forbidden to enter.

The passage was soon completely dark, but she could feel she had reached another platform. She banged into a trap door above her head, it lifted a couple of inches, then fell with a hollow thud. A thick layer of dust tumbled about her cheeks, a dead, turgid smell, she shut her eyes and held her breath, and in that moment she heard distant sounds, not distant in space but in time.

Astrid waited until the air was breathable again. Then she set the back of her head under the trap door, pushed her way through it and carried on climbing, ascending through a cloud layer of the ages.

Up in the belfry she rested on her knees. Dust caressed her face as it fell. The room was dimly lit by the gaps around the narrow wooden shutters.

She put the trap door back in place. The bells were visible as two heavy black shapes in the hazy shards of light. They were bigger than she had expected, and they had a strange smell. An acrid odour like dried chicken muck. She groped over to the shutters, opened their latches and pushed them ajar. She stepped carefully towards the bells, which seemed more vibrant in colour now, a green sheen over the dirty grey metal. Light and shadow played on them, and they seemed so powerful, so vigilant. The slightest move, and they might ring out and warn of her presence. Their surface was decorated with two bands of flowers, between them lettering engrained with verdigris.

She crouched down and looked up into the vault of one of the bells. A pitch-black void, an endless night. Along the inside rim she could see that someone had scraped at the metal. It was true what Klara had said about the Holyblight, and she saw now that beside two such church bells logic shrank into insignificance.

A blast of wind blew through the windows, and with a creak they opened wider. Daylight streamed in with the fresh icy air. The tower swayed a little. She had never had such a view of the village. It was dizzyingly high, she could see both ends of Lake Løsnes and far beyond the Løsnes Marshes. Through another window she could see the parsonage. And down there, between gravestones, the German stood staring ahead.

All at once she feared that the bells might ring of their

own accord and deafen her. She went to close the shutters, but stopped when she saw her footsteps in the dust-coated floor.

Such thick dust could only mean one thing.

I must be the first to have been here in twenty, maybe forty years.

The dust shone in the shafts of light, making glittering pillars in the air. She got the feeling that there was someone else in the belfry, someone who wanted something of her.

The shadows dissolved in the stronger light, and some of the letters on the bells were now legible. A lump rose in her throat, and she started to shake, as she saw what was written there:

"IN LOVING MEMORIE OF HALFRID AND HER MOTHER ASTRID."

Then she heard a faint humming from the bells, like the buzzing of giant bumblebees, rich and manifold. She held her breath until it had stopped, crouched down, ran her little finger across the bronze and brought her tongue to its tip. A sharp, salty taste.

Astrid moved carefully over to the other bell.

"IN LOVING MEMORIE OF GUNHILD AND HER MOTHER ASTRID."

She began to hear stray sounds from another time, echoes that had lain in a daze, a rumble that went deeper and deeper into her, until it found the last remaining straw of rationality and took the form of a voice that twisted the inscription on the bells, and a woman's voice said in an ancient tongue:

"Thou art their mother."

Astrid felt herself change. It was murky and cold, a strange smell tore at her nostrils, and somebody was talking about her. The character of the air shifted, everything grew older, and she had the feeling she was *expected*. She felt wiser and stronger, as though she had suddenly grown up and lived a lifetime. A figure started to emerge before her, it sucked in the shifting grey of the dust and shaped itself into a darker, more solid form, then became invisible, yet was still present. The veins in her neck trembled, her pulse ran up to her temples, all at once she was tumbling through the ages, and out in infinity another being was also tumbling, and in the next nothingness she suddenly stood firm and knew that half of her was another.

She felt herself being guided to the bells and placed both hands on the coarse bell rope. The forces within her did not want her to ring them, only to show her that she could. She let go of the rope – the slightest movement raised a faint vibration in the bronze, from the deepest octaves, a wandering, lost chime from a long-ago funeral Mass.

For an instant the bells looked new and shiny, and there, reflected in their curved surface, she could see herself. An unfamiliar woman, from another time, in a red dress of coarse cloth with a silver buckled belt, holding both hands over her belly. A hazy light shone on the bronze surface, before it grew dull and old again, and the tremors inside her faded, like marshland mists lifting.

Gifts from Latakia

"Did your work go well today?" asked Kai Schweigaard in his reliable German.

"Satisfactorily, I suppose. I . . ." Schönauer coughed into his hand. "I was trying to draw the internal structure of roof. But it's so dark in there, and I have so little time. And it didn't feel quite right to work on a Sunday. Although, I suppose, people may not count drawing as work?"

Kai Schweigaard drummed his fingers on the table. When on earth would Oldfrue Bressum arrive with the supper? He was finding it impossible to concentrate, his thoughts flew between Astrid Hekne and his duties as a pastor. He had received no reply to his letter to Ida Calmeyer. And Schönauer had received nothing from Professor Ulbricht either.

"But you were left to work in peace, at least?" said Schweigaard.

"Absolutely."

"Nobody disturbed you?"

"No. The only person I met was that young woman, who wanted to borrow the key to the church. Does she work here?"

"No. She used to. She's from the farm who originally donated the church bells. She has a romantic relationship with them, *ein bisschen*. It's best you don't talk to her more than necessary."

"Oh. I drew the portal for her."

"You did? When?"

"A few days ago. She came into the church. Early one morning."

Schweigaard screwed up his nose. She had made no mention of this.

He felt a certain respect for Gerhard Schönauer. But he would never like him. Their meals together had become rather staccato. In the beginning the German had seemed so brisk and light-footed, with a slight swagger even, as he walked along with his tall easel and dapper coat, but now he seemed rather gloomy and strange, and complained of not being able to *understand* the church.

At last Oldfrue Bressum arrived with the dinner plates, clanked them down on the table and went. There was more weight in the porcelain than the food. Like all their previous suppers, it was made of winter-stored ingredients; gnarled potatoes, salt herring and thick flatbread.

Schönauer took three potatoes. His mind was elsewhere and he dropped the serving spoon on the table. They talked briefly about something Schweigaard had read in the papers, about Britain's introduction of a standard time across the whole country, making train timetables easier to use, and Schönauer told him about his trip to England. He went into exorbitant detail about the shelving system in some Cambridge bookshop, but Schweigaard chose to enjoy the fact of having a man of the world to visit.

Then, all at once, Schweigaard put down his knife and fork. Was this long-winded story about shelving systems in Cambridge merely a ruse, so as not to talk about his encounter with Astrid Hekne? Had she done something in the church, something the German preferred not to mention?

Schönauer broke the silence first. "I thought that, as a 'thank you' for your hospitality, I might give you something."

He fished a square tin from his pocket, snapped it open and pushed it across the table.

"Grousemoor," he said. "I bought two pounds of it while I was in London, and I've still got half of it left."

Schweigaard hesitantly picked up the box.

Pipe tobacco?

He put his nose to it, sniffed twice and instantly knew this was a *superior* blend. During a study trip to Copenhagen, he and the other young theologians quickly discovered how spoiled the city was for good tobacco houses. He had stocked up with half a kilo of tobacco from Wilhelm Øckenholt Larsen and his wife in Amagertorv, and from then on every word he read in the faculty library was read through clouds of the pale-blue smoke from one of Larsen's mixtures, usually the "1864" or "no. 05". But, unable to get hold of it in Norway, he had to content himself with Tiedemann's blends, which had a rather harsh flavour and stung your tongue.

He took a pinch of tobacco and sprinkled it into the palm of his hand. The fragrant, golden-brown flakes which comprised most of the mix had most undoubtedly come from Virginia in the United States. The thick, black shreds that gave off a rich, almost nauseatingly sweet odour must be the precious and inimitable varieties that were shipped from Latakia in Syria.

Schweigaard filled his pipe and lit it.

Truly, a magician had been at work here. The mixture had backbone and strength, but a faint exotic aroma which made it completely bewitching, augmented perhaps by that "little secret" Larsen had let him into, namely finely ground *Yenidje* leaves.

The conversation had stopped. On the other side of the table he noted that the German was lighting his pipe too, while he himself was already under the pleasurable influence of the tobacco.

The two men smoked in silence. Kai Schweigaard felt a deep sense of peace and comfort that could only be compared to the early phase of an opium rush.

And then she was back. The whore from Pipervika. "You're not a priest yet."

Schweigaard came to himself. The smoke had settled over Oldfrue Bressum's thin coffee and the problem of the burned portal. And a bigger problem perhaps: that the man he had invited here might start to take an interest in Astrid Hekne.

He put his thumb over the bowl of his pipe, and, although the glow burned his skin, held it there until he had snuffed it out.

"So, what else did the woman in the church say?" he asked. The German looked up. "Hm? About what?"

"About this portal. You said you drew it for her. A few days ago. How did she react?"

"She seemed to recognise it."

"She did?"

"Yes, I was rather surprised too – it was *ein bisschen merkwürdig*. You said it was burned almost forty years ago. She can't have been alive at the time. Unless, of course, she's rather older than she looks! I'd say she was twentyish? Nineteen, perhaps?"

Kai Schweigaard folded his napkin slowly in two and discreetly wiped his mouth. "In a couple of weeks we'll be finished with the funerals," he said, making a gesture to indicate that supper was over. "Then you'll have free access to the church, Schönauer. But in the meantime it'll be busy. So busy that you ought to take a little break from your work. Wasn't that a fishing rod I saw in your luggage?"

The Stain on the *Stabbur* Wall

She sat in the barn, shivering, and wished she had a travel blanket to wrap around her shoulders. It was getting late and she still felt troubled. Her body had felt numb when she came to herself in the belfry, as though she had woken up before a cold, darkened campfire.

The shaking gradually stopped, although not in her mind. She ambled over to the farmhouse, went up to see Emort and felt his forehead. He was even thinner than before, and his skin was wet and glassy.

"I found your traps," Astrid said. "Two squirrels."

"Oh."

"That were some days since. Ye have na' been awake afore now."

"Oh."

She wished she could tell her brother everything that had

happened, but he was too ill to really take anything in. She had a sleepless night, and the following morning she saw to the cows and then went outside for a walk. That moment in the belfry had left a searing scar where there had never been a wound. Someone had called Astrid Hekne's name and required an action of her.

Down by the wash house two cats lazed against the sun-facing wall. She went up and took one onto her lap. Over at the farmhouse the sun glinted on the buckled window panes. On the wall of the *stabbur* was a greasy black stain, at the corner that was always first to be warmed by the sun when winter was over. Klara had always rubbed the corner with butter, dollops of it, year after year, an old custom meant to guarantee the coming of the spring. Back then Astrid had been irritated with Klara for wasting butter, in the season when everyone was so thin. Nobody had done it this year, and the weather was unusually cold.

Her thoughts leaped about. Between retribution and sin and love and regret and curiosity and the vibrations of two church bells, whose will she did not fully grasp. She ran down to the farmhouse, slipped into the larder to fetch some butter and rubbed a big patch into the *stabbur* wall.

Then she sat and let a big question grow bigger. Why had her grandfather never told her about the inscriptions on the church bells? And why had he never mentioned the Door Serpent? She went back down to the farmhouse, climbed the stairs and went "up". The door was never locked, nobody dared go in when her father was not there, but she let herself in now, and, looking steadfastly away from the bundle of birch twigs, lifted the basket down from the shelf and opened her grandfather's notebook.

His writings from decades past. Sweat, farm labourers' hands, back pain and womenfolk's toil. 1833. 1834. Sowing. Calving. Taxes. Horses. Ploughs. 1835. 1836. Crofters. Fires. Potato-setting. Ground rent. Slate roof. Breaking new ground. 1842.

Crofter's cottage in Halvfarelia. Wrought iron. Harrowing. 1844. Trade with Bergli and Hallum. Two specie dollars.

She frowned. "Trade"? He had never used that word before. Anything else was "payment". And the year was . . .

"What be ye up to?"

Astrid snapped the book shut. Her father filled the whole doorway, angry and strange.

"Astrid, answer me now. Tell me what ye be doing."

"I been looking in grandfather's book."

"What be it wi' ye, Astrid?"

"I just wanted to read it."

"Nay, lass, ye were stood talking to yersen."

"Oh?"

She expected him to tell her to leave. But instead he sat down.

"In 1844," said Astrid, "he bought summat from two men and paid two specie dollars for it."

Her father reached his hand out for the book. He read the entry, remarking that two whole specie dollars was a lot of money back then.

"It be very queer that he didna write what it were for," said Astrid. "When he were as particular as ye with his account keeping."

Her father looked back at the book. On the next line it said that new crofters had moved into Halvfarelia and that a byre had been built there for their sheep.

"Halvfarelia," said her father. Astrid knew what was going through his mind. It was one of the few crofts still owned by the Heknes, although they allowed their tenants, Adolf and Ingeborg, to live up there without making any great demands. It was the "Hekne way", as her father called it. A sense of fairness and kindness to older folk. Adolf and Ingeborg had six children, but they had all gone to America. Adolf got off lightly at harvest and sowing time, because he paid his dues in meat and fish; his skills as a patient hunter were of greater benefit than if he had worked himself to the bone on the land. In winter he set snares for grouse, and in the early autumn he occasionally shot a reindeer which would be served at Hekne on festive occasions.

But her father's expression told her that he was not thinking about Adolf or Ingeborg now.

"That time in the church," said her father. "What were it ye said our Klara spoke of?"

"Summat she called the Door Serpent."

"Not 'Svartormen'?"

"Nay. What be that?"

"The Black Serpent. The only thing I ever heard of that reminds me of this Door Serpent. And it had summat to do with the sheep byre over at Halvfarelia."

"Tell me."

"First, I mun know what ye be up to."

She told him what she could without causing him shame. He sat for a moment and finally said "hmm", and after that he looked back at the notebook and said:

"This be summat I heard of long since. Long before Adolf and his wife took over there. There were an old man from Mikkelslåa visited us. He said summat that stuck in my mind. Rather, it were my father made it stick. 'Cos he laughed so queerly when he heard t'other fella saying it."

"Were it a joke?"

"Nay, it were about the sheep. I was only a lad then, eight or ten. That year all the sheep in the village went down sick. Got sores on their hooves, they did, and some got white froth round their muzzles. All the farms had it bad, and some had to slaughter their sheep. But not Halvfarelia. The sheep at Halvfarelia went unscathed. One and all."

"Halvfarelia be a long way off from folk," said Astrid. "Happen they wasn't infected."

Her father shook his head. "Folks thought this sickness was some sort of curse, I remember them talking of it at table. And this old fella, he were a canny one. He said the sheep in Halvfarelia stayed well 'cos Svartormen watched over them. That be the only time I ever heard of such a thing."

A Fisherman without Bait

The next day, after milking, they started work on the top field. Astrid stood with the barrel of ashes they had collected from the stoves during the winter, and after pouring the ashes into buckets she showed her younger sisters how to sprinkle them over the remaining patches of snow, to make them melt faster.

She still hadn't managed to find a good excuse to go up to Halvfarelia. But then suddenly the sky darkened, and the year's first thunderstorm came. This was a sure sign that the sap would be rising in the trees, and she announced that she was going up to the birch woods near Halvfarelia, to see if she might harvest some branches for basket-making. But first she had to fetch the carry strap and sharpen the knife, and as she stood in the work-shed with the whetstone and honing steel, she heard the door go behind her.

"Astrid?"

Emort was standing in the doorway, thin and pale. She took two steps back, then walked towards him and placed a hand on his chest.

"Why be ye doing that?"

"To check ye be alive."

"I be alive alright," he said, running a finger over the anvil. "I got up just now. So much snow has melted!"

She put her arms around him, hugged him and said how glad she was.

"Were it ye rubbed butter in t'*stabbur* wall?"

She nodded and hugged him again. He went back inside to rest, and she set off towards Halvfarelia.

On her way she got distracted by the sight of the young German. He was carrying a small brown leather-covered tube. She slowed down and followed him with her gaze. He took off along the stream and then disappeared into the forest. Why is he going there, she thought, when the path is on the other side?

She looked around. Nobody else there. She left the path and followed him on the other side of the stream. The stream had no name, despite being quite wide. It was one of the many streams that gushed from the mountainsides to fill Lake Løsnes, and she had no idea how long the water stayed here before it trickled down to Fåvang and out to Laugen, where the water gathered force and rushed towards the sea, a thing too vast to conceive.

Everything she had felt in the belfry seemed more distant now, but still real, something between a thought and a vision. Over the years, she had sometimes seen creatures in the dark, especially up at the seter, but she had always brushed them off as imaginings, and scoffed at the old folks' explanations of *huldrers* and underground spirits. She knew that for countless hundreds of years, the Butangen folk had needed explanations for anything strange, or a void would open up that made them afraid of the mountains and forest, and since they had to pit themselves against nature in all weathers, whether in the grips of hunger or pain, they *saw* things; after all, it was easier to cope with a *huldrer* than with not knowing what was hidden in the dark, and these beings were named so that they could be spoken to or about, treated with respect or warned of, and then life could go on.

But for her, these strange feelings refused to be dislodged. Life had to go on, yes, but now it was as though she were being accompanied by something.

The German was wandering in the thicket on the other side of the stream now. She spotted him and crouched down. He was carrying a canvas bag which kept getting caught on the twigs, but having freed it he stumbled off the track and headed straight for a sudden drop, which she knew would take him unawares.

What if he just disappeared? Would someone else be sent to Butangen, someone else from this city called Dresden? Her thoughts nestled up to Kai Schweigaard, and she took a grim pleasure in torturing herself with this dead hope.

"Would you like some coffee, my dear Kai? I thought so. There you go. 'Tis freshly made. Have you finished with the newspaper? Thank you, dear. Oh, goodness me. Have you seen this? 'Still no trace of the German painter who disappeared in Gudbrandsdal earlier this spring.' Isn't it awful? Yes, I agree, dear! Oh dear me, winter's on its way already. Yes, there was rime on the lawn this morning. I'm so glad, by the way, that we kept the old church. It is so delightfully warm with the timber cladding on the outside, just like the church at Fåvang."

The German fell down the slope, letting out a scream that faded as he went. A rock loosened, and she heard something that must be a German oath. Then silence. She watched him clamber up again. Muttering to himself, he crouched down and fiddled with the curious-looking leather tube, before staggering on, his knee clearly causing him pain. He disappeared into the undergrowth, but she could hear him as he went. Branches being bent and springing noisily back into place, pebbles clattering. On the slopes the sounds were drowned out by the stream's burbling, but as the terrain levelled out she could hear him again, and he finally re-emerged from the thicket and then waded across the stream, further up.

She had always believed that if ever the outside world came to Butangen, it would sweep in like some great and wonderful parade, and set up camp with colourful banners and ride off in a cloud of dust, leaving only the certainty that times had changed.

But now the outside world sat there on a rock, in the form of a young German with rounded shoulders.

He looked so alone.

In a sweat, his footwear and trousers soaked through. He rested briefly and continued up towards Daukulpen.

Daukulpen – the dead pool – had not got its name because hopeless folk ended their lives in it, but because the fishing was dead. It might look as though it was full of trout, with black and shiny deep waters, but no fish ever bit. Some folk thought that Daukulpen was like the mountain lake at Breitjønna, which was crammed full of trout, but where line-fishing was useless, doubtless because there was something good at the bottom that the fish enjoyed more than grubs and maggots, although nobody knew what.

He rummaged in his shoulder bag, and soon a gentle puff of wind brought an unfamiliar smell towards her. A lively blend of rich, spicy aromas that allowed themselves to be divided into components and were nonetheless one. One ingredient was like the marshes and cloying, another resembled freshly cut hay, the third thread in this weave of fragrances reminded her of Christmas, and finally, floating over everything, there was something she remembered from Kai Schweigaard's newspapers, not the smell of the ink or paper itself, but the *expectation* that resided in such smells.

Halvfarelia. If she did not go there now, she would not get home in time for the cows.

But there before her was the German. A rare species of animal at close quarters.

His pipe had gone out, and he relit it, flicking the match up into the air. He had to relight the pipe several times over. She thought it unseemly to be so wasteful, at home it was unheard of to use more than one match a day; they lit the stove in the morning, and for the rest of the day they put twigs to it to fetch a flame when needed. She was sitting downwind of him, and against her own will she began to enjoy these aromas that had taken a detour through the stranger's breath. He took out an oblong book and a pencil, and she grew instantly restless, for she had seen him stand for hours drawing outside the church, but then it was as if the wind turned and carried her impatience up to him, and he snapped his book shut, opened the leather tube and pulled out a dark-green canvas case. Soon he had an elegant, lacquered fishing rod in his hands, with a worn cork handle and a reel out of which he pulled a thick, pale yellow fishing line.

Fishing? Now? The water was too rough for the trout to bite, everybody knew that, you only had to see the meltwaters racing past. And there were still patches of snow in the shadows; where had he found bait, when the ground was so cold?

Again he did something strange. He knelt down beside the stream, rolled up his sleeves and turned the rocks under the water over, as though he expected to find something beneath them. Then, crossing over to the leafless bushes that hung over the stream, he shook the branches and quickly gathered up something that dropped from them, took out a small brass box and fastened a strange feathered hook to his line. He walked up the slope, stood at some distance from Daukulpen, and then the pale-yellow line flew out from the rod; but rather than letting it land on the water, he reeled out more and more with each cast, and the shining line flew high into the air drawing letters against the side of the valley, a sideways U that stretched into a sideways J and then shot forwards to become a new upside-down J, before finally straightening out and landing in the water near the edge of the ice.

He soon reeled the line back in and cast it again. Sometimes he fell out of rhythm, so that the line made an untidy loop – and then, even if the hook landed well, he would reel it back in. It seemed he was only satisfied with *beautiful* casts, and soon she was as caught up in the excitement as him, more so perhaps, gripped as she was by springtime hunger: she imagined a trout flapping about in the water and then curling up on the bank before it flapped and curled in a hot frying pan, its pink meat falling from the bone, a fork, salt, a fresh boiled potato, butter.

How long is it possible to watch a man fishing where there are no fish?

Infinitely long, she realised.

His next cast landed just under a round boulder, grey and dry on the top and black where the water splashed against it; the rod bent, and she heard a grating sound as the line ran out from the reel.

Windswept February Red

The stream churned before him, it was swollen from the melt-water coming down from the mountains, more like a small river. The mountains further up were still white. It was probably only now that the snow had started to melt that far up. He knelt down and stroked the case of his fishing rod.

Earlier that day he had given up on his work. Neither the

pastor nor the church seemed keen to have him around. He had flung his drawing materials aside, grabbed his fishing rod and followed the nearest stream. His rod was made of carefully prepared split cane, a tangible connection to civilisation, a shining spear forged in the British empire, especially for outposts and rugged terrain like this. He had purchased this fishing rod during his study trip to London. Seeing it displayed in a shop window in Jermyn Street, he had fallen for it completely, even though the rod-maker was only newly established and far from well known. It had been made by two brothers by the name of Hardy, a prototype for a series which the shopkeeper thought they should call "Smuggler", since it was made in six sections and easy to transport. Gerhard looked long and hard at the rod and pictured himself in ten years' time. A fully fledged architect, travelling, prestigious contracts for elegant buildings, staying in smart hotel rooms, barely any luggage apart from his drawing materials and fishing rod, spending uplifting moments by meandering rivers, while his ideas matured for the next day.

That day in London he had asked to see the rod assembled, he tested the flex, then let the shopkeeper dismantle it again. It was beautifully packed in a sailcloth pouch of dark green, sewn with a row of pockets of increasing size, one for each section; and when the pouch was rolled up tightly the wine-coloured silk emblem of the Hardy brothers was visible on the outside, along with two cords to secure it, and then the pouch could simply be slipped into a leather-covered tube which protected the rod against the challenges of distant climes.

He was sold, and the rod was sold too.

Now he took it out of its tube and found to his relief that his fall down the slope had not damaged it. He untied the cords, and the pouch rolled open revealing the sections of the rod, the cork handle to the far left and then the increasingly thin sections going to the right, like a sentence on a line, and soon he had the elegant fishing rod in his fist. He turned the rocks over and tried to identify the flies that were hatching there, but started with a common wet fly, Greenwell's Glory.

He already felt calmer. This was exactly how a fly rod should be used, British perfectionism meeting the wilderness. Imitation of a living insect, an honourable game, an honest meeting of man and nature.

He fastened the fly and lit his pipe. It was lovely to surrender to the spicy smoke of the Latakia tobacco, feeling the light stimulation of the nerves, how the nicotine caressed and calmed him. It was his need for the latter that meant he had relatively little left, and his hoard seemed likely to dwindle quickly, since the pastor clearly felt the same need.

Even before his second cast he got the feeling that someone was watching him. A movement from under the spruces, a branch swinging independently from the rest of the tree. The stream's babbling was no longer monotone, it formed strange words whispered in a bygone tongue.

He shook himself.

There probably *were* fish here, they simply weren't biting. His sense of expectation and excitement rose, driving out his troubling thoughts about the church. He switched to a Quill Stone fly, and dared himself to try a Black Gnat, but when he still didn't get a bite he assumed that the trout were going after stone flies at the bottom, put on a Windswept February Red and aimed his hook far out into the pool.

Not a soul to be seen. The water was phenomenally clear. He could count every stone on the bottom. What a country!

Suddenly he felt a weight and resistance at the other end of the line. The rod stretched in a curved arc, and something tugged hard on it under the water. Soon he brought in a fine brown trout. Not very big, but beautiful. He put the rod aside, knelt down by the shoreline and grabbed the fish with both hands.

Then he heard it, lost in the stream's burble, a rustling from the juniper bushes. He turned and glimpsed a flash of red lower down – someone was approaching, and the sight of it caused a long, steady shudder to go through his whole body. The hair rose on the nape of his neck, goosebumps spread down over his shoulder blades, running up and down his body in waves, it was terror, it was awe, but when he finally had to blink, there was nothing red there, just the camphor-drop girl, walking along in the same dark clothes she had worn in the church.

Is it her? he asked himself. And in a flash he felt that his thought was echoed, as though she was asking herself the same question. It was as if their thoughts were thrown from one to the other, and that they were tacitly agreed that this moment would be destroyed if it was explained.

"Nay pictures today?"

He shook his head. "Today I am a fisherman."

She sat down, gesturing for him to continue. He cast the line a few more times, but he felt uneasy with her watching him, and reeled in his line.

"How did ye learn to speak Danish?" she said.

He did not understand her dialect and had to ask her to repeat the question, and then to talk more slowly. He told her that he had taken lessons, "and I have this," he said, holding up a little book. The title glinted gold against the brown cover: Meyer's *Sprachführer für Reise und Haus*.

She asked him how he caught fish without insects.

He looked at her, at the trout, at his fishing rod, at the mountains behind her, then held out the brass box of fishing flies, wondering if his Danish lessons had given him enough vocabulary to tell her about the Windswept February Red, but she had already looked in the box and answered her own question. She held up a fly and inspected it from various angles, a Sawyer's Nymph.

"The pastor says I must not talk to you so much," he said, and gave a little laugh.

She seemed surprised.

"And I still do not know your name. What's your name?"

She said nothing, and looked at him quizzically.

Surely, he thought, my Norwegian isn't that bad? He flicked through the phrase book.

"Your name? What's your name?"

"Astrid Hekne. And yours?"

"Gerhard Schönauer."

They stood and looked at each other.

She took the phrase book from his hand and curiously leafed through it. Then she asked if he knew anything more about the old door of the church.

"It is a catastroff," he said. "Your pastor is sure it was burned. I wait now to hear from Dresden about what to do."

She continued to flick through the book.

"Take it," he said. "The book. Put it in the studio when finished!"

The Gas Lamps in Dresden

When Astrid Hekne came home and opened Meyer's *Sprachführer*, she knew that this was the moment in which her life would be firmly divided into a before and an after. She had curbed it for years, but now it had been reawakened – the urge to travel, to go on a railway train. Just as one twin sister always had to drag the other along, two wills were aroused in her, and neither could outlive the other. For Butangen had taught her one thing: it required one will to travel far, and another to stay.

Now Meyer's *Sprachführer* flung the doors open onto the world. A long list of phrases contained sentences for German travellers in Norway. But she could equally well use the list in reverse, and then it transported her the opposite way, to Germany, offering her a direct view into the country that wanted to save a Norwegian stave church from Kai Schweigaard.

At the very back there were advertisements for hotels, from Kristiania to London, Geneva to Cologne, the largest showed a drawing of the Hotel Kaiserhof in Dresden, before it a row of elaborate wrought-iron posts with lamps on top.

Going back and forth between the vocabulary lists and the German caption, Astrid worked out its meaning.

"At night the beautiful glow of gas lamps is seen along the promenade near the Brühlsche Terrasse."

Light, she thought. Light at night.

Light indoors to read by. Light outdoors to walk by. A change that must be like the one in Genesis. When there was no longer just darkness on the face of the earth. To be able to go outside when the moon was thin, to meet someone and recognise them. Liberation from the darkness of the forests. The terror of *huldrers* and forest bandits, the gatherings around the fireplace, the stories retold and exaggerated. Such was the dark. You had only to venture out on a winter's night, and the question would come to you: Am I really alone?

Fear would evaporate in light. Dark corners would hold nothing creepy. There'd be no more scurrying close to the houses in the winter.

She folded out the maps of northern Germany, Denmark, Norway and Sweden, worked out how to order in a restaurant, and what it cost to take a steamship or train.

It was forceful and potent, this urge. More forceful now than when she had read Kai Schweigaard's newspapers – the desire to travel, to travel far, to be warmed by the sun behind the sun.

Here and there she found jottings made by him in the margins. His handwriting was beautiful and easy to read, and in the chapter on "Practical Advice for Travellers" he had tried to construct sentences in Norwegian. "I look for the street to Gudbrandsdal." "Where can everyone the lunch buy?"

A drawing had been slipped between the pages, dated some time in January. On that day, he had sat in the very place about which she now dreamed, and pictured Norway. His imaginary landscape had sharp mountain peaks, and the trees were an odd round shape, but beautiful, and cutting diagonally through the terrain was a wide road, with a horse-drawn carriage driving through deep snow, the weather fit for a sledge not a carriage, and right in the background was a church.

She read further in the chapter on "Advice for Travellers" and imagined that she was one of those travellers. She procured leather suitcases and travelling clothes, and made Gerhard Schönauer's journey in reverse, and in a bonnet tied with a ribbon under her chin she stepped aboard a steamship. She asked to be taken to her cabin ("*Meine Kabine, bitte!*"), and quizzed the captain about whether the sea was rough ("*Ist das Meer rau?*"), she switched to a horse and carriage and begged the driver to go faster ("*Schneller! Schneller!*"), she swept past the petty criminals trying to overcharge her ("*Sie fordern zuviel*"), arrived at a six-storey hotel and asked for a room on the ground floor, because the stairs would be onerous ("*schrecklich anstrengend*"), then demanded a better room with a water closet, and did not rest until the maid had brought fresh drinks, water to wash in and had closed the door behind her.

But she kept leafing back to the advertisement for the hotel with a view onto the promenade near the Brühlsche Terrasse. To the yellow light of the gas lamps. This was not merely the delirium of the moth around the flame. She realised how deeply the light went inwards, that it did not merely light up the houses, it also illuminated the mind.

But when she closed the book she was sitting alone in a dusty hayloft; outside she heard her mother barking at the children and farmhands, and Osvald rounding the men up to groom the horses, workhorses that had been born on the farm and would never go anywhere else. And she wished she could return to the minute before, when she was dreaming, but knew that she must give back the book, that *afterwards* would soon come – by Christmas – and then *before* would contain a mute echo of this spring, and the German would be gone.

She thought of the two men who had offered her marriage. Amund last spring, Sverre in the autumn. Two seasons, each bringing a smartly dressed man, a meeting outside the church, and an honourable declaration in the parlour. One suitor from Nordrum and the other from Lower Løsnes, both respectable farmsteads. There was nothing wrong with either. Not with Amund, the better-looking, apart from a knocked-out tooth. Taciturn, a bit old, almost thirty. Nor with Sverre, coarser and heavier, but cheerful and always well turned out.

In truth, it would all be the same. For some time she did not know why she had said no. But it was precisely because it would all be the same. Into the farm, up into the bed, then out into the kitchen. Their mothers and grandmothers were still alive and kicking. She would battle for her own farming methods, which were not unlike those of her predecessors. She would instruct the old women bakers. Christmas, Easter, ploughing and sowing time, autumn harvest and then Christmas again.

She enjoyed farmwork – it wasn't that. Pulling out lambs that got stuck, chastising wayward cows, working dawn to dusk in the hay-making season, such long days of potato-lifting that she woke up bent double. But she had never forgotten what her grandfather said:

"Ask yersen what ye want to be remembered for, Astrid. When we tell the story of a person's life, and many a year has passed, there in't room to say much. Myseln, I don't reckon as I'll be remembered for nought. More than having tried to be kind-hearted, maybe, and 'tis difficult to make a good story out of that. The things folks are remembered for are cast in metal or carpented or woven or painted or written. Wickedness and foolishness, not in a small way but big, these be oft remembered too."

She went to her bedroom and took out the drawing Gerhard Schönauer had given her. He had come full of such admiration, for a church that Schweigaard wanted to tear down. The drawing was so beautiful, and she had watched it come into being in the space of a few minutes. If he had a whole day, a month, a lifetime, what couldn't he achieve?

There was love in the drawing. A love that had a price in German money, which, she had learned from Meyer's, was totted up in marks and pfennigs.

Once again she wondered at how many things could run back and forth in her head at one time. Each thought like a busy ant. The change that had come over her in the belfry, the sense of duty, the fear of retribution. Then she eyed something that she knew was vital, and she studied the idea from all sides. A memory from the belfry stared back. *There had been no footsteps in that thick layer of dust*. The last person to be there must have been the old bell-ringer, when he collected the Holyblight. This meant that nobody, and certainly not Kai Schweigaard or the German painter, had any idea what the church bells looked like.

Finally it was clear. She knew how she could save the Sister Bells.

The next day she asked to take the day off after milking, and went up to Halvfarelia.

No Bell Tower in Your Name

Kai Schweigaard stared out across the courtyard. There was no talent for jubilation or shouts of hurrah in his parish. His "glad tidings" had awakened little enthusiasm, nobody realised it was the result of months of planning and letter-writing. Still, folk were probably not as morose here as in Østerdalen, where it was said their facial muscles had wasted away because they had been taught for generations to express neither sadness nor joy. But praise was certainly never forthcoming in Gudbrandsdal. You knew something was good, when the complaints stopped. He suspected that the building of the new church was going to be another lonely journey.

Besides, there was something going on in the village. He had heard rumours in the last few days, strange rumours that *sin* had taken hold. The day before yesterday two unmarried girls had each given birth to a child precisely at midnight, and neither would say who the father was. Somebody – probably the schoolmaster, Giverhaug – had spread the idea that these girls had conceived in sin because they had attended a Mass during which the "new pastor" used tallow candles. Church candles had always been made of beeswax, because the bee was monosexed and thereby free from sin. Because beeswax was so expensive, the old pastor had always held his services in fumbling semi-darkness. Schweigaard had brushed off the churchwarden's warnings and ordered him to procure tallow candles and light them throughout the church. It was irrelevant, he said, that they were smoky and smelled, since they were cheap and gave a bright light, and yes, *of course* they could be used as altar candles.

Was this the thanks he got? Foolish, blasphemous twaddle. Clearly it had been two night suitors, or two big, fat, wealthy farmers who liked to dip their wick in young girls. Besides, bees were not mono-sexed, not in the least, he knew that they coupled high in the air, that the male's genitals were ripped off, causing him to die, and that the female laid eggs which she left to her workers; hardly an example for a healthy family or sex life. Such drivel had to be discredited, but the subject was unworthy of being taken up from the pulpit. A pulpit that was soon to be torn down.

Besides, he felt spiritually depleted right now. He was more concerned with what he might do to mollify Astrid Hekne. He entertained the idea of tearing open Schönauer's door, slamming the table and saying, "Listen here, you can have the church as agreed, but I had no authority to sell the Sister Bells. I'm sorry, we'll reduce the price, as with the portal, but we'll have to sort this out some other way!"

That was how it should have been; one brave axe-blow to cut a bond and forge a link.

Just then, as so often when she was on his mind, he saw her walking along the path in the pale morning light. Reluctantly, he admitted that such coincidences occurred because she was, in fact, always on his mind.

She was heading purposefully down the hill, and as she turned towards the parsonage he felt a flash of joy. His forearms tingled as she opened the gate. In the middle of the courtyard there was a large muddy puddle, but when she reached it – wasn't she going the wrong way? Instead of walking on this side of the puddle and heading for his front door, she walked on the far side and headed towards the cottage where Schönauer was lodging. Was she going to . . . ? And if so, how did she know he was staying there?

She knocked and walked in, and as she vanished from view Kai Schweigaard filled with something painful and bitter. Indignation – a torrent of rage and jealousy.

Astrid re-emerged from Schönauer's cottage after a length of time that seemed not to tally with any particular errand.

His anger ebbed away, but left a dull silt. Her visit had been too brief for her to have had a conversation with Schönauer, too long to have established that he was not there. She crossed the courtyard, walked out of the gate, and vanished from view. Schweigaard rushed through the hallway, to the other side of the house that overlooked the path, and there he saw her turn. She stood looking for somebody, but then, changing her mind, headed back towards the parsonage.

She came in quietly this time, without Oldfrue Bressum discovering her, not flustered or in a stamping fury, but calm.

"Good morning, Astrid," he said flatly.

"Herr Schweigaard."

He coughed, smoothed his hair, and said, "Astrid. Please don't think I'm insensitive about this matter. After our last talk, I looked into the possibility of changing the agreement. Just for your sake."

"Ye did? But then—"

"I'm afraid it's too late. I'm duty-bound to the cross. As well as to a contract. There's no going back."

"That in't so certain," she said.

"Oh?"

"Ye said that he were looking for a portal. The German."

Kai Schweigaard sighed through his nose. "You already knew that, I suspect." He turned to the window. "What are you talking to him about?"

"Who?" said Astrid.

"The German, of course. The architect."

"I thought he was a painter," said Astrid.

"No doubt he's a bit of both," said Schweigaard flatly.

"Were ye ogling me just now?" she said.

"Was I . . . what?"

"Ye knew I were looking for him."

"Well, I saw you down there in the courtyard, and you knocked on his door."

"So ye was ogling me then?"

"I . . . it's my . . . the parsonage's courtyard."

"I didna talk to him. I wanted to return this," she said, holding out the copy of Meyer's. "Summat he loaned me. A German dictionary."

"I see. So he's lending out . . . dictionaries?"

He did not ask Astrid to sit down. She took small, restless paces as they talked, and now she was standing near the wall under the crucifix. She was flicking at a callus with her nail. "Last time, when we had that . . . chat, I understood that the new, small church bells—"

"They're not particularly *small*. They're quite average."

"But they be here already now?"

"Yes. I told you they were brought over the ice this winter. They're in a barn."

"Tell me, Kai Schweigaard. If the German were unlucky enough to take the wrong church bells, would that trouble ye deeply?"

"Astrid!" He turned on her, and hissed: "Don't drag me into such a thing! I can't be privy to fraud!"

"It in't fraud if we get him to take the wrong bells of his own will."

"And how exactly would that happen? By having that will implanted in him? Which I greatly suspect is *your* will?"

"I shall persuade him to mistake them."

"I can't listen to this. Trickery? I can't swindle them out of the portal *and* the church bells! Are you aware that Gerhard Schönauer is here on a royal mission? The Queen of Saxony herself is paying for the church. People like that don't accept anything less than they've paid for."

"He has na' seen the church bells! I were up in the belfry, the floor were thick wi' dust, that means naebody knows how they really look!"

"You simply can't go wandering about in the church, Astrid! Besides, the German has a key and can see them at any time! And he'll see the bells during the demolition anyway."

"Not if they be wrapped up. In canvas. And placed next to the new ones. Down in the barn. With a label on them."

"No. It's out of the question to do anything so . . . devious. Besides, I've already said the old ones are too big! The bell-ringer will go deaf and the entire congregation with him!"

"They has a separate tower in Ringebu. Just for the church bells."

"Frøken Hekne. There will be no bell tower built in your name."

"Nay, but happen there might be a mortuary chapel with space for some bells? The dead canna be deafened."

Schweigaard slumped back into his chair, red-faced. Finally he said:

"What makes you so sure that the German will accept the idea of taking the wrong bells?"

"'Cos the portal still exists."

"What did you say?"

"It be right here in the village!"

"Here? Has it been here all along?"

"No carpenter would have burned summat so fine. They tricked the pastor."

"Yes, that's something you villagers do all the time."

"Them bells was a gift. Now I shall take that gift back. Trading it for the portal. All ye has to do is make sure that the new bells is placed close to the old."

Kai Schweigaard bit his lip. This might just salvage his whole plan. Perhaps the German would in fact be satisfied with this exchange. But this deal appeared to include more than just a couple of bells. With what would she pay the difference? What was her currency?

"Has he accepted this?"

"Not yet. Just give me the say-so. That we can do it like this?"

He was silent. You're falling, he thought. So obsessed with rescuing the bells that you're tumbling into the cauldron yourself.

Then he gave his answer. A barely visible nod. "I might just be away on the day the bells are taken," he said, shaking his head. "Hmm, you must be careful, Astrid. This man is—"

"Dishonest?"

"Not exactly. But he . . . embellishes."

They looked at each other.

"Astrid. I can't help you to persuade him. A pastor cannot lie."

"Nay," she said quickly. "But a pastor's wife can."

She stepped towards him, just as she had done when they were last alone, but this time she did not hesitate, she continued all the way around his desk, and as he pressed himself back in his chair she bent down and kissed him on the cheek. Afterwards, he tried to tell himself that the kiss had just been well meant, that it was a thank-you kiss on her part, though he was terrified that it might be a farewell kiss, and that the taste of her would be the taste of poison.

He could not sleep that night, and judging by the flickering candle in the log cottage neither could the German.

Kai Schweigaard got out of bed to fetch the paraffin lamp and lit it. Its light scattered across the floor as he went over to the bookshelf. He pulled out a thick, well-thumbed book which he had come across in a Copenhagen bookshop. Schweigaard often found solace in the works of John Donne. And since nobody in his congregation could possibly have read them, he often stole quotes from Donne's sermons. It was to one of the meditations he turned now, lingering in particular over an old favourite, "No man is an island ...", before moving on to the *Paradoxes and Problems*. There, in one of his essays, the young poet mused over why nobody died for love anymore, and why sinners and outlaws always had the best luck with women.

As usual, Donne answered his own question: "Because fortune herself is a whore."

Kai Schweigaard's grip loosened and the book fell limply between his fingers. For a long time he stared into the lamp, trying to convince himself that Astrid Hekne was not worth the paraffin. He closed his eyes, but the flame had burned into his retina and remained visible to him. He blew out the lamp, and still saw it in the darkness, whether his eyes were open or closed.

The Artillery Officer's Son

Gerhard Schönauer put down his pencil. He still couldn't get it right.

It was not right *at all*. It had been difficult to draw the church, but now it was utterly impossible. It contained a riddle, as hard to unravel as a mangled coil of wet rope. He could not work out what the arches over the central room of the church rested on, how the scissor rafters were fixed to each other, or even whether the diagonal braces in the passageway shared some of the weight of the arches further up.

The weather was dismal. Mealtimes conversationless. His body trembled every time he looked up at the spire. And his concentration melted into a welter of confusion, in which the camphor-drop girl was the scariest yet only comforting thing.

He had been instructed by Kastler not to reveal all he knew, particularly in relation to the legend of the bells. At one meeting, Ulbricht had taken out a roughly bound wadge of papers, which had been found among Dahl's possessions after his death. "An unpublished manuscript," he said, "on the cultural history of stave churches, written by a Norwegian, a certain I. Kveilen."

According to Ulbricht, Kveilen had translated his own text into German, a world language back then, hoping to get it published in the printing city of Leipzig, but it was repeatedly turned down, growing tattier each time.

"Not that its title helped, exactly," he said, pointing to the title sheet: "Evidence and Apocryphal Reports of Legends and Popular Beliefs, Including Personal Experiences of a Metaphysical Nature, Associated with the Oldest Churches from the Innermost Territories of Norway."

"The author talks about the same churches that Dahl visited," said Ulbricht, "and the title suggests to me that he followed in Dahl's footsteps and hoped to profit from his work, since there is some evidence of plagiarism. Here and there, however, the book verges on the fantastical and downright crazy, with long sections describing how invisible forces can inhabit old buildings and objects, forces that can be invoked with para-suggestion. Naturally, it's just folklore, but in the chapter devoted to *our* church, he offers a sparkling analysis paired with verifiable details, including dates, sums of money, family names, farm names, et cetera."

Ulbricht cleared his throat and read out a lengthy account of the "Schwesterglocken von Butangen". When he put down the manuscript, there was silence.

"Not bad," said the burgomaster's representative. "Precisely the sort of fable we'd expect from a primitive people like the

Norwegians. But that makes it no less important. We want to attract visitors to the church, and what we can *show* them is one thing, what we can *tell* them is another. With these bells, the church and the sound that comes from it will form a greater whole of esoteric history. They will ring across the city and be a reminder of our great achievement."

There in Dresden, surrounded by brilliant city planning, modern maps of the world, cafés and a fully developed railway system, Gerhard had smirked at this legend with Kastler and Ulbricht.

Now, he no longer felt so assured.

The girl by the trout pool seemed to be the key. The fleeting glimpse of her when he had believed she was wearing red, her hair piled up. It was in such moments that he had seen something. The motif for an artwork? Or something of her inner self set free? Perhaps both. Because the moment vanished for the outside world, leaving a trace to be transformed into a work of art. What was a work of art, if not the capturing of a moment?

That evening he started to draw her. But her image flowed into the chaos he felt when he tried to draw the church, compass needles going into a spin. Another drawing wanted out, one that demanded he surrender to a deeper and wilder imagination, that could contain both her and what he felt when he looked up at the bell tower. He began on a ghoulish picture, partly to grasp his fear and partly to banish it. "Yes," he said to himself, "whatever this is, it's a warning of sorts, a messenger with great wings, an injection of undiluted *terror*." He went on making sketches until he fell asleep over his sketchpad, and when he awoke the visions were gone, but a finely finished pencil drawing lay before him.

It depicted a woman with deep-set eyes, wearing an outfit from a past era. She radiated an alluring power, the same he felt when he stepped to the edge of a precipice to see how far down it went, and, realising that the drop would be fatal, felt the impulse to jump.

The drawing conveyed it all. Yes, it was a fine work. Too wild to show anyone at the academy, but among his best. It encompassed the ethereal breeze that blew about her.

His teachers at the Academy of Art had taught him to draw all that was solid; on paper, he could depict a steamship, a locomotive, a medal-decked admiral, a dying tiger, a church. He could draw a heart, a brain, a vertebra. He had studied anatomy in the stone-cold basement studio, known to all as the "horror chamber", where chimpanzees' heads and snakes were suspended in jars of alcohol. Although still more gruesome were the remains of twenty human beings. In one glass case there were fire victims, dried and cut into cross sections, in another a row of human skeletons, probably typhoid victims, among them five children.

But the teachers always sought realism. He had never learned to draw anything intangible, the misty stuff of the heavens, the vibrations of things – such as the creeping feeling that he violated these dead human beings, rendered them onto paper without their being able to protest, and that someone in the kingdom of death was putting a mark against his name for later.

Not until now.

Again he looked at his drawing of her.

He had actually caught this sense of otherness.

It was Astrid Hekne and yet she was another. That radiance – it was the spectre of a human being's inner self. But she should not be clothed, she had to be outside time and place, she had to be naked. He made four sketches of her, full length, then drew details of her neck and hair, which she wore loose in one drawing and up in another, and he tried to dress her in a long evening gown before returning to draw her naked, wandering among large boulders.

It's good, he said to himself. But the magnetic field that radiates from the bell tower still evades me.

I need colours, paint.

He already knew that he would limit himself to four colours – Indian yellow for the glowing light behind her, burnt umber for the shadows, purple-brown *caput mortuum* for her face, a blend of all three to add nuance to her features and elsewhere, and finally he must have vermilion for her garb.

He had a motive for choosing these colours. They were all natural pigments from almost obscene sources. *Caput mortuum* was originally extracted from human skulls. In his lessons on colour at the academy he had learned that Indian yellow was made from the urine of cows fed on mango leaves, and in some languages the word "umber" meant a glimpse of a ghost or poltergeist. Finally, the tube of vermilion was not only the most expensive he had ever bought, but it was highly toxic, containing pure mercury sulphide.

The painting was completed in just one session, as if he had been standing on a reef with only hours before the tide would take him. With stained fingers he took a step back and looked.

The finished image was like nothing from the real world. It had issued from the attic of his mind, where all his fears were stored. Yet it was not the work of a madman, quite the opposite, it was restrained, and beautifully executed. He often felt a little tingle when he completed a work, but this time an enduring shiver ran through him, just as when he had seen her at the trout pool.

The next morning Gerhard Schönauer longed to go home. Far from Butangen and Dresden, back to the apartment safe within the old walls of Memel, to the two spacious floors above Frau Henkel's music shop, to the familiar morning smells from Herr Mannlicher und Söhne, the bakery on the other side of the street, to the breeze from the Baltic Sea that carried the sweet fragrance of fresh pastries up to the window of his boyhood room, filled with Faber pencils and sketchbooks.

He sat up in bed and looked at the painting that was still drying. He was gripped by a sudden urge to talk about his hometown, to tell *her* about it. To tell Astrid about Memel, about his father, an artillery officer at the coastal fortress, about his mother, Lenka, who was originally from Lithuania, about his brothers Winfried and Matthias, both of whom were recently qualified officers. He himself had no military bent. His childhood took place through pencils and paper, with few friends, and encouraged solely by his mother. He only ever tinkered aimlessly with the tin soldiers his father bought for the boys. Every year Captain Schönauer brought cannons and ships home for them by the kilo: he followed the build-up of Europe's armies and navies and re-created this arms race in miniature at home.

His father and two older brothers used the entire living-room floor for their re-enactments of famous battles. With the aid of a measuring tape, and all strictly in accordance with historical detail, the cavalry, artillery and foot soldiers moved as they had at Waterloo and the *Völkerschlacht*, the Battle of the Nations. To re-create the hilly terrain, they helped themselves from their mother's library, the Feldherrenhügel – the commanders' hill – was reconstructed with a volume of the *Andrees Welt Atlas* surrounded by other books in descending order of size; novels for the most part, with the finer contours created out of poetry collections or unread folios that had finally found a use. Deadly cannon shots were fired from the Bible and a first edition of Goethe's *Epilog zu Schillers Glocke*, and fleeing French officers were slaughtered or captured on *Hermann und Dorothea*, by the same author.

Thus hundreds of tin soldiers fought in the living room, while the firing of cannons was re-created with guttural sounds and hand movements, and the best – or the worst, in Gerhard's view – came when their father bought a tin whistle and sat under the table trying to simulate an Austrian reveille.

Meanwhile Gerhard sat with his pencil and paper, and later a paintbrush and canvas.

"Mutual resignation" might best describe his relationship with his father. Until, one day, Gerhard sat in front of the tin soldiers and painted the Battle of Metz.

His father had not followed his youngest son's progress, and was surprised.

Very surprised.

The battle was shown from the enemy's defence line, the only angle that could give a full-frontal view of the resolute Prussians' faces as they advanced. And, as Captain Schönauer quickly realised, this perspective spared the viewer from all the blood further back on the battlefield – this was the front line, the decisive moment. The boy had produced a little work of art. In a form that Captain Schönauer was amply qualified to appreciate. The spiked helmets were rendered accurately, there were no blunders in the officers' insignia, and the men held themselves as officers would. Neither were there any other silly errors; Dreyse rifles with levers on the wrong side or unrealistically short bayonets. Doubtless there was room for criticism with regard to the painting of the shadows, the perspective and anatomy, but far more important to Captain Schönauer was the fact that the painting captured the Prussians' fighting spirit which he held so dear, and their strict code of honour in war, which meant that it was immoral to aim at any individual as he moved forwards, especially an officer. This "battle ethic" was both abstract and fleeting, yet Gerhard had succeeded in putting it on canvas; it was there to see in the faces of the Prussians as they moved towards a collective enemy.

Gerhard's father twirled his moustache; he realised that his son's paintings might, if bigger and improved, have some monetary value. Later Gerhard would discover that military art, in particular the painting of historic battles, was the most popular art form in the whole of East Prussia.

The living room, which the housekeeper had for years been prohibited from dusting, was transformed into the scene of other battles too, and Gerhard painted them all. The resulting pictures were sold to his father's officer friends for their dining rooms, or anywhere that could do with a large painting of a historical battle, which in practice included any living room in the capital of Königsberg and the rest of East Prussia. After a couple of years sales dried up – they had exhausted the market of buyers who were interested because the pictures were reasonably priced and painted by Captain Schönauer's son. His horses, when viewed critically, had rather too much in common with donkeys, and when his cavalrymen leaned out from their saddles with swords outstretched, cutting down Frenchmen, they looked stiff, as if they had been frozen into position and then glued onto their horses. Gerhard's talent clearly needed honing, and when he turned eighteen he applied to the best art school in the new united Germany – in Dresden, where the education was so broad that he instantly lost interest in military painting, and immersed himself in architecture and the decorative arts.

This was Gerhard.

His story thus far.

But it was still untold up here in Norway, as though it had never happened, because nobody could listen to it, because nobody apart from the pastor could understand German, and he was only interested in international news.

The only possibility was Astrid Hekne, and he knew that he would return to Daukulpen tomorrow, in the hope that she might come.

What makes me want that? he wondered. Why is it important that this Norwegian girl should know who I really am?

The sadness he felt, the sense of lack, the longing, the deep craving in his body for someone to embrace, for someone who understood, who was not hostile, but interested – all this he substituted with ever more drawings of her, he brought her to him, into the cramped cottage. He slept with his sketchbook at his side, while his drawings of her continued into his dreams and turned into fantasies in which she lay at his side, and he knew that the more he drew her, the more dangerous she became.

I Swear on Meyer's Phrase Book

Astrid saw that the trout was not properly hooked, and when Gerhard knelt down to pick it up, it freed itself. It thrashed about on a rock at the water's edge, with one flick of its tail and a second's contact with the water it would escape. She leaped forwards and shot her fingers under its gills, pulled it up and broke its neck, the blood ran over her hands and they exchanged glances.

She went over to a patch of melting snow, drove her hands into the coarse, watery crystals and rubbed them so hard they turned a flaming red, she shook them and pressed them against her skirt, took off her scarf and tied it back on neatly, and for a moment he stood looking at her curls, shamelessly, and when her hands were dry, she took his sketchbook, sat down on the rock and looked through his drawings.

Back at home, they were resting after their mid-morning snack. She had sneaked off, in a rush, afraid that somebody might see her. She opened up the sketchbook at a drawing of the church and asked him which was the most valuable – the church bells or portal? He shook his head and said they were *different*. "But I know what the portal is worth in money," he said.

"Oh?"

"We've had a letter. My clients are demanding that payments be reduced by three hundred kroner. The pastor was terribly upset when I told him."

She put the book aside. "He were mistaken," she said. "The pastor. The portal was nay burned."

Gerhard Schönauer put down the rod, and began leaping about, waving his arms in the air. "*Du sagst* – I mean, you're saying . . . the portal . . . *ist nicht in Flammen aufgegangen*? It still exists? Is it intact? Where is it?"

"I have seen it. It was na' spoiled. It has been used as a door, on a . . . a building."

Gerhard Schönauer continued to pace about, uttering half-phrases in German.

"And you've seen it? Yourself? But what will . . . who owns it now?"

"It be somewhere belongs to our farm."

He stopped.

"Have you known about this all along? But . . . what do you want in payment?"

"A promise."

"A promise of money?"

"Nay. That ye shall never look upon the metal of the church bells. Never."

"Is that all?" He knitted his brows and smiled.

She got up.

"*Unglaublich*," he said. "I don't believe it. You're not teasing me, are you? The portal *does* really exist?"

She nodded and let the silence work for itself.

"But then I need to know *why* I'm not to see the bells," he said.

"'Cos of the old village legend. 'If an unwed man sets eyes on the Sister Bells naked, he shall die.'"

"Die?"

"Aye. Die."

"But it's impossible to demolish the church without seeing them! And I can't lie to the people who sent me. I must have the church bells."

"In't no reason for ye to lie. Dresden shall have its church bells. Old church bells. They shall be ready to load on the sleds when winter comes. Ye just have to do't right. The way the legend says."

"Which is?"

"If the Sister Bells mun be moved, an unwed Hekne maiden shall wind them in canvas. Then after they be lowered to the ground, a wooden casket shall be built round each, and naebody may open these caskets till the bells are safe inside a church once again. When they be pulled up again in Germany, ye mun find an unwed woman to take off t'canvas. And afterwards, the belfry doors mun be locked."

Gerhard Schönauer scowled.

"And, if he *does* see the bells?" he asked, smiling. "How exactly will he die?"

"He will be struck down. Then taken by illness. Over weeks. As he wastes away."

"*Jawohl. Jawohl.*"

"Happen ye think I be teasing? I nay do this to make ye afeared. But to *save ye.*"

"Yes, but . . . I really don't make the decisions, there's a professor, he's called Ulbricht, I'll have to consult him!"

She pursed her lips and shook her head. He dismantled the fishing rod, put it carefully into its pouch, and spun the reel, though the line was already wound in, and stood listening to its whirr.

He stopped spinning it. "And anyway. I must see the portal first."

"Soon," said Astrid. "I shall come and fetch ye by and by, when the time be right."

He deliberated, then nodded.

"Alright. We'll do it – we'll do as you say."

"Exactly as I say? Ye mun promise!"

All playfulness drained from him. He shifted his gaze, gestured with his hands. Moments passed, and when he looked at her again, he was a different person.

"I promise. I shall *never* look upon the church bells. If I had a Bible, I'd swear on it now. But I don't usually bring a Bible on fishing trips."

"Swear on this, then," said Astrid Hekne.

His eyes opened wide in surprise.

"Alright." He nodded. "Why not?" The book she held out was so small that their fingertips touched. "I swear on Meyer's *Sprachführer für Reise und Haus* that I shall never look upon the metal of the Sister Bells. I swear on our friendship. On the friendship between Germany and Norway."

She hurried home. Even more excited, even more fearful. He had gone along with it. The German had actually accepted it. But he had done so without hesitation. Was he quite honest? And as to Schweigaard, humph! All yesterday she had worked on the farm like a woman possessed, trying to forget that stupid kiss. It had just burst out of her, she was so happy that everything had fallen into place, that her plans seemed to be blossoming. But he was so stiff, as cold as a draught from a well, and there on the wall above them hung Jesus, watching everything, undoubtedly already measuring out her punishment.

Astrid hurried on.

Near Røvlingen farm she met two children with a flock of goats. They wanted to stop and talk, but she dashed past them saying she had to hurry home.

They stood watching her pass.

Hurrying homewards? With no tools in her hands, no birch branches loaded on her back, no animals before her?

Struck down. And then taken by an illness.

She had just made it up on the spot. She was amazed at how believable it sounded. Like a forgotten legend from Butangen.

Forty Fox Skins for a Faithful Wife

Kai Schweigaard lost many kilos that spring, and not just because Oldfrue's Christmas fare had run out. The fat beneath his skin went first, and then as he grew thinner his sinews became more pronounced. His shoulder blades started to show under his cassock, and he seemed older. In dim light his face looked a bluish hue, the skin on his hands seemed thicker, almost scaly, and his neck went nubbly when he shaved.

Suppers with Schönauer were now deafeningly silent, even when the German had come back with a fine trout, which, remarkably for the time of year, he had caught on his line. But it was the endless funerals that were wearing him down most. Organising these new services had almost cost him his life. He had misjudged how much work it would take to write eulogies about folk he barely knew, and there was an awkward time lag between the thawing of the earth and the thawing of the dead. The cemetery grounds were still frozen long after the sun melted the snow. Just centimetres beneath the grass the churchwarden's spade struck what felt like solid rock. Meanwhile, the bodies in the outbuildings and barns had been soft for weeks, and eventually the stink from their coffins crept over the forest and fields. Red foxes prowled around corners, and dogs howled day and night.

Once again the forces of nature were doing their victory dance atop the coffin, and he slept badly at night, occasionally Astrid Hekne wandered into his dreams, but every morning he woke up to more funerals. The woodshed grew empty, and the tenant on the parsonage farm sent folk out to collect dry branches. Schweigaard cut the ceremonies down, so that folk did not have to endure the stench for too long, and left all the church doors open. It was customary in other countries to put heavy scented flowers around the coffin, especially lilac, bird cherry or lily of the valley, which drove out the smell of the dead – they needed some flowers up here now, but it would be weeks before even any leaves burst forth.

He often thought that the stink of death would pursue him all summer. The sweet, nauseating odour of decaying corpses, the earth that received them so gratefully. He performed six funerals a day, and let the bonfires burn on even while he was scattering the earth, not least because the smoke veiled the smell of rotting under the coffin lids. He was tempted to hold the last funerals outside, but resisted, and when the last of the winter's dead was finally committed to the earth, he delivered a splendid speech.

He staggered up to the parsonage, informed the German that he now had free access to the church, then collapsed into bed, fell into a deep sleep, woke up late the next day with a headache, and asked Oldfrue Bressum for some coffee. Schönauer wasn't around, and he settled in the parlour to read the international news in the *Lillehammer Tilskuer*.

Later that afternoon he began to feel better.

He took out the large, leather-bound *Kirkebok* – the church register – and entered summaries of the village's recent struggles. The influenza that had raged in January and February had killed twenty-six people. Whooping-cough and scarlet fever had taken nine children. He glanced through earlier *kirkeboks* and found the same misery recorded year after year. The old pastor held little back in his descriptions of the causes of death.

"Pauper woman found dead near Slovarp. Haugen's child burned when struck by lightning. An old tramp fell into a furnace. An unknown woman's child found dead. Jensen's whore-child stillborn. Erik and Knud Myhr, both fell into a mill at Løsnes. Moen's child, died during the labour. An old woman killed accidentally by a falling timber in Bjørge's cottage."

The list of misery grew under Schweigaard's fountain pen too, although he tried to be more sensitive in his descriptions, and give a name to each victim. Life did not seem to have improved in Butangen. Illegitimate children, pneumonia, sudden deaths caused by farm accidents or bad weather up in the mountains. Such short lives, so many emigrating to America, yet the village was still overpopulated. He would often have to spend an hour on baptisms in any one week, yet many were baptised just to be laid in a coffin a year later. It was the sheer banality that gnawed at him most. Farms changed hands in a game of poker, liquor offered the only comfort. Drudgery waited outside the door, disappointment waited inside, and the results all landed in his lap.

Could nobody see what he was trying to do?

He went to the window. Why stay here, when everything was so impossible? Why not just look for another parish, find a place he could call home, stop fencing his way through the night against the rapiers of death and nature and ignorance, find peace, strength and flowering gardens, find one who touched him as Astrid Hekne had touched him.

What a relief it would be when the church was gone. He was so sick, so utterly sick of it all! Of how he associated it with her, this leaky, sunken wreck, that could never be warmed or cooled, that was dark and cramped, scarce better than a cave, and this building was meant to house life's important moments.

A grieving mother was colder when she came out of God's house than when she entered it. These were the conditions under which *animals* lived.

He fell on his knees and prayed for strength. Better times must come, through common sense, moderation and a clean, warm church. And please God, give me a sensible pastor's wife to help me. Send her to me. Please.

He took the next day off too, nourishing his soul with pipe tobacco, coffee and the *Lillehammer Tilskuer*. He had just begun to surface, when a latecomer knocked on the door. His visitor was an old man who lived in a tiny cottage on the road to the summer meadows. He told him that his wife had died earlier in the winter, "sometime before Christmas".

The funeral, the day after, was the worst of all. The old man sat alone in the front pew, and Schweigaard could barely remain composed because of the stench. The coffin was discoloured and weighed almost nothing, and the churchwarden and a helper carried it out hastily. Later, Schweigaard heard that the man had, on the previous day, gone to Vålebrua, where he sold almost forty fox skins, and that it was on his return trip that he had visited the pastor's office to report the death. Oldfrue Bressum served the pastor with weak coffee and a detailed rendition of what had happened in the cottage in the late winter. The widower was a keen hunter, and as the spring came the smell from the outhouse attracted the foxes from the surrounding forest. After years of his failing to hit them, they were finally in close range of his old muzzle-loading rifle. Not until the foxes stopped coming, and he had killed and skinned the entire population, did he think it worth delivering his wife.

Kai Schweigaard rushed up to his room, tore off his shirt and slammed his head into the wall. He needed to give vent to these torments, to get this filth *out*! Out of his head! If only he could escape, just once, go out one Saturday to a barn where folk took a drink, hang his cassock high on the wall, join the revelry, dance and drink straight from the bottle, tell yarns with the others, have a grope and a cuddle and a kiss and a laugh, take another swig and slobber, get worse and worse, as crazy as the rest, kick his legs in the air, click his heels together and land with a thud on the floor, point at the cassock on the wall and say:

"There hangs the pastor and here am I!"

A Green Shoot at Last

The cow bellowed. The only one with the strength to do so. The others glowered, thin and bony, with barren udders.

Astrid released their teats, pushed her milking stool back and lifted the wooden pail to the light. A pathetic splash of milk swilled about in the bottom. She still had two more cows, but they gave so little that it was scarcely worth the bother.

Besides, Gerhard Schönauer was somewhere out there.

But the cows could not wait. The spring-pinch was worse than for years, despite it having been a good autumn. The farmhands had cut leaves, collected moss from the mountains, mowed the grassy marshes in Samdalen, carrying load upon load of thick hay down to the farm, and the fields closest to the farm had given a fair yield too, but now the barn was as good as empty, and there wasn't a green thing in sight. She got up and went down to the farmhouse.

"Mother. Ye mun come to the barn."

When it came to the animals, her mother never contradicted her. She went with her, placed a hand on the cows' backs and squeezed. Their skin hung so loose she could hold it in her fist.

"She be nowt but bones," said her mother, shaking her head.

Astrid showed her the milk pail. "It be scarce wet in t'bottom."

"I can see. It in't good."

Astrid and her mother went out for a think. All around them the birches were bare, and the fields were bleached yellow and brown. It was the same on all farms, big or small. The ground had finally thawed, but the air was still cold and raw, particularly at night, and there were still light snow showers. This time last year, the cows had been put out to pasture long ago, but now she asked herself whether they were fit enough to go out at all. They would have to fatten them up before letting them out of the barn. A couple of weeks ago they had, as a last resort, fed them horse manure, horses being unable to digest everything, good oats passed right through them. But now even the manure heap was finished. Not that it had been very big, since the local crofters were quick to collect their horses' muck and take it back to their crofts. It was at the foot of the slopes, where the horses pulled their loads and stopped to shit, where the most manure was found, and where they stooped. This spring, the Hekne bairns were forced to stoop there too.

There was an art to foddering hungry cattle in lean times, and they had done their best.

There was also an art to living together with hungry folk. The womenfolk might feel like complaining, knowing that the men fed the horses at the expense of the cows, but they generally held their tongues. Osvald was the worst, but Emort and his father were not without blame. Though whining was useless in the short run, for they were in it together for the long run. If the horses weren't strong enough, the ploughing wouldn't get done, and then that autumn would be their last.

"I mun go up to Hellorn and cut some young branches," said Astrid. "I can na' see another way."

Hellorn was a steep area of land at the top of the village, which still belonged to Hekne. It was said that folk and animals had lived up there once, before the Black Death. But it was no longer fit to farm, for an avalanche had left the slope strewn with rocks, giving it its name –"Rocky Hill". But spring always came early to Hellorn. In late winter, avalanches of snow could be heard rumbling down from the mountains above, and the April sun melted the rest. Nothing grew between the rocks here now, except dwarfed birches and willow thickets, these were too spindly for firewood, but their foliage made good fodder, although carrying it back down was heavy work.

Astrid fetched a sickle, a small lunch pack, a carry strap and set out.

Hellorn was so steep that she almost found herself clambering up it. She leaned across a little birch tree and cut off a twig. There on its surface she could see the minute shift in colour. A bud. A green bud. She chewed on it. It had some flavour. Within a week, as long as there were no hard frosts, leaves would burst forth, the size of a mouse's ear.

She started cutting twigs, armful after armful. Later that day, Osvald came with a cart and they drove back to the barn with their load. Soon the lowing of cows could be heard, and their mother nodded. They agreed that Astrid would go up again next morning and carry more bundles down to the cart road, ready for Emort and Balder, the old workhorse, to pick up in the evening.

"Ye mun take someone with ye to help cut," said her father.

"Nay," Astrid replied. "We ought not to take too much from

up there. And I cuts faster than the cows can eat. I shall go early tomorrow."

The Door Serpent

Gerhard Schönauer shifted the easel on his shoulder. He had only brought it for appearance's sake, in case he met anybody. He had followed her directions, and at the agreed meeting place she slipped out from the shadows and pointed to where he must go from there. She herself went into the forest. He continued down a slope, so steep that he had to walk sideways, and far down, above a river that rushed over pebbles and fallen trees, he saw something that looked like a flattened pile of rocks, but which he soon discovered to be the slate roof of a low building.

She reappeared, and together they walked towards a medium-sized log shed, so old and sunken that the logs followed the unevenness in the terrain. Tiny trees were growing out of the sagging peat roof. Inside he heard the bleating of sheep.

"This is a—"

"We call it a *fjøs* – a byre."

Again he looked at her. Noted her clothes, with the same gaze as when he drew her in secret. Her naked body, was it as he imagined? Fine skin, sinewy, yet supple?

The byre was unusually tall and narrow. There was a small arched door in the shorter wall, darker than the grey log walls. Its shape was perhaps reminiscent of Dahl's drawing of the portal, but its frame was of plain timber and the wrought-iron hooks were simple and short.

"Surely this isn't a church portal?"

"It be back to front."

"What do you mean?"

"What ye be looking for is on the inside. The carved patterns was hidden behind some planks, but I had someone take them off."

"Tell me who owns this place?"

"'Tis a Hekne croft. An older couple do live here. The man gives us wild game now and then as payment. Ye mun take summat from your travel money and give them money for materials for a new door."

"Have you been inside? Seen it?"

"Nay. The man that lives here has took away what was shielding the carvings. It were done yesterday, and that be all I know, save that it were once part of the church."

He felt the pulse in his temples. The byre *was* curiously high.

"'Cos I wanted to wait," she added. "And look upon it with ye."

From the waistband of her skirt she fished out a matchbox and a half-burned tallow candle. The doorway was so low that it barely reached her bosom, she stepped aside and invited him to go in. As he pushed the door, it let out a long creaking sound of rusty iron and swollen pine. He heard bleating and recognised the heavy, sweet odour; it was dark inside, and it was into this darkness and sweet smell that he now crept.

Fleetingly, he got the sensation that he was climbing into the church as it had been many centuries ago. A sky glowed with the dawn and shifted to night and glowed again, he was sure he stood naked in the rain, then, just as quickly, he was back in a sheep byre, warm and dry, looking at Astrid Hekne's face in the shimmer of a tallow candle. He could see that she was also in a trance-like state, but she was looking at him, not the portal.

Her dreamy contemplation ended as a summer ends, ebbing away reluctantly.

"That *is* it," whispered Gerhard Schönauer.

He stood open-mouthed, pointing at the myriad carvings that were faintly picked out in the candlelight. A giant serpent writhed on either side of the door, but this was no mere design cut into a wooden plank, it moved upon the surface, thick and muscular, carved from a single hefty log. It twisted and slithered along the door frame, and at the top its head snarled with a flicking tongue, and beside it a massive tail was poised to strike. And now he saw that this beast consisted of countless thinner serpents all biting at each other's tails. Around it was a throng of dragons, lizards, gaping wolves and horsemen with longbows.

The tallow candle suddenly sputtered and went out. The sheep bleated a little, but barely moved, like mythological beasts at rest.

"*Einen Moment*," he said, as Astrid went to relight the candle. It was almost dark, and he went close up to the portal and placed a hand on it and searched its surface with his fingertips.

"Carvings. You must touch them to understand them. Your hand. *Gib mir die Hand*."

She did.

"Can you feel them? *Hier – nein, hier* – the scales of the lizard?"

"Aye. I . . . I can feel them."

"*Und hier* – a sea serpent. And this . . . is a dragon. Can you feel this – a wolf?"

The carvings were worn by the weather and centuries, but in the dark, against their fingers, they felt distinct, crisp and new. She let him hold her hand and guide it over these ancient powers, her fingers brushing against Fenris the Wolf and Odin's ravens, over *Naglfar*, the ship of the underworld made from the nails of the dead, over flames, with a heat that was past or still to come, a battle betwixt darkness and light, from the time when light had been divided from dark. He spread his hands and felt the warmth of hers beneath his, and ancient forces pulsated against their fingertips. Together they traced the endless serpent in the dark, and its power tingled against their skin, as they followed its contours, inward and outward, in an endless, bewitched flight.

Towards Enemies Greater than Him

Kai Schweigaard went out into the courtyard to meet the horse and cart. It was carrying a large, flat, dark-brown object. The workhorse snorted, as a farm boy led it by its harness. Beside them ran Gerhard Schönauer, issuing constant instructions, as he ducked down behind the cart, then leaped to the right side, and then the left, checking the load.

Schweigaard recognised the horse. It came from Hekne. And the boy leading it was Emort, Hekne's *odelsgutt*.

Astrid Hekne was not there herself. But the signs were that she had been busy again.

Schweigaard had no idea what the exact bargain was, whether this was simply an exchange for the church bells, or whether any difference had been made up in cash, or worse, emotions. Yesterday Schönauer had told him that "someone in the village" had offered to sell him the portal, prompting a whole host of possible barbed questions: with whom did you make this deal? At what price? And how did it come about?

But Schweigaard asked none of these questions, which just made things more awkward. There they sat, each with his own half-truth, which together comprised a lie. And what was a lie to the Queen of Saxony, compared with a lie to the Almighty?

He ordered his tenant farmer to fetch some workers. Four men were needed to lift and carry the portal into the cart shed. Three hundred kroner went back into the accounts for the new church. Better that these men remained ignorant of the amount, it was as much as they each earned in two years.

Emort left and Schweigaard walked reluctantly towards Schönauer, who was raving about what a historic event it was, that such an invaluable artwork should be brought into safe-keeping at last. The portal had looked like any old timber-load on its arrival, but now it was standing upright, and as Schweigaard drew closer its huge surface came to life. This really *was* a severed part of the church. The labyrinth of carvings seemed arbitrary at first, but it led his gaze through a clear hierarchy of creatures from a smoke-laden past. The serpent peered out past Schweigaard and into eternity, towards far greater enemies than he, enemies who inhabited deep waters and dark caves. Schweigaard turned to leave, but had to go back, to stop and stare. Pagan, wild, exuberant. Months of work, years. Intricate and painstaking, the smallest figure must have taken as much work as the plans for a bishop's New Year's service. An infinite number of tiny details, guided by one huge, overarching idea.

Once, seven hundred years ago, an enormous burst of creativity had been born of sincere faith. Perhaps it had been made by an artist from here, an artist with a lot of Gerhard Schönauer in him.

"Folks need summat beautiful too . . . Not like an ornament. But beauty they can feel inside of them."

He gazed at the portal for a long time. It *could* have stayed in the village. Been exhibited somewhere. As a memorial – a word he could not remember ever having rated too highly – a memorial to all those things he could not understand, but which were of value nonetheless. In much the same way as he could experience love, but never explain it. Walking down the aisle of a church with her arm in his, he in black, she in a new shop-bought dress.

Standing behind him was Gerhard Schönauer. Until now he had never understood what Astrid Hekne might see in the German. But he knew now that he had the chance to draw weapons on an equal battlefield. When Astrid finally had what she wanted, she would be able to see the change in him. A greater openness and a new generosity of spirit that he could cultivate in himself.

He must break his engagement with Ida Calmeyer. The Sister Bells would remain in Butangen.

And he would build a bell tower for them in the name of Astrid Heknes.

He looked at the closed door, crouched down and took the handle. But the door swung inwards and hit the wall behind it, and he never got to walk through the portal.

The Word with a Capital K

They walked down from Daukulpen. The days were longer at last. Noticeably longer. Spring had finally taken hold, and streams burbled on every hillside.

"I'm so glad," he said, "that we rescued it. Up there it would have been just – humph, just think about all those sheep! I've sent a letter to Professor Ulbricht."

She nodded, but said nothing. Everything had felt so right in the beginning, but now that beginning was over. Who was she, Astrid wondered, to sit in judgment over the past, to ignore the warnings in her grandfather's silence? On that day in Halvfarelia the centuries had breathed on her and asked: who really *owns* the door of a church? Is it truly possible to own a door? After all, only the door itself can be owned, never the opening, and without an opening a door is not a door. And who can govern a church bell, who *owns* their sound as it travels along riverbanks and up across mountains, who can truly own something that is older than the kinfolk we can remember, and which will survive the kinfolk who will soon have forgotten us?

But what was done was done, and all the choices and all the questions left a restless emptiness that longed to be filled. Her thoughts about Gerhard Schönauer had settled. There was a warmth about him, with an eye for what she herself thought lovely. A lonely soul who wandered about Butangen, and whom nobody quite understood.

"Have they night lamps in Dresden?" she asked.

"Night lamps?"

"Aye, do they light up so folk can walk between the houses at night?"

He realised he could best answer her question with a drawing, and so it was that he made his first sketch of Dresden for her.

"And be the roads covered with stone? So folks can go with . . .", she pointed at her boots, making a cutting motion with her finger below her ankle.

Help from Meyer's was required before he understood the question – whether folk could walk outdoors in low-cut shoes? He had no idea how exotic this seemed to her, how, even in summer, such a thing was unthinkable here, as the muddy roads were constantly churned up by cartwheels, and the paths intersected by streams and marshland. She asked him about where he came from, about how he had discovered his talent, and how he had honed his skills. She was disappointed on hearing that girls were not admitted into the academy, but wanted to know how his homeland could let him sit for hours with a thin pencil instead of working the land – how did they order their affairs in this faraway country? How, she asked, were great painters like him discovered?

"I'm not a great painter," he said, "I'm just a stu . . ."

He swallowed.

"I am an architect," he said, correcting himself. "First and foremost an architect."

They took a break, it was a tough walk, as she was choosing paths where they would not be seen. They stopped in one of the few places in the valley where there was still snow, as though stopping at the divide between winter and spring, and she felt lighter at last.

It had gone to plan. The deal was done, the bells were secured. And here she was, walking with a man, who, whenever he thought she was not looking, stole a glance at her, who purposely slowed his pace so as to walk behind her, causing her to walk with a new sway in her hips.

Happiness. Was this happiness? Sent to her from a country faraway in the south?

She sat on a rock and took out Meyer's *Sprachführer für Reise und Haus*.

"Will ye show me some German?"

In a column on the left were the German words, on the right the Norwegian, and he sat on her left, as though they themselves were an extension of the book. Each put an index finger on a word, choosing in turn, and then alternately helping each other to pronounce the words correctly in German or Norwegian.

She looked up the German for "mountain range" and tried to say "*Hochgebirge*", but he wanted to be systematic and went back to the letter A.

"*Abend*?" she asked, and he made her pronounce the end with clear T.

"Evening," he said in Norwegian, and she tried to make him say it in her dialect, the result making them both laugh.

"*Aber*?" she asked.

"That's almost right," he said. "Not such a sharp R."

She repeated the word, softening her R.

"*Abergläubisch*," she said. "Superstitious," he said.

"*Abfahren*," she said. "To depart," he said, suddenly going quiet.

They continued with A, but the letter seemed somehow loaded, and they went to B, but were soon bored with following the alphabet and started to skip about between words as the fancy took them.

"*Strudel*?"

"Whirl."

"*Leiden*?"

"Suffering."

"*Lippe*," he said.

"Lip," she said, slowly, and they both saw the words printed just above: "*Leben*" and "*Liebe*" – "life" and "love".

It was his turn to choose now, but he took his time, and tipped the book on a slight angle, so that she had to lean closer to see; she felt his warmth, her cheek against his stubble.

They landed on N, playing with *Notschuss* – "emergency flare", *Nordlicht* – "northern lights" – before she took back the book and turned to K.

"*Kühnheit*?" she asked.

"Daring," he said.

"*Kurzatmig*?"

He cleared his throat. "Shot of breath," he said.

"No, *short* of breath. Try again."

"Shot of breath."

"*Short-short-short* of breath," she repeated, laughing.

"*Shorrrt* of breath."

As she moved her finger to the next word, his trembling must have reached deep into the ground, and he tried to look away, but the book was still in her hands, and no earthly power could guide her finger away from the word starting with a capital K.

"*Kuss*," she said.

He hesitated, as he had at the word "*Liebe*", and again he did not say it, but put his arm about her neck and, as Meyer's *Sprachführer* fell to the ground, he acted upon the word.

She arched backwards in response, supporting herself on the rock. Then she grabbed him and twisted her fingers through his hair, he stroked her back and drew her close and she grew as pliant as a willow.

Now at last she felt the difference between a kiss and a kiss. Between kindness and love. Boiled water and a mountain stream. Kai Schweigaard and Gerhard Schönauer.

Through the Tip of His Pencil

Gerhard Schönauer was standing in the church. The light from the windows high up trickled over him and his drawing of the altar. He was still unable to convert the church into Saxon feet. It was like trying to find the head measurement of a ghost. He no longer dared lift his pencil for fear of producing another poor drawing. He escaped into thoughts of Astrid Hekne, and paced about the church, and finally sat down on the wall end of the pew, where she had been sitting on the morning they had met there.

He rested his head against the wall and closed his eyes.

The pulpit and *andreaskorsene* flickered between his eyelids, and then he had the feeling that he was back on the little croft where Astrid had shown him the portal. She was standing outside, but now she was wearing a red, ankle-length dress, and with her hand outstretched she bade him walk through the door.

He crouched down and crept into a sheep byre, but stood up in a stave church. *The* stave church, as it was when it was newly built. The pine walls were freshly hewn and luminous. There was a smell of resin and fresh turpentine, on the floor lay a broad-axe and scraping-iron, a break in the work perhaps, he could hear voices, but saw nobody around. There was no roof yet and the sun shone in through the open structure. Walking on tentatively he recognised the *andreaskorsene*, saw how they were fixed to the rough-hewn staves that ran up from the floor, looked towards the main gallery and realised that the workers were probably two years into a job that would take four.

This was no physical transfer, rather a falling through the centuries, entering the swirls of the past, steering through mirages of forgotten events. This was Butangen stave church, but seven centuries ago. When they had so few tools available to them. Long treenails of hard wood, whittled by hand, lay alongside a mallet. Axes and iron scrapers, black, rough-forged, with glinting edges. He found himself in an era without saws, little cuts and long grooves were the only marks left by these craftsmen. He heard hammers beating through time, everything became jumbled, and a procession passed through the night with dancing lanterns.

And he came to himself.

He got up and looked up at the horseshoe-shaped *bueknærne*, the braces that linked the staves. It occurred to him then that the church got its elegant sense of length because the distance between the staves on the long sides was double that on the short sides, and that the *andreaskorsene* were not part of the supporting structure, but were *suspended.*

All at once the church seemed welcoming, the smell of tar, even the creaking of the floorboards felt strangely homely to him.

He grabbed a pencil and made a sketch. For the first time in ages he nodded approvingly at his own work. The drawing was technically perfect, its proportions precise, yet it retained the mystery of the church. He looked around. He was no longer frightened by the sighs he thought he heard in the stairwells, the movements in the gloom. It was as though he was preparing to move a building with folk sleeping in it. And this feeling flowed into his work that day, infusing his drawings with soul. These were not cold, technical illustrations; through his play with shadows, his delicate hatching, he conveyed a whispering, flickering legacy of building and craft.

That afternoon his thoughts returned to Astrid, and he gave free rein to ideas that he had tried to drive out with good reason – because he would leave soon, return to Dresden and never come back – but now, here in the aisle of the stave church, these thoughts opened like flowers and revealed their beauty.

Hesitation changed into certainty.

Money awaited him in Dresden.

Sabinka did not.

When the church was re-erected with a plaque bearing his name, architecture firms would compete to hire Herr Gerhard Schönauer. In Dresden an architect's salary could give them a good life.

And it seemed she wanted the same thing. She had asked him to make another sketch of the bridge over the Elbe, of the illuminated promenade. Her very presence made him grow, it would give him the mettle, not only to rebuild the church, but for new buildings, great architecture. He could already feel the urge to create something that might be remembered, not just for a hundred years, but for seven hundred! Without her, he was not Gerhard Schönauer, the artist, he was merely Gerhard Schönauer, the copyist.

He would leave *die Schwesterglocken* here.

But he would take something else with him to Dresden.

She, a kindred part of the legend, would accompany the stave church to Germany, and when it was rebuilt they would walk together through this portal, walk down this aisle and be married with the chiming of church bells.

Passion's Braid

Two weeks later he presented her with a ring and asked her to go with him to Dresden.

It was a delicate braid of copper-brown metal threads, and as it glinted in the palm of her hand Astrid saw that it was a miniature of the Door Serpent, a criss-cross of slender serpents biting each other's tails, coming together to form one powerful, endless serpent. The ring was made of thin fly hooks. He must have heated them over a candle, twisted them into each other and threaded the barbs through the eyes of the hooks, before hammering them tightly together. The ring represented hours of painstaking work, and Astrid saw it as proof of a thought that had neither faltered nor faded with reason, but which persisted and demanded: I must have a ring.

As she slipped it on she felt a few little pinpricks, from the barbs he had not quite managed to hammer smooth, but it was so ingeniously put together that it held its form despite not being soldered. She could not fathom how he had made something so exquisite from something destined for another use, and she said this to him, and then she saw how much he wanted an answer to the really big question.

"Well, ask then," she said.

But he asked in Norwegian, and she stopped and looked him in the eye.

"Ask me in German," she said. And when he did, shivers went down her spine. He had come to *her*, he had come *here*, full of admiration for the leaping trout, for the silence, and for the stars that were so clear. He explained that the stars were never as bright in the Dresden sky, because such pitch-black darkness did not exist there.

She stood on tiptoe and kissed him.

There were probably street lights in Kristiania too, but why dream of Kristiania when she could dream of Dresden? Yes, she thought, give me gas lamps in Dresden, before all else. I would snuff out the Plough for a single glimpse of a gas lamp, I would darken the Great Bear to be kissed under a street light.

At both marriage proposals the Hekne farmhouse had bustled with folk. Each suitor had stood in the doorway before ten or fifteen villagers of all ages, and nervously, but pompously, declared his wish to talk with her father, so that everyone knew right away what his errand was.

It was altogether different with Gerhard Schönauer, who said "*Ich liebe Dich*."

Love. This word, which did not exist in her dialect, which no Gudbrandsdøl had ever been able to say without feeling like a liar – which even she could not say. It swelled in her mouth and wanted to return to her lungs, it sounded like a lie, it was too grand, against her nature. She could show it, through loyalty and devotion, and through actions, but to *say* it was impossible.

But in *his* language, oh heavens, how good it sounded! What a ring German had to it! She had overheard him speak irritably once, and his words were like sharp mountain ridges, his

Is and Ns crackling and sparkling: "*Nein*!" But usually there was nothing gentler or softer than German, and when he said "*die Schwesterglocken*" or called her "*Fräulein*", his voice was, to her, like grass on warm valley slopes, that bent softly in the summer breeze.

And now, just as Gerhard had said "yes" when she asked him to leave the *Schwesterglocken* in Norway, she now gave him, as church bells chimed in unison, an answer which chimed with his "yes":

"Aye," she said. "I shall come with ye to Dresden."

Back in time for supper, she stroked the ring, it had no beginning and thus no end, and neither, it seemed, did the serpents that comprised it, and since it was impossible to see which serpent's head bit which tail, they defied counting.

She turned in bed, rubbed the ring and pretended her pillow was Gerhard Schönauer.

No man had ever seen her naked. In fact, she had never seen herself naked either, not in her entirety. There was only one full-length mirror in the farmhouse, and that was in the hallway. Her body tingled and throbbed, and she wished she could show herself to him.

Because you, she thought, are beautiful. When you suddenly gaze into the air, or leaf through that little phrasebook, or move your lips when you think I'm not looking, and when you silently try out new sentences in Norwegian; you're so eager to improve, and yet still your Rs grate hopelessly and your As are much too long.

In his sketchbook, Dresden now emerged. He drew Memel, his parents and brothers, and the apartment he and Astrid would have in Neustadt, he drew the promenade along the Elbe with its gas lamps, and then, dizzy with love, he began to draw the two of them, as their life together might be, and these imagined moments filled page after page. Executed at lightning speed, yet always precise, his drawings took the place of all he would have liked to say to her, but did not possess the language for, and through them he shared his dreams for the future: a little brick house with a veranda, the two of them together, Astrid in a smart town-dress with her hair piled up, or in bed with tousled locks and a come-hither smile – a drawing so immodest that she grabbed the page to rip it out, but it was too beautiful and she let it be, and those that followed were more respectable or dream-like.

When should she tell her mother and father that she was leaving?

They were going to have a fit.

Or perhaps not. They would probably be glad to get her married off. Her mother's three brothers had gone to Canada. Folk left the village all the time. Now it was her turn. Emort was the one she would miss. Long summer days on the seter. The cows.

But she refused to check herself, to entertain obstacles. Something good was waiting for her somewhere in the world. With him she would find what was hers, whatever that might be, and she would defend it so that she could call it "mine".

One evening he told her he would soon be finished with drawing the church. They walked through the forest to avoid being seen together, down to Lake Løsnes. He was curious about the fishing there.

"Are there any shallows here?" he said. "Where I can wade out and fish?"

She nodded and pointed over to the other side. "Where that beck flows out. A little to the left of those boats. But I can na' go there with ye. Folk will see us."

She followed him a little way until they glimpsed the lake between the tree trunks, and she pointed him towards the shoal, then sat in the forest to watch him from a distance. He waded into the cold water with his black trousers rolled up to his knees and his white shirtsleeves rolled up to his elbows, and again and again the glossy fishing rod bowed in a supple arc and sent the pale-yellow line out to draw letters against the sky.

That evening, under cover of dark, she went to him in his log cottage on the parsonage grounds. He hung his coat over the window and locked the door.

"Let me make a better drawing of you," he said.

He put a tallow candle on her left; she realised that her profile was more pronounced that way, with a sunny and a shadowy side, so that the curve that ran down through her forehead and nose and mouth became a boundary between shadow and light.

She had her clothes on but felt that he could see right through them, and for her, too, he was naked.

"I used to believe," said Astrid, "that there were an explanation for everything. But now the more I try to make sense of things, the less I understand."

"There's a poem," said Gerhard.

"A poem about what?"

"About *that*."

"I have nay heard many poems."

"Beautiful are the things we see," he said, "more beautiful still the things we understand, but the best of all are—"

"Stop," she said. "Say it in German."

"I'm not sure I remember quite how it goes."

"Say it anyway."

"*Schön ist, was wir sehen. Noch schöner, was wir verstehen. Am schönsten aber, was wir nicht fassen können.*"

They blew out the candle and crept under a sheepskin rug. A little below the parsonage ran a swollen stream, and they lay listening to the rush of the meltwater.

He began to touch her, and she him. Hands on backs, hands on thighs, hands up over bellies and down again. She discovered that his breathing grew heavier when she touched him near his groin, and she pursued this until they both lost all grip on themselves.

They awoke in the early hours, to find that it had been snowing again and that the entire spring landscape was white.

"I mun go home now," she said. "But he mun nay see my footprints."

Gerhard opened the door and carried her in his arms to the edge of the forest, where the snow had landed on the branches but not the ground, and on a carpet of last year's leaves he set her down, and she disappeared like a deer into the forest. She muttered prayers to God as she ran, and worried lest they had been seen.

She woke to a new working day. Touched the ring and hid it.

The night's snow melted before noon, and that day the spring came to stay. The sun was baking-hot, as if it were the middle of summer, and the ploughing and sowing got under way. Not an inch of earth must lie fallow, and where it was too steep for a workhorse to go they had to break the earth with hoes and smooth it down by hand. They ate, rested, and after food, it was out again. Bare fingers in cold soil. The steady pull of the Døla horse. Out to collect more branches. Fodder for a restless cow, clean-scrubbed hands against teats, also cold, the echo of squirting milk in a wooden pail, a more saturated sound as it grew full.

The sight of a hard-working man down by the church, in and out of doors.

A grandfather clock in an empty parlour, slowly ticking in anticipation of something to come.

Love Might Take the Same Path

The pain of what had been and what would be, a leaden-grey shadow landed in her mind as he thrust deep inside her, and she slapped him. He stopped abruptly, and she stared into his eyes until he grew fearful, grabbed his rump with both hands and made him go on, her eyes still fixed on his, and they continued until the flat rock beneath them melted away. She came to herself when a tear dropped from him onto her cheek.

They lay for a long time on the rock. This was not crude, she said to herself. Not crude. All animals coupled outside. Let it happen when it happens, as the water in a river flows towards the waterfall.

His weight, his strength, the heat from his body, and everything this weight, strength and heat did when it invaded her, and the joy it prompted when she allowed it to invade.

She dressed and sat beside him.

He clasped his hands about his knees. Nearer the edge of Daukulpen lay a Hardy Smuggler. The line was dry. The sun had shone brightly in the last three days, bursting with heat, and the rock was dry and warm.

Her mind wandered. Everything had such tempo and weight that it rolled of its own accord, refusing to be stopped in time.

The church would be torn down. She would not.

"From now on we mun meet up at the seter," she said. "I be taking the cows there in a day or two. I shall put a candle in the window each Saturday night when I be alone."

"And if you're not alone?"

"Then ye mun listen for the cowbells. Look for me. When ye be finished we shall have the whole summer."

He seemed not to understand.

"Or if ye find the cows," she said, "ye mun holler."

He had gone quiet. She stroked his arm.

"What be the matter?"

"Didn't you hear that?" he said.

"What?"

"I thought I heard a church bell."

"Be it already time for church?"

"No. It's too early. Listen, there it is again."

They both leaped up, Astrid so fast that the blood thumped in her ears. They ran to the top of a hill, and as they left the river's noise behind them, they heard the chimes louder and clearer.

Down in the village, the Sister Bells boomed. Ringing as though they were declaring both the fulfilment of something and a warning. It was a frenzied din without tempo or rhythm, like runaway thunder, and for the first time she heard a clear difference between the two bells, they were no longer in unison, this was the sound of two separate bells, and as they sprinted downhill, the bells rang and rang, until they suddenly stopped.

They came down to such chaos that none of the old gossips noticed that they arrived together. Everyone must have rushed from their houses, even bedridden old folks staggered across the way, all with one goal, to join the growing throng outside the church. Folk stood between the grave mounds flinging their arms about. It emerged from the frantic shouts that the Sister Bells had rung themselves. Rung in a wild unrelenting frenzy, that scared the birds out of the trees and the badgers from under the stone walls to the four corners of the earth. The farm dogs howled, and the first to arrive thought an extra Mass was being called, but could not understand why the cemetery was empty or why the bells kept ringing, nor could they confer with each other, since the noise was so deafening that nobody could make themselves understood. An old cavalry officer remembered the rule that church bells should be rung if Norway was at war. He flung out his arms and told folk to turn and spread the word that a conqueror was on his way, and thus the rumour of "War! It's war!" was broadcast to the same four corners to which the badgers had fled, and was not quashed until late next day. Children scrambled up onto the stone wall, old folk squinted and yelled into each other's ears, while the chorus of gossips split into yet smaller coveys, for they also gossiped about each other, and lived in fear that the gossip might turn upon them.

Meanwhile Kai Schweigaard and the bell-ringer came running, but since both assumed the other had let himself in and rung the bells, neither brought the key.

And still the bells continued, louder and stronger than ever, sending out seismic vibrations that made pebbles rattle. While the pastor and bell-ringer ran for the keys, folk pushed towards the church doors to see if they really were locked – which they were – so that on his return Schweigaard had to push through the crowd, an arm stretched out and the key in his hand.

Then something happened that was seen as an ill omen, and that rekindled latent superstitions: at the very moment Kai Schweigaard put his key in the lock the bells stopped.

Several villagers saw it.

The instant the pastor's key slid into place, as metal met metal, the bells fell silent, leaving a humming in everyone's ears, and an echo that rang over the valley and shattered into a thousand little echoes against the mountainsides. And just before the door was torn open, three women – who had all lost their first-borns in labour – thought they heard deep sighs rising from beneath the cemetery.

Everybody rushed after the pastor into the church, which was soon so packed that the culprit could easily have slipped out from a hiding place and mingled with the crowd. But this was only noted by the few who sought a logical explanation, and never won any real interest.

*

Despite the pandemonium, Schweigaard held a powerful Mass, which curbed the panic and confusion. The church was already full, and he got everybody to settle in their pews, and began a much-rehearsed sermon, in which he said farewell to the village's church. This day, he told them, resembled a full stop, an insignificant mark to which few attached any meaning, but which ended all the finest sentences in literature.

Honed into shape over weeks, it was sharp, dignified and inspired, and he delivered it with authority and elegance, he had no need for a script, he had practised it in his office using the grand three-tiered stove as his audience. He had helped himself liberally to passages from the world's great preachers and poets, in such a situation he permitted himself to be one of Christendom's gentlemen thieves – that Sunday, both Martin Luther and Donne were heard from the pulpit in Butangen. He even dared to allude to God's promise of resurrection, as he talked of the church's future in a new land. But as his sermon drew to an end, its tone became more vulnerable, almost intimate, and his voice was so filled with sorrow that it threatened to falter, but it held steady, steady until he said "Amen". Then it cracked.

These emotions were unrehearsed. They came when Kai Schweigaard spotted Astrid Hekne sitting in the pew where Klara Mytting had died.

It was then that he saw it – that it was probably too late. That it might not just be the old church that left the village. Love might follow its path. And as he shut his Bible and let the bells ring out, their sound was heavy and sad, and he feared that God might shut the door to that innermost chamber within him, and, unlike the Bible, shut it for good.

Second Story

THE FALL

The Deconsecration

SUNDAY IS A DAY FOR THE SOUL. MONDAY IS A DAY OF work.

Shortly after sunrise they were gathered, twenty-two men from the village, highly respected craftsmen, with a diversity of skills, some young and fearless, others old and shrewd, all under the supervision of the oldest and most skilled among them, known simply as Borgedal the Elder, leaving the pompous title of Master Builder to the self-aggrandising Lillehammerites and other town folk.

They were about to demolish the church that their work-brothers, almost certainly their ancestors, had raised many generations ago. An hour passed with them standing hands on hips, looking and talking, before they climbed the church steps, deposited their hats and knives in the porch, and spent another hour inside, looking and talking. Nobody pointed at anything, but there was much nodding. They came out again and divided into teams of three, and began work, without marking a single timber or consulting any written plan.

Gerhard Schönauer tried to get Borgedal the Elder to remind his men that this was no ordinary demolition job, the church had to be rebuilt, it must be done carefully, attention paid so that no finely crafted joints were damaged or timbers split. Borgedal nodded, but did not pass the message on. Not one usable timber had ever been wasted in the village during his lifetime.

As on the day before, the cemetery was surrounded by onlookers, but they were astonishingly quiet. Nobody would ever know who had rung the bells. Several villagers had keys; the churchwarden had one set, Gerhard Schönauer had his, and no doubt a number of replacements had been made over the years, and it was not that difficult to force a lock forged on the same anvil as a plough blade. But there was no earthly explanation as to why the bells had stopped at the very moment when the priest's key entered the lock, and everybody knew that the "wild ringing" would live on in the memory for years to come.

Folk had time on their hands now. The early summer was hot, the sun had been bounteous, the potatoes and seeds were in the ground, and the first net-fishing had been fairly good. The villagers should have felt that something momentous was about to happen, the challenging demolition of an old church and the building of a new one, but the lean years had made the idea of anything *great* alien to many. And as they moved around the church, the carpenters felt a sadness. They knew they no longer took the same joy or pride in their creations as past generations. It was hard for them to say it aloud: we could work like that once, and we are the same, but we no longer do. And, adding to their sadness, they wanted to build with staves and logs, not dull planks and a timber frame.

The doors had just been lifted from their hinges, when Kai Schweigaard suddenly dashed up to old Borgedal and took him aside. The men were ordered to stop work, and the crowd looked on in bewilderment as Schweigaard ran back up to the parsonage.

He had forgotten to deconsecrate the church!

Back in his office he ransacked book after book with little hope of actually finding anything about deconsecration. As trainee priests they had never been given any instruction about this ritual – after all, it was impossible to cover *everything*, exorcism, for example, had been skipped, despite three of his fellow students expressing curiosity about it. He left books lying open as he pulled others from the shelves. John Donne was not of much help now. Strictly speaking he should have consulted Folkestad at Hamar as regards the correct procedure, but that would take three or four days.

Schweigaard laid a sheet of paper on the table and unscrewed the lid on his inkwell.

Something symbolic. Something . . . visible.

He stared into the tabletop. Pen poised.

What if I'm committing a capital offence? He shook his head. Forgiveness afterwards.

Fifteen minutes later he was back in the church with blue-stained fingers and a sheet of paper in his pocket. He found a large beeswax candle, and with the workmen as his public he knelt before the altar. He lit the candle, got up and went over to where the sailboat hung from the ceiling, the traditional symbol of the journey of faith, and now understood by all to symbolise the church's forthcoming journey too. He nodded towards the four corners of the House of God and said:

"We thank this old and once proud church for serving the Christian faith for hundreds of years. We thank God for protecting it from the perils of fire and war, and give thanks for its welcoming of our pious prayers and humble hopes, for having housed baptisms and liturgies. We thank this church building – for all this. I now liberate it from its duty."

He took a deep breath and drew the burning candle, which he held in both hands, closer. As he was about to blow it out, he interrupted himself, adding: "And we thank the church bells for calling us to Mass and ringing at times of joy and sorrow. I liberate them too from their duty." Then, as he blew out the candle, a drop of wax splashed onto the nail of his index finger, and hardened.

And with that Christianity moved out after seven hundred years.

The contents of the stave church were carefully brought out, the men like silent pallbearers, who wanted to spare these objects from witnessing the forthcoming brutality of the demolition. Richly decorated religious objects were carried out, never by fewer than four hands, and always by respectfully bareheaded men, out they came, the soapstone font, the statue of St Laurentius, the plaque dedicated to a German captain – for which nobody seemed to have an explanation – one by one they were taken to the parsonage and put in the parlour under the watchful eye of Margit Bressum. Every fifteen minutes more objects were brought into the open, objects that the villagers had stared at in the semi-dark, all the mysterious things that folk had, through the centuries of changing beliefs, found it proper to fill a church with, which, as time passed, it seemed wrong to discard. Folk sighed in wonder at each object, artefacts that came into the light like pale prisoners released after many years: heraldic lions with gilded manes that guarded King Frederik IV's double monogram in gold, the sailboat from over the aisle with its crisp paper sail. Four men lifted the great cross down from the chancel arch and took it onto their shoulders, until they saw a likeness with Calvary, and decided to lay it flat on a cart and drive it up to the parsonage. Into the parlour they went, rose paintings and woodcarvings, all those things that Pastor Schweigaard had kept out of the contract with Dresden.

"Everything else is going to Germany," said Schweigaard. "Including the pews." By "everything else" he meant the pulpit, the altar and various carvings in the old Norse style, including the staves depicting Odin and Thor. These were to be taken down to a large barn beside Lake Løsnes, which had been rented for the purpose long ago; its roof had been repaired and it would house the church itself and these objects until winter. A row of water pails stood outside ready to be passed down a firefighting chain if the worst happened.

"There is one exception," said Kai Schweigaard. "If you find a roll of fabric, something resembling a tapestry, hidden under a floorboard maybe, or up in the rafters – wherever – do *not* touch it. Stop all work and fetch me immediately."

The men nodded and continued with their work. They had been issued with two hundred metres of sailcloth, which they cut and wrapped around anything delicate. It took six men to lift the pulpit, followed by the altarpiece, so precious that they made it a protective wooden crate of its own, and padded it with sheepskin. They found an offering bowl, an incense burner and an engraved silver goblet under the altar, a hint of other treasures that might be under the floorboards, together with the skeletons that were probably there, and Kai Schweigaard took all these objects with a rather surprised nod.

The pews were stacked and loaded onto the cart, and Gerhard Schönauer made notes in a logbook of each removal so that he could re-create the interior precisely.

After a long day's work the church felt curiously empty and naked. A strange, hollow echo followed each footstep. The Hekneweave had not been found.

"Good," said Schweigaard, nodding. "Early tomorrow morning you must move the bells. Lower them gently and put them at the back of the barn, next to the new ones that are there already."

But outside a sense of unease had taken hold. Until they had seen the church pews being taken to the barn, the villagers had not fully grasped what was happening. Up to that point it had all just seemed like a simple refurbishment, few knew what a spartan building their church would be replaced with, nor had it seemed worth asking, as their objections were never heard anyway.

No-one had imagined that the old pews, on whose doors were painted the names of respected old farms – Flyen, Kinn, Hjelle, Hilstad, Romsås – would not be kept in the village. Yet here they were, being carried down to the barn one by one, whence they would disappear for good. And gradually the mumbling turned to muttering. There had been an absolute belief that the pews would be used in the new church, and now it felt as though those things not bound for the parsonage crossed the divide between the living and the dead.

All eyes fixed themselves on Gerhard Schönauer. The demolition was due to start the next day, and it was as tense now as before an execution. The only foreigner, the German in their midst, became, alternately, both executioner and sentenced man.

Even Astrid Hekne wasn't free from such feelings. Standing alongside Emort and Oline, at the fringes of a band of villagers, she felt a shiver of doubt every time she caught sight of Kai Schweigaard and Gerhard Schönauer. They went about the church, pointing and nodding, with no eyes or ears for the grumbling crowd on the other side of the stone wall.

She had known them, whispered with them, been close to them.

They were men who lived and sensed and breathed.

But they were also men who heaved and crushed and disrupted. Men who demolished churches and sold church bells. They strode about the church of Butangen's ancestors in their tall boots, as though it were a reindeer to be driven into a pit and slaughtered upon its knees. They laid plans, and did as they planned, with ice-cold precision – and it was this coldness, the draught that issued from it, that was intolerable to her, as it made the scar in her ache, and every glimpse of them was a blow on a crowbar that prised the scar open.

My Name beneath Sailcloth

"It'll be by the stairs up to the belfry," Gerhard had told her. "A roll of sailcloth and a coil of rope. I'll leave the sacristy door open."

The men had packed up. Emort said there was no more to see that day, and Oline needed to go into the forest for a pee. Astrid parted ways with them, saying she wanted to take one last walk around the church. They walked on, and she gazed after them, wondering if Emort had noticed anything strange about her.

Villagers hung around the church saying their final farewells, in large and small groups, and the odd lonely soul. She knew each by name, and, to some extent, could anticipate their thoughts. She lingered behind the crowd, and then, when she was alone, she sneaked into the sacristy.

For some minutes she stood in the empty, stripped church and took in the resonance of peace, of high days and holy days, and all that had been. She thought of the countless people who had sat here, of Eirik Hekne and his ancestors, and all those whose names had been forgotten. The Hekne sisters must have stooped to come in through the old door. *Everyone* in Butangen had left traces of themselves, traces she felt sure had been collected by some tireless, unknown being, a being who still moved in here, and had transformed all the sighs and whisperings, the grief and joy, into the fine haze of dust that ran in the shafts of light from the narrow windows high above.

And it forced her to think whether it was possible. To move a church to Dresden. To move a girl from Butangen to Dresden.

But I have given him my word, and so it must be.

With the roll of sailcloth clamped under her arm, she groped her way up the creaking ladders, through dark corners that smelled of age, grabbing at old wooden rails from which the odours of the hand-sweat of generations seemed to be emitted simultaneously to hers, and then she was finally up in the belfry and pushed the shutters ajar so the evening light poured in.

The Sister Bells were waiting for her.

Two dark vaults above her head, two ropes attached to axles at the top, ropes that disappeared down through a hatch, towards an infinity in the church room below. The silver-bronze ready to react to the least change in the air.

She took a deep breath.

"Do nay ring," she whispered. "Be good to me, do nay start to ring."

Astrid looked over her shoulder. She touched the bell rope, thought she could see brown hair twisted into the pale grey hemp. She was present. Close. Like a faint breath. A being too dead to move her eyes or give signs of life, but who followed events and had thoughts about what would happen.

Astrid crouched down to unhook the clapper. She felt as though she was about to empty a gun of its powder. She reached high into the sound bow, but then let her hands fall. Again she asked herself if she had the right to rob the bells of their ability to ring.

Then she did it. Raising her arms again she felt the iron orb fill her palms. Soon its entire weight was in her hands, heavy and cold as a stone bismer weight. The clapper was suspended inside the bell on an iron stem with a hook at the end; she lifted it and twisted it free, but the hook touched the side and a dark, humming sound surrounded her. It shifted tone, then dissolved. And she thought that if it were visible it would look like drops of blood in water.

She lowered the clapper. The iron stem wavered, it was like holding an upside-down sledgehammer, but it came out without scraping the bell. She laid it on the floor and released the breath from her lungs.

She felt a gust of wind, and her body swayed. Every movement in the church was magnified up here, the wind ran through the wooden framework, making it whisper.

Astrid wiped the sweat off her hands and unhooked the second clapper and laid it carefully down so that it would be clear which bell it belonged to. Then she unrolled the sailcloth, attached one corner to the cannons of the first bell, *Halfrid*, and tugged it down to cover it. She had to stretch the cloth around it while holding the edge of the bell, and it had to be done without any sudden movement, otherwise the bell would vibrate, but as soon as she came halfway the sailcloth slipped, making the inscription "Astrid" visible again, and when she had finally got the sailcloth in place and had covered her own name, she knew that nobody in the whole world had ever done such a thing before and neither would she wish it upon anyone.

Struck down

A frequently asked question, when large objects are taken down, is how on earth anyone managed to put them up. Hundreds of years had passed since the Sister Bells were hung in place, when they were probably hoisted through four hatches, one below the other, which, when they were all opened, formed a long downwards shaft. Later a new platform was built for the bell-ringer, which did not rest on the construction, but which by some ingenious method hung from somewhere higher up, doubtless connected to the point from which the bells were suspended.

And now Gerhard Schönauer was staring at this very point. He had, for the first time, ventured into the belfry. His gaze wandered between the two bells, both wrapped in layer upon layer of sailcloth, secured with hemp rope in tight knots.

Her knots.

Gerhard took hold of one of the bell ropes and rolled it into a coil, but just as he picked up a knife to cut it free from the bell's axle, one of the windows blew closed with a bang. He pushed it open again, put his knife aside, and instead unscrewed the attachment from the ropes.

Old Borgedal came up the ladder. He grunted approval, saying it had been wise to wrap the bells. They stood for a while studying the timber structure from which they hung. Wooden beams crossing this way and that, cracked with age, their seamless joints covered with bird dirt and firmly locked together by their own colossal weight, each timber like a molar in the gums of a giant jaw. Eventually Borgedal pointed to a beam high up and said that a leak had made it rotten, so they must remove any weight from it before lowering the bells, and to do that, they had to remove parts of the spire right away.

Outside long ladders were put against the eaves. The youngest lad on the team went up onto the roof, a hammer and tongs in his belt. As he crawled towards the steep spire the gasps of the crowd, which was even larger than the day before, were so loud that the sound carried all the way up to him. Nobody could see how he was getting a grip on the tiles, which from a distance looked like tiny fish scales, but they all assumed he was there to fetch the weathervane down, which was so high that its top was barely visible against the sky.

A sharp-eyed reindeer hunter saw how the boy was climbing, and told those who stood nearest him. Sticking out from the spire was a row of little wooden wedges. They were loose, and before stepping on them, the boy pulled them out one by one, spat on their ends to make the wood fibres swell, then knocked them in and continued his journey upwards. He must have been able to see across the entire village from up there, but he did not wave, and nobody dared to say anything. Just as he got halfway up, there was a sudden gust of wind, and a sharp creaking sound went over the gravestones and towards the onlookers, and the boy swayed with the spire.

At the top he tied himself securely, freeing both hands so he could get at the top of the spire and reach the weathervane, tall and slim like eight longswords. Two men climbed up to take it from him, and as he passed it to them they were surprised by its weight, but they managed not to drop it and it was soon lying on the grass. The onlookers surged forwards against the cemetery wall, and then looked at each other speechless.

What they had always believed to be a weather cock was a raven. It had a powerful beak, and cruel, cunning eyes; it was a raven, gnarled with rust and clearly ancient.

Then Schönauer did something he ought not to have done. He rushed over to the weathervane, as though he were taking possession of it, giving neither the lad nor the other workers, nor the crowd, a moment to wonder at it. Instead he stood astride the raven and measured it with a ruler before fastening a label to its beak with string.

Then the cracking of crowbars was heard, and everyone's gaze turned towards the men who were now balancing up on the roof's ridge. Several teams were working in unison at breath-taking speed. There was never a dull moment for the onlookers now, as roof tiles sailed down to the ground, to be gathered up by the men below and packed into wooden crates, which another team was busy making as required. Old Borgedal stood beside Kai Schweigaard, who was his calmer self again, as Gerhard Schönauer dashed about recording the number and position of each part. As the tiles were removed, more and more load-bearing beams were revealed, and he regularly demanded a pause in the work so as to draw some hidden detail of construction. The carpenters had to glue a label on each thing they dismantled, on which he wrote a code in thick pencil before he smeared the label with wax to make it rainproof, and then entered everything into a logbook using an intricate system of numbers and letters. Later that afternoon a deep-blue sky peeped through the timber framework, and suddenly the church seemed less majestic, and the interior of the spire proved unexpectedly rough-hewn, a powerful centre stave with crosswise supports of decreasing size, reminiscent of the skeleton of an adder, and inside that again, two church bells could be seen, enveloped in sailcloth.

The next morning the tools had moved from where the men had left them. A coil of rope appeared in the sacristy, and when they unravelled it they saw seven blood-knots in it, the distance between each being one *kvartstaur*, a local unit of measure that had gone out of use before the Danish era, but which presumably related to the inner dimensions of the stave church. Strange occurrences of this kind were not uncommon when they disturbed old buildings, and they untied the knots and got on with removing the platform below the bells. Gerhard Schönauer had prohibited the use of any cutting or scraping tools in the church, so there wasn't a double saw or axe in sight. The carpenters tried to loosen it by prising a crowbar in here and there, but with each jerk came an ominous groaning in the timber.

This was bad enough. But still more ominous were the strange vibrations emitted by the bells. Despite being packed so tightly, the bronze and Hekne silver absorbed any activity, and whenever pressure was applied to an iron crowbar, the church was darkened by a stifling dissonance.

It was late in the afternoon by the time they got the platform down. Then they erected a beam from which the bells could be lowered.

It was soon afterwards that the first accident happened. It

was heralded by the shouts of a carpenter, then came the scream of timbers being ripped apart, then a beam loosened and thundered to the ground making the whole church shake to its foundations. A cloud of fine dust cascaded from the ceiling and filled the church, making everyone invisible to each other. Coughing was heard in the fog, and there was a long silence before the first workmen dared emerge, one as grey as the other, a new communal uniform for these men who were no longer carpenters, but the opposite, and they went at it again with even greater force, as if the building had become the enemy, and from their mood Gerhard could see they had forgotten they were in a church, and they had begun to curse when things went skew.

Above them the bells continued to murmur. Each time a crowbar was inserted and a timber torn loose, the sound was answered with an eerie tremolo, a damning judgment on every movement that broke the ancient silence.

Gerhard Schönauer set up a tall ladder so as to get a good view when the lowering of the bells began. The new platform was of newly cut pine and thick as a roof timber, yet it bowed slightly as it took the weight of the first bell, which swayed a little as it was guided downwards. It was the first time in centuries that the two bells had been parted, and a gentle moaning sound issued from both.

This was followed by a creaking, then a loud cracking. A split second's warning that the platform would not hold.

The timber broke and the rope went slack.

Then the bell fell.

The sailcloth caught on something and was torn off like the skin of an animal. The sunlight touched the bare metal and Gerhard Schönauer saw the bell fall through the air, leaving the hemp rope hanging like a writhing snake. The bell crashed into a beam and broke it in two without losing speed or direction, and continued downwards, bringing any loose tiles and timbers with it, and then, as witnessed by those present, it *changed direction* in mid-air and headed straight for Gerhard Schönauer. He fell off the ladder and went into free fall with the bell tumbling after him, until it hit an *andreaskors*, where it became wedged, while Gerhard Schönauer continued to fall before landing with a smack on the church floor.

In the falling cloud of splinters and dust there was also a long, thin rod that dropped vertically down and hit a young carpenter in the stomach, the same lad who had taken down the weathervane. Blood slowly spread across the floor, while the bell that still hung high in the tower above rang with a heavy and sustained warning sound, more naked in tone now since it chimed alone.

A Last Resort

The workmen buried their young companion in a nice spot in the cemetery. They chose it themselves, dug the grave themselves and held the ceremony according to their old customs. There was no consecrated church in which to hold a funeral. Kai Schweigaard scattered the earth, but was so shaken by the death that he was not his usual self. The carpenters helped themselves to wood that was intended for transport crates, and built a long, six-sided coffin, which they planed and crafted to the best of their ability as the villagers looked on. And into the lid they carved a beautiful design. When the first fistful of black earth fell onto the coffin and filled the grooves in the pattern, the twisting shapes emerged even more clearly, acknowledgment that they were burying a young carpentry talent.

Gerhard Schönauer was found unconscious in the dust and blood. They put him on the cart and took him up to the parsonage. He was unconscious for so long that they feared he might die of thirst. When he finally woke up, Oldfrue Bressum gave him some brandy for the pain, and the next day the doctor came to see him and check whether he had any broken bones.

He reeled in a languor of sips of water, thin soup and brandy. A few days later he staggered to his feet. His thighs, chest and arms were blue and swollen, but he grabbed a chair and hauled himself up. New pains declared themselves in his ribs and wrists.

"What day is it?" he asked Oldfrue.

"Saturday."

"Has anyone been here while I was asleep?"

"Who might ye be thinking of?"

He muttered something and stumbled out. He could see the church further down the slope. It had no roof or doors. There were no work teams to be seen. Higher powers had, Oldfrue Bressum informed him, released them from the task. The story of the accident had spread as fast as young legs could run.

"Accident?" said Gerhard.

"A carpenter died. The youngest in the team."

She gave him a walking stick, and he hobbled down the hill. The graves in the cemetery were covered in wheel tracks, and the interior of the church looked like something between a building site and the scene of an accident, and in what seemed an impossible place, in a corner just above the choir, he saw the bell, firmly wedged.

I have already seen you naked now, he thought as he fought his way up a ladder. The dull bronze was covered in scratches, which glinted against the green patina. Then he spotted the inscription.

"IN LOVING MEMORIE OF HALFRID AND HER MOTHER ASTRID."

He shuddered, closed his eyes and turned away. The sailcloth was lying in tatters at the foot of the ladder. He smoothed it and carried it up to the bell, still reluctant to look too directly upon the metal, fearful and ashamed, as though obliged to tend to his own mother. Pain seared through his ribs, and his neck and knees, and he only just managed to pull it in place.

"You shall be left here," he said. "I promise you that. You and your sister. Please don't harm me."

While Gerhard Schönauer lay in a delirium, Kai Schweigaard tried to get a new work team together. But not a single man from Butangen or any neighbouring village would set foot in the church, no matter how much money he offered them.

What he had not foreseen either, was that stories of the stave church's innate powers would begin to spread through the village. It seemed another life-view lay in wait at the forest's edge. Since ancient times a church had not just been a house of prayer, but also a living shield, a buttress against the dark powers.

This was a feeling shared by all. As they set out for the mountains or the seters, it became clear to them that folk were not the only beings on two legs. The highland meadows were inhabited by creatures who emptied milk pails, or led otherwise sensible milking cows into the marshes. Two farmers in the next valley had been obliged to move barns that they had only recently built, when the cows grew ructious, bellowing and refusing to go in. Opinion was that the barns had been mistakenly built over entrances to the world of the underground spirits, and they took them down and rebuilt them a hundred metres away – after which the cows had instantly settled.

Down in the village, however, there were never any such difficulties. The reason was simple: the church *building* kept them at bay, it was the building itself that protected folk against other powers; the Mass and God's word were no more than a light in the windows. Kai Schweigaard could see now that this was true of the faith of all Gudbrandsdøl folk. They respected God, but set their churches high.

Nowhere was this more evident than in Butangen. Now that the spire had fallen, ancient methods of warding off evil reappeared. Folk started to put out porridge to gain protection, and rumours flew that Kari På Vona, a woman as tall as a house, her face hidden behind rags, had started walking once again at night to catch children who were out alone. Ancient legends were being revived too, among them the story that explained the white rocks which lay scattered around the church. It had long been dismissed as a folk tale that the *jutuls*, a race of giants, had thrown the rocks at the church in a fit of rage when it was first built, until they finally gave up and wandered up into the fells, where they still lived. But now this story had a recent follow-up, namely, that when the Sister Bells had first arrived their sound reached deep into the mountains, where they woke the mountain troll, who threw the three gigantic boulders that now stood in the middle of the Høystads' farm, before he loped off to Grøtorhøgda and Gråhøgda, far enough away to escape the chiming of Christendom's bronze bells.

These had, for generations, been stories for children. Now even rational folk felt that something "other" was closing in. At night, badgers and wild cats fought in the church's remains, and strange powers moved in from the caves and valleys. Old men resumed the practice of leaving dried meat on the boulders that stuck out of the river, offerings to the Butangen water sprite, a naked, grey-coloured creature that leaped on all fours and accompanied the fish to their spawning grounds. Better to be on the safe side, than take the risk of *not* believing.

Kai Schweigaard noticed the change with each passing day. He saw villagers rummaging about at dusk, before they disappeared into the forest together, nodding, and re-emerged later, separately. Even everyday Christian traditions were being subverted. And with no church in which to hold funerals, his orders began to be ignored.

If only people had *light*, he thought. If there was a strong lamp in every home, which could illuminate faces and edifying books, I could banish these mad notions in a few years. But at sunset the village grew dark, and with it folk's minds, and these unknown powers ruled until sunrise.

Kai Schweigaard went to Vålebrua to seek the advice of the mayor. On the day of his absence somebody from the Hågå farmstead saw the opportunity to bury an old woman without consulting the pastor or churchwarden. They fetched the schoolmaster, Giverhaug, who sang more loudly and beautifully than ever, and when Giverhaug died years later, he left behind a saying from that summer, namely that "a priest that tears down his own church, can nay expect much of a congregation".

Kai Schweigaard had to admit Giverhaug had a point. He had ordered his own pulpit to be carried out, and knew that eventually, when the new church was ready, he would not have to make up for just one, but *ten* years of spiritual darkness. To re-establish reason would be more difficult than pulling a cow out of the marsh. He sat there with a ruined church, a distrustful congregation – *and* a broken agreement, since according to the contract it was entirely *his* responsibility to get the church demolished. Outside the sun blazed, as it had for weeks, and such abundant sunshine could mean only one thing, that it would soon end, and rain would come pelting down onto a church with no roof.

There was only one thing for it.

He had to resort to the Bergenites.

The Hekne Sisters' Coffin

The following day he travelled to Lillehammer, to send the first of many telegrams to Bergen. He ought to have paid the senior rector a visit, but instead he booked into the Hotel Victoria, where he gorged on rich food between trips to the telegraph office. These dishes – fillet of pork in cream sauce, hearty beef goulash, and thick pea soup – strengthened him in the belief that his plan was a good one and achievable. Schweigaard knew that a stave church in Bergen had been taken down in the year before, no doubt in the naive hope of rebuilding it elsewhere, and he contacted a local rector to ask if anyone could offer the same team to do the work in Butangen. Food and lodgings would be arranged – if they came quickly.

Over the next weeks Butangen was filled with growing numbers of strutting Bergenites, who made so much of themselves that although they were only twelve in number it felt more like sixty. Schönauer set to work again, and limped about making sketches and recording each timber as it was taken down. The foreman was a hard-working and efficient fellow by the name of Michelsen. He could even speak German, and within one hour he had grasped Schönauer's numbering system and put a quick-witted young lad from Fana in charge of marking the materials.

They applied the exact same method as the local carpenters had done in lowering the bell, but strangely enough *their* platform held, and soon *Halfrid* came swinging down, as if all it had needed was for someone to ask her nicely. They made a wooden crate for her transport according to Schönauer's instructions, with handles so that four strong men could lift her, carry her out and set her down near the foundation wall. Next came *Gunhild*, whose descent was accompanied by a minor chord, which fell silent the instant she reached the ground with a thud.

"Put them in the barn. Next to the new bells," said Kai Schweigaard. He met Gerhard Schönauer's gaze, and they gave each other a quick nod.

The crowd of onlookers was smaller now. The villagers tended to pass by once a day, stand for a while, arms by their sides, say "hmm" and then head off home.

Kai Schweigaard started to do the same. He might have found the Butangen folk irritatingly obstinate and difficult, yet he felt slightly defeated by the fact that the boastful Bergenites had succeeded where the local carpenters had not. Yet he had to admit that these west-coast men were perfect for the task. Not only did they have recent experience of demolishing stave churches, they were, as all Bergenites, equipped with an intolerably buoyant confidence and arrogant rationality that meant that they were not fazed by any task. These descendants of shipwrecked Portuguese and Hanseatic folk did not believe in forest spirits, did not attribute meaning to a change in the wind or inexplicable echoes from the mountains. With icy coolness, they studied the church's construction, prised out the theory behind it and set their crowbars in exactly the right place. They took over the parsonage, occupying beds and floors, and annoying Oldfrue Bressum by tramping about in dirty boots and demanding fish at every meal.

Day by day, Butangen's stave church disappeared. Walls fell, so that you could see in, and from some viewpoints you could see right through the church to the rippling surface of Lake Løsnes that glittered between the timber framework. Soon it was unrecognisable as a church. Plank after plank, timber after timber, one by one they were laid out on the ground, given a number in the logbook and driven to the barn; damage was minimal, and soon Kai Schweigaard realised: this will go to plan.

He saw nothing more of Astrid Hekne. The village was as good as empty of young girls, they had all been sent up to the seters as dairymaids – a little early perhaps, with the spring having arrived so late, but no doubt someone had suggested it might be wise to keep the girls safe from the bragging, itchy-fingered Bergenites.

He imagined her alone on the path, walking up to the seter at sunrise, a branch of rowan berry in her hand; he had a notion that she wanted to avoid seeing the church's demolition, or perhaps his part in it. She would return later in the summer. The village would have changed, she would have changed, and she would have got her way.

And he would surprise her with a newly built bell tower.

The demolition work continued. Soon only the staves were left, around which the entire church had been built. Twelve evenly spaced, rough-hewn pillars stretched up to the heavens, a scene that conjured images of the church as it must have looked when it was first being constructed under King Magnus. Calmly the twelve staves were detached from one another, then rocked loose from the foundation wall and laid down.

Butangen church was finally lost to the world. Only the floor was left, and nobody knew for certain what was under it.

"I think it's time, Herr Pastor."

"Right," said Schweigaard, rising from the breakfast table. "Was everything made ready last night?"

"Just as you asked, sir."

They opened the front door and stood for a moment watching the dawn.

"Ten chests?" said Schweigaard.

"We've made twenty, to be on the safe side. There'll always be a use for them."

Schweigaard nodded, and they headed off towards the church.

"Is the German out of the way? I want the way clear, with as few people around as possible."

"That Schönauer chap is still asleep, and Oldfrue's been instructed to hedge him busy all day."

"Is the churchwarden down there?"

"He is, sir. There are six of us waiting, and we've filled and cleaned the oil lamps."

"Good," said Kai Schweigaard. "This is going to be a long day."

Down at the church site, he straightened his cassock, turned his Bible in his hands, and nodded in Michelsen's direction. He had imagined that everything within the ring wall would be hidden under a gigantic duvet of dust, covering the centuries of forgotten deeds, the complete range of dubious customs, an assembly of skeletons, and the images of the gods in line with the shifting beliefs in Butangen. And what worried him most were the contents of the coffins which he knew they would find under the floor. It would be best if the dead were sorted out quickly and reburied without fuss. Nothing could be worse than if the building site was invaded at night by Giverhaug and his muttering associates carrying barn-lights, on a quest to "preserve the past".

He had wondered how fresh the coffins would be, and scoured the royal decrees which the old priest had received. Here he read that an end had been put to burials under the church floor in 1805, with a statement that he might have written himself: "It is unseemly that buildings dedicated to the Worship of the Highest Being should be used as hiding places for bodies given over to decay."

Schweigaard shook his head. *Decay*. All spring he had been nauseated by the sweet, intense odour of corpses, and these bodies must have lain rotting under the floorboards for weeks on end. The statement went on to suggest that this custom presented a "health risk for the living". Didn't folk *care* back then? Or were they so reconciled to death that they tolerated the stench?

But now, when Kai Schweigaard climbed up onto the stone wall, he was surprised. A third of the church floorboards had been removed that morning, but beneath them there was no dust at all. Instead the foundations resembled a freshly tilled field full of pebbles, early in the spring, before the appearance of any new shoots. The pale morning light sloped in. He spotted the first coffin, grey with age, its corners crumbling.

"Stand aside," said Schweigaard.

He folded his cassock about his knees and descended a small stepladder. Having reached the coffin he put the Bible on its lid.

"We shall move you now," whispered Kai Schweigaard, towards what he assumed to be the head end. "May you continue to rest in peace."

Crouching down, Schweigaard went between the coffins in the gloom. Several had split, so that the remains of bones stuck out. Others were in such good condition that it was clear that the 1805 regulation had been ignored until quite recently.

He walked back over to the men. "Go ahead. Remove the rest of the floor," he said to Michelsen. "As carefully as you can. You must lift all the undamaged coffins up gently. None are to be opened. And you," he said to the churchwarden, "transfer any loose bones into new coffins. One skeleton in each. Have more coffins made if needed. Work carefully, but don't dawdle. They must all be reburied before nightfall."

Even the Bergenites lowered their voices during this task. The first coffin was lifted over the wall, but somebody lost his grip and it tipped. First, there was the clatter of bones sliding about, then a rolling sound, followed by a thud as the skull landed at the foot-end.

It was a mistake they only made once. From then on the

coffins were transferred horizontally, in deep silence, into the crisp, early summer air.

Schönauer was not around. Schweigaard went up and changed into rougher clothing, and he took a rake and, together with the bell-ringer, collected coins, amulets and rarities which had been lost between the floorboards or put there for luck.

Later that day, fourteen old coffins lay outside the ring wall, shrouded in grey blankets. Next to them stood a row of newly made coffins, but these too were soon covered. The work was done in such a muted fashion that the spectators beyond the cemetery wall did not stand around for long.

Then Michelsen walked over to Kai Schweigaard.

"We've been waiting to take up the last coffin. It's rather . . . odd."

"Oh?"

"Its shape. It's very wide. As if it holds two short people."

"A married couple?"

"Seems too short to be adults."

"They were shorter back then."

Michelsen cleared his throat. "We had to wrench it loose from the ground, but there weren't any . . . clattering noises."

"And so?"

"There's something in it, though. Judging by its weight."

Kai Schweigaard put down his rake. Michelsen led him over to the corner where two men were standing at a respectful distance to a wooden box.

"As you can see, it hasn't disintegrated," Michelsen said.

Kai Schweigaard went down on one knee in the crumbling soil. Before him was an elaborately made coffin in greying pine, still perfectly intact. Smooth timber. One and a half metres long, and almost as wide. Carved in the centre of its lid was a little H. The coffin did not have a clear head or foot, and seemed somewhat small for its purpose.

Michelsen crouched down. "It's made from ore-pine. It doesn't rot. It could be centuries old."

"I'm not sure if this is a coffin at all," said Kai Schweigaard, running his fingers over the treenails in the lid.

"Shall we open it?"

Kai Schweigaard both did and did not want to, as though he was holding something murky in a glass.

"No," he said, getting up. "We shan't disturb them. There may be nothing but their bones, resting in peace. Let's bury them."

"*Their* bones?"

Kai Schweigaard nodded. "Yes. Let's get them buried quickly."

The workers were slow to respond. Some looked skywards, others kicked the ground. Finally, Michelsen said:

"The day is wearing thin, Herr Pastor."

"I'm well aware of that."

"To put it bluntly, sir, I fear we'll still be doing this when it's dark. There were more coffins here than we expected."

"If we're short of time, I'll join in and dig myself," said Kai Schweigaard. "I don't want these coffins left out here tonight."

The sound of shovelling and heavy lifting could be heard late into the evening, and it was by the glow of an oil lamp that Kai Schweigaard scattered earth on the last coffin. He had placed the wide casket in the furthermost grave, and he was still unsure whether or not he had made a mistake.

The men stood about with their hats in their hands.

"Let us sing 'Kjærlighet fra Gud'," said Kai Schweigaard.

The New Assignment

There is no greater quiet than when Bergenites have just left a place.

Gerhard Schönauer stood looking at the church grounds that no longer had a church. The sun was warm and he had his sleeves rolled up. The birch trees were dense with green foliage. There were wild ducks down on Lake Løsnes, followed by long lines of young ones.

He turned the logbook in his hands, and walked down towards the barn where the materials were being stored. At the gate of a field he met some villagers, he nodded politely, and they responded with something resembling a "Morning". Mosquitoes, flies and bees buzzed everywhere, even the air felt thick and luscious. He had never thought Butangen could offer such temperatures, but now he felt that the valley collected heat like a cauldron. Everywhere the villagers were busy, on the slopes he saw horses at work, farm animals grazing, a calm had settled over them all in the heat, and life seemed less harsh.

The hot sun was beating down on the slate roof of the barn. The odour of tar could be smelled from long away. He let himself in. Ran his hand over an exquisitely carved beam, studied the paler wood where it had been attached to another beam, thought back to his coded system to find the part that matched it. The materials were cleverly stored, with a wide corridor down the middle, so that when winter came it would be easy to access everything and load the sledges.

At the very back he could just make out four church bells. Two large and two smaller. He swaddled the smaller church bells in sailcloth, and placed some planks at an angle over the Sister Bells so that they appeared to belong to another cargo, and let himself out.

It was done.

On the other side of Lake Løsnes two men were busy in a boat. They were fishing near the shallow grounds where he had been with his fly-fishing rod earlier that spring. Back then she had hidden at a distance so as not to be seen. *That* now seemed to be a permanent state. He knew she was up on one of the seters, but even up there, with the way folk talked, she must have got word of the accidents. Yet she had not found any pretext to come down to him.

He turned and looked up. Even he had grown accustomed to seeing the church there. Now he mused over its absence, and wondered how it would look down in Dresden. In his last letter, Ulbricht had said that they had agreed upon where it should be rebuilt, a magnificent site among the conifer trees in the Grosse Garten, beside an artificial lake named after Queen Carola. The church too would bear her name.

He felt a sadness. The stave church could never be the same in Dresden. Neither would he be the same when they arrived there. For something was confused, had lost its way, like a swallow robbed of her nest, swooping invisibly over the cemetery. Thirty metres up in the blue, where the old bell tower had once stood, he thought he could see that the air was still disturbed, as though something was desperately seeking to regain solid form.

Astrid.

His thoughts became wreathed in worry. Wild unpredictability was the base-colour behind the shimmering tones that surrounded her. And he knew now for certain, having been away from her for so long, that the colours in him would dry out without her. Dry in their tube.

A few weeks ago he had sent a letter to Professor Ulbricht, telling him that the church's demolition was finally going to plan. He had asked if he could have a travel grant against his future salary, to "visit my parents in Memel and return here at the start of the transportation process".

It was a ruse. He had no intention of going home, he needed the money to pay for Astrid's ticket to Dresden.

Gerhard Schönauer turned his face to the summer sun. It mattered no longer that he had toiled all summer until his clothes were threadbare, and had nearly been killed. The church bells had been rescued. Right now, he was *here*, and he wanted to be *here*. What was the rush? There was none. Go and find her up at the seter. Let their engagement be known. Get a money order for a little of the reward that awaited him in Dresden, buy a roll of fabric for Astrid so that she could get some travelling-clothes made. He could rent a summer cottage, spend the mornings painting landscapes and the afternoons fly fishing, visit her when it suited her, sweaty and loving encounters in violet-blue nights. Old Borgedal had said that the route over Lake Løsnes usually opened up in late November, when the northernmost section froze over with blue ice, after the winter's first full moon.

He and she. Together on the last sledge, crossing the ice, into something new.

What a life! He felt an overwhelming urge to tell her about all these plans of his. How wonderful it was, that his first thought was to share his joy!

Gerhard went up to his log cottage, tidied his drawing materials and sorted out his fly hooks. He lost track of time, and when he arrived at the table Schweigaard had already finished eating. He was sitting there, legs crossed, studying a letter.

"Ah, there you are!" said Schweigaard.

"Morning!"

The pastor watched him as he made his way around the table. "I've had a message from Professor Ulbricht. I assume you've got it too." He nodded towards Gerhard's white plate, beside it a long envelope with a familiar handwriting and a stamp from the Deutsche Reichspost.

Gerhard grabbed it and opened it with his table knife.

"I get the impression," said Schweigaard, sipping his coffee, "that the two of us need to take a short trip to the bank. And that, from there, you'll be setting out on a much longer trip."

Dresden, July 1880

Herr Schönauer!

Congratulations on completing such a superlative enterprise. Thank you too for the beautiful drawings you enclosed. We have discussed the contents of your letter, presented it to Courtier Kastler, and have another proposition for you which we consider both generous and of enormous benefit. Formally, you are still required to deliver a number of artworks for external examination, and we need accurate drawings of more Norwegian stave churches to further emphasise the importance of the reconstruction here in Dresden. People need to understand that we have performed a rescue mission of historic proportions, rather than having just moved an arbitrary medieval building. We are already looking to the future! More Norwegian stave churches will be demolished in the coming years - probably all - and they must all be recorded. Yes, that's right - you, Student Schönauer, are to complete J. C. Dahl's work! Your name will be ensured a place for ever among artists and architects.

You may withdraw a generous sum from the bank in Lillehammer to cover your travel expenses. Buy a money belt to avoid any worry about being robbed. Send regular updates about your work. Start right away. Do not waste your time on this place. We have enough rustic landscape paintings and sketches of farmers with goats. We have instructed your priest friend to put any goods from the church in safekeeping. Return on the 1st of December to accompany the transportation. Always remember that you are on a royal assignment, and that in representing Courtier Kastler you are subject to Queen Carola's command. Any deviation will be subject to the strictest examination.

Your friend,

Ulbricht

Gerhard put the letter down. On a second sheet, in an unfamiliar hand, was the outline of his itinerary. Over the next four months he was expected to visit seven stave churches, spread across several counties. It would take days to travel between each.

"We must go into Lillehammer and each collect our monies from the bank," said Schweigaard. "The payment for the old church has come through, and I understand that you're to get more in travel grant. My crofter here will arrange a horse and cart for us. Tomorrow, preferably. I assume you have nothing else arranged?"

Needs Must

The sun beat against the timber wall.

From the gap under the cheese-making shed, Black-Rag leaped out with a mouse in his mouth. It was not dead and he released it onto the slate pavings in front of her, patting it with his paw to liven it up. Astrid got up and killed it with a log. She'd been annoyed by the mouse-plague on the seter, and Emort had made her a box for her favourite cat so that she could carry him on her back when she went up with the cows.

She did not wear the ring. She told herself that it would not survive the heavy work, and hid it in a little leather pouch. Its tiny barbs had scratched her skin, and when it was off, the soreness disappeared from around her ring finger.

On the way up here she had turned only once to look at the demolition of the church. The spire was bare, the tiles gone, and she saw the workers around the church, they looked minute from so far away, and nothing in the village looked like itself.

The cows found their own way, some so eager they bounded up the slopes, as they knew where they were heading – up to the seter, then further into the mountains, to feed on the marsh grasses and new shoots on the dwarf birches.

That first evening, Astrid stopped halfway through milking the first cow, shoved back her milking stool and gulped the warm milk straight from the wooden pail. In the weeks that followed she churned butter and ate, and then ate more – butter, flatbread and *soll*, and then more flatbread, butter and *soll*, and once a week Emort and Oline turned up to help her make the cheese, which they then gobbled down in huge quantities.

Black-Rag brought her another mouse. Astrid grabbed it by the tail, and as she flung it over the wooden fence, she saw a man walking down from the mountain carrying a rifle and a large kill strapped to his back. Adolf from Halvfarelia. He changed direction on seeing her, she opened the gate for him and he sat down so that he could rest his burden on the ground and ease himself out of the straps. The animal's horns were cut off. "Be that a reindeer doe?" she asked.

"Nay, 'tis too early in the year to shoot a doe. She might be carrying a calf. This here is a little buck."

"Oh, aye."

"'Tis too early to shoot a buck, really," said Adolf, "but needs must."

"Needs must."

"Aye, 'tis the same with most things."

He carried his kill on a wooden packframe that he had made himself, and told her that he had been in the mountains for two whole nights before seeing any animals. Astrid lifted his rifle and said it was heavy; he told her it was an old chamber loader from the Kongsberg gun factory. She gave him milk, butter and flatbread, so much that he was unable to eat it all.

"Thank ye kindly, Astrid," he said, wiping his mouth on his sleeve. "I be well fed now for the trip down." There were, they agreed, probably enough folk on the road for him to meet someone with a horse who could give him a ride.

He put on his packframe and got up to leave. "She be gone now," said Adolf. "The old church."

"Aye, that she has," said Astrid.

"It'll be queer."

She nodded.

"I can see, ye didna like it. That they took her down."

"I dread going down to the village."

"Did ye hear that the bell fell down?"

"Emort was up here and told me."

"Strange goings-on."

"Strange goings-on, aye."

She asked if he had built a new wall and door for his sheep byre yet.

"Aye, that I have," Adolf said. "And it all turned out right for ye?"

She said that it had, but in such a way as to deter any further questions. She gave him a piece of cheese for the road – the freedom they gave their crofter was a small price to pay for meat of an animal as wild and free as this reindeer. Astrid felt there was something more they ought to have said to each other, a kind of promise she needed, but it slipped away from her, like a thought that was forgotten immediately after the realisation that it was so important that it ought to have been noted down. He went on his way, this stalwart man with his rifle and gunpowder and slaughtered reindeer. Before leaving, he had cut a fine chunk of neck for her. And she fried it in her own freshly churned butter, made soup with the bone, and for the first time since Christmas she ate fresh meat.

The next morning the cows needed little encouragement to leave their stalls, they gorged themselves on the grass outside the barn with lolling tongues, and she hollered and chivvied and drove them up to the marshes. The smells changed the higher she went, from the cool resin-laden fragrance in the shadow of the spruces near the seter, to the bitter odour of the new shoots in the little forest of mountain birch. The herd settled on a plateau and licked lazily on the dew.

Her thoughts drifted to Gerhard Schönauer. She put the ring back on and twisted it around her finger.

Life was so new now.

Yet she felt a void before her. She had tried to picture herself in Dresden, in Saxony, the land on the other side of Meyer's *Sprachführer*, but it was as though a sudden clarity surged down from the mountains and filled her mind.

She still wanted to travel.

The price was that she would have to stay there.

The farewells to her mother, father and siblings. The question of whether she would ever return home. The odd joke, that Gerhard had got her with the purchase of the church. He had promised that she would be an architect's wife, but did she really want to be an architect's wife? It sounded just as old-fashioned as being a pastor's wife. She could neither speak German nor *be* German. She might just seem to the locals like something he'd found under a bush. Somebody who smiled at her guests, but didn't understand a blind thing. And how would things differ down there? How would her day-to-day reality differ? What real difference could there be while she was a *wife*? And was Gerhard Schönauer the sound, honourable man she hoped he was? What hidden stranger might lurk within him, this man who sketched the world as he wished it to be?

The cows were settled, and none of the lookouts had warned of wolves or rogue bears; she headed back down, greeted familiar faces and continued, surrounded by animals and pastures, past greying log cabins and seter life.

As she rounded a ridge she saw him. There he was, far below, in a fox-coloured coat, with a fishing rod. He seemed uncertain about something, wrote a message on a slip of paper and stuck it in a crack in the barn door. Then he walked towards the gate, glanced back again, and disappeared in the direction of the stream.

Then she knew she would have to answer that big question.

I feel happy when I see him.

But happy enough to go with him to Dresden?

He disappeared behind the turning, and she stood staring after him.

Then she hurried down. Just before she reached the barn door, a little puff of wind caught the note and it fluttered down onto the doorstep, before another gust lifted and carried it away.

Listen, Astrid! she said to herself. That be him! Right there! Gerhard Schönauer! 'Tis now that the smelting pot be boiling, 'tis now ye mun step forwards and go toward the heat with all ye have.

She ran after him, and it felt so free, so real, as she yelled his name out across the meadows – "Gerhard!" – without caring if anyone heard, and she yelled his name again, took a shortcut through the nettles and junipers and yelled even louder: "Wait!"

The sun crept in through the narrow window. She snuggled into him, this was how they had lain throughout the night. Half-afraid that somebody might come, half-afraid of his leaving.

"Come in here with me," she had said. "Just this once let us lie indoors in the dry. From now till sun-up. For one whole night."

He told her he had to leave, and leave soon. "The last week in November," he said. "I'll be back then. But I can write."

"Donae write. Just come up to Hekne. Right up to the door. We shall be going away together anyhow."

In the middle of the night she sat astride him, eager, hungry, and did something she had conjured up during those long nights alone, and discovered it was both possible and pleasurable for them both. Afterwards they dozed off, and he woke her at an hour that did not exist in real time with something that *he* must have conjured up in his long nights alone, and the next time it was *he* who was woken, and the next time that they woke was now.

She lent against him, stroked his shoulder and gave his hand a little squeeze, this hand that could transfer a thought or a hope onto paper, and she knew that she had a greater ability than he to transfer thoughts and hopes into reality, and thus her thoughts continued to drift around like clouds in the sky.

He had persuaded the pastor to wait one more day. But a horse and carriage would wait for him at the parsonage the next morning, and now the next morning had turned into this morning in which they lay side by side, now.

They got dressed and she gave him some fresh thickened milk, from a pail she had left to stand in the cellar.

"November," he said.

She nodded, and sniffed. "November."

Then he was gone, and she knew he felt much as she did, half-mournful and half-excited, surrounded by a maelstrom of something unknown. He left his fly rod and fishing bag behind with some drawings. She hid everything behind a cupboard, went out into the sun and felt like a satiated bee.

Her day out with the cows was hot and strange.

In the night she woke up.

It was dead still. She got dressed in the dark. The only sounds were those she made. She lit the fire, put on the coffee pot, then let the flames die. The embers slumbered around the old blackened pot.

It was then that she noticed it.

Noticed it in the same way she noticed two church bells that were no longer there. She felt him now, just as she felt the church that was not there.

And deep within her, in a place she had never known before, she knew that he had been there.

"So *Much* Happening"

Kai Schweigaard was struggling to sleep. It was midsummer, but he thought he could feel an icy draft around his bed, the air coming in gusts, as though from the beating wings of some cold, majestic creature. His bedspread felt oddly coarse, the tiny wool hairs pricked his skin, as thin and searching as insect legs.

He went downstairs into the living room, still in his nightshirt, opened the door onto the apple orchard and sniffed the summer-night air.

The apple trees had finished blossoming, and he walked between them down to the churchyard with no church. A few remains lay scattered about. He had put all the coins and rarities they had found under the church floor in a casket in his office. On impulse, the bell-ringer had dug his fingers into the postholes and found small discs of gilded metal. Brushing off the earth they had discovered pagan figures hammered into their surface. One showed a helmeted man with a raised arm, another a marriage ceremony between a jøtun and a human being.

It was then that he realised that this had been a place for the worship of gods since time immemorial. For rituals, even sacrifices. Perhaps a pagan altar had been torn down to make way for the stave church. Perhaps the discs had been placed here so that the pillars of the new Christian faith would rest on the ancient Norse faith. Or, then again, had the intention been that the new church should keep the old faith down?

Regardless, some seven hundred years ago a priest must have said the same things as he had: "We cannot build our new church in an inferior place to the old one. Pull it down!"

Ida Calmeyer had written to tell him that she "understood". Her letter was as reserved as her acceptance of his marriage proposal had been. Ah well, he thought, get back to your mission, Kai Schweigaard. There's nothing else for it but to push on. With or without love.

Further inside the house he heard Oldfrue Bressum opening a door, followed by the familiar sounds from the kitchen.

"Oldfrue Bressum!" he shouted.

"What do the Pastor want this early?"

"He wants a big plate of bacon and eggs and fried potatoes."

"Right ye are. So ye plan to eat more heartily now the German has left."

"It has nothing to do with him. By the way, make the coffee stronger from now on. Put two handfuls in."

"Two handfuls in one pot?"

"And ask the stable boy to get the driver and two horses ready for nine o'clock. I'm going to pay a visit on Herr Gildevollen."

He emphasised the phrase "pay a visit", and not without reason. The team who should have demolished the old church had originally been contracted to build the new one too. But after the ensuing chaos the deal had crumbled, and a landowning farmer, Ole Asmund Gildevollen, had eyed his chance to nab the best team in the village, on haggled-down wages, to build him a new farmhouse.

Gildevollen was the nearest thing to a grand farmstead in Butangen. Its lands had been plotted according to an ancient custom; the would-be settler was put in a boat with nothing but an axe and steel fire-striker, and he would then run alone from Lake Løsnes and up the valley side, where he lit bonfire after bonfire to mark his boundaries. It was not enough to be greedy and light one fire and then another miles away, he had to run between each and keep them burning, since the boundaries were not valid until darkness fell, and he could only claim the land encircled by the fires that he managed to keep alive. The fires that had marked the land that became Gildevollen glowed in a large square that stretched from Lake Løsnes and up the steep slopes at the top end of the village, an achievement never surpassed.

In more recent times, Gildevollen was admired for its avenue of white-flowering hagberry trees that led up to the courtyard and farmhouse. It was nigh on impossible to grow these in Butangen, but Herr Gildevollen still knew the traditional way of sowing them. His family were used to thinking big, so he had ninety holes dug on each side of the avenue and forced his workers to eat the berries in their porridge. Being slightly poisonous, the berries loosened their bowels, at which point they ran down, did their business in a hole and covered it with earth. This porridge was served for days on end, until all one hundred and eighty holes had been sown and fertilised, and later that summer little trees started to shoot up.

It was along this lush avenue that Kai Schweigaard travelled that morning, in his freshly painted cart drawn by two golden-brown Døla horses. The driver had clean clothes on and swung proudly round the flagpole before asking a young boy to fetch Ole Gildevollen out to see the pastor.

In a sun-drenched spot with a lovely view over Lake Løsnes the work team was busy with the new building. They stopped, touched their hats and stood there. Schweigaard could see that they had made good progress. The foundation wall was made of neatly hewn granite, and the horizontal log timbers already reached the men's shoulders. They were using raw timber as was the custom, and the newly stripped pine blinked in the sunlight.

But Ole Gildevollen did not come out, instead he sent a reply saying that the pastor should come *in*. Schweigaard would discover later that Gildevollen had not meant to be rude, but was listening to Trond Stenumgård tell him a story about the weekend. The sheriff of Øyer had gone to stop an impromptu after-auction dance, but had got drunk himself and thrown Einar Garverhaugen's hat onto a roof. Stenumgård was in midflow when the pastor's message arrived, and Ole Gildevollen forgot himself and sent the boy back with a careless response.

This aroused Kai Schweigaard's sudden wrath. All his life his fiery temper had brought both benefits and problems, but this time it exploded like perfectly laid dynamite. His voice thundered out across the courtyard, and as though he was God's last man on earth he yelled that he would give Ole Gildevollen a thorough thrashing if he didn't come out this minute!

A heavy timber crashed to the ground. Eight carpenters stood open-mouthed. Ole Gildevollen came out and apologised, and after a brief discussion under the flagpole it was settled. Schweigaard would have his team back, ten men initially to lay the foundations, the rest following as soon as was practical.

"The framework and walls will benefit anyway from being allowed to dry and shrink for a year before the windows and doors are put in, isn't that right, Herr Gildevollen?"

"Aye, that's a fact."

"We're agreed then," said Kai Schweigaard.

The next day, as the new church wall was being marked out, another problem cropped up. The best burial plots had always been located close to the church, and for centuries families had paid substantial sums to have their family graves there. Moss-covered and impressively big, some of the gravestones bore thirty names, but now they had to be moved to make way for the bigger church, they had to be ripped from the earth and put some place else.

"There's nothing for it," said Kai Schweigaard.

Soon he was visited by eight landowners, who had never been contradicted in all their lives. Two were set on easier solutions, for example a plaque in the new church, since, in fact, their ancestors would rest beneath the new church floor. The other six refused to move their gravestones to the spot suggested by Schweigaard, despite its being on a sunny and attractive slope, since local gossip had snapped up the plans, and there were already scraps over how best to name it: Grandees Pile or Biggety Hill.

Schweigaard brought the eight families down to look at the site. The graves *had* to be moved, or they'd end up with a church that was no bigger than the old one.

"You see," said Kai Schweigaard, "we've no choice."

The farmers stood there with their arms crossed. Schweigaard looked about him. This cemetery was governed by . . . yes, by blessed chaos. The wooden crosses were weathered and all the gravestones were crooked. The grass was straggly, and the earth lumpy after decades of the villagers doing their own thing. Few had dug deep enough, the graves were not in rows, and some did not even face towards the sun of the resurrection in the east.

Schweigaard cleared his throat. "Very well, gentlemen. Let's pull your gravestones further out so they're still near the church, in the same position as before. We needn't throw aside all the old customs."

The farmers exchanged glances. They seemed to doubt that this was really Schweigaard talking.

"But how will the Pastor do that? Are we to move the dead?"

"The dead have returned to the earth long ago, and this earth will not be touched. It is their memory we honour. Not the dust. We'll redesign the cemetery and place the stones more neatly. Into neat rows with walkways between them."

Over the next weeks the foundations of the new church were raised, and fine-quality materials were fetched from the sawmill at Breia, while further down the slope, in a small area set apart and surrounded by large hanging birches, six men worked with bearded axes to build a beautiful free-standing bell tower. The bells were to hang directly beneath the roof, housed in a box-shaped room with large openings to ensure that the sound carried well, and nothing was said about what the large room below it was to be used for. The village blacksmith forged the locks and hinges, strong and highly ornamented, the like of which folk had rarely seen before, and they wondered why Schweigaard insisted that the door handles and handrails should be made of brass, especially since it had to be brought all the way from Hamar.

The carpenters who were building the new church had a bigger, but less pleasurable, task ahead. They studied the plans and asked themselves if the construction wasn't rather over-simple. Wasn't it dreadfully . . . plain?

Soon, however, the knocking of hammers sounded across the village. When it rained, sawdust ran between the gravestones, when the sun came out the fragrance of fresh pine floated on the breeze, and some weeks later the framework was in place and a row of trusses ran like the teeth of a saw against the clouds.

"There be so much happening," said a little boy who was following events. Oblivious of the fact that, for many, this was cause for alarm.

The pessimists gathered outside the cemetery walls to spread their forebodings, determined that every little mistake, every bruised thumbnail, every missing saw-blade, be seen as an ill omen. But Schweigaard held them in check. He asked old Borgedal to make sure the carpenters did not mumble any old spells during their work, and kept the church work going in the makeshift chapel in his parlour. He distributed the hunters' bounties every Monday as before, and the villagers stopped calling him the "new pastor".

He inspected the building site each day, and oversaw the churchwarden's work equally carefully. Gravestones were straightened and put in regular rows. Strictly speaking none of the stones stood over the right graves anymore, but since nobody had ever been quite sure who lay where, and since there was no great tradition of visiting graves, no strong objections were raised, except by the schoolmaster, Giverhaug, who griped and grumbled, but Schweigaard paid little heed to his protests. They sorted out the bumpy ground and the overturned gravestones that folk had stumbled over, and later that summer Kai Schweigaard saw something he had never seen before. A widow came to sit by her husband's grave. She chatted away as she lay a bunch of columbines framed by ferns. Then she moved to the cross that stood over a daughter who had drowned, and beneath it she laid a bunch of water lilies that she had probably fetched from the edge of the lake.

By the autumn the new building was recognisable as a church, and the raw timber walls gleamed under boughs of yellow leaves. But the hammers beat less methodically, many of the men had to help with the harvest and seemed unworried about exactly when the church might be finished, so long as the joinery was good. When the potatoes and grain had been brought in, work was resumed and the October frosts came. But increasingly Kai Schweigaard wandered about in the autumn chill, wondering why he saw nothing of Astrid Hekne.

The Crossbar

That autumn darkness closed in quickly. And in the darkness another darkness took hold, a darkness that no daylight could drive out; she was in the blackest of black nights, and she knew that not even the gas lamps in Dresden could shine through it.

She remembered it now, with more clarity each time she conjured it up, that evening with her grandfather, which she had partly forgotten and partly suppressed, because he had become so strangely morose. But now she remembered it, and she touched her belly and knew why she remembered it. What one sister had said to the other. "When the weave be woven we two shall return."

She knew there was a way to find out more about unborn children, but it had to be done at night when there was a moon.

And right now it was shining over the fields.

Astrid walked between the brewhouse and the barn and into the forest. The farmhouse was dark and hushed, the animals were calm. She walked where nobody would see her. Stepped carefully over the beck, and went up to the cart-road at the top of the village. Here she quickened her step and stopped looking over her shoulder. The road narrowed between the tall spruces. A breeze came and went, and with it the clouds came and went before the moon. Whenever it went dark, she had to peer up between the treetops to check that she was heading in the right direction.

All at once she became unsure of the way, despite having been here so many times. She began to think of Kari På Vona, who could suddenly appear out of the forest. She had always ridiculed those who believed in her.

Just before the road split in two, she heard the babbling of a stream, and knew that she was almost there. She took off to the left, and following the stream upwards she came to a log cabin in a clearing in the forest. She lifted her hand to knock, but the door slid open, and Widow Framstad came into view, lit by the tallow candle in her hand.

"So, ye have come, Astrid Hekne."

Astrid nodded and looked down.

There was only one reason why young girls came out to this cabin alone, and that was because they were with child. The village midwife was as ancient as an ore-pine, she could make medicines from plants, her usual advice to folk with headaches was to drink a decoction of goat-willow bark – *why* it worked nobody knew, but it worked. It was said that she knew ways to stop a life before birth, but nothing was known about how she actually did it. What was certain, was that she had brought most of the children into this overpopulated village, some claimed she had attended five hundred births, others that it was many more.

Astrid had a friend who had gotten with child when she was fifteen, she had gone to Widow Framstad to remove the infant while it was still small, but the old woman had refused, saying it was too dangerous. The only solution, she said, was to give birth, register the child in the *kirkebok* with all the other illegitimate children and make the best of the rest of her life. On her sixteenth birthday the girl gave birth to a son, and this boy was now four years old. The girl was still unwed, and Widow Framstad never let slip who the father was. Her births were accomplished without any scolding or commotion, no matter how protracted they might be. A sense of security would descend when she arrived at a farm, and she even succeeded in saving women whose babies were breech, though *what* she did nobody knew, since she demanded to be left alone when things got difficult; and usually, after an hour or two, a scream would be heard, and the door would open onto a pale, sweaty mother with an infant at her breast. There were times when there were no screams, then she just left the farm with a heavier midwife's bag and nobody ventured any questions, they just adjusted to the silence.

Widow Framstad went to a spinning wheel and turned it. She rocked her upper body from side to side.

"I have heard tell," said Astrid, "that it be possible to find out if it be a boy or a girl."

"We can find out more than that."

Widow Framstad took her hands. Feeling the rough skin against her own, Astrid started at the old woman's closeness and the suddenness of the touch. She began to sway and thought she could hear a clanking sound, echoes from another life, of something that had wandered through the generations and was here in the cabin with them now.

"Ye be filled with doubt, poor lass. About what the future may hold."

"That mun be true of all the girls that come to ye. That they be in doubt."

Widow Framstad continued to hold Astrid's hands and started to hum. She was known for such eccentricities, both before and after a child was born. The instant a child arrived, she would demand that a hymn book be placed at the head of its crib. It had to be dressed right arm first, or it would be left-handed. And she always took care to throw a glowing ember into the water in which the baby was bathed and ordered that it must not be emptied out before the following day, when the sun was up. Otherwise, the *jordfolk* – the earth folk – would smell it and take an interest in the child. Particularly now that there was no church in the village. Newborn babies had to be protected in the old ways until they were baptised. A pair of scissors was always laid beside a girl, and a knife beside a boy. Only when they had been baptised could the hymn book and the scissors or knife be removed.

"I have followed events down in the village," said the old woman. "It be the German, aye? Or be it the pastor?"

Astrid pulled her hands away and did not reply. The old one guided her to a stool and comforted her.

"I just came for advice," said Astrid.

"And ye shall have advice. But what ye fear, in *here*," she said, banging her bosom, "is whether there be two bairns inside ye, and not just one."

"How can ye see that?" asked Astrid.

"'Cos I knows there be twins in your family. I donae suppose anybody ever told ye, but your great-grandmother gave birth to twins."

"She did?" said Astrid. "Nay. That canna be right. Naebody has said ought of that."

"That be because your grandfather's twin brother died at birth, and there were nay more bairns after that. The Heknes told naebody, but I know how hard it were for your grandfather. He always asked himseln if his brother might have been a better farmer than he."

Astrid took a deep breath.

"I came here mostly to find out how best to prepare myseln," she said. "If ye can find out what time of year the bairn will come. And, aye – whether there be two."

"Naebody can know if there be two till the first be out."

Astrid swallowed.

"Ye be afeared, lass," said Widow Framstad.

"Aye," said Astrid. "Afeared as never before. I – I who do nay frighten easy."

The midwife asked what she feared most, and when Astrid answered, the old woman flinched.

"Be there ways?" said Astrid.

"Ways to take a child?"

"Nay. Ways to know if they shall be born healthy."

Widow Framstad placed her hand on Astrid's belly, and seemed for a moment to be debating with herself, before saying:

"There do be an old way. But ye must believe in't."

"Be it dangerous?"

The old woman shook her head. "Nay. Not in that way. But it'll start ye thinking, and that too can be dangerous."

"So, what be this way?"

"The crossbar. Ye mun ride the crossbar."

Astrid said she did not understand.

Widow Framstad nodded towards the corner, where there was an old warp-weighted loom. Astrid understood less and less. The old woman pointed at the long shaft that ran horizontally through the warp yarns. The loom was ancient, the wood had shrunk so that its grain was like raised veins, and it was imprinted with the sweat of hands, just as the bell ropes had been.

The old woman handed her some yarn, Astrid asked no more, sat down and threaded it through. It was a solid green, she knotted it firmly, then added a red yarn, and a pattern began to emerge of its own accord. The old woman went out into the late evening, saying nothing more, and Astrid was left alone in the log cabin. The clanking sound she was sure she had heard persisted, and she went on without knowing how long she was meant to continue or what was expected of her.

Eventually the old woman returned, and Astrid stopped.

"Now ye mun rise and take out the knife ye have in your waistband."

Astrid looked at her. Her knife was under her shawl and out of sight.

"And cut off the running yarns," said Widow Framstad.

"But then I shall surely ruin it all?"

"That's what mun be done," said the old woman, and Astrid did as she was told and slashed the yarns so the weave collapsed, then Widow Framstad freed the crossbar and led Astrid onto the floor and put it between her legs like a hobbyhorse.

"Now ye shall ride it. Put it well up into your crotch. Aye, just do it, there be naebody looking. And go like *this*," said the old woman and drew a pattern in the air.

Astrid did what she was told. It did not feel as though she were riding anything, rather it was as though all the possible forms that a weave might take on a loom were talking to the unborn life within her.

"Keep going. Aye, in a circle."

Astrid went round six times before the old woman told her to stop. "Now come with me."

She guided Astrid out onto a grassy bank and to a stool near the grindstone. Through the hazy moonlight Astrid could barely see the cart-road below that led to the seters.

"Ye mun wait now," said Widow Framstad and took a step back. "If the first person who comes along this road be a man, ye shall give birth to a boy. If it be a woman, it shall be a girl."

"Stay with me," said Astrid.

"Ye mun be alone."

"Naebody has reason to go out so late at night. And there be barely any moon tonight. There be nought to see."

"Do ye understand nowt, lass? Someone shall come. Do nay spoil this with your chatter."

She padded off, and Astrid sat and waited. She fidgeted, expecting her familiar clear-headedness to return, to tell her to get up and go home. Then the layer of clouds thinned, and the moon cast its light over the forest and the cart-road below.

She glimpsed something moving. A man, a huge man, with an oddly shaped body, who looked as though he was carrying something heavy, a kill perhaps. She tried to see the man's features, but suspected he was not from the village.

Then Astrid realised that this person was not from any village. Only she could see him. And as he drew closer, she saw that he was not struggling with some burden. What she was seeing was a young man stuck to another young man. They were coming down the mountainside, slowly, in a halting but steady rhythm. Suddenly they looked in her direction. Astrid was startled and raised her arm, and they instantly fell in a heap. They did not separate, but staggered to their feet and stood staring at her, until she slowly lost sight of them; they dissolved, and all she saw was the cart-road as before.

After Four Wet Months

Gerhard Schönauer was standing in front of the Hopperstad stave church when the first snowflake fell. It was mid-November.

He had spent four wet months shivering outside stave churches all over Norway. Horses and carts, treks, rowing boats, church spires, leaden skies. A mire of time. Bleak hours spent sketching on damp paper, endless mix-ups over travel timetables, leather soles that never dried, a nasty cough deep in his lungs.

But he had finally done it. He looked at the church, and

looked at the leather portfolio which held all his drawings, and knew that these buildings were now preserved for eternity. His trip was over. He had fulfilled J. C. Dahl's work, having completed studies of eight stave churches, which would comprise the last volume in *Exemplars of an Exceedingly Sophisticated Timber Architecture from the Earliest Centuries, in Norway's Interior Landscapes*.

The church which it had been most urgent to capture, and had been first on his itinerary, was Garmo. He had arrived late in the evening, only to find that it had already been demolished, the altarpiece, framework and entire contents already scattered after an auction, and so he had headed straight across the mountain and managed to draw Reinli. The Hedalen stave church was in a terrible way, but still standing. In Ål he drew the church during its actual demolition – a brutal and undignified affair – after which the materials were sold off as timber frames and cladding, while the decoratively painted staves were destined to be used as supports for the roof of a farmhouse. Two beautifully carved staves were thrown on the back of a cart before he managed to draw them. He had a wasted journey to Tuft, where the church had been removed the year before, although he was told that if he followed the River Numedalslågen he would find several churches that were not on Ulbricht's list.

Schweigaard had had the foresight to supply him with a letter of recommendation; it was surprisingly complimentary and gained him access to bare attic rooms in draughty parsonages, with local pastors who were amiable enough. Although they all had the same chilly grey air about them as Schweigaard. They were ashamed of the churches they administered, and none asked for copies of his drawings, they preferred not to think about these houses of God with rotten floorboards, leaky walls, sinking foundation walls and crooked spires. They had real problems to deal with. Hunger, alcoholism, suicide.

Schönauer travelled on. The larger parsonages were well preserved and situated high up on grassy slopes. Meyer's *Sprachführer* had presented Norway as an old-fashioned but proud and splendid place, but it made no mention of the harrowing differences between rich and poor. He passed through iron gates, knocked on doors, sat upon stools with his hat in his hands, waited an hour, waited two, and was finally allowed in to see a worried-looking priest and present his errand.

In Borgund he had been given peace in which to work and a lovely warm room, but to get there he had travelled by stagecoach for two whole days in the wrong direction, after a misunderstanding at a staging inn. This was his last real setback, however. Every day he forged a deeper understanding of the locals, he tackled the dialects that changed at each stream he crossed, and soon he felt that, despite his cough, he had mastered his task.

Out he went among the gravestones, up went his easel. In the raw autumn air, his paper grew soft and his fingers grew cold, and he usually only spent a couple of hours outside and completed his drawings indoors. His workdays were haunted by a face. Any dark-haired girl he saw made his pulse quicken, kindled a hope that was instantly dashed, because it was not her.

Of course it was not her. His pencil strokes would loose their power, and often in the evenings, by a solitary lamp, it was *she* who took shape on the page.

A summer love in Norway. The taste of her, so complete. A precipitous promise in the mountains. A great task. To move a church. To switch the bells. To deceive a queen. To marry on the whim of love. Two bodies on the same sun-warmed rock. An oil painting that was still drying. Unseen forces in wind and bronze.

His sense of loss and his painstaking work made the architect in him grow. His understanding of the construction that had so eluded him in the church in Butangen deepened. The word *stav* – "stave" – was too flimsy, surely a more suitable word was *søyle* – "column". Columns that had once been proud, tall trees. Yes, they should have been called column-churches. As high as a pine tree could reach, so too could the nave in a stave church. Cut down these pines and set them out in a rectangle. Link them with *andreaskorsene*, then make walls and floors, add a chancel, a spire and a roof that reached as high as you dared. The forests were endless, time and human endeavour unlimited, and the building would last for ever.

As long as times did not change.

But without her his longing had nowhere to go, it gathered in his pencil and transformed into a creativity, the equal of which he had never known. He began to draw these churches at tremendous speed, with uncanny precision, yet with spirit. He started to dream about stave churches. Arches and pulpit doors, portals and aisles drifted through the night, they started to assemble themselves in the form of one perfect church with features from each, and in this church he saw Astrid Hekne in an exquisite Prussian wedding dress. Then one night, as he lay on a hard bed in a loft in a parsonage in Sogn, he suddenly woke up and knew what he must do.

In the flickering light of an oil lamp he began to sketch it out. A stave church with the best of all those he had seen. A single, tightly unified construction. The lines came of their own accord, for half a year he had done nothing but live with stave churches and an all-consuming love, and now these things came together in a belief that he could design a modern stave church, and he worked on the new while visiting the old.

When he finally reached the end of his itinerary his shoes and trousers were worn out. Water seeped through the soles of his shoes, making it almost impossible to stand still, and turning his feet white and wrinkled. His overcoat no longer kept the wind out, and in his draughty lodgings a sore throat and cough were his only companions. Each church he left behind, he said farewell to for ever. They would all disappear in flames or under the crack of the crowbar.

But this new church – it could actually be built.

As a rule he was mercilessly critical of his own work, but this – he said to himself as he looked at the drawing he had laboured over for so many hours – this is perfect. The church rose up into the heavens, a pact between building in wood and faith in God. Magnificent yet temperate, as stave churches might have been if the art of building them had been allowed to mature over the centuries. A perfect development of the wild play with angles and jutting roofs. Simpler and purer, with judiciously selected embellishments. A giddy spire, tall and slender windows that followed the building's desire to stretch upwards, a shout towards heaven, a tower in which the largest of church bells could ring, ring to awaken the last soul in the universe.

The snowflake was not alone when it came. Soon white granules settled on his drawing. He looked up at the clouds, folded his easel and went to pack. With a protective sheet of thin paper between each drawing, and cardboard for support, he made a large parcel of brown paper which he smeared with grease and sealed with wax to keep out the damp, then he lay wooden panels on it to form a case, which he secured in a canvas cover with rope handles.

Yes. He would always remember Dresden, but more than that, Dresden would remember him. The fairy-tale adventure had direction now, solidity. Norwegian ages transported through snow and mountains.

Finally he gave free rein to his homesickness, a homesickness no longer linked to Butangen, Memel or Dresden, but to some future home, the residence of the church architect, Herr Gerhard Schönauer and his Norwegian wife Astrid, with chrysanthemums on the window ledge, schnitzel on the plates, and oil paintings displayed on papered walls. And soon, sons and daughters playing *bro-bro-brille*.

He was taken by rowing boat deep into the Sognefjord, where the last drawings he made on his trip were of the old stave church in Fortun, which had been modified so greatly that it looked like a grain silo in the United States. It was still impressive on the inside, but a new white church had been built beside it, and it stood forlorn and cold and dark and ready for demolition, and the local pastor said it would be on offer for eight hundred kroner. Gerhard enquired about help in crossing the mountains back to Gudbrandsdal, but the pastor frowned.

"You really want to go there?"

"Yes. By the 1st of December."

"That'll be difficult. If you've enough money you should take the boat round instead, to Kristiania."

"But surely that will take weeks?"

The pastor shrugged. "Winter's on the way and I doubt you'll find anyone to take you over the Sogn Mountain. I assume you don't have any experience with skis?"

"Skis? No. But it's only just started to snow."

"Down here, yes."

He had to pay double to get a guide and packhorse to take him over the mountain to the Bøverdalen, and early next day he set out on a journey that nearly killed him. When they reached the treeline the snow fell, heavy and wet. His guide unhitched two pairs of skis from the packhorse, but barely looked back when Gerhard lagged behind. In the mountains they followed the cairns, which were so close to each other they would have been visible in a violent blizzard. Indeed, not long afterwards, when the weather worsened, they found themselves in just such a blizzard. They stopped for a moment and ate slices of dried ham with their backs to the wind, and his guide spat in the snow for luck, saying that if they got to Røysheim all would be well.

As the evening closed in his guide turned and shouted that they *must* get to Røysheim. Gerhard hung limply from his ski poles, jabbing them into the snow and dragging himself onwards, while his coughing fits got worse. After an eternity he heard loud knocking on a door in the darkness, and when he awoke next morning, his guide was gone.

In Ottadalen it was viciously cold. He was poorly dressed for the time of year, delayed by several days; his cough turned into a fever and the journey became a bitterly cold torment behind horses with ice crystals in their manes. At Fossheim a bright moon shone over the frost-night as they waited for a change of horses.

Then off again through the icy air.

The wind was sharper than ever, it found its way into his throat and through his clothes. The sledge continued its descent past Bredevangen, driving along narrow valleys. The wind pursued him right to the door of a staging inn, where he collapsed, unable to manage any food. He had to lie there a whole day, almost forgot his portfolio as he left, and remembered very little before he reached the middle of the Gudbrandsdal, where he spent the night at Skjeggestad. He got to Fåvang church, found no coach going further, and began to walk the last stretch.

Behind him he heard a thin, metallic ringing. Sleigh bells. He saw two horses approaching, light brown and frosty. They turned a corner and disappeared behind a ridge, but re-emerged surprisingly quickly. Clumps of snow dangled like pendulums from their manes in rhythm with their movements, two men sat on the sledge, jovial fellows from Hjelstuen who offered him a ride. Little was said in the biting cold. Over the next ridge he confirmed for himself that the northern end of Lake Løsnes was frozen, while the southern, deeper stretch lay open and steaming. The men did not stop to check if it was safe, and as they sped out onto the ice the sound shifted to a sharper tone, as the hooves of the winter-shod horses came out onto the ice.

Halfway across the ice, he thanked them for the lift and said that he'd prefer to walk the rest of the way. He gazed about him, and stopped for a moment in the middle of Lake Løsnes, in full view of Astrid Hekne, and thought: This is how it looks when an architect returns.

Up on the side of the valley, where he had first seen the stave church earlier that spring, stood Schweigaard's new church, freshly hewn and pale. Its tower was nothing special. Just a little pointed cap. J. C. Dahl would have said it was devoid of any style.

And now he, too, had – or soon would have – the status and experience to pass such a judgment.

The men were clearly not finished, to judge by the sound of hammering and sawing up there. Below the church he saw an odd log building whose purpose was a mystery. Seven or eight metres high, a smaller top floor with large openings onto the sky in every direction.

He reached the shore and looked towards the barn. There were no footsteps around it, nor did he set any there. It was a clever move, leaving the deep snow untouched near the barn. The pastor's idea no doubt. A perfect seal, in which a footprint would reveal any attempted theft.

He walked past the new church, and as he approached the parsonage he thought that he would light a fire in the cottage, shave and warm up.

Then go up to see Astrid at Hekne.

Entering through the gate, he was taken aback. There was smoke rising from his chimney. What a friendly welcome!

Schweigaard must have got word from the sledge drivers that he was back. Perhaps Oldfrue had even made his bed?

He knit his brows. The snow in front of the cottage had been trodden flat. A half-used stack of birchwood stood by the door, and judging from the large quantity of bark and sawdust the stove had been lit in there for several days. He opened the door and was met by the smell of strangers.

The parsonage itself felt familiar, he remembered the resistance in the door, the creak of the floorboards, the oppressive silence and Oldfrue's gaze. But something had shifted. The house seemed different. In the dining room he heard humorous banter and laughter, and as he came closer he heard German being spoken, very loudly.

The voices of enlightened men with fine phrases and continental habits. The loudest voice transported him back to a high-ceilinged hall at the Dresden Academy of Art, and his confidence withered and he knew that in a second or two he would be like an obedient dog on a lead.

Kai Schweigaard was sitting at the dinner table with his back to him. On either side of the table sat Professor Ulbricht and Courtier Kastler, smartly dressed in Saxon city-clothes and holding fine-china cups in their hands. They talked with a biting self-confidence, and shouted "Schönauer!" the instant he appeared in the doorway.

But what really made Gerhard sense trouble was how Schweigaard leaped up, and was so spectacularly happy to see him.

The Astrid Church

Kai Schweigaard stretched out in bed and studied the flames. Early in November he had had one of the small first-floor rooms refurbished as a bedroom, not just because it had pretty flowery wallpaper in soft shades of green, but because there was an open fireplace in the corner, the greatest luxury imaginable in a bedroom. A new maid was employed and told that she must light the fire at six each morning, without clatter or to-do, so that he could wake up to a warm fire; and that at half past six biscuits and a pot of coffee should be left outside his door. He indulged himself with a morning ritual of sitting barefoot in his housecoat before the hearth, in a wine-red armchair – also a new addition – with his coffee and newspapers. The post came more regularly in the winter, and he could now trust that his parcel containing *Lillehammer Tilskuer* and *Morgenbladet* would actually arrive each Wednesday.

These comforts were not a luxury, they were essential to his recovery after such an appalling year. He had put a few kilos back on, regained the colour in his face, and before the snow had come he had visited his mother – a stay that he had intended to last a few days but cut short, because she had nagged him about Ida Calmeyer and been generally unbearable. On his return home, he struggled with the fact that his confidence in life had been displaced by an increased mistrust, and he tried to curb his temper when things failed to go to plan. His clerical duties, the care of the poor, the temporary church in his parlour, the renovation of the cemetery, the delays on the building site, all helped the days to fly by. The most markworthy thing to happen was when an old woman from the top of the village, who must have been quite a beauty once, appeared in the doorway holding a wheat-sheaf the day after the harvest. With downcast eyes, she said, so quietly that her words were barely audible, that she was bringing him *skrøfterugen* – the "shrive-rye". Schweigaard had no idea what she meant, but after his initial awkward confusion he realised that she wanted him to take her confession, for which, according to an old custom, the pastor could be paid in rye. He led her up to his office, sat beside her and heard her confession; it was relatively innocent: in recent years, she had started to regret having had carnal relations with a married man who had later gone to America. He prayed with her for the forgiveness of her sin, sent her home with the certainty that God would look upon the matter generously, and hung the wheat-sheaf out for the songbirds which would soon be heading south.

He began to feel that he had things in order. Later that winter, the new church would be ready, and not only that: he would celebrate Christmas with a certain German out of the house for good. Once more he saw a glimmer of light in the shadowy room within him that he had believed had been closed for ever, and he even allowed himself to think that God was on his side in the fight over the girl from Hekne.

He had seen nothing of her all autumn, the girl who had always been so quick to find a pretext to visit him. When he fished for news from Hekne, he always seemed to draw a blank, even Oldfrue Bressum failed to come up with any gossip. Then a surprising letter arrived from Dresden, with a postmark that bore witness to a severe delay.

"*Sehr geehrter Pastor Schweigaard*" – all very courteous, yes, yes – "*Student Schönauer*" – yes – "rebuilt in the *Grosse Garten*" – I see – "*das Portal*" – yes – "*Transport der Kirche* ... sledges" – yes – "*Schwesterglocken*" – hmm ... what?!

They wanted to come themselves.

Here.

The professor and the courtier.

Soon.

"Nach Norwegen und Gudbrandsdal, um die Region zu studieren und dem Transport zu folgen" – to investigate the region and supervise the transportation work. It would be invaluable "in communicating the stave church's original cultural habitat to our public". They would arrive at the beginning of December, to tie in with Student Schönauer's return.

Kai Schweigaard bit his lip. It was one thing to violate the Seventh Commandment, another to stand face to face with someone and break the Eighth too.

After all, it was clear that they were coming to enquire about the bells.

He immediately sent a reply to say that the letter had arrived late, and that Herr Schönauer had his full permission to show them around, but that he himself would "be away for most of the time, attending clerical meetings".

They arrived promptly on the first of December, not just two, but *four* men with large quantities of luggage. Kastler and Ulbricht had each brought a manservant, one a bustling Dane in brown tweeds, who bossed folk busy wherever he went.

They collared Kai Schweigaard immediately. They wanted to see the materials, the portal, the church bells – and where, they asked, was Schönauer? They were pompous, demanding and *very* hungry. They would be in Norway for three weeks, and while it was still possible to cross the ice they would take a look around Gudbrandsdal, and then go on to Kristiania, where they had already visited the Collection of Ancient Artefacts and the remains of the Viking Tune ship.

Kai Schweigaard nodded and apologised, and said he knew no more about Schönauer's whereabouts than they, ordered his tenant farmer to slaughter a pig in their honour, and stalled them the next day by showing them the portal, still stored in the carriage shed. But Schönauer's delay was agonising.

"And what about the church bells, Pastor Schweigaard. Where are they being kept?"

"Down in some barn. Behind all the other materials maybe. Schönauer's been the one dealing with it. I'm really not privy to his storage system."

He made himself look busy and disappeared down to the new church, but by lunchtime they were at him again.

"This portal," Kastler said. "It raises a very interesting question. Why exactly did the doors swing inwards? It seems so completely illogical."

Schweigaard cleared his throat and explained to his guests, who stood with their hands behind their backs, listening and nodding, that, as they could see, Norway was a land with lots of snow, and that it was easier to go in and out if you didn't have to shove your doors into snowdrifts.

"Besides," he said, "doors can get stiff. If they swing inwards, they can be kicked in. And then be closed again with another kick."

"Hmm!" said Kastler. "The first is logical. But the second makes no sense at all." He went over to the dining-room door. "Look. I can surely just grab the handle and pull it towards me, irrespective of whether the door swings in or out?"

Schweigaard scowled.

"It takes some strength to open a Norwegian door," he said, sharply. "Especially when the weather turns. A door that swings inwards can be shoved with a shoulder at the top or kicked in at the bottom. If it swings outwards, well, you'll just yank the handle off."

Ulbricht interjected with an enthusiastic "ah!" before Kastler could say more. "*Fantastisch!* A whole world in miniature! We'll make sure to mention that in the book we're planning about the church."

Schweigaard excused himself and went out to Oldfrue.

"No sign of Schönauer?"

"What?"

"Schönauer – is he coming? Have you seen anyone coming across the ice?"

"Not another German in sight," said Oldfrue Bressum.

In a bid to quieten them down, Pastor Schweigaard invited Mons Flyen, the foreman of the sledge drivers, round for coffee. With the pastor acting as interpreter, Flyen set out their plans for the church's transportation. Not that they had any real plans as such, they simply intended to carry the main structure like any ordinary timber load, only more carefully, and put any fragile items onto smaller sledges. Flyen had made a good impression, despite being unaccustomed to drinking from dainty china, and sweating because he was too heavily dressed. He reassured them that his men would take care not to scrape the timbers against each other, so that the "marks of grizzled age", as he described the centuries-old patina, were not worn away.

Flyen left, and then, as if by magic, Schönauer appeared in the door.

He was emaciated and coughing badly. Professor Ulbricht bombarded him with questions, and he seemed completely dazed.

Then Kai Schweigaard understood.

They had given him no notice. In an instant, he saw what Schönauer really was: a pawn on a chessboard.

Kai Schweigaard stared into the hearth, finished his coffee and tossed the grounds into the flames.

He had recognised it in himself recently too – and did not like it – a certain hardness to which he resorted to get things done. If he were with Astrid, he could soften and regain the colour in his life.

He settled back in his chair and let his imagination roam; he saw himself waking up beside her, a mild summer morning that turned into a warm summer day, in another parsonage, in a town, with a bakery and a twice-weekly postal service, far from Oldfrue Bressum, and strongest of all was the image of the slender, bare calves of the young pastor's wife, near the white-painted chair-legs in the parlour, her embroidery on a corner table, laid aside because they had important issues to discuss, her competence, her sound judgment, her hand on the helm as their ship passed over the rocks beneath the water.

New Year, he thought. Then *they* would be gone, leaving Astrid Hekne and the church bells behind. All he wanted was for them to leave, for this fuss to be over with, to let Schönauer tell his lies about the bells and cart all the old stuff away, so that he could hang the Sister Bells in the new bell tower, ready to ring Christmas in.

He lit a paraffin lamp to light his way along the hallway. He could hear Oldfrue Bressum banging about in the kitchen. He found her tired and grouchy.

"We should have a farewell dinner tonight," said Kai Schweigaard. "Perhaps you could make something in the German tradition?"

"We know nowt about German traditions here."

"Pork ribs will do fine. And stuff some sausages for lunch. They like those."

Oldfrue Bressum moaned and said she did not have the staff to do anything so fancy.

"Get someone to help you then," he said. "Astrid from Hekne, for example. As before."

She shook her head and returned to her work, muttering something that was half drowned out by the clatter of pans.

Kai Schweigaard left the kitchen. It was almost as if she hadn't wanted him to catch what she said, as though it would be too painful for him to hear. What was it she had said?

Something about Astrid soon being "unable to do any heavy work"?

He went up to the bedroom in which Schönauer was staying. They urgently needed to talk. About how they should fix things. Today, they would all go together to inspect the barn, after which the haulage would be set in motion.

He knocked, gave Schönauer time to wake up, then knocked again.

Carefully, he pushed the door ajar.

"Herr Schönauer. Are you asleep?"

He walked in, lifting the lamp.

The bedroom was empty, but the air was thick, he recognised *his* odour, in a corner there was a chamber pot. He knocked against it with the toe of his shoe. Dark-yellow urine slopped about at the bottom. But there was no overcoat on the stand, and his leather boots were gone.

Out already? Now, in the December dark, as cold and tired as he was after his travels? He had looked so forlorn yesterday, as though looking to be rescued.

The swaying lamplight fluttered over two open cases, one filled with clothes, the other spilling over with paper, sketchbooks and artist's materials.

Kai Schweigaard bent down and picked up a brush. Long and worn. Used and cleaned, used again and cleaned again. Tubes of paint, flecked and crumpled. Pencils, sharpened until they were mere stubs.

There were some drawings of Butangen, truly beautiful they were, one was almost certainly of Norddølom, another seemed to be of Spangrud. Summery, verdant, lively. For the first time he took in how skilled Schönauer actually was. How meticulous. These drawings were not just good – some were so exquisite that Kai Schweigaard lost himself entirely in them. He put down his lamp and spread the drawings over the floor, he paused at a series of sketches of a church that was unknown to him, it was uniquely beautiful, but was not set in an identifiable place like the rest.

So unusual – so lovely was this House of God! Tall, narrow Gothic windows that stretched upwards towards the tower, topped by a row of smaller windows, like flames on the tips of other flames. The main door was big, but surrounded by ornamental details, and a thick undulating form, which he gradually realised was a serpent, although there was no head to be seen, instead there was just this undulating movement, as though a serpent had flung itself about the door and dived into the ground.

But where in Norway was this church?

Then he recognised the grassy bank, the cluster of birch trees nearby, the parsonage above it to the left.

It was here. Schönauer had situated it here in Butangen! This opulent bouquet of Schönauer's imagination had been inspired by *this* place! A searing pain went through Kai Schweigaard as he realised the opportunity that had been missed. To think, if such a building could have been erected here!

Above the drawing was a title in small block letters.

"*Die Astridkirche.*"

He went cold. Then his eyes welled with tears. Then he grew angry.

The Astrid church?

He rooted on through the drawings.

And then, painted in oils, he found a portrait of Gerhard Schönauer and Astrid Hekne, shamelessly recognisable, in front of a brick villa. He pulled it over to his oil lamp on the floor, but it had other sheets stuck to it, so that more were dragged with it.

Finally, he saw what he longed to see, but could not bear to see.

Astrid Hekne.

Not just her face. The whole of her. Without clothes.

Dozens of drawings and paintings. As she was, but as he had never been permitted to see. Naked, young, clever, smiling. Willing.

She smiled just like the prostitute in Pipervika. And as with her, someone else had been there before him.

And she would soon be "unable to do any heavy work".

He would never see Astrid Hekne naked. Other than in the memory of this wretched moment, down on his knees, on the floor of a room that stank of Gerhard Schönauer's piss-filled chamber pot. An odour he felt might always surround her.

Those Who Are Leaving Butangen

"*Vielen Dank* for a delicious breakfast, Pastor Schweigaard! First-class milk and eggs!" Kastler drained his coffee cup and clapped his hands together. The manservants crammed the last morsels of pork into their mouths.

Gerhard looked about him. He could not make eye contact with Schweigaard, who was just sitting there drinking his coffee, sip after sip, in a strange, almost compulsive rhythm. As for himself, his throat was so sore that he could barely swallow.

"I'll second that," Professor Ulbricht said, clapping the napkin to his lips. "Thank you for everything, Schweigaard. It's been fascinating for us to see this country, with its snow and timber and those amusing skis the children play with, but we must get back to reality now. The time has come, Schönauer. Your time. We shall go down now and view the treasures. If you only knew how proud I am of you!"

Play-acting, thought Gerhard. I should have known. Take a final-year student, one of the best, with ambitious Prussian officer's blood in his veins, who works for months on end, in the belief that he stands to get the credit. A young man raised away from Saxony, with no family to intervene. Coming here in secret, the two of them, for a fun little demolition-holiday in the *Norwegischen Gebirge*. They'll climb down from the freight train when it pulls into Dresden, where the applause will ring out for this quirky gift for the queen. A professor and a courtier, both at the height of their careers. They'll lift their hats and nod to the brass band to strike up, as the hissing of the steam valves fades. Make neat comments to the reporters from the *Deutsche Allgemeine Zeitung* and *Dresdner Anzeiger*. While I will be as insignificant as the humble stoker.

"You look rather pale, and you're perspiring, Student Schönauer," Kastler said. "Aren't you well?"

"I have a cold. From working outdoors."

"Well, well, you'll survive," Ulbricht said, giving him a slap on the back. "I went through your drawings last night. Two or three were slightly water-damaged at the corners, and some need a touch more work, but nonetheless: the collection has turned out even better than I ever hoped for. And now we'll be home for Christmas!"

Mons Flyen was waiting outside. In the hallway, Kai Schweigaard was the first to button up his coat. He went out onto the stone steps, freshly cleared of snow, and led the group down to Lake Løsnes. It was a crisp, winter-white morning, with bright sunshine. They walked three abreast, footsteps creaking: Pastor Schweigaard, Kastler and Ulbricht in their polished leather boots and hats with tall crowns, Mons Flyen following at a distance in his black work gear, and at the very back Gerhard Schönauer in his threadbare coat. The deep virgin snow around the barn had been cleared, presumably on Schweigaard's orders that morning, since there was now a wide and neatly cut pathway leading straight to the door.

"*Meine Herren*," said Schweigaard, stepping aside. "Herr Schönauer! You have the key. You must show us our old church now, and then we shall say our last farewells and wish it luck on its journey!"

They swapped places in front of the barn door, and Gerhard unlocked it. The smell of tar and age were fainter now in the cold winter air. The drowsy breath of a dragon, this, the last air it would breathe in the place it was about to leave. Behind him, Gerhard heard impatient chatter as the others craned their necks, kicked the snow off their boots and followed him into the narrow gangway between the materials.

This, he thought, was the smell of summer. This, and the smell of Astrid Hekne. For a moment he forgot the others, forgot the shocking encounter he had had with Astrid earlier that morning, and he used a few quiet seconds to just look. It was as though the entire church had been caught in the shards of a broken mirror. In the light that crept through the gaps in the log wall he made out carved objects alongside half-rotten beams, here and there an ornate stave behind a church pew, and hundreds of labels, all numbered according to his own ingenious system.

Kastler and Ulbricht pointed and talked excitedly, but he was not following what they said. His attention was focused on the patches of snow he saw on the floor, snow from the sole of a shoe. Someone had been here earlier that day. Behind him, the door had been shoved wide open, so that sunlight flooded the gangway all the way to the rear wall where the altar stood. An elaborate carving of gilded flowers glinted from the deep shadows, and Kastler pushed past him to get further in, followed by Ulbricht.

They stood in the middle of the barn and gazed about them,

in hushed silence, as though they had been let into a bank vault. Ulbricht lifted the corner of a sailcloth to study some carvings on a stave, Kastler spotted the pulpit and stood there nodding, they put their heads together and exchanged some words, before Kastler pointed towards a corner of the barn.

"Ah, there they are. The famous bells. *Die Schwesterglocken*," said Professor Ulbricht.

He headed for the two smaller church bells.

Gerhard followed the two men, and felt his heart start to thump when he saw that someone had moved the planks that had hidden the Sister Bells further back in the barn. He pushed past Ulbricht and Kastler and stepped towards the small bells, but before he could turn to the two men and say anything, Kai Schweigaard had rushed over to the Sister Bells.

"You are mistaken, Herr Schönauer!"

He picked up a knife and sliced off the knot with which Astrid had tied the sailcloth.

"*These* are the Sister Bells," he said. "Those who are leaving Butangen shall take the goods they rightly deserve."

He grabbed the sailcloth, and it slid over the silver-bronze, allowing them to see the inscription that ran around the rim. At the back, where the letters on the disrobed bell went into the shadows, the last word was barely visible: "ASTRID."

Months without Blood

Gerhard had promised her Dresden. Kai had promised her a stroll. But Astrid Hekne knew that these would come to nothing, that nothing would come of anything. And on the day she realised this, a flinty obstinacy gripped her. She walked alone, she hid away in the barn, and she stopped asking questions, for the answers would mean nothing anyway.

Her belly grew larger and larger. She said it before they saw it. Her father was resigned, her mother angry. Emort cried with her, Osvald shook his head, her younger siblings understood nothing.

"Aye, a fine fix ye have put us in," said her mother, and with that she had said it all. Illegitimate children were always undesirable, but for ordinary folk they were less of a catastrophe, in the greater scheme, than if the intestines of a workhorse got blocked.

It was very different for a girl from Hekne, moreover the eldest.

For Hekne was still, despite its crooked slate roofs and rickety barns, a farm held in high esteem, the seat of an honourable family whose tenants knew they would not be thrown out, and whom the blacksmith could rely on to settle its bills, a family whose reputation meant that the father was never contradicted.

She was now a black stain in this acanthus pattern. The girl who had run into the forest with a stranger. She might get married, but never well married. And, whatever the case, the baby would have to be placed with another family, so that she could start again with the new man.

The day after her visit to Widow Framstad, she had walked upstream to Daukulpen through the autumn leaves, to the flat rock where she and Gerhard had lain that summer. The sun still warmed it during the day, and she sat there and prayed. Then she knelt before the pool. The water was still and black and seemingly bottomless. She pointed a finger at her reflection, at the eyes – it was impossible to distinguish whether she was pointing downwards or had been swallowed up by the water and was pointing up towards herself, and she thought: This is how I shall look when they find me.

Clenching her fist, she punched her face; her fist broke the water's surface and she shattered her reflection. Her face remained distorted and trembling for a long time, and she got up to leave, before it could right itself.

In the days that followed, she often gazed down at the large building where she knew Kai Schweigaard was well fed and warm. Below the new church was a handsome bell tower, and she taunted herself for not having said yes to his invitation to take a stroll. This stroll would pretty quickly have led to a church aisle, with the senior rector's gaze upon them both.

But only small bells would have rung for them.

Months passed with no blood, and then came the cold, her belly grew, the ice hardened, and then came that week in early December. A week devoid of any good. The week of Gerhard Schönauer's return.

He had set out for Hekne early on the first morning of his arrival. His return to her was not as he had imagined just a few hours before. But he mustered the courage, which Schweigaard had never had, and walked across the snow-covered farmyard to hammer on her door, in full view of everyone. He shared his bad news, and stood strong when she gave him *her* bad news. He wanted so much to keep to his promise of taking her to Dresden. And he would one day. But his employers had come to the parsonage, he was being watched closely. And he was less sure now what the future might hold, life as a poor, unknown architect could be hard. He bowed under the weight of her news about the children she was carrying, looked tortured and strange, went from feeling sadness to feeling dismay. They parted, and she was glad when he left, the combined weight of their fears was so huge that the ground would have given way beneath them if they had come too close.

She stood and watched him go. Brushed the others aside and went into her room, and there she had to face the image of herself in the streets of Dresden. I'll be there with two children, they'll be hungry, and how will I find food for them, there in Dresden?

Then she heard what Kai Schweigaard had done. There was a time when she would have torn open the door to his office and asked if he had forgotten who Judas Iscariot was.

She remembered her grandfather's words: "Wickedness and foolishness, not in a small way but big, these be oft remembered too."

"One day ye shall bleed," she muttered. "One day Skråpånatta will come, Herr Schweigaard, and *ye* too shall be swept to your doom when the earth has been scourged. *Your* face appears somewhere in the Hekneweave too."

The next day she went back to Daukulpen, wading through snow that clung to her and dangled from her thick woollen stockings. She went out onto the ice, it creaked, she knelt down and swept away the snow with her sleeve, and stared down into the black water that reflected her face; but, obscured by the ice, it was hazy – her face was without definition. She was like one of Gerhard's unfinished sketches.

All was snow and silence. The Sister Bells would never ring in Butangen again. Why had they rung on that day when she and Gerhard had been lying on the rock by Daukulpen? To announce that children were inevitable, put there by fate? Or did they want to warn her that something even worse lay ahead?

The nights were not to be counted on for rest. Tossing and turning in bed, she sifted through future possibilities, but they would melt into the night, and return, looking forlorn, only to disappear again like children desperately seeking food.

Should she go down to where the sledges were, get one of the drivers to take her, follow him to Dresden? What shape would defeat take there? She turned and felt the bodily warmth of the best possibility: America. But then she must travel before the children were born, or she would have to pay for three tickets.

Best to stay on the farm perhaps, make the most of her stubborn determination. She was from these parts, she would be talked about, but she'd have it easier than the girls of humbler means who trudged about alone, and only got work during the harvest. She had seen them, these girls who wrapped their babies in rags and left them on the edge of the field while they raked the hay, and then occasionally went to the forest to suckle them. They existed, these women who survived alone, but they grew dissatisfied and bitter, and she knew that such a germ lay within her too.

She took the ring Gerhard Schönauer had given her and turned it between her fingers. Don't do this to me, she thought. God, be good to me. Don't harm them. Not my children.

Thirty Fur-Clad Men

Døla horses and sledges were gathered near the barn. Ten men wearing thick furs – most with chunky moustaches, the hallmark of a skilled long-haulier – began work.

Their responsibilities were clear, the plan simple. There would be about three hundred loads in all. Eight sledges, four trips a day. Ten days. First down to Fåvang church, where they would reload onto larger sledges, before crossing Losna, free-riders on a sleeping river, over ice so thick that you could not hear the breath and heartbeat of the streaming water below. Then onto firm land at Tretten and down to Lillehammer, before going out onto the ice again, across Lake Mjøsa, by-passing Hamar and straight to Eidsvoll, where the goods would be reloaded onto a freight train for transportation via Sweden to Germany. They had considered going via Hamar, but this would involve reloading twice, since the tracks on the Hamar to Eidsvoll line were owned by a different company and had different gauges, besides which there were doubts as to whether the hand-brake freight trains were safe for such a precious cargo.

The most difficult stretch would be the first. Haulage over Lake Løsnes had followed the same route for centuries, across the black ice on the north side of the lake. Here the sledges would travel at a good speed, but after that there were steep hills and slopes to be negotiated to get up to the marshes, and only the lightest loads could be taken that way. Heavier sledges had to be pulled along the riverbank all the way to the southernmost end of the lake, a dismal roadway where the steam from the open water turned into rime on the horses, turning them into grizzle-bearded beasts.

The men started leading the horses back and forth in front of the barn to tramp the ground hard. There were ten in the team this morning, they expected a further twenty, and many more sledges to arrive later in the day. Quickly and unsentimentally they carried the materials out into the snow, so as to plan their distribution. The staves that had held the church up for centuries looked helpless and lost in the white snow, old and gnarled, the same brown as the workhorses.

The usual flock of onlookers gathered, their gaze wandering between the new church and the barn. Suddenly they caught sight of the long procession of horses and sledges speeding over the ice towards the village, sleigh bells ringing. It was not the speed or magnificence of this sight that surprised the villagers; it lay deeper: it was unknown for such a big procession to come to Butangen to *fetch* something. Cast-iron stoves, glass for windows, blades for saws, always came *to* the village, and, having arrived, remained there until they crumbled or rusted away.

Gerhard Schönauer stood with his logbook and recorded which sledge each batch of items was loaded on. Nobody could catch his eye, he said little. Professor Ulbricht and Courtier Kastler stayed close, dressed in elegant bearskins, purchased at great expense from Hallstein Huse.

The first load went off without ceremony. Up onto the sledge, secured with rough hemp rope, driven from the village and out into the world. The next followed swiftly afterwards, without need for any directions or instructions. Each sledge returned after a few hours, and later in the afternoon Gerhard Schönauer accompanied one of the sledges to Fåvang to check how things were going. He took out his logbook again and began making notes. One of the workhorses came up and nudged him from behind, a giant of a horse, reliable and gentle, when he patted it it was like patting a fur-clad mountain. The Gudbrandsdal horses reminded him of the workhorses of his childhood in Memel, which used to come down to the docks carrying timber from the forests along the Russian border, plodding steadily through life, without any expectation or thanks or the capacity to accept thanks.

At the evening meal, Professor Ulbricht, wearing a grey suit with a tie tucked into a waistcoat, announced that he and Kastler would go to Lillehammer the next day, they would accompany the sledge carrying the portal, book into a hotel and undergo "a historico-cultural study of the region". They had, it was revealed, collected an entire chestful of trophies from the "untamed north", treasures that Gerhard assumed would come in handy when they were bragging in Dresden over a glass of cognac. Wooden platters decorated with traditional paintings of flowers, silver-mounted hunting knives, carved spindles and flour scoops, filigree bridal broaches and finely embroidered women's bonnets.

They thanked their host for their supper and left early for bed.

Gerhard Schönauer stayed at the table, while Kai Schweigaard followed them into the hallway, saw them out and then stood in the doorway of the dining room.

"Look at me," said Schönauer.

"I am."

"In the eye. Have you any idea what you've done?"

"There's nothing unique about them," said Kai Schweigaard. "Take them with you. It's just a bit of bronze."

Gerhard Schönauer started to cough. He rose and went up to him. "You thought I was some sort of weakling. A pathetic little artist."

Kai Schweigaard scoffed. "Go to bed, Herr Schönauer. You're talking above your station. The fact is that you have seduced an innocent young girl, and now you shall have to carry your cross. That's the real crime that's been committed here, and the sound of those bells will remind you of that when you're down there in Dresden."

They stood there.

"You already regret it," said Gerhard Schönauer. "That much I know you. But now you'll see what I am capable of."

He left, leaving Kai Schweigaard staring at his own reflection in the dining-room window.

The next morning, Kastler and Ulbricht left after making sure that the hauliers knew which were the correct bells, and taking Gerhard's drawings "to study their qualities in good lamplight". The Danish manservant waved his arms about, issuing orders, and then they were up on the sledges, bright-eyed and bushy-tailed, snug in their bearskins. They seemed to relish the trip like a Christmas sleigh ride.

Gerhard Schönauer continued.

He was used to the noises now. The grunts of the men as they drew breath before lifting, the snorting of the horses, the rasping of sledge blades, the thundering of hooves on ice, and, further up, the ceaseless hammering from the new church. He filled line upon line of his logbook, sent more and more of the church on its travels, and in the evenings he stood looking out over the landscape with an impenetrable gaze. He often looked up at Hekne, but thought of the day when the church bell had changed direction in the air and fallen towards him, and knew that these powers were the only ones he could talk to about this.

Down by Fåvang church the dark-umber loads arrived for reloading, piles of mysteriously carved tree trunks, like a shipment of logs from an enchanted forest. The men brought load after load, without a grumble, sweating as they led the horses uphill and shivering as they came down the other side. Snow-caked men and horses emerged from the forest's edge with an old church and set it next to another, newer church. Since he was needed both at the barn with his logbook, and at Fåvang to check what was being reloaded where, he was driven back and forth every day. All the horses knew the way now, and once or twice he took the trip back to Butangen alone, with the sledge empty, the Dølas strolling gently home across the frozen marshland.

Thus the traffic continued, like a shuttle on a weave, back and forth. Then one day Gerhard Schönauer took a small load on his own. He stayed some hours at Fåvang, then turned back. The next day he did the same thing, returning with new entries completed in his transport records. He continued doing this until the others had come to expect it. The movement of the crampon-shoed horse became lodged in his spine. Dependably, it swung off before the steep hillside and continued alongside the open water, near the shoal where he had fished that summer when everything had been different.

This is not over yet, he thought as he gazed over Lake Løsnes. A spiked tail may still lash out.

There in the Grey Frost-Smoke

Sleep spread the travel blanket over her at last, and in her dreams she walked towards enticing flowers, only to find that they pricked her and wound their stalks about her. Then all at once it was winter, and she went out onto Lake Løsnes, to where the ice was thin, and the deep took her and her children.

The nightmare receded. A gentle hand stroked her cheek, as her mother might have done if she were kind, but this was someone else, a woman who carried a great loss. Astrid blinked, thought she saw the stranger at her bedside, and the stranger said: "Ye nay be the sort who goes to the edge of Lake Løsnes."

Ye nay be that sort.

I nay be that sort.

She slept deeply that night; it was daybreak when she awoke and thought she heard church bells.

She sat up in bed.

Church bells sounded over Butangen. But they were not being rung, this was one endless sound, chime after chime was carried out beyond Lake Løsnes, flung against the valley sides then meeting its own echo that was multiplied and multiplied again. Then it was as though the bells were packed in, tighter and tighter, until only the echoes were left, and when she dashed to the window and saw the snow floating down, she felt a kick in her belly, and knew it was not an illusion.

She had heard the Sister Bells.

Folk had seen a black horse galloping across the ice on Lake Løsnes, its harness dragging after it, so fast that they had soon lost sight of it in the swirling snow. Having finally caught the runaway, they had to walk it gently for half an hour so its heart wouldn't burst. Onlookers flocked round, the hauliers returned from Fåvang church, and it was then that the story – the first version, at least – gradually took form:

The sledge carrying the Sister Bells had turned over on a slope above Lake Løsnes, at the southern end where the water was deepest and ice-free, and Gerhard Schönauer had been dragged down with them. The bells must have vibrated with each bump as they tumbled down the valley side, and their loud ringing had continued under water, fading as they sank until they reached the bottom and were silenced for ever. It was hard to tell exactly where the horse had broken free, since the warmth of the open water had rendered much of the shoreline snow-free, and the snow on the road above had been stamped down by all the freight sledges that had gone back and forth.

The snow went on falling in heavy, lazy flakes, melting into slush where the water was open, but everywhere else the new snow did what new snow always does – the ally of those in flight – it spread its white blanket over any sledge tracks or footsteps.

Some went out onto the ice, to its dark, steaming edge, to see if the German was floating there, but no-one dared go all the way, to the abyss that resembled the end of the world at a time when even wise men believed the earth was flat.

Two men shovelled away the snow outside a boathouse and

set out in a rowing boat. The morning light grew stronger and gleamed grey through the falling snow, but visibility was too poor for anyone to count on finding the body. They rowed along the shore, in a steaming no-man's-land between broken ice floes and open water, through sinister grey slush, and frost-smoke that veiled the dipping oars. The boat was visible to onlookers for seconds at a time, and then disappeared again, now and then folk heard cracking sounds as the keel hit ice, and it was at just such a moment, when the boat was out of sight, that a shout was heard. The boatsmen had found a rope, and on returning to shore they found, close to land, a leather-bound journal bobbing in the water. They opened it and the water trickled over the signature of the man who had arrived there in April: "Gerhard Schönauer".

The legend of the Sister Bells' end was moulded and then rendered solid that day, as quickly and irrevocably as when the bells themselves had been cast. That morning the villagers were agreed, more than ever before, that these were *their* bells, the *village*'s bells, because this had happened now and in their midst, and thus the old story of the bells was fused with the new. The need for an explanation led to all sorts of conjecture, and just as the stave church was a mix of faiths, old and new, the legend was also a blend. They agreed that God had been opposed to the removal of the bells from Butangen. Many expected that, on the coming Sunday, they would hear the Sister Bells ringing beneath the lake. The stories spread from one group to another, some crossed themselves, and nobody noticed that it was Astrid Hekne who ventured furthest out onto the ice, closest to the open water, even though most folk were now sure that he must have been dragged to the bottom or beneath the ice, and that it was doubtful he would surface there.

She went there because she wanted to be there.

She stood on the narrow stretch between the saw-toothed ice and open water, where the frost-smoke quivered over sleepy wavelets, because it resembled the place where she found herself now in her earthly life, midway between security and catastrophe.

"Out there lies your father," she said to the children. "The bells mun 'ave rung for him all the way down, as he sank and sank, and 't will be easier to remember him like this, and I shall be here, happy that he be so close to us."

A Mild Death, in the Circumstances

Rumours are the seeds of legends, light enough to spread on the wind, and quick to grow. By the time a truth has put down its root, rumours will have blossomed and become their own truths, because even the wildest fantasy has been told by someone, and this – the fact of something being told by someone – gives it a veracity, even if what is told is more than a little unlikely.

The first thing people should have asked themselves was, why a team of skilled hauliers, masters of sledge transport, weight distribution and the securing of loads, would allow a young stranger, a foreigner, to go off with the most valuable cargo of all, entirely on his own in the driving snow, with no other sledges ahead or behind, to offer him help should anything go wrong. The next thing that should have prompted questions, was that the ropes had come loose. The bells had been secured by men with forty years' experience, and should have survived the capsizing of the sledge.

These questions were only seriously raised when Mons Flyen

and the two oldest members of the haulier team arrived on the scene. Flyen sent to Lillehammer for Professor Ulbricht, and then walked the route from the barn to the site of the accident. The sledge's tracks were covered in fresh snow, but here and there he knelt down to dig beneath the surface, went to various viewpoints from where he could calculate distances and angles, took off his glove, brought his hand to his chin and tapped his finger on his lips. Word reached him that Herr Schönauer had been acting strangely on the previous day, and had insisted that morning that both bells be fastened onto the same sledge. Two other loads had been prepared as an accompanying convoy, but the black horse that had been harnessed up to the bells had grown restless. It bolted and took off, and the German had thrown himself onto the load, but could not – or did not want to – stop the runaway horse. Later the horse and sledge had been glimpsed between the trees on the other side, then the church bells had, it was said, started to ring loudly and the horse had come galloping back.

The case against Schönauer was convoluted and required an understanding of driving-reins, traces, whippletrees and clevis hitches, together with a knowledge of the terrain on the far side of Lake Løsnes, where nobody liked to go. It seemed that Gerhard Schönauer had caused the accident himself, and then either escaped or drowned. But such suspicions could never challenge the magnificent legend that was spreading, as clear and compelling as the sound of the bells themselves; namely that greater powers had intervened to fulfil the bell's intentions when it fell in the church, and killed the man who wanted to abduct them. This explanation was much better; it honoured the village, pointed the finger, was wise-after-the-event, and was impossible to disprove. Besides, it was inconceivable that this foreigner would sabotage the mission he had worked towards so eagerly and diligently since April. The truth had to be that this man had been punished by God. And to add grist to the mill: he had been seen with Astrid Hekne, from the farm that had donated the bells, and who was now with child.

But the hauliers investigated further, revealing ever more reasons for suspicion. Trodden into the snow, they found a rope that had been slashed with a knife. They stopped their work and refused to continue until they were guaranteed payment in full, contending that the deceased Schönauer had destroyed his own cargo.

Shortly afterwards something happened. Arvid Halle, a boy who was too simple to go out alone, was reported missing. He had gone down with his brother that morning to look at the workhorses, but had disappeared in the ensuing commotion. There was huge confusion out on the ice, and it took time before his brother noticed his absence. The crowd was busy working itself up, and Arvid's brother ran around yelling out his name, searching in wider and wider circles until he eventually caught sight of him in the forest on the other side of the lake. He was trudging through the snow from the north side, at some distance from everyone else, and he was dragging something heavy and bulky. It turned out to be a coat that had been wet and was now frozen into a formless lump with reddish creases. Arvid was pulling it along by the sleeve, leaving tracks in the snow behind him, and when he reached the crowd, it was instantly recognised as Gerhard Schönauer's fox-brown coat with the figures of eight embroidered around its buttonholes.

Arvid Halle had trouble making himself understood, but with his brother's help it was revealed that the coat had been found at the north end of Lake Løsnes. A long, thin line of villagers set off, the quickest first, with the stragglers at the end. They numbered almost a hundred, and when they got there they realised, somewhat reluctantly, that the day wasn't such fun anymore; that the casting of a legend is one thing, its material is fluid and workable, but the sight of a frozen man is something quite different.

He was lying face down, curled up with both hands tucked into his crotch, on a pitiful bed of fir branches, with wet boots and ice in his hair, before a heap of twigs that seemed to be the makings of a fire. A bloated matchstick box with a German label lay near his fingers. The mountain folk elbowed their way to the front, knelt beside the coatless body, and announced that the cold could play tricks on the brain, causing the victim to feel warm and tear off his clothes, after which fatigue would numb his brain, so that the poor wretch died what was, in the circumstances, a mild death.

But the prevailing powers, whoever they might be, had greater plans for Gerhard Schönauer than for him to die beside Lake Løsnes under the curious gaze of ninety pairs of eyes. He mumbled something in German, turned slowly, like a fly on a windowsill waking from the winter cold, unable to defend himself or understand where he was or who was observing him. There were more than enough men to lift him, and the same sledge which had transported the Sister Bells, was now used to drive him up to the parsonage, where they were met on the steps by Kai Schweigaard, who looked strangely troubled. Schönauer was carried into a bedroom, Schweigaard himself undressed him and gave instructions that the stove must not be fired up too quickly. When Margit Bressum saw Schönauer's fingers and feet, she said they must send for a doctor and a saw, since an amputation was on the cards.

Schweigaard knelt down and took Schönauer's feet. He held them for a long time. Then he grasped his hands and held them for as long.

"Fetch the crucifix in my office. And hang it over the bed."

Oldfrue did as he said.

"We shan't fetch a saw before we know that something must be sawn off," said Kai Schweigaard. Oldfrue was at a loss and flapped about the room, pulling the curtains and sweeping in front of the stove.

"That's not necessary," said Kai Schweigaard. "You must fetch Astrid Hekne. To look after him."

"Her? Here? Whatever can the Pastor mean?!"

"I mean what I say."

"But what'll folk say?"

"Let her sleep in the next room, send food up and give her the key to the door. I don't care what people say. From now all that matters is what God says."

Kai Schweigaard was on his knees in his bedroom.

And now murder, he thought.

If he dies, it's murder.

Shortly before this, Astrid arrived at the parsonage, he recognised her footsteps in the hallway below, but could not bring himself to go out to her. Instead he sat there, alone, so ashen-faced that the charwoman did not dare come in, writhing with regret over the moment he had betrayed Astrid Hekne and himself. Everything that had seemed so promising lay smashed and scattered. He might as well try to put the needles back on last year's Christmas tree.

He clasped his hands and banged the knuckles of his thumbs against his forehead until his skull vibrated.

Answer me, he prayed.

Answer me, God, why this pitch-black swill flows through my veins. Ashes, vinegar and bile. Tell me how to rid myself of it. Tell me whether I can be a priest at all, whether you *want* me to be a priest.

Hard floorboards. Bare walls. A darkened fireplace.

Answer me!

He knew very well – he preached it himself – that faith was only faith when it required no answers or proof. But this boulder lay so deep within him that he had no idea of its size, perhaps it filled him so entirely that the layer of earth in which something might grow was thinner than it might seem.

Once again he took out the worn volume that was not the Bible. "Never send to know for whom the bell tolls; it tolls for thee."

The next morning Ulbricht and Kastler arrived in a foul mood. He tried to pacify them with the explanation that the bells had sunk in an accident for which Gerhard Schönauer could hardly be blamed.

"I really am terribly sorry," said Kai Schweigaard. "But there's not much to be done. The contract has been fulfilled."

He said that Gerhard Schönauer had, despite a debilitating cold and headache, worked as meticulously and energetically as the first day he had arrived in Butangen, and now he was suffering from a terrible fever, unable to offer any explanation other than the most obvious: that the sledge had hit a tree stump under the snow and turned over on the slope, and that Gerhard had ended up in the water when he tried to stop the bells from rolling out.

"We'll talk to him," Kastler said. "Where is he?"

"He's in a state of confusion," said Schweigaard.

"He's *ours*!" snapped Ulbricht.

Schweigaard sent Oldfrue to get Astrid out of the sickroom, and then took them to him. The room smelled sickly and strange, and Schönauer was lying in a blue sweat under white sheets.

"Would you leave us alone, Herr Pastor?" said Kastler.

The professor and courtier stayed with Schönauer for a long time. When they came down to the living room, Ulbricht said, "He must have a proper doctor. As soon as possible. And we must find the church bells. We will offer a reward. Make it known that we will pay a hundred kroner for each of the Schwesterglocken if they are found within two days. Everyone must look for them! Now!"

"I doubt that anyone will be able to find them," said Kai Schweigaard. "I've no idea what happened, but Lake Løsnes is extremely deep. I can say this, though: we've been given two bells for the new church from another parish. I can offer you a swap."

"A swap?" Kastler said.

"Like for like. Bells are bells."

Kastler stared at him. Smiled faintly and scoffed. They left without saying where they were going or what they planned to do.

Next evening, Kai Schweigaard caught sight of something from the parsonage window. Far out in the dark, on the other side of Lake Løsnes, he could see a yellowish, flickering light. It seemed there were people with torches along the shoreline. He buttoned his overcoat and went down to the boathouses, where he met a group of villagers who also wondered what was going on. Four of them had headed off across the ice to see, but when the torches went out, they returned from the dark still ignorant of who the strangers were.

Envelopes between Psalms

Gerhard Schönauer woke up that evening but did not recognise Astrid. She managed to get a drop of milk into him, then he mumbled something in German and lay there trembling. She locked the door and crept in beside him again, to warm his frozen body. All night she lay at his side, alternately behind and in front of him, until she too began to freeze. Then she got up and went over to the stove to warm her own skin again, and thus she continued throughout the night. His fingers were badly frozen and she put them under her armpits, then on her belly, against the children therein, constantly moving them to keep them warm.

He became wet with fever. He tried to sit up, but fell asleep again. As it grew light she no longer dared to be naked; she unlocked the door and sat on a stool.

Margit Bressum came in with coffee and took the chamber pot away. Then there was another knock on the door, and Astrid called out that Oldfrue Bressum was welcome to come in.

"It's me," said Kai Schweigaard.

He stood close by the door. He was carrying his cassock.

Astrid's gaze wandered back and forth between Kai Schweigaard and Gerhard Schönauer, she swallowed and got up, but he shook his head and told her to stay seated.

"The bells," she said. "Ye—"

"Please don't say anything, Astrid. I have so much to regret, so much that it's a matter between myself and the Almighty."

He went over to the sickbed and asked if Gerhard had managed to eat anything. Astrid told him about the drop of milk. Schweigaard pulled up the duvet at the foot end of the bed and inspected Schönauer's toes.

"The professor and the courtier suspect him of having sunk the bells deliberately," he said. "Not that they understand why."

"The children," said Astrid.

"What?"

"He did it for the children."

"Why do you say 'children'?"

"There be two. I know there be two. Widow Framstad showed me."

A little time passed.

"Were you planning to leave with him?" said Kai Schweigaard.

She said that she had indeed considered it.

"You can't go back with him to Dresden now. The Germans know that the bells come from Hekne. They'll realise that he did it for your sake."

"I want to be with him. But we have nay the money to travel."

"He'll have to come back to fetch you all. But—"

"But what?"

Kai Schweigaard shook his head. "He's so ill that I'm not sure he'll survive. It would make a huge difference to you and the children, if they were widow-born. Do you understand?"

She said she did.

"I mun follow him later," she said. "He made the journey from Dresden to Butangen, I shall manage to make the journey from Butangen to Dresden."

"But do you *want* to marry him?" asked Kai Schweigaard, a lump in his throat so large that he could barely get the words out.

Astrid looked at Gerhard and said, "I do indeed want to marry him. Naturally I'd want to marry such a man as him."

A little shiver went through him. Then he shook himself, and said, "You don't have much time. The Germans may arrive with a doctor and a sledge as early as today. They need him for the reconstruction of the church. And precisely for that reason his life may be saved."

Gerhard Schönauer turned in bed.

Astrid got up and went to the mirror, and ran a hand over her hair in a gesture that said a life-weary farewell to the past. "I wanted it to be in a church. To wear a shop-bought dress. And to have proper wax candles all about us. With the bells ringing out for us."

"Nothing has turned out as it might have," said Kai

Schweigaard. "And it's all my fault. I don't suppose you have a ring, but—"

"I do have a ring," said Astrid.

"Send for me when he wakes up," said Kai Schweigaard, getting up. "The minute he wakes up."

Astrid went to fetch her Sunday clothes, and when her mother asked what she was doing, she replied they could all carry on as usual, since there was no church with an aisle for her father to lead her down. They had no idea that she was being serious, and she went back down alone. Gerhard had sat up in bed and eventually he managed, between coughing fits, to say a few words. Oldfrue put Astrid's hair up, and found a suit for Gerhard that she still had from her deceased husband. Moments later Astrid heard folk down in the hallway. Standing there were her father, Oline and Emort.

They helped Gerhard down the stairs and into the makeshift chapel in the parlour, and in front of the depleted remains from the old church the couple and onlookers took their places.

Kai Schweigaard stepped forwards. Inside the Bible, tucked between the first and second verses of the Book of Psalms, were two small envelopes containing marriage certificates.

They were wed in the middle of the room in the winter's light from the window, but as Kai Schweigaard said "God has instituted marriage", his voice broke.

Astrid Hekne put a hand on his shoulder, and with all three of them connected through her, she said, "Please say it all in German."

Kai Schweigaard nodded and completed the wedding ceremony in Gerhard Schönauer's language. He said "*ja*" to Astrid Hekne, his lungs gurgling, and put the latticework ring on her right finger.

A little later they were alone. She lay close to him and listened to him breathing. He gathered his strength and turned to her.

"Astrid."

"Gerhard?"

"*Schön ist, was ich sehe.*"

To Dresden with You

The torches flickered again on the other side of Lake Løsnes that evening. The next morning it was clear that at least eight men were involved in the hunt. They were led by Kastler and a stranger in a black coat, exceptionally tall, and those who saw him close up said he had a pockmarked face, which looked like porridge left to stand for so long it had begun to ferment.

The villagers formed an unusually united front during these days. No-one in Butangen would lend a stranger a boat from which to dredge the lake, nobody had a spare bed for the night, there was no food for sale, and absolutely no dry wood for a bonfire. The discovery of Schönauer was interpreted variously. Some thought the Sister Bells had taken their ultimate revenge on him, while others now saw him as their saviour, so that for some he was a guilty man who had paid the penalty, and for others a hero, but this quiet stretch of Lake Løsnes was now the Sister Bells' burial ground, and each dip of an oar into the water was a desecration.

A large crowd followed the strangers' activities, others went on feigned errands by horse or skis to obstruct them. Regular parties of villagers came and went across the ice, bringing fresh supplies of rumours about what was done and what was said.

Later that day, it seemed that a broken plank had been found at the water's edge. On it, marked in pencil, was a weight written in bismer pounds, identifying it as part of one of the crates made to protect the bells. But nothing else was found, and that evening there were no torches to be seen along the shore.

The next morning things turned.

A boathouse had been broken into, a boat taken, and on the opposite shore five men stood in a huddle, excited and pleased. They were gathered around a church bell. Still warm from the water, the falling snowflakes melted on the bronze.

"We've got you! It's to Dresden with you now!" said a man.

It was *Halfrid* they had found. Like a matriarch reindeer, the oldest and wisest of her herd, freshly slaughtered, she lay on her side.

The parsonage was quiet. All that could be heard was Oldfrue shuffling about and the clinking of coffee pots. Outside there was a thick snowdrift. The door to a bedroom was locked. A newly wed couple agreed on names for two children.

The day brought *kakelinna*, the annual spell of mild weather that hailed the coming of Christmas and triggered the baking season. And so it was, through slushy snow, that the Danish manservant drove up to the parsonage in a horse-drawn sledge to fetch Gerhard Schönauer.

He told Schweigaard that *Halfrid* had been found in the shoal, on the edge of the shelf that dropped abruptly into deep waters, and they assumed that the other bell must be at least twenty metres down, since the entire shelf had been trawled. The Dane said that the offer of a reward for the second bell still stood, but that they would in any case send people next year to locate it.

The villagers were watching every move, and when the sledge carrying Gerhard Schönauer set out from the parsonage there was a crowd on either side of the track, come to wish him farewell in the dialect he now understood.

Up at the parsonage, too, everyone had come outside, Kai Schweigaard and Astrid Hekne had followed him into the courtyard and they now stood at a distance from each other, their eyes fixed on the sledge, as it headed down towards the frost-smoke on Lake Løsnes.

I am losing him now, thought Astrid as the sledge set out on the ice. Now I am losing him.

The horse and sledge swung around so that it was in full view from the side, but it was too far away now for anyone to see whether Gerhard Schönauer turned to look back at Butangen.

Chain Brothers

Only the finer details were left to be done on the new church, and the sounds of saws and chisels were tamed now that the snow lay so deep. But the work was slow, carried out by pernickety carpenters who informed the Pastor that the church could not possibly be ready for Christmas, and they were likely to continue well into the winter.

Kai Schweigaard accepted their explanations. He made daily inspections, but on the whole he stayed in his office, near the stove.

Soon the villagers' talk turned to other things.

The freeze took hold. The *blåmørke* – the bluedark of winter – had already driven folk behind log walls. The sheep were scrawny that year, which meant that the cottages were gloomier than usual. The tallow candles were few and poor, and in their flickering light the stories grew longer and wilder. The frost penetrated deep into the ground, but at last Kai Schweigaard could see the fruits of his labours, as the coffins were taken into the mortuary and the door locked behind the dead.

In the parlour he baptised babies, one after the other, so many that his head reeled with their names. He invited the villagers to a Christmas service at Fåvang church, knowing full well that few would come. It was only a short trip to Fåvang to go to a *pols* dance or card game, but a long way to go for Mass. Nor did folk want to turn up like some homeless crew, to sit on pews warmed by others or suffer the bodily odours of strangers. So Kai Schweigaard held Christmas Mass that year in an almost empty church, and thus yet another new word was introduced that unhappy winter – a *Butangenmesse* – a Mass so empty of folk that it echoed from the walls.

But lying in the depths of Lake Løsnes was something that the villagers could rely on. Something with great powers, cast in grief and longing. Word spread that when the stave church was rebuilt in the faraway land called Saxony, and *Halfrid* had been hauled up into the belfry to ring out over the new city, *Gunhild* would answer her from beneath the water. And the sisters would go on calling to each other, lamenting and complaining, so that events in Dresden would be echoed in Butangen, and likewise the bell in Dresden would ring whenever anything significant happened in the village.

That January, the final chapter – and eventually the most important – was added to the legend of the Sister Bells. Arvid Halle, the simpleton who had found Gerhard Schönauer, said that he had been lured out onto the ice by a voice. He had made corn sheaves for Christmas, and wanted, out of kindness, to place one on the spot where he had found the frozen German. His sisters told him it was a mad idea, there were no songbirds out there, that he was too aggerheaded to go there alone, but it was busy before Christmas and Arvid went anyway. He hung the sheaf on a pole in the deep snow and then headed home. He had been ambling along as usual, sucking the snow from his mitten and gazing about him, when he heard sounds coming from the ice-free part of Lake Løsnes. At first he thought it was the lapping of water, but then it changed into a whisper that said his name.

He went to the very edge of the ice, and there the voice could be heard more clearly. It was a woman, a grown woman, he could not see her, but was sure "she were harmless", for she spoke in the Butangen dialect and seemed to know him, saying:

"Only seven chain-brothers can bring the sister bells together again."

Arvid's tale was believed – children like him who had difficulty counting and reading were thought to have other, rarer talents. In particular, it was the word "chain-brother" that convinced folk, since Arvid could never have come up with it himself. Many, even the very old, shook their heads and said they had no idea what it meant, but Widow Framstad had been called to a birth on a neighbouring farm, and when news of this event reached her, she remembered hearing the word from her predecessors, the oldest midwives; it was an ancient term, not used for decades.

"Chain-brothers," she said, "be brothers born without sisters between."

This awakened hope in folk, and they looked at each other and wondered if the bells would perhaps be reunited some day, one being fetched back from the land in the south, and the other raised from the depths of Lake Løsnes, and they pondered which was more difficult, and some whispered that Astrid Hekne was with child, but none dared to prophesy further.

Almost simultaneously – so close in time that she could not have heard this story from anyone – Gyda Braastad, a bright girl of sixteen, came running home with a very similar tale. This time the voice took on a shape, a woman on the ice in a long red tunic who called her to follow. She, too, seemed harmless, and she turned to the girl and said the same thing that was said to Arvid. Gyda said that the woman spoke "plain", and since Gyda had never been outside the village, they reckoned that must mean the figure had spoken in the Butangen way. Some folk asked her straight out whether it had been Astrid Hekne she saw, but Gyda shook her head.

Gyda Braastad quoted the same words as Arvid Halle, but with a slight difference. Gyda was sure that the woman had said *two* chain-brothers. This was explained by the fact that in the Butangen dialect "seven" and "two" sounded similar, and since "seven" made for a greater legend, it became the accepted truth that only "seven chain-brothers could reunite the Sister Bells".

The woman on the ice was seen a few times. Soon she was given a name, which alternated at first between the Woman in Red and the Lake Spirit, although eventually folk called her the Bell-Witness, a name someone professed to remember old Klara Mytting, who took so little space on this earth, going about mumbling to herself.

An Architect among Architects

Gerhard Schönauer was waiting for sunrise. He had slept for a few hours, dreamed of her and the children, and woken again. In the weeks when the fever consumed him, he was terrified of falling asleep, since whenever he gave way to his exhaustion he would stumble about in a snow-white hell in Norway, in a nightmare of tumbling church bells, black, frostbitten feet, of a faceless girl searching a lake for her children, before he woke abruptly, his stomach hard with fear.

He had lain for days in a sickbed, he had no idea where, and the doctor decided not to amputate his frostbitten toes and fingers, not that it made much difference, since even in the slightest chill they were stiff and without feeling. When they got to Dresden he was admitted to the city hospital in Friedrichstrasse to treat his pneumonia. He lay there through Christmas and woke up one morning in January and talked to himself in Norwegian to be sure that the previous year had not been a dream. His fingers hurt at the tips, and the first thing he did was to check if he could still draw. Three weeks later he could use a pencil almost as well as before. He was discharged, but the pneumonia persisted. His chest felt tight and wheezy, and the fever came and went.

One memory kept him going. Her face. His drawing stood on his bedside table, in a small frame in which he used to have a picture of his mother. As soon as the church was rebuilt his salary would be paid out. Then up to Norway again. Meet the children. Put things in order. Before coming back down again, together. On the first train with the last of the money.

He had promised this to her in two letters. He had received two replies and in both she agreed.

Soon he limped down from his loft room and out into the raw morning air. He had got his old room back in Lärchenstrasse, and in pain-free moments he felt grateful for all the noise that made his lodgings so cheap. These city sounds felt safe and homely. The noise of the railway and the reveilles from the military camp drowned out the silence of the north that clung to him.

His heels clicked on the cobblestones – even that was an

alien sound to him, in Norway the ground had always been soft. Mud, snow or grass, mute wherever he went.

On his left was the drill-ground. The soldiers came running and fell into line for inspection, nervous about the officers, and he thought about his father and brothers and regretted his tardiness in writing. He continued over Carolaplatz and onto the Albertbrücke. The bridge was arched, to let ships through; the climb that met him was only a slack curve, nonetheless it exerted him. Five men hung over the railings – he passed them there every morning, fishing in an open channel in the river, passing a bottle from one to the other, pulling up their lines whenever a barge glided beneath them.

Here over the Elbe the air was colder and sharper, he felt a prickling in his chest, a warning that a coughing fit was on the way. He bent over, grabbed in his pocket for the brown medicine bottle, took a swig and barely managed to swallow it down before the fit started. His shoes skidded on the ice as he descended the bridge, not because they were very slippery, but because he was unsteady.

The centre of Dresden was waking up. He took his place in the bustle, among the pedestrians and horse-cabs, avoiding the street-sweepers who stood there with their brooms, half-asleep; past the cafés where candles were being lit, past the newspaper vendors and the police constables who kept watch over it all. Being in the big city, he no longer turned to look when somebody shouted. Here, he was a small dot, too small to see, in the magnificent work of art called Dresden. Nearer the Grosse Garten the city sounds faded, and finally he reached the tall conifers. He passed the grey house where he lingered each morning, because there was always somebody practising a woodwind instrument inside, an oboe, a musician perhaps in one of the city's philharmonic orchestras.

Today he heard no oboe, and the window was dark.

He walked on.

Down at Carolasee he saw the tall hoarding around the building site, erected partly to keep thieves out, and partly to heighten the excitement when the church was unveiled. But perhaps most of all, Gerhard thought, to hide the difficulties involved in rebuilding a Norwegian stave church.

The nightwatchman, a grey-haired man wearing the palace's dark-green uniform, came out of the hut at the gate. A beautiful German shepherd dog rose from its lair and came, tail wagging, towards Gerhard.

"He likes you," said the nightwatchman.

Gerhard nodded and crouched down. "I like him too."

He got up and walked through the gate.

Before him stood the Butangen church, no more impressive than a skeleton. The *Dresdner Anzeiger* had published a long article about the church, in which only Ulbricht and Kastler were mentioned, as though they had single-handedly, in honour of Queen Carola, gone to the wilds of Norway and rescued the wooden church from oblivion and spiritual poverty. Gerhard himself was no more than a living packing slip, and he knew that ultimately he would be rendered as useless as just that – an old packing slip. Although all the materials and drawings were in place, his logbook had been spoiled when it fell into Lake Løsnes. The minute he had been discharged from hospital, he had been ordered to study the building materials and create a new overview, and just days later the reconstruction had begun, although somewhat haphazardly.

The foundation wall was now laid, built of rough-hewn stone – a fine piece of workmanship – and the twelve columns soared towards the sky. He had begun to call them "columns" rather than "staves". But from here the church refused to be rebuilt. The materials lay waiting in sheds and under tarpaulin. Ancient and warped, black or umber-brown, blond where they were supposed to meet another timber – points to which they now refused to find their way back. The joints either proved too tight, or the timbers fitted in one place but then jutted out at the wrong angle for the next joint. They tried this way and that, and an already suspicious Kastler was growing increasingly angry each time he visited, despite Gerhard's repeated assurances that beam no. H38 *ought* to fit against chancel arch no. F21. There were eight carpenters on the job, but they just stared at his drawings, none of them understood the principle, the thinking behind the church, they were a bullish lot and a couple were even a little stupid.

Halfrid was stored in the basement of the city museum, alongside a vast collection of statues from Italy and Greece. Of the bells, Gerhard said that the horse had been scared by something and that someone – no doubt someone who did not like the church being moved – must have filed through the ropes. When the sledge capsized the haulage crates containing the bells had started to slide. He had tried to guide them away from the water, but it had been impossible for him to control two of them; he became overwhelmed by their weight, was injured, fell out of the sledge, and then lost consciousness.

Ulbricht calmed Kastler down for a bit, and praised Gerhard for his drawings, but did not mince his words in telling him that he must oversee the rebuilding of the church, he must rack his memory and work out where each part fitted, after which he would receive his salary, and could return and take his examination.

"Then you'll be done," said Ulbricht. "Free to go out into the world. An architect among architects."

Gerhard shook his head sadly. He tried to regain some of the spark he had felt that December, when he had first crossed Lake Løsnes to fetch a church and a fiancée. He sat on one of the pews that was now in the middle of the building site. On its hinged door, in golden-brown letters, was the name Vestad, the name of a family who had once paid for permanent seats in the church.

He started to study some drawings, his gaze wandering between them and the stacks of timber, as though searching a map for his own location. Then his cough erupted again. Coming from deep in his lungs, it seemed to subside at first, but a tickling sensation warned him of a prolonged attack, which shook him until his vision grew blurred and he lost hold of his pencil and drawing, and grabbed the pew, coughing.

At the gate he heard the German shepherd barking. A rare event, since it was a good guard dog, and had got to know the whole team early on. But the barking continued, and he could hear raised voices from behind the fence.

Gerhard wondered who would want to argue their way in this early, and went over to the gate.

"Herr Michelsen?" murmured Gerhard. "Is that you?"

"Of course it is!" said Michelsen. "We want to see how it's going with our church!" He gestured towards the man alongside him. "I take it you remember my companion?"

Gerhard nodded and held back a cough.

"Good God!" said Michelsen. "You've got very thin, Herr Schönauer."

The three men stood and looked at each other. Michelsen was wearing a new long overcoat, a tall hat, and a beautiful green brocade vest with a silver chain leading to his pocket watch. The other man wore a brown suit with thin red stripes and a flat cap.

The guard tightened the dog's chain and let them in.

"Who sent for you? Ulbricht?"

"Nobody!" Michelsen said proudly. "We came from Leipzig yesterday evening. There are," he said, his Bergen Rs bowling out across the building site, "a great many Norwegians in Leipzig. Herr Grieg, Bergen's celebrated composer, stays there regularly with his darling Nina. They have close friends there, including a doctor, Herr Sänger, who recently got engaged to a young music student from Ålesund. They were here in Dresden to see the *grande entrée* of the church, with the brass band and flags, et cetera."

Gerhard looked at them quizzically.

"Well, I heard of its arrival via a letter to a mutual acquaintance. And we knew you'd need our help, but that you Germans would be reluctant to consult an outsider. A Bergenite recognises arrogance and pride when he sees it!"

The three men walked over to the church. Michelsen bent down and inspected the foundation wall, let his gaze glide up over the staves, uttering the occasional enigmatic "hmm!" or "well, well", before saying: "The church was transported by train, yes?"

Gerhard nodded. "And then taken by ship."

"Hmm."

"It doesn't fit together," Gerhard said. "It's as if it didn't like being moved."

"Of course it didn't like it!" exclaimed Michelsen. "We took the church down in Norway in early summer. Now you're trying to put it back together in the winter in an altogether different climate."

Three of the work team came through the gate. They surveyed Gerhard and the two strangers, crossed over to one of the sheds and stood waiting.

Michelsen's companion took a pipe from his pocket. He turned it over in his hand, and pointed its black mouthpiece towards the twelve tall staves. "The problem is," he said to Gerhard, "that the staves are twisted. Not warped, but twisted. If you could look at them from above, you'd see that the points where they are going to join the other timbers are at the wrong angle. But that's hardly something these moustachioed fellows would notice," he added, nodding towards the men near the tool-shed. "They've grown up with straw roofs and Bavarian beer."

"So . . . we have to wait until the summer?" said Gerhard. "For them to twist back into place?"

Michelsen shook his head. "No, we'll need to do something rather more drastic and labour-intensive. It involves steam and tension belts. Take us to your employers, and we can discuss payment."

A few weeks later, the staves were re-erected. And when the arches between them came into place, Gerhard Schönauer felt as though the church had been resurrected. It had regained its proportions, it began to live again, and with every passing day it grew before his eyes.

"So, it's going to be alright?" he asked Michelsen.

"Yes. It'll go pretty quickly from hereon. Then there'll be a few fiddly bits to do on the roof. But you'll manage."

"Are you sure?"

Michelsen nodded. "You've moved a stave church, Gerhard Schönauer!"

Gerhard walked up the steps. He stopped for a moment on the huge, flat rock that they had brought with them from Butangen, which now lay in the same place as before. He went in, crossing the temporary plank floor, and sat on a wooden crate near the back, close to where Astrid Hekne had sat when they had met in the church.

He looked around him. The evening sky shone through the open framework. But it had the shape of a church, the place already had the power of a church, and he put his hands together and prayed for her and the children.

He started to cough again, and he leaned over.

He must go there now. Help her through this.

He had shrugged at death when he was in Butangen, because

it did not affect him, but now that it did the torments that Kai Schweigaard had struggled with made sense, things were no longer black and white, but shades of grey. Shades that Gerhard Schönauer knew he would, after these ordeals, learn to draw and to paint; there *was* a great artist within him, and from hereon he also had the weight of the dead and living in his hands: two sons he must guide through life.

These thoughts were just taking shape when he felt a coughing fit building up again, it came like a horse at full gallop and bowled him down.

He sat in the church for a long time when it had passed, listening to the whining in his lungs. He thought of the day when he had arrived in Dresden and first seen the Academy of Art. The building was so big that it had taken him ten minutes to walk around it. He'd had to stroll to the other side of the Elbe to really take in the true magnitude of this brooding colossus. He had stood there admiring the roof adorned with a huge glass dome, lit from inside so that it sparkled against the sky, and at the top of the dome a gilded angel balancing on one foot with outstretched wings and holding a trumpet. He had gone back, he remembered, on that first day in Dresden, to look at the columns on the facade. Each bore a name, the letters chiselled into the stone and filled with gold.

STEINBACH – LEONARDO – DÜRER.

He wondered why there was no name on the outermost column, just a smoothed area, as though it had been left unfinished.

Sitting in the framework of the old church now, he finally realised the purpose of this empty space.

A master shall come from here some day, and that master may be you.

His name slid into place on the column. In honour of the Astrid church. The last breath of a thousand-year-old tradition in stave churches that had flowed through him and met in one unique building.

His memories of the stave church as it had been in Butangen began to merge with the framework he saw now. He imagined the spire rising, and high above he heard the sound of a solitary church bell that forgave him.

The church started to expand, growing in width and in height, the roof shifted form, took on the angles and shape of the Astrid church, it stretched out and lifted itself higher, the row of Gothic windows slid into place, and colours glittered through the leaded glass, and when the vision came to a close, he was sitting in the church he had drawn, and it was this vision that was sent with him as he folded his hands and slumped over, an architect among architects.

Kaiserschnitt

The frost lay over Butangen. The air was dry, and down on Lake Løsnes the north wind invited the snow to dance. In the winter's bluedark children played on their sledges, speeding down the valley slopes until their eyes watered, hollering as the blades rattled over the bumps.

At the bottom of the hill a sledge swerved into a snowdrift and the children tumbled off and laughed. They had almost mowed down a man who was walking towards them. He had quickly stepped aside, and seemed almost oblivious to the event. They stopped laughing when they saw his expression, and pretty soon they stopped playing, for they knew that he who travels with the lightest baggage carries the heaviest news.

It was the postman. He would usually have gone straight to the post-house, but this time he was heading for Hekne, because he had spotted a letter bearing a Leipzig postmark, a thick letter with a black mourning edge.

She cried for him all evening and long into the next morning. When she finally stopped, it was because she was worried that she might get cramps and harm the babies.

All you could have accomplished, she thought. You and I and us. Each day and the next. Your talents and strengths, all turned to dust, gone in a flash. Your smile, your hands, the voice that spoke so softly in German. So many blank canvases waiting, so many caresses, so many children, so many fly-fishing rods to be cast. All that you could have filled the hours with, the days, the weeks, the years. But they threw you into the earth and walked away, and strangers shall rot around you, you are dead now and alone, with nobody to say "*Ich liebe Dich*."

She sat there with his paintbox, the box that contained life as he had hoped it would be. She picked up the sketchpad and a pile of drawings, looked at the picture of them both standing in front of the fence, Herr und Frau Schönauer, the children, the brick house. And the strange painting that reflected what she had felt in the belfry, eerily sinister, but proof that he had seen into her very being as nobody else ever had.

Over the course of the evening she managed to collect herself. Collect herself with the same strength that the women before her had collected themselves, through avalanches and floods, tuberculosis and dysentery, frost-ruined harvests and barn fires.

The letter had been sent by a man named Michelsen. The envelope had been opened and resealed. The paper was filled on both sides, with his signature at the bottom. After introducing himself, he told her how he had visited Gerhard and about the weeks they had worked together. Everything was consistent with the last letter she had received from Gerhard. But he had not mentioned how ill he was. Michelsen wrote that Gerhard had been admitted to the city hospital with an untreatable infection in both lungs.

> We put a halt to the work that day and took Gerhard to the hospital, but on the way he insisted we go into the bank. We said that we had to hurry to the doctor, but he forced his way to the counter, even though he was coughing so much that they almost seemed reluctant to give him the money. He withdrew eighteen marks and sixty-two pfennig, and I have, as you will see from these two receipts, exchanged these for Norwegian kroner. From what I understand, this was his entire salary from the academy.

Astrid looked at the banknotes. This was reality. Money left by a dead man. He had passed away two days later and been buried at the Alter Annenfriedhof, with Michelsen, the work team and Professor Ulbricht present.

She slipped the letter and receipts into Meyer's *Sprachführer für Reise und Haus*, and reread a separate little note, also in Michelsen's handwriting.

> Dear Astrid,
>
> I am writing this at the Leipzig post office. Something occurred to me last night. Gerhard told me that you are pregnant. That twins run in your family. That you are worried about some kind of repetition of history. Leipzig is very near Dresden, and I meet many people here. I recently visited a German obstetrician who is engaged to a Norwegian woman. He regularly goes to Kristiania as a guest physician at the Rikshospitalet, and will be there in the spring. His name is Max Sänger. For years he has been developing a method for difficult births called a "*Kaiserschnitt*" or "Caesar

Cut". Unfortunately, it is still very risky. But I took the liberty of mentioning your situation and he is not uninterested in overseeing your birth. Ask for him at the birthing clinic in Kristiania.

Your friend, Michelsen.

A Ewe Will Nay Have a Better Birth

"I heard he be dead," said Widow Framstad.

Astrid nodded and walked in. Without any preamble she took off her shawl. The old woman put her hand on Astrid's belly, pressed, then moved it and continued until she had covered the entire area.

Astrid said, "There be two, right? Two children."

The midwife shook her head. "In't possible to say. Happen it be a hefty boy. We shan't know before the birth."

"But be there no way – no signs?"

Widow Framstad cleared her throat. "Only the crossbar. And ye know what it told ye."

"Do ye believe in the crossbar?"

"It has proven right. Many times."

"More than half?"

"Well over half."

"It told me there be two," said Astrid. "Two boys. And I had a vision."

Widow Framstad frowned, although it barely showed in her wrinkled face; then, sitting forwards on her chair, she said that Astrid could, if she wanted, tell her what she had seen.

"They was . . . together. Like they was carrying one another. Limping forwards."

"Did they walk towards the mountain or from it?"

"Down from the mountain."

"Was they pulling a load or summat behind them?"

"No. One dragged t'other close to him somehow."

The old woman shook her head, saying she did not know what to think. "Happen it were a guardian spirit ye saw. Or summat that has happened or will happen. How old were they – these two?"

"About as old I be now. Maybe a little older."

The midwife cleared her throat and fetched two cups that hung from hooks under a shelf. In one corner of the room was a very sooty fireplace where a blackened coffee pot hung from a thin chain. She lifted the pot and filled a cup with coffee for Astrid, handed it to her and filled a cup for herself. It tasted bitter, but it was hot.

"It be important to listen to signs," said the midwife. "But ye mun na' let them control ye. The bells have the family silver in them, so ye may have taken a peek into your family's path, a trail alongside your own. Though I reckons it *were* your bairns ye saw, but it in't certain they be joined e'en so."

"I . . . I been wondering," said Astrid. "About a kind of operation. Where they take the children out through the belly, if the birth do nay go as it ought."

And why would it nay go as it ought? she hoped the old woman would ask.

But she did not, and Astrid shivered.

"Be ye thinking of the Caesar Cut?" said the midwife. "Wipe that idea out of your head straight away, lass."

"But there be doctors—"

"Astrid, Astrid! They canna do anything in Kristiania that we canna do here. The child mun come out in the same place as its father went in. And if it do nay want to come out, then . . . aye, I do nay want to show you this, but happens I mun."

Widow Framstad crossed the floor and kicked an old rag-rug aside. Beneath it was a trap door. She crouched down, opened it and from a hook at the side lifted out a grey bag. From it she took out an object that looked like some kind of a fire-iron or tongs. She did not take it over to Astrid, but held it out at a distance. The metal instrument was greyish in colour, tarnished and stained. It had a long, thin shaft, with two prongs shaped like big kitchen spoons.

"In my time here as the village midwife fewer and fewer women have died. Ye may know that. Ye may also know that when it gets difficult, when the babby be lodged sideways or the mother starts to bleed, I ask folk to leave the chamber. They think 'tis because I want to work in peace, but 'tis because I need to take this out, and naebody mun know about it."

"But what is it?"

"My forceps."

"Forceps?"

"She do help me pull out the child. She were specially forged in Åmotsfors in Sweden. There be eight of us midwives here in Gudbrandsdal who have them. This one has saved the lives of forty bairns . . . aye, more."

"But why do ye hide her?"

"'Cos I be forbidden to own her, never mind use her. Here in this country only doctors are allowed, and I promise ye there be none as *likes* to use her, and few as *knows* how to use her."

The midwife packed her tongs away. They were dreadful to see, and Astrid could not bear to think how they were used, much less how it would feel to have them used on you.

"But some be born dead anyway," murmured Astrid.

"Oh, aye," said the midwife. "We canna govern that."

"Do ye use the tongs then too?"

"Astrid, if the babbies be stuck, I shall get them out. Rest easy. I shall get them out."

*

That was all Widow Framstad would say on the matter. What Astrid did not know was that she had other tools at the bottom of her bag, tools that the law allowed her to use, but no-one in the village must know about. They were taken out when babies could not be pulled out with the tongs. When the only goal was to save the mother. Sometimes the baby lay crosswise or had the umbilical cord wound round its neck. At other times, the child was completely stuck or already dead and the mother unconscious. Then she had to dig in the bottom of her midwifery bag for the instruments she could scarcely bear to look upon, despite having used most of them. The best was a large hook fixed on the end of a stripped birch stick, which she regularly soaked in water to keep it flexible. Another resembled the forceps, but instead of two spoons at the end it had two curved knives. The thing she used most, however, was a strong, plaited cord made from a fishing net, which she would wrap round the child before she cut it up. She was always alone when she did this, both hands working, sometimes she could feel life in the baby before it was stilled, and that night she would be tormented by the sounds, sounds of something wet and heavy on the floor or in a pail. But before she steeled herself to do this, she always put her hand on the mother's belly and baptised the child, whether it was alive or not. She gave them old-fashioned names like Bolette or Jakup, swaddled the remains and put them in her midwifery bag, and her explanation was always that the child had been dead long before birth and that there was nothing to see. But in truth she took them home and buried them in a little flower bed outside her log cottage, and in this flower bed lay more than thirty babies whom she had removed like this.

But the mothers survived. In her hands most of them survived. She got the babies out, scraped out the remains of the afterbirth without damaging the mothers' wombs, and a year later they were with child again, and thus they continued to give birth every other year, until age finally brought a halt to the springing of the seed.

Astrid got to know nothing about this that night. Widow Framstad closed the cellar flap, went to the window and looked out.

"I mun go now," said Astrid.

"Do nay go to Kristiania."

"But surely they in't doctors for nought?"

"Men shouldna see births. It in't right. And it be wrong to gather womenfolk when it be time for their confinement. They comes down with a mortal fever. Sometimes one in twenty dies, and a few weeks later every fourth girl. I believe there be summat – in the air or the blood – spreads between them. A disease. They can be right as rain in the morning, but as the day passes the fever sets in, and then there's nought can be done."

"Does that nay happen here too?"

"Nay. Nay here in the village. We keeps the women from each other and wash and clean all the time. And I always ask for boiling water and fresh cloths to wipe with. They can be rags, but they mun be clean. Menfolk donae understand these things. They stand with their aprons cagged with blood. Leastways it were so before, and I wouldna chance it that things be much altered."

Astrid felt the tears welling up.

"Do nay fret, Astrid. They can do nought in town that I canna do here. A ewe will nay have a better birth just 'cos ye drag her to Kristiania."

The Stroll

Late in February a mild spell came to Butangen. Astrid sat by the stove upstairs, knitting the first of two little coats. It felt strange to her to sit like this. The babies were kicking more and more, one calm, one restless as before.

Astrid heard footsteps in the hallway downstairs, and there it was again, the impossible hope that Gerhard had come, a reflex still not quashed, but on the way to being so.

A man had come in, and soon she could distinguish the rhythm of the footsteps below, and she heard her father coming up the stairs. She straightened up and put down her knitting needles.

Her father knocked, a little tap, and said she had a visitor.

It could only be one person.

And there he stood, down in the hallway, snow on his shoulders, stared at by dumbfounded adults and gawping children. The time had come, she realised, for Butangen's pastor to fulfil his promise of a stroll.

Astrid fetched her shawl and laced her boots. They walked across the courtyard together, but said little before Lake Løsnes came into view.

He asked her when the birth was expected.

"Some time in April," she said.

She shot him a glance and saw that he was counting back to the summer's day on which all chance had slipped from him, and she added hastily, "Though it may come sooner. I donae know if it takes an exact nine month, like the Bible says."

"The Bible? I didn't know it said anything about the length of a pregnancy. But then I don't know everything that's written there."

"Everyone knows it takes nine month. It be a simple matter of counting the time from Lady Day to Christmas Eve."

They reached the new church, and he handed her a huge key. They kicked the snow off, went into the weapons porch and there she unlocked the door. Everything was timber-white and high-ceilinged and the sunlight streamed in. The stoves were unlit. They were both wearing woollen mittens, which they kept on.

"So queer with it smelling so new," said Astrid, her gaze flitting about.

"The bishop will come soon," he said. "To consecrate it. Right now it's just a building. The carpenters still have a few little jobs to do, they say, but they've said that since Christmas."

Astrid started up the aisle, caught herself and stopped halfway. She stroked the back of a pew, the same bright pine as the floor.

"She be beautifully crafted," she said. "She turned out just as ye wished."

"Yes, it's beautifully crafted."

"But?"

"But we should have built another."

"Another?"

"The one Gerhard drew. I saw his drawings."

She walked over to a window that looked down over the slope towards Lake Løsnes. There stood the new bell tower, pale and gleaming, the log walls would have to be left to dry for a year before they could be painted with tar. The snow had been cleared all the way to the door, but there were deep footprints leading up to it, it was clear someone had carried something heavy there.

Schweigaard moved a little closer to her, stopped and picked at a window ledge that still needed moulding, turned and walked towards the austere white-painted pulpit, and up to the old font of worn soapstone, which now seemed so out of place. The new altarpiece was the only colourfully painted thing, and above it was a simple, dark cross.

He shrugged.

"It be easy to regret things," she said. "The new always lacks summat, and the old vexes us."

He nodded gently. She looked at him and saw that her words, that to her were light-hearted, were of deep comfort to him, and that he had a yearning to hear such words every day.

"If only you knew how much I regret things," said Kai Schweigaard. "He died because of what I did."

She said that he was judging himself too harshly. "Ye betrayed us, Kai. That be the truth. But I didna make things easy for ye either. And it were Gerhard's own doing when he overturned the bells, and were dragged out with them."

"Still. It's as though I pushed him."

"So why did it happen – if ye wish to tell me?"

Kai Schweigaard could not answer her. But from the length of his silence Astrid understood that he was grateful for her discretion, asking him why it had *happened* and not why he had *done* it. He cleared his throat. "I'm not sure how long I want to remain here as a pastor. Or be a pastor at all."

"You can na' mean that. With all ye have managed to do?"

"It's all got too much. No-one can force me to be a priest. It makes no odds what I do or how well-meaning I am, it goes wrong."

"Ye be the best pastor the village could have. A little strict maybe, but folk expect that of their pastor."

"Perhaps I'd make a reasonably good teacher."

"Here in Butangen?"

He shook his head. "Far away. In America perhaps. They say there are Norwegians in Brooklyn. Lots."

Astrid told him about the letter from Michelsen and about the vision at Widow Framstad's cottage. "If summat do happen," she said, "if the worst do happen, ye mun come and baptise them in my belly."

He coughed nervously. "Then I must know their names."

"Jehans and Edgar."

"Oh – really?"

"Gerhard wanted Edgar. Doubtless he knew someone by that name."

Kai Schweigaard did not ask if they had chosen any girls' names. He just asked: "And Jehans – is that someone from Hekne?"

"Nay. Or aye. He died long ago. He came to us as a little boy. From a farm up in Dovre. His mother couldna take care of him. He took the Hekne name and were a great reindeer hunter and trapper. It were from him I learned to tell the difference between all the animal claws and pelts."

Kai Schweigaard repeated the names and said he would remember them.

"Jehans will be born first," said Astrid. "He be lying lowest and be the most restless. Edgar only kicks now and then, but harder. I wish ye to baptise each with their own name, even if they be joined as one, and if I die."

They looked away from each other. Eventually Astrid said it was time for her to go back up.

"There's just one thing first," said Kai Schweigaard, moving closer. "If things had been different, if Herr Schönauer had died out there in Lake Løsnes, then I could have . . . I would have—"

She nodded for him to continue.

"I would have thrown off my priestly robes and declared myself the father."

She blinked. "But that would na' have been the truth."

"No. But neither would it have been a lie."

"Be that possible?"

"It's possible when the truth is greater than the untruth."

"Kai, my dearest. I no longer know up from down. Tell me. What be the truth, then?"

"The truth is this, Astrid, that I . . . that I—"

He cleared his throat and stared down at the ground.

"Ye canna say it, more than I?"

"No," he said, shaking his head. "But I bought a ring. A fine ring. Earlier this summer."

This time, it was she who could not look at him. She heard the wind outside, coming in from Lake Løsnes, as though common sense was trying to blow in through the walls.

A common sense that told her she no longer had many men to choose from. That she must cling to whatever might secure clothes for the children. That she must reignite her love for Kai Schweigaard, for the young priest who had leaped from his carriage that day with two suitcases.

She wanted to ask if he'd already considered these things, when he had arranged for Gerhard and her to be married. Did he have it at the back of his mind, that a pastor could not wed a girl with bastard children, but could wed a widow?

But he had clearly suffered enough and she held back from saying it.

"Kai. I shall have my little 'uns. Only after they come shall I know what I feel. Things mun take their own course."

Inside her mitten she stroked her thumb against the jagged ring.

"I wedded a dying man. If the birth go wrong, ye canna wed a dead woman. But one thing ye shall know about wedding rings."

"What's that?"

"That a woman's ring finger be made with room enough for two."

They walked down the aisle of the church, but he did not hold out an arm for Astrid to link hers with. He stopped her in the porch, and said: "I want to know whether you've forgiven me. Whether you *can* forgive me."

She took her hands out of her mittens and placed them on his.

"Ye *shall* feel it. I can promise ye that, Kai Schweigaard. Ye shall most surely feel whether I forgive ye or nay."

Echoes of Ancient Bronze

February turned to March, and she found it hard to get about. Her younger siblings were instructed not to mention her "condition", and conversations became muted whenever she joined in. Anxiety came well before she went to bed, it woke her while it was still dark, and the night hours were filled with worries.

About where she would give birth.

About the days that would follow.

About the answer she had given Kai Schweigaard.

About the village talk, which she could almost hear at her window.

The claws that held about her were strong, as though everything had been decided long ago. She was not so afraid that life might end, but more how this end might happen, and whether it really was over when it was over, or whether she would be taken to some other place, and have to watch what happened to her children from afar. She wished her grandfather was alive, or that there was an old person who, less busy, could sit by her bed.

The house woke up. Doors were opened and shut, wood and water were brought in. She sat listening to the farm's little noises, the mice hiding in walls, the Buhund barking outside. She waited for the others to go out before she ate, and then went upstairs to her father. "Ye must drive me to the district doctor," she said.

"The doctor?"

"I mun ask him what to do. About a kind of operation."

Her father had seldom heard the word before. She told him about the letter and the German doctor, but she knew he'd had his fill of Germans and outlandish plans, and couldn't bring herself to bother him with her fears that there were probably two babies and that they might be joined.

Her father cleared his throat.

"I were planning to go to Vålebrua to look at a mare," he said. "I wants to look at her soon, or she'll be sold. Ye mun be ready early tomorrow, Astrid. Before light. We shall have to take it slow so the ride in't so painful for ye. 'Tis a bumpy road. But ye know that."

"Listen Fru . . ."

The district doctor leaned forwards over his notepad.

"Hekne," said Astrid. "I be a widow. Took back my maiden name after he died."

"And why did you do that?"

"If my children mun grow up without me, it'll be easier with a name from these parts. Besides, I wants them to remember me."

The district doctor lingered over the latter statement, but did not pursue it. He refused to examine her other than by eye, and put the size of her belly down to her carrying a large boy. He made no mention of forceps. She continued to question him, and he lit his pipe and was thorough in his answers, but she demanded greater and greater detail, until he eventually interrupted her:

"I understand that the midwife up there hasn't told you everything. She was wise. There are things a mother ought not to know about her coming confinement. It's not good for her to know everything. Nonetheless, I shall ask you this: did she tell you about the 'destructive method'?"

Astrid shook her head.

"She was right not to. But since you're so persistent, you must brace yourself for the truth. You're in safe hands with your midwife. If the child doesn't come out, she'll put every effort into saving you. But that'll be done at the expense of the child. It'll have to be removed. Dead. Through your birth canal. Piece by piece. Hence the word 'destructive'. I shan't explain in more detail. You will survive and be able to give birth to more children."

Astrid put her head in her hands and looked at the floor.

"Such children wouldn't survive anyway," said the doctor. "And where did you get the idea that there were two? As I said: it's probably just a big boy."

"In Kristiania," she said, "I've heard there be a big birthing clinic. With doctors."

"They have midwives there, just as we do. They only fetch a doctor when they have to. But you live here! I shall come if the need arises. Would you really go all the way to Kristiania and install yourself there and wait?"

She asked about the sickness that was rife in the city. He said that the midwife must have been describing childbed fever, but that they had beaten it now.

"But this operation?"

"No. No. You won't find a single doctor who'll undertake it. Not even if a mother signed a document saying that she would gladly offer her own life so that her children would be born healthy – as I suspect you want – no. I don't like the idea of anyone even thinking of such an operation. People say that the ancient Roman leader, Caesar, was cut out of his mother, but that's an impossibility. We know that Caesar's mother lived to a ripe old age. If she had been cut open, she'd have died."

"So, why do they call it the Caesar Cut?"

"Because the word 'Caesar' resembles a Latin word that means 'cut'."

She got up to leave.

"It will all be alright," he said. "If anything happens, then the midwife or I will make the choice for you. We'll relieve you of death and pain."

"But not of grief."

"No. We have no hand in grief, nor do we destroy it."

She travelled home in silence with her father. The mare had been sold the night before and they stood in the March weather near Fåvang church, each nursing their own defeat. She glanced to the south over the River Laugen and towards Kristiania, and then they started up the slopes back to Butangen.

That evening she fetched Meyer's *Sprachführer für Reise und Haus* and asked herself what Gerhard would have done. Not the man who drew so beautifully or fished with a fly-fishing rod, but the man who had risked his life for her.

A thin sheet of paper rustled to the floor. A receipt from the Søstrene Scheen's guesthouse in Kristiania for one night's stay. A woman's handwriting, beautiful and legible. It hadn't been *that* expensive. She made a mental calculation, adding this amount to the district doctor's estimate of the cost of giving birth in Kristiania, against the money she had received from Gerhard. She went outside, stood on the doorstep and stared into the darkness. The surrounding black was only pierced here and there by a flickering light in a neighbouring farm. The night concealed Lake Løsnes, the valley sides, the forests, and the cemetery.

The next morning she put on her scarf, walked down to the moorings and out onto the ice. Half of the lake was still open, and as she drew closer to the edge of the ice she heard the steady lapping of water under the clouds of frost-smoke.

Astrid crossed over to the other shore. The tracks from the sledge convoy were gone now, only faintly discernible as shallow dips that stretched out into the landscape. No heavy loads had been driven there since, and she had to wade through deep snow to get to the spot where Gerhard had let the church bells tumble out into the water.

He had told her where the second bell lay. It was close to the shoal where he had gone fishing last summer. He had tried to guide both bells so they would sink onto the shelf, where the water was only two to three metres deep, so that they could both be hauled up again. *Halfrid* had rolled down as planned, but *Gunhild* had thundered to the side and ended up in the deep.

Had the Sister Bells spoken to him again? Were they pleased with him? The old and the new were crashing into each other, and the space between them was so tight that she felt crushed. Perhaps she must leave Butangen, and perhaps, in a few weeks, leave this life.

A flurry of sleet came and went.

Further out, where the water was deep, she saw circles rippling out from a tiny ring. Like the wake of fish that would have had Gerhard Schönauer bowing his head and preparing a cast.

Around her a doleful sound rang out, in harmony with her own despair. It was a muffled sound, and seemed to rise from the water. She had difficulty keeping her balance, and stamped a new foothold into the snow. The babies started to move inside her, both were kicking, but now she thought she felt a new kind of movement, a harder, more decisive thrust, before they reverted to their usual pushing and shoving. Then suddenly they were still, before she felt it again, a single kick, powerful and lasting, as though they had joined forces. And it felt to her that they had three legs, not four.

Fear was closing in from all sides. She tried to block out

the sound, but it persisted until she had to accept its presence; stronger and closer it came, like the reverberation of ancient bronze, like the rumbling of ice when it gives way in spring, or the rattling of pebbles before an avalanche. The fear stepped in and announced itself, and she knew it would stay with her until she gave birth, from now on it would poison everything, it would govern the air she breathed, it would be in her food, in the water and in the smell of blood and the sight of a cross.

The House of Bowed Heads

She had expected it to be a resplendent brick building where scientific knowledge and daylight ruled. But the instant she stepped into the Birthing Institute in Kristiania, and stood in the gloomy, mildewy hall and was told to wait for the head midwife, she saw it clearly.

This was no house of joy.

It was a house of bowed heads, of hardship and suffering.

A house of events that were not to be spoken of. A house of turning points in life, where women were reminded of their place in the animal kingdom.

She sat on a stool near the front door, waiting for so long that she grew hungry, and when she asked a nurse in a white coat if the head midwife would come soon, the woman expressed surprise and said that *she* was the head midwife, and that nobody had mentioned that someone was waiting. She was guided into a small room with grey walls and asked to sit down. The head midwife went out, and through the half-open door Astrid heard someone say: "I can carry out the interview." The second woman was tall and beaky-looking, she was also in a white coat. She was stunned when Astrid told her where she came from, and sceptical when she said that she was a widow and could produce a marriage certificate. She began writing in a notebook and asked Astrid if she knew the day of conception and whether she was sure who the child's father was.

"Speak properly, so I can understand," she said, interrupting Astrid the instant she tried to answer.

Astrid held her tongue and did her best to soften her dialect.

"Give me your letter," the other said.

Astrid said she did not understand.

"The letter!" she repeated, stretching out her hand. "Everyone has a letter."

"Who from?" said Astrid.

"From the Poor Relief Association," said the other, her hand still extended. "We must have a letter if you're to be admitted for free."

"But I have the money myself," said Astrid.

The woman looked her up and down, and put her hands on her hips. "Have you been examined for syphilis?"

"Why do you ask me that?"

"Because you're here with your own money."

"I have neither a letter nor syphilis," said Astrid. "I be— *am* here to see a doctor."

"You want to see a *doctor*?"

The woman took a deep breath, releasing the air noisily through her nose, and left the room muttering to herself.

Time passed.

Nobody asked her to leave, and nobody asked her to stay. She got up. Her back was aching. She wandered about the room and glanced through a book lying on the edge of a table. There was a chapter entitled "Pregnancy with Multiple Foetuses". She read: "The lower the place of an animal in the animal kingdom, the more fertile it is, and the smaller an animal, the shorter its gestation period, and the lower the resistance of the foetus."

Astrid had read a great deal by the time she heard footsteps in the corridor. It was the head midwife.

"I don't quite understand why you've come here," she said. "This place is for women who live in Kristiania, and it costs money. Besides, you're meant to come here when it's your time. Why don't you just give birth at home?"

"Because I've heard about this operation. If the birth gets difficult."

"And what makes you think it would be . . . problematic?"

"Because there be— *are* two," said Astrid.

"Nobody can know that," said the midwife gently. "Nobody. It's probably just a large baby. Your problem now is that you've come to Kristiania in vain. It must have taken two days?"

"Three. But that in't far if it can save my babbies."

"But you're perfectly healthy, as far as I can see!"

"There's a doctor," said Astrid. "From Germany. Herr Sänger."

The two women looked at each other.

"*You* have heard about Herr Sänger?"

"He knows my name and that I am to give birth. I know that he is wed to a Norwegian lady and that he is coming to the Rikshospital this spring."

They seemed not to know what to do with her. A third midwife took her into a room and examined her. It was unthinkable to send anyone to search for Dr Sänger. The doctors stayed in the hospital and were never called out before "all the usual methods had been tried". They asked her when she had felt the first contractions, and again when the child had been conceived. Then they looked at each other.

"There are still three weeks to go," Astrid said.

"And where will you stay in that time?"

"In a guesthouse. Which I will pay for myself."

They fell silent. They had seen it all before, thought Astrid. That when a pregnant woman had made up her mind, it was impossible to change it.

"You'd have to share a dormitory with the others here. We have a few single and double rooms, but they cost a good deal more."

She thought about the smells. About the grunts. The shuffling when they had to get up and walk about to ease the back pain.

"You're from up in the valleys?" asked the midwife.

Astrid nodded.

"So I take it you've been doing farmwork?"

Astrid nodded again.

"Up until now?"

"Aye."

"Well. If you are carrying two children, you will go into labour long before nine months are up. I was going to tell you to go home, but you'd better go back to the guesthouse. Come here when it starts. Can you read?"

"Thank you. Aye, I can read."

"You can borrow a book from us."

Astrid thanked her again. As she walked out, she glimpsed the door to the adoption office. It was next to the exit.

Outside a crew of sweaty workmen were clearing snow from a cart. They scraped the sides, fetched brooms and swept the rest of the snow out into the road, where it turned a dirty grey from the horse-cabs that clattered past. A rough cart loaded with clinking bottles followed. It was being pulled by two gigantic workhorses.

Astrid thought about Balder and Emort, who had driven her as far as Lillehammer. They had been told that the spring sun had softened the ice on Lake Mjøsa, so that the next leg of her journey would have to take place at night, when the temperature dropped. The sledge travelled at lightning speed across the ice, with a panoramic view beneath a huge moon. The blades sang, sonorous against the hard ice, rasping as they cut through crusty snow, and hushed as they pushed through water. Near Skreia the ice threatened to give way, and they had to go onto a bumpy road, but by then she was too tired to be afraid. When she woke up, they had come to a halt, and the two drivers wearing thick furs offered her some cocoa and a piece of chocolate. They told her that they had reached Eidsvoll, but that the morning train had already left. They suggested she drive further with them, since the road to Kristiania was good, and it would be both faster and cheaper than taking the evening train.

As they harnessed up new horses, she caught sight of the railway lines. Two dark tracks that stretched around a bend.

Later that day they reached some stables, and the drivers told her that she was in Upper Vognmannsgate. As she got out she felt dizzy. Horse-drawn cabs rattled past, folk were strangely dressed and nobody looked at her, she was surrounded by the city that she had read about in Kai Schweigaard's newspapers. Somewhere in these brick houses, behind the tall windows and thick walls, there must be auctions of paintings, lectures about the Atlantic expeditions, dance parties and oranges from Valencia. A boy in rags clung to her and helped her to find the Søstrene Scheen's guesthouse, it was barely any distance, but when they got there she realised that he expected some money, and she gave him an øre. She signed in as Astrid Hekne, and wondered if she should mention Gerhard to them, but realised that nobody in this city would want to be bothered with the death of a past guest, nor that she was standing there one year later carrying his children.

*

The next day Astrid returned to the Birthing Institute, and the head midwife told her that they had enquired with a doctor who worked with Dr Sänger, but there had been no word from him, which there would have been if he was interested in her case. She went back out, trudged about in the streets to keep her backache at bay, always staying close to the guesthouse.

Rectangular signs informed her of the street names at each corner, and her gaze was constantly turned up towards the tall buildings. Like confident women in fine dresses, they seemed to say: If you want to know what true beauty is, then look at us! She felt like a rolling stone in a river, which for one brief moment peeps up above the water. And she walked on a little further, caught the smell of the salt air and rotten seaweed, a smell she had never encountered before, but which she somehow knew was the smell of the sea – and where there was sea, there had to be ships.

Near Bjørvika a steamship lay waiting, a raging colossus, black and brooding, a horizontal red stripe its only adornment, so heavy and powerful that the seawater seemed despondent as it splashed limply around it. It smelled of smoke and rancid oil, everywhere she saw streams of people, all too busy with their own lives to wonder about her. Emigrants. Whole families with everything they owned in homemade wooden travel chests, bearing their names, which they lifted between them as they shunted forwards in the queue with small steps, clinging to each other's sleeves so as not to lose each other.

So here I am, she thought. The ewe that dragged itself to Kristiania. He won't come. Sänger won't come. He may not even be here in this city. And nobody believes me at the Birthing Institute.

The fear made her tremble, and the thought was so close: If I go back home, my life will not be at risk. Widow Framstad knows I have twins inside me and that the birth won't be easy.

She won't hesitate. She'll grab hold of those ghastly instruments. The tools that always save the mother but never the children.

But she had made the choice long ago. It had been made down by Lake Løsnes, where she had touched her belly and asked herself: Me or you? And her answer had been as strong as the clang of bronze.

Astrid Hekne stood watching the women near the ship, at the way they kept their raggedy little ones in order, and thought: Some say we should not bring children into a world like this. But then who will give birth to them, the children who will in the end make the world better?

The pain returned in her lower back.

She turned from the ship, went back to the guesthouse, and it was there that it started.

The inside of her thighs went warm and then cold, and she leaned over her bulging belly to look and turned her ankles to stop the waters running into her shoes. When she went to pay her bill, the woman in reception stared at her, slammed the guestbook shut and said that she would accompany Astrid herself right away, there was nothing to pay for this night, and they would send her luggage on. At the Birthing Institute, she was given a bench in the waiting room to lie on, and a young midwife in a freshly ironed blue uniform introduced herself as Frøken Ørjavik, saying that she wanted to carry out a second interview since the previous one had been incomplete.

"Do you have the money with you?"

Astrid nodded.

"I'll lock it in a cupboard. Is it right that you wanted a bed in a double room?"

"If it be still available. I would prefer not to give birth in the big hall."

"You know it'll cost four kroner a night?"

"Is it the same price whether I have one babby or two?"

Frøken Ørjavik's pencil stopped in its tracks on the page; she looked at Astrid and said that if there were two, the second birth would be included. "And you're alone here in town?"

"Aye."

"And the baby's father. Is his name known?"

"It would have been known, if he had lived."

Ørjavik cocked her head.

"He was an architect, and we were wed, but now he is dead. His name was Schönauer, but I want the boys t'be baptised Hekne."

The midwife nodded and entered the name of Gerhard's hometown.

"We chose names," said Astrid, "in case they were sick and needed to be baptised quickly."

There was no space on the form for this, and Frøken Ørjavik made ready to write in the margin. Her writing was neat and she used a newly sharpened pencil.

"Jehans and Edgar," said Astrid. "Jehans is the one who be coming first."

"So it'll be Jehans if there is only one?"

"Aye. Then Jehans."

"And if they're girls?"

"They will na' be . . ."

"What?"

Astrid cleared her throat. "Gunhild and Halfrid. Gunhild is the one that shall shuttle close."

"What?"

"Nay, I meant . . . Gunhild first. If there be only one girl."

"That's a nice name. I've written that down now. All of it."

"And what about me?" asked Astrid.

"You?"

"Where shall I be buried if things donae go well?"

"Oh." Frøken Ørjavik cleared her throat. "That's a bit sudden."

"I want things in order."

"You mustn't think like that. It'll go alright."

"We must write down a name in case it doesna go well."

"In the *Krist kirkegård*," said Frøken Ørjavik. "The cemetery nearby."

"Do I get a gravestone? So they can find me if I pass away?"

"Your parents?"

"Nay, my children."

Frøken Ørjavik lowered her pencil and rubbed her brow.

"I don't know," she said. "But it will be done according to proper custom."

"And if the children die?" said Astrid. "What happens then?"

"Then . . . if we are fearful of that, we call a priest to carry out an emergency baptism. If the priest doesn't come, we'll do it ourselves and the baptism will be confirmed in church later. When you all get home."

"But where be the children taken if they die?"

"Don't fret about all this now. It's not good for you to get worked up."

"The only thing that works me up," said Astrid, "is when I in't told everything."

"Very well. They too will be laid in the *Krist kirkegård*. Within the wall."

"There be two paintbrushes in my bag," said Astrid. "Put them in with the children if they die."

Silence fell between them.

"There's something else," said Frøken Ørjavik, and this time she picked up another book, bigger and more worn. "Since you're a widow, may I ask – do you have any prospect of someone who can provide for you?"

"Aye, I do."

"But you are not engaged?"

Astrid shook her head.

"Then you'll receive a visit from another lady soon. From the adoption office. She'll ask you whether you're able to take care of the child or whether it should be placed elsewhere. They have their ways. Discreet. They know parents of good standing. Who will take care of the child as though it were their own."

Frøken Ørjavik closed the book gently, saying that there was no rush, but that the decision should be made during the next day. She led Astrid up to a room on the first floor and told her she could lie down. The other bed was empty and she said that if Astrid was lucky nobody else would claim it, so that Astrid could give birth in this room alone. She shook the duvet and spread it out neatly, put an extra pillow under Astrid's back and tucked a little blanket around her feet, before fetching some coffee which they drank together. Her cup empty, Astrid said, "Have you heard anything more from Dr Sänger?" Frøken Ørjavik shook her head and said she had never heard of a Dr Sänger.

During the night the contractions grew stronger. The midwife was sleeping, and a nurse popped in sporadically. Astrid did not have a watch and there was no clock in the room, so she started counting her breaths to work out the length of each contraction, she was certain the time between them was getting shorter. At one point the contractions were almost overwhelming, but the babies refused to move down, and she knew that all she could do was what women had always done in the birth chamber.

Hold out.

Wait.

Then came a huge surge of pressure, and she staggered out to the lavatory in the hallway, where she sat for a while before realising that she had misinterpreted her body. Returning to her room, she found an elderly midwife and another woman in there. The woman was dressed in a light-green embroidered gown and sat on the edge of the other bed, and close to Astrid's bed were some big suitcases and a light-blue cardboard box tied with a silk ribbon.

"Who is this woman?" asked the stranger, pointing at Astrid. She was quite old, well over thirty, and swallowed hard several times, as though she had just been sobbing. Her hair had been recently put up, so perfectly that she could not possibly have done it herself. As the midwife replaced the cork in a medicine bottle, the woman grabbed her by her white coat and said, "I was supposed to have a single room! I have paid for a single room."

"You will have a single room," said the midwife. "It will be available in a few hours. As soon as it's light. I told you that a moment ago."

"Oh. Right."

The midwife left. Astrid sat on her bed and shunted herself into place. She did not look at the other woman or say anything. It was dark outside. The room had large windows with dull, cream-coloured curtains. A light breeze streamed in, making them flap gently. The only thing happening in the room.

The other woman sniffed. "I'm sorry," she said. "Sorry that I was so churlish."

"Aye," said Astrid.

"I'm not accustomed to being alone."

"Then happen ye shouldna have asked for a single room."

"I mean, I'm not used to being with people I don't know."

"Nor I," said Astrid.

The woman went to answer, but was gripped by a contraction, and when it passed, the sentence had gone out of her head.

"Did ye come here in the night?" said Astrid.

"Yes. It started early."

"Oh. It be so wi' me too."

The other woman did not answer.

"D'ye come from the coast?" said Astrid.

"From Møre. But I've been living abroad these past ten years."

"But ye prefer to give birth here in Kristiania?"

"Don't you understand a thing, girl? You really are quite intolerable! My room *must* be ready by now!"

She started to cry again. When she showed no sign of stopping, and nobody came in, no doubt because a crying sound was as normal in this corridor as the sound of footsteps, Astrid wriggled out of bed and sat down beside her.

"My previous ones all started like this, much too soon."

Astrid asked what she meant by her previous ones.

"Other women manage it. But not me. And now I'm thirty-two. He's disappointed in me. I know he's disappointed in me."

"Your husband?"

"We should have been back home twelve days ago. But he's on a fishing trip near here, and he's been delayed. I'm staying with my aunt in Briskeby. Then tonight it started. The baby wants to get out. It's not doing well there inside me. And he's busy fishing for salmon!"

These men we fall in love with, thought Astrid. Who manage to catch fish in the cold waters of the early spring.

Now it was Astrid's turn to battle with contractions. They started getting closer for both women, and lasting longer, and with this in common they talked between contractions. The woman said her name was Elisabeth; she was the daughter of a district judge, and had met her husband at a party with eight other Englishmen who had come for the fishing. They had exchanged letters, and she had returned with him in the autumn she turned twenty-two. "He seemed so exciting. At our first dinner, I learned that he had been involved in the annexation of the Transvaal, I had no idea what the annexation of the Transvaal was, but I fell for him instantly. Now he'll probably take me to Ceylon, he wants to buy a tea plantation."

"Be that in Africa?"

"No, south of India. A little island."

"And now ye both live in England? My husband liked London," said Astrid.

"We're closer to Scotland."

"Oh."

Astrid lay in thought. Then she asked Elisabeth about the house they lived in and the surrounding buildings. "D'ye truly have three floors?"

"Yes. It's built of stone, but it's in a dreadfully desolate place. *He* doesn't care a jot about that, of course, because there are trout rivers right near the house. Luckily we get visitors in the hunting season. The place is teeming with grouse and pheasants, which he shoots with the other chaps, and then we ladies get plenty of time to talk."

After a while, she asked Astrid to tell her about her pregnancy.

"His name was Schönberg, you said?"

"Schönauer."

"And he drew churches?"

Astrid nodded.

"There can't be too many people who go out and draw churches that late in the year."

"In't too many draw churches at all."

The other woman was in pain again and Astrid dozed off. Daylight was shining brightly through the curtains when they came in to say that the single room was ready. Elisabeth walked over to Astrid, she let her know that she didn't really want to leave, but that whatever lay ahead of her now was something she had to face alone.

"Good luck, Astrid."

"The best to ye too, Elisabeth."

"Thank you."

They touched hands and said goodbye. Then the door opened again, and in came two girls with bulging stomachs, neither looked more than fourteen, and they both had wet hair from having been washed and scrubbed. Astrid understood from the midwife that this had not been voluntary. The girls were shrill, unbothered that somebody was already in the room. A third bed scraped the floor as it was dragged in.

That's how it goes, thought Astrid. Here we lie.

Those who don't want children, get them. And those who want them, don't.

She fell asleep, and when she woke up the two girls were gone. A contraction came that was so strong that she groaned with the pain. It had finally begun. The midwife came in and fetched the stirrups. Astrid was repulsed at having to sit like that, wrenched wide open, with clammy skin and soaking-wet hair, feeling ugly and angry. Later that evening they concluded that the baby was wedged in sideways and no matter how she sat in bed or strained, it would not come down, and her belly refused to change shape. Her mind drifted to thoughts of nights spent with Gerhard Schönauer. The memory of him made her close her eyes and return to her old dreams of Dresden, and she had almost reached the promenade when the pain grew stronger than the daydream, and the cramps in her pelvis extinguished the Dresden gas lamps.

When she woke up, the lamps had been relit – she had no idea where she was, until she realised it was night, and that the light was coming from a carbide lamp on the wall. It grew larger and hazier, and the yellow flare began to dance before her eyes, and it felt as though a heavy fish was stuck inside her, and in front of the flare a dark figure moved suddenly, it vanished and then came another, and she heard the clank of metal against metal, and something being dropped on the floor and picked up again.

Then came the terror.

With the sound of men's voices.

"How long has she been like this?"

"Half a day now. The midwife said something about her cervix. That it's been dilated for several hours."

"Yes, that means she's fully dilated. And she's not strong enough to push the child out?"

"No. She said she thought there was more than one."

"Well, she can't know that."

"Her mind has been wandering. She said something . . . er . . . rather strange."

"Strange? This isn't the time for delicacies. Just say it, man!"

"She reckoned they were conjoined. Presumably it's happened in the family before."

"Good God. That would be a sensation."

"But it can't be excluded?"

"No. Just as it can't be excluded that there are three foetuses in there."

"Oh, is that possible?"

"No, of course not. I'm trying to get you to handle this situation calmly and collectedly, from moment to moment. Work from what's probable and what your fingers tell you. Do what's needed. Feel inside. Can you feel what's coming first?"

"I can feel something soft. Something soft and squishy."

"That's its bottom. The legs are folded up against its stomach. Move over. I'm going to go in with my hand and whip the legs out."

Astrid felt something being pushed deep into her, impossible to know where, thrusting into a swollen and tender mass. The voices around her faded, and she realised that she could no longer separate out the sounds.

She woke up and felt a little better. The voices had returned, she blinked and could see them clearly, two men, one old and the other young, and now she recognised the head midwife too.

"The head's stuck. There's no way back now."

"Tell me what to do."

"Get the tongs. The newest."

"Yes. Alright."

"What's going on?"

"The new ones don't seem to be here."

"Then you'll have to fetch the tongs we had a moment ago!"

"They're still being used in the other room."

Astrid slipped out of the world again, and was woken by the slam of a door. She saw a man enter, his clothes were caked in blood and he was carrying something.

Astrid opened her eyes, she was suddenly wide awake.

The forceps lay in an oval metal dish, long and bloodied, like serving tongs lying on a platter from which meat had been served.

The doctor grabbed the forceps, but they slipped from his hand and clanked against the metal dish. He shifted his grip on them, trying to find the balance in this long tool. The metal was tarnished and dull, and semi-congealed blood glinted in the glow of the carbide lamp. Astrid heard the sound of a stool being pulled across the floor. The doctor lifted the tongs high, and Astrid could see a thread of mucus hanging between the spoons, which, when he opened the tongs fully, snapped, and dangled back and forth before gluing itself around the shaft.

"You in't never gonna stick that into me!" Astrid yelled.

Then she pushed.

She heard a baby's scream far away, and something gushed out, leaving a cold gust of fresh air deep inside her. She felt something running out of her, but did not realise how much until she heard the dripping in the dish beneath her change to a steady trickle.

"You need to take control of this now. Can you feel a heartbeat?"

"I'm not sure."

"You're not sure? Move over. He came bottom first, so they might have been lying with their necks and heads close."

"How do you mean?"

"I mean chin against chin. That's why the first one didn't come. She has actually pushed both of them now."

"It's slipping. I've got so much blood on my hands."

"Move over now! Let me do it! No, wait."

"What is it?"

"She's pushing again."

Astrid Hekne gathered herself once more, harnessing the strength of a faraway place, the strength of bare mountains and craggy slopes, of every mother back to the woman who bore the Hekne sisters. She was exhausted now and frightened, the only thing that might make her feel safe was a man's voice speaking German, but the voice never came, and finally her instincts took over, and no thought or word had any place in what she now did.

Third Story

THESE SOME MUST BE SOMEBODY

Ye Shall Shuttle Wide

ASTRID HEKNE LAY WITH THE TWO BOYS AT HER breast, hoping they would suckle before it was too late. So here you both are, she thought. Finally the words "to come into the world" made sense. They turned like lazy cats, close to each other, as they nudged their way over her, each in his own way, and looked into her eyes and into each other's eyes and then all around them, in those first hours of life in which a mother and a brother were no more unusual than the water jug on the table or the curtains at the window.

"Jehans," she said. "Ye be out at last and they didna get to harm ye. Already keen to go, with the selfsame strong movements ye had in my belly, but freer now and further-reaching with each passing hour. Legs made to walk. Though it be ye who shall shuttle close.

"And ye, Edgar. I do see him in your face. Your father. Ye play with your fingers as if ye be seeking a paint brush. Ye who clings tightest to me now, ye mun shuttle wide."

Edgar wriggled, his movements belonged to one who would take time to realise he could walk on two feet. She leaned closer to them both, and said, "I thought I had lost. But I have nay. I have lost so ye can both win." The boys found a breast each. And as she felt the nourishment leave her and enter them, she slipped into a doze. When she woke again, Frøken Ørjavik was sitting next to her.

"It in't looking good, is it?" mumbled Astrid.

"Just keep calm. You can't afford to lose more blood."

"Have ye been in the other room?"

"Yes. Her baby didn't survive."

Astrid swallowed. "But she canna take both?"

"No. Her husband mustn't know."

"Then it mun be as we said."

"Sleep now, Astrid. We'll know more tomorrow."

Astrid drifted off, then suddenly opened her eyes wide and flailed with her arms.

"Calm yourself, Astrid," said Frøken Ørjavik. "I'm here. I'll look after you. They shan't come to grief."

"Ye be sure they be healthy? Ye looked them over thoroughly?"

"I have rarely seen two such fine, strong boys. You should be proud."

"Though I donae think they be much alike?"

"No, that much is clear. Fine in their very different ways. Wait, I'll straighten the pillow behind you."

"D'ye see how he has such curly hair?"

"Just like you. And this one has smooth hair. From his father?"

"Aye. From his father. Were ye there when they came?"

"I was there the whole time. One of the doctors fainted."

For a second Astrid dozed off again.

"Frøken Ørjavik?"

"Yes, Astrid."

"That talk we had."

"Don't worry. The boys will get milk."

"Nay, after . . ."

The midwife shifted on her stool and took Astrid's hand. "About how happiness may be brief and great?"

"Aye."

"That's not how it is."

"Nay?"

"It is far longer. And far greater."

Astrid drew the babies closer in to her, cradled their heads, and fell asleep.

Deep within her sleep, past and future parted ways, and a view opened up to her. She saw herself dressed in a fine dove-grey coat, at a train station at home in the valley. The conductor held out his hand and helped her up into her compartment, which resembled a small cabin, freshly cleaned, a touch of chlorine. Facing each other were six deep chairs with high backs, covered in a light-grey weave. The seat was soft, with a cushion sewn in for her lower back. She rested her arms, stretched her feet, wriggled and made herself comfortable. Stared out over the busy platform and compared it with the quiet of the compartment.

Edgar and Jehans were not with her. Only she had to leave. The whistle blew. She felt a sustained pressure against her shoulder blades, as the powerful motion of the train kicked in, with enough force to change the world. The train picked up speed, they passed a field and came out onto a bridge, to her left she could see the train reflected in the familiar green river, and the long row of windows where her face must also be reflected, invisible because they were in motion, but nonetheless reflected. She trembled at the thought of how she was part of this motion, this great forward movement, fast and steady, yet so comfortable that she would be more refreshed on arrival than when she left, forward, forward, forward.

Speeding along. The view opened up and shifted to a new, foreign land. The whole world was presented to her through the windows, left and right. She could see a storm brewing on the horizon, and she pulled the collar of her coat close around her neck, the clouds were already above them, and she hunched her shoulders; then she realised: she was warm and dry here in the train, and no rain could ever get in now. Water droplets slid sideways across the window, and soon the storm had passed.

Then she was in a hotel room. The day passed, the sky changed colour and darkness enveloped the strange city outside. She went out and watched two long rows of yellow, shivering street lamps being lit, one by one, into the distance; floating on iron posts, they formed a winding path through the darkness. She walked on tentatively, stepped under the street lamps and stood there, quietly watching the crowd pass by. She headed along this path of light, taking a turn down to the bank of a river, where the lamps threw a quivering reflection over the water. Facing the river were the statues of those who had achieved fame. She walked among them, a shimmering silhouette of monuments mirrored in the river. Then a church bell rang out, and she saw the Butangen stave church mirrored in a little pool. The bell rang again, and far away, as in a hallucination of tone colours, she seemed to hear its sister answer.

Ants and Flies

"I thought," said Bishop Folkestad, "that I might offer you gentlemen some cigars. Not that we should fall into hedonism. But this is worth celebrating."

Fifteen smartly clad gentlemen sat at the long festive table at the Butangen parsonage. They had finished their four courses, including meatballs in broth and ox tongue with vegetables, listened to nine speeches and an equal number of toasts, each followed by a little sip of sherry. Bishop Folkestad continued:

"Tell me, Herr Schweigaard: how long have you been here? Is it three years now?"

Kai Schweigaard lifted his eyes from his half-eaten pudding. "It's coming up to two, Bishop."

"Two? Yes, that's right. All the more impressive! You've achieved so much! It was a pleasure to stand in your newly built church. To observe the congregation gazing about in contented wonderment. Sturdy pillars for future faith. The bell tower proved rather a frivolity, standing there for so long with no bells in it, but, er, it has its uses as a mortuary. Anyway, the time has come to mark our personal appreciation. Mayor, Herr Bank Director, gentlemen, please join me in raising a glass to Kai Schweigaard!"

The ceiling oil lamps had newly trimmed wicks that burned brightly and steadily, and the sherry sparkled golden-brown in cut-crystal glasses as they were raised. They put the glasses down and then the cigar box was sent round. The mayor and the dairy chief nodded with satisfaction on discovering that they were Havanas from Conrad Langaard. One after the other, the guests helped themselves, each man contentedly sniffing his cigar. The box was coming back round towards Kai Schweigaard, who was sitting on the bishop's right.

Suddenly his ears pricked up. There was talking in the hallway. Then the front door closed. He got up and his chair scraped on the floor.

The bishop looked at him. "In a hurry?"

"I'm afraid so. I'll be right back." He went out of the dining-room door and into the kitchen. Here the womenfolk stood, their hands red, washing the dishes in steaming hot water. Standing in one corner was a freshly iced *kransekake*, a perfect pyramid of baked marzipan rings. Oldfrue Bressum asked if it was time to bring it out.

Kai Schweigaard shook his head, and signalled to her to

come into the hallway. Wiping her hands on her apron, she followed him.

"I heard someone out in the hall," he said.

"That were Emort from Hekne."

"And?"

"She be down in Kristiania."

"What did you say? Kristiania?"

"To have the child. Got some notion in her head that it were urgent, and he had to drive her to Lillehammer."

Kai Schweigaard sighed. "When was this?"

Margit Bressum cleared her throat. "A few days since. They drove without stop, and when he turned to come back, he realised the sledge blades were done for and the horse were half-dead."

"But why exactly did he come *now*?"

"That be the Hekne way, no doubt."

"What do you mean?"

"According to Emort he gave her his word, that he'd get a message up to ye. But happen his mother was ashamed and didna want the whole village to know she were down there."

Kai Schweigaard stood motionless in the hallway.

A moth came to life on the windowsill. Earlier that day, the women had opened the windows to let out the smell of frying. The moth must have hidden itself in a crack during the winter, and now it took wing and began fluttering around the lamp. He grabbed a newspaper to swat it, but ended up catching it in his hands and releasing it into the spring evening. As it flew off, he saw that it was a butterfly.

Back in the parlour he heard polite, expectant laughter, and he returned to the festive table. The others had cut their cigars, but out of courtesy they had waited to light them. The box stood open next to his plate. He nodded and apologised for keeping everyone, and as he cut his Havana the bishop struck a match and held it to the stick of cedar that accompanied each cigar, giving Schweigaard a large, pure flame in which to roll his cigar until it glowed evenly and strongly. The others followed suit, and soon smoke was rising towards the lamps in swirls that dissolved in the turbulence of the heat.

Kai Schweigaard sat staring into the lamps, saying little. Oldfrue Bressum arrived with the *kransekake*, followed by two maids with silver coffee pots, who started to serve.

Schweigaard held a hand over his cup and shook his head, and when the maids had left he stood up and said: "Bishop, Mayor, honoured guests. I am grateful for all your kind words today, and all your support during the past year. Something unexpected has happened, something directly related to my mission here, and I'm afraid I must leave you all. Do feel free to stay and see the evening out. I'm most awfully sorry."

He walked calmly towards the door, as surprise turned to confusion around the table. At the door he bowed and apologised again, then dashed along the hallway, pulled on his tall boots and overcoat, and ran down to the carriage shed, where his tenant farmer and two farm boys prepared the sledge as fast as they could.

He reached Kristiania late the following evening, and it had already been dark for some time when he finally entered the Birthing Institute and was led to her. She lay under a thin white sheet that was stretched from her feet to her neck. A single candle burned on a tall candlestick.

She was the only one in the mortuary.

Kai Schweigaard stood there a while. Her hair was washed, her eyes closed. She lay with her arms at her sides, the slightest bulge in the sheet over her belly.

His first impulse was to go and warm her up – she must be ice-cold down here under this thin linen cloth, and this cellar was so draughty and grey. But then he realised that she would never be cold again, and, stopping in the middle of the floor, he let his tears roll, and the nurse who had brought him down left him to be alone.

He cried silently. He went over to her and took her hand, and looked at her face and thought how she had never looked like that in life. It seemed as though she was dreaming. And he thought, if we had come together, I would have woken up one night, perhaps in this coming summer even, and I would have propped my head in my hand and lain there and looked at you like that in bed, and in the morning you could have told me your dreams. But now you will sleep for ever, and you will always look as you do now, while I shall age without you.

Glinting on her other hand was the ring that Gerhard Schönauer had made for her. Kai walked around the bed, and from his pocket he took out a brass box containing a ring. But when he lifted her finger, he could not bring himself to do it.

He put the gold ring back, folded her hands over her stomach, stroked her hair, bent forwards and kissed her on the mouth.

He had prayed for her throughout the long journey here, always with folded hands, apart from when the road was so bumpy that he had to hold on to something. Now he wanted to fold his hands in prayer again, but found his fingers closing into a fist.

Kai Schweigaard went to the foot of the bed and squinted up at a small cellar window with an iron grille. The glass was hazy, but he glimpsed a tiny patch of sky between the buildings outside, and to this scrap of heaven he muttered:

"You think you are so great. So great and powerful. Yet you have nothing but pain to cast upon us. Nothing but pain."

He tried to loosen the dog collar from around his neck. He had worn it during the journey, because it gave his words authority when he asked folk to hurry. But his hands were shaking too much to get a grip, and he yanked at it so the button burst off.

He threw the collar to the floor, set his foot on it, and lifted his gaze again.

"There is no reason to take such a fine human being. No reason. None."

He shifted his weight onto his foot and ground the dog collar into the floor. "This Bible of yours. All these poor souls. Looking for meaning. Blind idiots whom you want us to honour. Because they obey you in everything. We are ants and flies, ants and flies that you hold between your fingers."

The door opened behind him, and the nurse came in. He swung around and she hurried away.

He turned to the little window again and said, "You're not the real reason behind things. I can't ask you if you're listening, because you *do not exist*! This church I built in your name – I shall let it stand. But only because a watertight roof is worth more than a cross."

He went over to Astrid and stroked her cheek. His gaze drifted to the floor. The wooden boards had been scrubbed with bleach and were so dry that his tears left small shiny blots.

Two women came in, and one said it was best they go now.

Jehans had his mother's mouth and his father's eyes and jaw. He lay in a room with six other babies, and he had his name on a band around his wrist. His hair was dark and slightly curly, as Astrid's had been, and he continually pulled his knees up under him and kicked out hard. When Kai Schweigaard bent over him, the boy met his gaze and held it steadily, and the two of them looked at each other for a long time. Kai held a hesitant finger out towards him, and Jehans grabbed it in his fist. His fingers were only tiny, and yet his grip was hard. He was dressed in a soft, knitted coat with three buttons, and little trousers with a drawstring at the midriff; Kai recognised the colours of the yarn that had been on Astrid's knitting needles.

He coughed to clear the lump in his throat, but it was too firmly wedged, and his voice took on another tone as he looked round at the other babies in their cradles and asked, "Which is the other one?"

"The other?" said the nurse.

"Didn't she give birth to two?"

The nurse shook her head. "I came on duty last night and this is the only baby I've heard about."

Kai Schweigaard coughed again and tried to steady his voice, but saw that she doubted he'd succeed.

"She always believed she'd give birth to two," he said.

The nurse shot a glance at the clock, it was gone one in the morning. She let him stay with Jehans a little longer, and then said that they must go out into the corridor. She disappeared for a while, and when she returned, she knew a little more. "There *were* two," she said. "But she was in labour for three days, and when it was over, the midwives were sent home to rest. First one doctor came, and then two more. They had to – do a lot. It seems that the second child was weak. The mother lived for a while, but then the bleeding started up again. This is the first child, the one who survived."

Kai Schweigaard asked if the other child had been baptised before it died.

"It was. Yes, I'm sure." She shifted, and would not say where the body was now.

"What happened to the other little coat?" said Kai. "She had two sets of baby clothes with her."

"I really don't know. It was probably given to someone who needed it."

"Yes, but who?"

"You'd do better to wait until the others come, early tomorrow." Voices could be heard from a nearby room, and rising over them a blend of growling and snarling.

Kai nodded towards the door of the room where Jehans was, and asked: "How is he getting food into him? I mean milk?"

She looked at him in astonishment. "The wet nurse, of course." An older midwife came over and insisted he come back the next day if he had anything further to discuss. "As you can hear, we're busy with births," she said. "That is what we do here."

They accompanied Kai Schweigaard out into the street, and the door was locked behind him.

In his hurry he had failed to bring any luggage. He got himself a room in a guesthouse, and next morning he was the first client in a barbershop, from where he went straight to the Birthing Institute.

"You're Schweigaard, I take it?" said the director. "Kai Schweigaard?"

"That's me."

"Yes. I heard that you'd been here. I understand that you wish to take the body home for burial?"

"Yes. I'd also like to pay a wet nurse to accompany the boy on the journey back to his mother's family farm, where he can grow up."

"Have they agreed to that?" said the director. "To taking care of a child?"

"Why wouldn't they?" said Kai Schweigaard. "It's their grandchild."

The director fumbled with some papers. "She was single," he said.

"Single? She was legally married!"

"Widowed, I see here. She signed a form. To say that the child should be placed with new parents if she died."

"Let me see this form."

The director laid the papers down. "These are just the notes our midwife made when she interviewed her. The form itself is with the adoption authorities, and is confidential."

"Then fetch the midwife, so we can hear it from her directly."

"She hasn't slept for three whole days and she isn't here now. Neither are any of the others who assisted at the birth."

"I can wait," said Kai Schweigaard.

The director couldn't get settled in his chair. He fiddled with his letter knife, even though there were no envelopes on his desk this early in the morning. "The deceased seems to have begun writing a note for you. The midwife found it. It's unclear—"

"But what's in it? In this note?"

"See for yourself," he said, handing him a small sheet of paper. "There's barely anything there. I'm sorry."

"*My dear Kai. Jehans—*"

"It seems she didn't have the strength to write more. She died when the bleeding started up again. Her womb was completely overstrained. It can happen with such a protracted labour. It fails to contract as it should. Then there's nothing to be done. Unfortunately."

Kai Schweigaard sat staring at the sheet of paper. The handwriting was unsteady. She had only managed four words. Nevertheless, she had gathered the strength to write "my dear".

"Did the German doctor come?" asked Kai Schweigaard. "Sänger?"

The manager was surprised. "Sänger? No. Nobody sent for him. He's not one of the regular doctors here. But the Rikshospital sent their best man over, with an assistant, and they did everything they could. They saved the babies, but there was no way of saving her."

"The babies?"

"Yes. Or, that was what they thought. But one ... hmm." He said that the second child had been buried quickly, being unfit for anyone to see, that it had probably been laid under the coffin of a recently deceased adult, according to usual practice. The main thing now was that they were left with a living child, and that he – Kai Schweigaard – was not listed as a relative of either the living child or the dead.

"You baptised him, I take it? Gave him an emergency baptism?"

"Yes, of course, if he was alive at birth. But as I said, none of the relevant midwives or doctors are here right now."

"Was it a boy? The other baby?"

The manager looked back at his papers. "Yes, a boy, as far as I know. Another boy."

Kai Schweigaard rose and placed both hands on the desk. "You can forget that so-called form of yours. I'm going to take this child with me, and I'm going to take Astrid Hekne with me. I may not be wearing my dog collar, but I am a parish priest in Gudbrandsdal, and Astrid Hekne was a member of my congregation. She will be buried at home, and Jehans Hekne will be entered into the *kirkebok* for my parish."

Three days later a horse-drawn carriage drew up in front of Lake Løsnes. The spring sun was warm, and the ice was grey and slushy. Two horses had been harnessed to a long sledge, and a black cloth covered the unmistakable shape of a coffin. Schweigaard sat alongside the driver. Behind them was a buxom, red-cheeked girl with a baby in her lap, wrapped in woollens. Few words were exchanged during the journey, his two new companions had the muted fear of those who are offered big money for a difficult mission, without quite knowing just how difficult it might be. The driver refused to venture out onto the lake and cross the ice since there were no fresh sledge tracks there.

"I'll not risk the horses," he said. "Nobody's driven here for days."

"The coffin has to go over," said Kai Schweigaard. "You understand?"

The driver nodded, and then shook his head.

Kai Schweigaard said that the driver and wet nurse could go the long way round, but that he intended to drive the horses and coffin over the ice. If they fell through, the driver would get the four best horses in the parsonage stables, and the wet nurse could bear witness to that.

"The ice won't give way," said Kai Schweigaard.

"And you *know* that, do you?" said the driver.

"I know the ice won't give way. Not today."

Kai Schweigaard took Jehans into his arms, whispered calmly to him and urged the horses on. The blades moved slowly through soft slush. The wet nurse and driver stood on the bank, and when they saw the sledge get over safely, they, too, ventured out onto the ice. But Kai Schweigaard did not wait for them. He rushed up the slopes to the parsonage, and folk gathered, just as when Gerhard Schönauer had left them. He realised now that the villagers saw straight through him and understood that he had brought Astrid Hekne *home*, and he thought: It is the truth, and for her sake it shall not be hidden. Nor shall Jehans be hidden. He hugged Jehans closer, and then the boy stretched out a little hand, as though he wished to take the reins, but he was reaching for Kai Schweigaard, who shifted his hold and took the child's hand and in that moment made his choice for the future.

All around them villagers looked him in the eye and nodded, and the realisation floated into his mind that they *wanted* him as their pastor, that nobody would try to square up to him. His story was forged now, and it had been forged among them. None of this would ever be used to cause harm, because all he had done was fall in love.

Astrid Hekne's funeral was the first to be held in the new church, Jehans Hekne's the first baptism. The driver had returned the evening before, and this was the last sledge crossing over Lake

Løsnes that winter. The wet nurse stayed for a while longer. She was a stoutly built girl from Halden, and Kai Schweigaard asked Oldfrue Bressum to give her all the food she wanted and to put her and Jehans in a good bedroom. Immediately after his arrival he went to Hekne and told them that they had a daughter to bury and a grandson to baptise. Some hours later a message came saying that her parents were opposed to the boy being called Jehans, but Kai Schweigaard said that since it was Astrid's and Gerhard Schönauer's will, it could not be changed.

In truth he needed only to confirm Jehans' baptism, but he woke the wet nurse at five in the morning to go down to the church, where he gave the boy a full baptism, also holding a little ceremony for the brother who had not made it. He prayed for Edgar in both Norwegian and German, and expressed, in the words available to him, his sorrow that nobody would know what this life might have held.

The next day Kai Schweigaard could eat nothing. He buried her in a sunny spot close to the new church, beneath the dripping eaves, where her grave would be nourished by the rain that trickled over the church roof, which thus, according to a custom she had once told him about, turned into holy water. When he came to say a few words at her graveside, it was hard for him to maintain the split between himself and his priestly duties.

"There are many of us who will miss Astrid Hekne," he began. "Miss her deeply."

He talked about her and Gerhard Schönauer, about the beauty of love between two people, and he made no mention of God or Christ, but spoke of courage and strength and determination, then, gathering all his inner forces, he said: "Astrid Hekne is not the first woman to die in childbirth, neither will she be the last. She travelled to Kristiania in the belief that the doctors there would save her and the children she carried, but the world had not yet come that far. For every little step the world moves forwards, some will fall in its path, and these some must be somebody, and this time Astrid Hekne was that somebody."

His voice cracked, and unvoiced cries echoed from the walls.

His gaze fell on her coffin, and he inhaled the smells of the new pine church in which he was standing; and he was filled with fear, for he knew that the new bells could never ring loud enough to drown out grief.

Sunrise

Kai Schweigaard never prayed for forgiveness, for having reviled God before Astrid Hekne's body. He never became a dean or bishop, and rejected any suggestion of promotion. Instead he became the best pastor Butangen ever had. He worked from dawn to dusk all week through, and folk seldom passed the parsonage without noticing a light in his window. He held Mass, confirmation classes, funerals and weddings with measure and sensitivity, more like a caretaker than a preacher. And in the *kirkebok*, line by line, he recorded everything that happened in Butangen. Sadness and joy waited in his inkwell; births, weddings and deaths flowed through his pen. He came to see God as a hands-off employer, the agreement being that Schweigaard should live a long life, and be allowed to continue his work without interference. He made a pact with God that they would talk again in forty years, and promised to ask his forgiveness if Astrid Hekne's death proved to have any meaning.

The following summer he got two carpenters to make a clinker rowing boat from good spruce, which was put out on Lake Løsnes. The villagers called it the priest-boat, and it always lay with its oars at the ready in the knowledge that nobody would ever borrow or steal it. He began to take long troll-fishing trips alone, giving him time to see more in the nature about him, more signs, a tighter weave of connections between nature and human beings, something greater than the Bible defined.

He had never been satisfied with the local teacher, so he started a Sunday school where the Bible hardly made an appearance, and he taught the children spelling and grammar, world history, geography and foreign languages, and when anyone asked why, he told them that when the future came to Butangen, it might quite possibly speak German or English.

He kept careful track of all the boy births in the village to see if there were any lines of chain-brothers; the longest was five, when it was broken by a girl. One summer he heard that six young men from an engineering school in Germany were camped in tents on the other side of Lake Løsnes, they had been there for several days and had borrowed a boat to go fishing in, but others had seen them sinking weights into the lake. Schweigaard rowed across to talk to them, but they had already broken camp, and no foreigners came the next summer.

Jehans learned to walk when he was nine months old. And from then on, he never stopped. If a door was left open for a minute, he would stray. He walked and walked, as though compelled, as though searching for someone lost, and in so doing he became lost to others. Sometimes they found him toddling among the dwarf birches above Hekne or threatening to clamber onto the stone wall that protruded from the steep slopes, some days Emort spent so long looking for him that he fell behind with his farmwork.

The wet nurse had been sent home after just two days, although Kai Schweigaard gave her a full month's pay and promised to continue paying her wages for as long as needed. He was powerless to do more, since the law gave the Hekne family authority over the child. Jehans was, for the most part, looked after by the elderly pauper-woman they had taken in after Klara Mytting. He was raised on warm goats' milk. At first she dipped a rag into the milk and squeezed it into his mouth, later he managed to suck on the rag himself, and soon he could sit on the floor and dunk it in for himself. Emort wanted him to be given milk from the same goat until he could eat solid food, but could not explain why, and was so busy working it was impossible for him to keep track of which goat's milk the boy got.

As Jehans grew, he grew too unruly for the old woman, a reminder to all of Astrid's own unruliness. On his second birthday he was sent to Halvfarelia, where Adolf and Ingeborg looked after him in exchange for half a pig twice yearly, ready-spun wool for clothes, and money for a pair of shoes every other year.

On the boy's third birthday, Kai Schweigaard knocked on the door of Halvfarelia. When they opened it for the pastor, they saw he was carrying a little suitcase, a leather portfolio and an old canvas bag. He greeted Adolf and Ingeborg with a nod and asked to meet the boy alone. He took all the luggage back with him when he left, but told them that everything that Jehans' father and mother had owned would be kept safely at the parsonage until he was old enough.

Adolf owned an old Buhund called Pelle, which followed Jehans wherever he went. The following winter Adolf made Jehans a pair of skis. He made them in the old way, with one long ski to glide on and one short ski, wrapped in coarse reindeer hide, to make it good for gripping.

Jehans went out skiing. The snow was so deep in the winter that old Pelle wore himself out with having had to leap about. Eventually Ingeborg hid the boy's skis, and only put them out after a fall of snow, so they could find him in the evening by following his tracks. When Jehans began to speak, it was of fire, trees, snow, dogs and knives, and thus he grew up in Halvfarelia without much talk of his mother or father.

In the summer of his sixth birthday, Jehans fell ill. He got a rash and fever and lay in bed mumbling to himself. Ingeborg was fearful that he might not survive. Adolf went to the Heknes to inform them, but their only reply was that the bairns up there had had a bad bout of something similar and were shot of it now. So Adolf carried Jehans down to the parsonage, to consult with Kai Schweigaard. They both knew it would take a day for a messenger to reach the doctor and another for the doctor to arrive – and that was if they were lucky and he wasn't out on visits. Keen to spare Jehans from an uncomfortable journey, Schweigaard suggested he row the boy over Lake Løsnes in the priest-boat, while Adolf drove a horse-cart around the lake and met them on the other side. It was late when they reached Vålebrua, and the doctor said that Jehans had what the villagers called *kufsa*, but which in his book was called measles – but whatever its name, it was dangerous. There was no cure and they could do nothing but wait and see if the boy survived the fifth day.

It was a Friday, so there would be no Mass that Sunday. They took rooms at a guesthouse, where their food was left outside the door, so as not to infect others. On the sixth day the rash began to disappear. They returned home later that week, and for the next few days Jehans stayed at the parsonage. He lay in the same room that his parents had shared, and Oldfrue Bressum gave him warm milk and fed him little morsels of meat, and then put the frying pan on the stove in his room, rubbed a crust of bread around the bottom and made sure that he ate all the fat.

Days later, Jehans was playing out in the apple orchard, though he was still not his usual robust self. Adolf and Ingeborg visited him, and arranged for him to return to Halvfarelia after Mass that coming Sunday. Afterwards, Kai Schweigaard took Adolf aside and exchanged a few words about the boy's future.

Later that afternoon Kai suggested to Jehans that they go out on Lake Løsnes in the priest-boat and fish for trout. His rod was made for trolling on Lake Mjøsa, it was one and a half metres long and as stiff as the barrel of a rifle. It looked unmanageable for one so young, but Jehans was undeterred and knew exactly what to do. He let out the line from the gigantic reel, and they rowed on for a while. Kai Schweigaard grew concerned because the boy was so quiet.

"You're not feeling ill again? Do you want to go back?"

Jehans shook his head. "There be summat here," he said, staring down into the water.

Kai Schweigaard said it was probably just the bait dragging along the bottom, and that trolling either gave you big fish or nothing, and suggested they head for deeper water where the largest trout were.

"How d'ye know when a fish has bitten?" asked Jehans.

"There's a tugging on the line."

"Hard?"

"Oh yes. If you get a trout, you'll feel it. I can promise you that. You shall most surely feel it."

They fell silent again, and Kai Schweigaard sat contemplating the young boy. He did everything he was told, but never revealed what he thought or wanted. As though he were in a larval state and would put on colourful apparel when the right time came.

Kai Schweigaard cleared his throat and broke the silence. "Have you got pencils and paper at home?"

"We has one pencil," Jehans said, pointing at his little finger. "It be just so long."

"I'll give you a new one to take with you. And paper. You should try to draw."

"Should I draw?"

"Every child should try lots of different things. Find out where its talents lie. I've a feeling you'd be good at drawing. You can sit up in my office afterwards and try a bit if you like."

"Oh."

"I've talked to Adolf. When you're seven, you can stay at the parsonage at the weekends. First we'll learn to read and give you nice handwriting. Then to count – and in time we'll try to speak languages from other countries."

"Other countries?"

"England and Germany. But one thing at a time. During the week you must learn about farmwork."

The boy turned and leaned the rod against the gunwale.

"Are you cold?" said Kai Schweigaard.

"I donae want to fish more now," said Jehans.

Kai Schweigaard rested the oars in the boat, took the rod and reeled it in for the boy, and passed it back to him. Jehans laid it in the bottom of the boat and took a step back to land in Kai's lap. He took the boy's hands and warmed them in his own, then reached over for the knapsack he had with him and said it was time to eat the chocolate they had bought from the store in Vålebrua.

"You mustn't get cold. Remember you've been ill."

"Aye. Will ye cover me with that travel blanket?"

"What did you just say?"

"I said 'aye'."

"But after that. What did you say after that?"

"Nowt after that."

Kai Schweigaard sat motionless. The knapsack was firmly tied, and had been the whole time. Just before they had gone down to the lake, he had, on impulse, fetched the blanket from the cupboard. It had lain there for years, and Kai was sure he had never even said the words "travel blanket" in all that time.

He pulled out the Scottish tartan rug, tucked it around the boy, put his arms around the boy's shoulders like a bandolier, then took out a bottle of strong blueberry juice and filled a cup for him. The boy drained his cup, and they sat like that in the boat gazing in the same direction, until Jehans tipped back and fell asleep, and Kai Schweigaard held him and looked out over the reflections in the lake.

When the boy awoke, he wanted to fish again. They turned the boat, put out the bait and rowed on. Soon there was a tug on the line, and Kai Schweigaard let Jehans reel it in while he prepared to pull the trout over the gunwale. The fish was dark brown with red spots and as long as the boy's forearm, it thrashed about, thudding against the sides of the boat. Kai asked Jehans if he wanted to kill it, but the boy said that Kai should do it so he'd learn. Kai took a little hammer with a round, polished head and killed the trout with a single blow between the eyes. When Jehans was older, he would explain that in England they called this hammer a "fishing priest" because priests were often present when someone died, but that he saw no reason to call it anything other than a hammer, and that he thought it was a good way of killing a fine trout, as it avoided the blood that came with a knife.

For a long time they sat and admired the fish, Jehans pointing at all its red spots. Kai Schweigaard said it was possible to find out how many there were if they sat down that night and learned to count. The boy sat scooping water from the bottom of the boat over the fish to keep it as shiny as when it was alive. When they put the bait out again, Jehans' gaze wandered between the dead trout and the hope in the line, and Kai Schweigaard asked what he dreamed of being when he grew up.

"A hunter like Adolf."

"Oh."

"And a fisherman like ye."

"I see. So you don't want to go out into the world and take a look around?"

"Nay, not me. I shall shuttle close."

Kai Schweigaard lifted the oars.

"Where did you hear that? Shuttle close."

"Mother said it," Jehans replied, gazing at the water's surface.

"Your mother? When?"

"In the room where I slept."

Kai Schweigaard stopped rowing. The only sound now was of water dripping off the motionless oars. The boat lost speed, and Jehans turned to see what was happening. They looked at each other and then at the fishing line, whose angle was getting increasingly sharp as the bait sank deeper and deeper into Lake Løsnes.

On the night Jehans went back home, Kai Schweigaard woke up with a feeling that someone was in his bedroom – not that it made him nervous or feel any need to defend himself. It was a moonless night and the room was dark. He sat up in bed and was about to strike a match, before realising that he had no desire to know what the darkness concealed. It was purer to live with his *belief* in what was in the darkness, then the feeling was more intense. A soft puff of air, a gossamer-like shift in temperature, waves that flowed with the movements of a person, a breath filled with love, a light shuffling of bare feet.

He said her name.

The footsteps stopped, and he heard a faint rustling of light clothing, sensed an intimacy in the air, pulled off his night shirt and felt a breath and bodily warmth against his skin.

When he awoke, she was not there, but he was content and fearless and longed for the next night.

He lit the paraffin lamp, dressed and went down to his office. During the week he always pencilled a draft in a notebook to be copied into the official *kirkebok* later in fine hand. Now he adjusted the wick of the lamp and took his desk key from the hook below the crucifix on the wall. His hands searched the top right-hand drawer in which he kept the book. But there was something strange lying on top of it – his fingers closed around a small brass box that was usually at the very back of the drawer. It contained the wedding ring he had bought that hopeful summer.

Slowly he opened the box. The ring was gone.

He left the box standing there open, and got up. And at last Kai Schweigaard smiled.

It was still night and dark when he went down to Lake Løsnes and pushed himself out in the boat. He rowed without direction or markers, feeling nothing but the rocking of the boat, hearing nothing but the splashing of the oars.

He rested the oars and leaned back. He felt the undulating and elastic nothingness of water in this kind of darkness. Black water under a black sky with black air to breathe. No distance between anything, in touch with everything.

He lay like that until the sun began to rise and he could just about see where on Lake Løsnes he was. As night gave way to day, a mist rose from the water and enveloped him. A mist that dissolved quickly in the sun, so that the farms in Butangen grew visible on the valley sides. The water's surface was broken by a sudden ripple, and he felt a gentle warmth touch his clothes and hair and face and hands, from the sun that warmed all those he could not see, and also the dead.

Author's Note

READERS WHO ARE FAMILIAR WITH THE AREAS AROUND Vekkom, Tromsnes and Brekkom, and also perhaps Dovre, will recognise the story about the sisters and the church bells, since it takes its inspiration from local stories, recorded by Ivar Kleiven and others. The same readers will have noticed that many of the surnames are taken from Gudbrandsdal, in particular some old farms in Fåvang. The descriptions on p. 10 are inspired by an article by Hans Aanrud from 1900. Works by Gunnar Bugge, Peter Anker and Håkon Christie have been important to the sections concerning church history. I would like to thank the following for their help and support during the writing of this novel: Lars Smedstadmoen, Per Børdahl, Even Hovdhaugen, Inge Asphoug, Ole Kristian Bonden, Olsen Nauen Bell Foundry, Dr Simone Fugger von der Fehr, Ole Vestad, Eva Avkjern, Ansgar Selstø, Ingebjørg Øveraasen, Asbjørn Fretheim, Levi Henriksen, Guri Ruste, my local garage Elverum Bil og Dekk, Tiro the dog, the distinguished Swedish coffee blenders Carlos Zoega and Arvid Nordquist, Gudrun Hebel, Oddvar Aurstad and everyone at Gyldendal. And of course Randi Mytting, as well as Tuva, Hedvig and Selma. Thanks also go to the many other people who are not mentioned here, but who have helped me along the way – they know who they are.

LARS MYTTING, a novelist and journalist, was born in Fåvang, Norway, in 1968. His novel *Svøm med dem som drukner* (published in English as *The Sixteen Trees of the Somme*) was awarded the Norwegian National Booksellers' Award and has been bought for film. *Norwegian Wood: Chopping, Stacking and Drying Wood the Scandinavian Way* has become an international bestseller, and was the Bookseller Industry Awards Non-Fiction Book of the Year in 2016. *The Bell in the Lake*, the first of a trilogy, was a number one bestseller in Norway and nominated for the Norwegian National Bookseller's Award 2018.

DEBORAH DAWKIN originally trained in theatre at Drama Centre, London, before turning to translation. Her translations include *The Blue Room* by Hanne Ørstavik and *Buzz Aldrin: What Happened to You in All the Confusion* by Johan Harstad, shortlisted for the Best Translated Book Awards in 2012. She is the co-translator of eight plays by Ibsen for Penguin Classics, and is presently working on a PhD about the life and work of the Ibsen translator Michael Meyer.